ISBN-13: 978-1-7320307-6-3
ISBN-10: 1-7320307-6-6
LCCN: 2022904365

Printed in the United States of America

Archangel Publishing
archangelpublishing@yahoo.com
http://www.tyffanyhackett.com

•Editing by Jesikah Sundin
http://www.jesikahsundin.com

•Cover Design/Illustrations by Gabriella Bujdoso
https://www.instagram.com/gabriella.bujdoso/
https://www.patreon.com/gabriellabujdoso

•Map Drawing by Gerralt Landman
https://www.instagram.com/dimensiondoor_maps/

For Ally and Hannah
and Chelscey,

❤❤

Who made writing this beast a little
more bearable.
And who regularly remind me what
true friendship is.

Numeryon

ACHMYN
MORTERNOS

RUINS
OF
INGRYST

Spiritwood Lake

LYTHARI

BERIENE

KINGDOM OF
VALLENWOOD

Aldmir Divi

Sedryn Lake

SINYTH

Castyr Lake

ELDORIS

Renian Sea

DEVAYNE
ESTATE

KINGDOM OF
GARENWRYNN

ZANDAMOOR

Madrion
The Land East of the Sun
& West of the Moon

PRONUNCIATIONS

CHARACTER NAMES

Sabrena - *Suh-bree-nuh*
Kiran - *Keer-in*
Nakia - *Nuh-k-eye-uh*
Bleiz - *Blay-ze*
Damara - *Duh-mar-uh*
Connak - *Con-nik*
Rhett - *Ret*
Amirah - *Uh-meer-uh*
Brielle - *Bree-ell*
Aldor - *All-door*
Rohana - *Row-on-uh*
Sloane - *Slow-n*
Avriel - *Av-ree-ell*
Edrick - *Ed-rick*
Hanelle - *Han-ell*
Roux - *Roo*
Niserie - *Niz-er-ee*
Aleksei - *Ah-leck-see*

Kirsi - *Keer-see*
Siyna - *See-nuh*
Nythal - *Nith-all*
Maryna - *Mare-in-uh*
Mintric - *Min-trick*
Cytherea - *Sith-air-ee-uh*
Syris - *Seer-iss*
Aurelia - *Are-ell-ee-uh*
Elentya - *El-en-tee-uh*
Fiore - *Fee-or*
Alyvia - *Uh-liv-ee-uh*
Oryn - *Or-in*
Faleen - *Fuh-leen*
Galryn - *Gal-rin*
Lyriath - *Leer-e-eth*
Rhadagan - *Rad-uh-gan*

Saryshna - *Sar-ish-nuh*

LOCATION NAMES

Numeryon - *New-mare-ee-on*
Ingryst - *In-griss-t*
Garenwrynn - *Gare-in-rin*
Lytharius - *Lith-are-ee-us*
Zandamoor - *Zan-duh-more*
Aldmir - *Ald-meer*
Beriene - *Bear-ee-en*
Vallenwood - *Val-in-wood*
Sinythell - *Sin-eth-ell*
Eldoris - *El-door-es*
Madrion - *Mad-ree-on*
Renian - *Ren-ee-en*
Sedryn - *Sed-rin*
Castyr - *Cast-eer*
Estaria - *Eh-star-ee-uh*

DRACONIC/MISC

Achmyn Morternos - *Ach-men More-tear-nos*
Ashyndah Talehn - *Ah-shin-dah Tall-en*

Mellek - *Mell-ick*
Mystarian - *Miss-tear-ee-en*
Ryntalen - *Rin-tall-en*
Vyrshal - *Ver-shawl*

Elysian - *Ell-is-ee-an*

CONTENT WARNING:

17+ recommended for mild adult
language and sexual content.

- Physical assault trauma
- Body dysmorphia
- Familial death
- Grief processing

PART ONE

Soft sand squished between my toes. The crashing waves of the ocean sent sprays of chilled water across my skin. My dress, fraying from wear, was sodden along the edges. The cotton skirt dragged through the moist sand.

A giggle sounded across the beach. I spun around.

Nothing.

An empty expanse of shore, assaulted by the dark sea, greeted me. The sun was already falling behind the horizon and I still hadn't found Nakia.

She had always been better at hiding than me.

A boom of thunder rolled across the sky. My heart skipped a beat, hammering a frantic rhythm against my ribs. Storm clouds loomed shadowy and ominous overhead. It was only a matter of time before they broke and released a torrential downpour.

If I didn't find her soon, Mama would have my hide. In contrast, Nakia's parents probably wouldn't even notice she was gone. They hadn't cared when she was three and nearly lost to the depths of Sedryn Lake. I doubted their care had grown much now that she was thirteen. We were young, by elven *or* human standards, being only eleven myself, but some people simply weren't made to be parents.

At least I knew that Mama's stern lectures and rules meant she loved her children, in her own way. She would notice if I weren't home for supper, let alone if I vanished for days.

"Sabrena." Nakia broke through my thoughts— her voice soft, taunting, and filled with mirth.

I studied the beach. The shoreline was mostly unblemished, a smooth expanse of white sand that glittered under the pink and orange sunset. To my left, a dark tree line loomed. While I wouldn't be surprised if Nakia had magically amplified her voice, deep in my gut I didn't think she was there. The trees were too unpredictable, the forests full of dangers we were unprepared to face.

"*Stick to the path, it will lead you true.*" Connak's words played in my mind every time we came to the shore. But my older brother would know. I trusted him.

Farther off to my right, a large formation of rock spread along the coastline, dipping into the water. We used it as a diving point when the ocean was calm. But tonight, the sea was uneasy, churning and thrashing around the jagged stone like an omen of bad news. I couldn't fathom a better hiding place—or a more dangerous one. But if there was one lesson Nakia had learned from her encounter with the lake, it was how to protect herself.

Nakia had grown incredibly talented with her powers.

Meanwhile, I had none.

Mald Magicae.

The magicless.

Among the elves, to be born without magic was the equivalent of carrying a plague. It wasn't a common condition. Less than one elf a generation was born with the defect. The elven community ridiculed and shunned those of us without power, treated us like outcasts. Best case scenario? They ignored us.

The call of her voice came again, a bit louder this time. At least I had Nakia. I moved toward the cluster of large rocks, scanning the sand for footprints. None. I shouldn't have expected her to leave a trace behind. She was too clever for that.

I picked my way across the coast, dodging skittering crabs and broken shells. If she wasn't hiding along the rocks, I had no idea where she might be. Her powers gave her a lot of options.

Sometimes, I wished she didn't have them either. Or that I was a little less alone in a world where nearly every being had magic, and I was the outcast.

But, inevitably, I couldn't fault her for wanting to use what she was born with. I would, too, if I were her. She had always been my best friend. And if anyone understood what it was like to be rejected, she did. So, I swallowed my jealousy and kept looking for her. Magic or none.

Unease rose inside me as the shadows lengthened around us. I would have to concede another loss. All because I couldn't find her. *Again.*

She would never let me live it down.

But the closer I crept to the massive stone, the quieter she became. Her muffled laughter was barely a whisper against the brewing storm. When I was mere steps from learning my answer, to finding her or failing yet again, fat drops of water had begun to spill from the clouds. I stared at my hand as one landed on my palm and admired the swirling colors of sunset reflected within. Another clap of thunder shook me from my reverie. I crushed the droplet in my fist, glancing up at the stone face. I didn't see her.

"Nakia, this isn't funny. It's getting dark. We have to get home before the storm breaks."

A soft chorus of giggles sounded from my left and I crept around the stone, crouching to peer beneath a low overhang. Green eyes met mine before I heard a soft splash. Nakia laughed as the water sprayed across my face.

"Lighten up, Sabrena."

"Mama will have our hides and you know it. Well, *my* hide since *you're* her favorite." I sighed. "How did you get under there anyway?"

"Very carefully," she said with a grin. Her long, ebony curls dipped into the ocean as she ducked below the stooped rock, only to pop up in front of me a moment later. "And it's not like it would be the first time she's denied me dessert for worrying her."

"Being denied one of her failed attempts at dessert isn't really a punishment." I rolled my eyes, then cast a worried glance toward the trees. A drop of rain splattered on my cheek. I wiped it away. "We need to go. I don't want to be caught in this."

Nakia's grin widened, deep dimples creasing her dark brown cheeks. She wagged her fingers above the sea foam that rushed between her ankles. "What's wrong with a little water?"

I ignored her, turning on my heel, and picked my way across the beach toward the tree line. The path back to town was wide, clearly marked. All I needed to find was the wooden sign etched with *To Eldoris*.

"Brena, wait for me!"

"Walk faster," I teased over my shoulder, even as I slowed my pace.

I looked for the patch of brush and grass that marked the sign. But a dark shadow in the trees caught my eye instead. My steps faltered when the form moved again, growing larger. Branches cracked. I pedaled backward, stumbling when I ran straight into Nakia.

"What's wrong?"

"There's something—" I pointed at the shadow.

Nakia's fingers curled tightly around my arm. "What is that?"

I took another instinctive step back. "I don't know."

Emerald leaves rustled around the stranger. The shadow took form, growing more defined with each step. A predatory snarl shattered the peaceful, natural sounds around us, followed by the metallic scrape of a sword being pulled free of its sheath.

Nakia tugged on my arm. I was frozen, unable to move, unable to look away from the man striding from the woods or the sword he brandished in our direction. Another angry sound rumbled out of him. Nakia pulled again, her fingers trembling, and this time I didn't resist. I stumbled several steps back.

When the man stepped out of the shadow into the lingering rays of sunlight, I barely restrained a scream.

Troll.

His skin was pale blue, the dense muscles of his arms and chest rippling as he strode toward us. He didn't see two young, fearful girls and feel sympathy. No. He saw our pointed ears and that we were unarmed—no other reason needed. Because trolls didn't care if we were fae, or elven, or even human. We weren't trolls. And to them, that was enough. To them, that meant we had to die.

The troll's tusks curved over his lips. His sharp teeth snapped in threat. He wasn't slowing.

My heart pounded in my ears. Nakia let out a soft whimper. I couldn't seem to pull my gaze from the troll, from the bloodlust that glimmered in his eyes.

Then he was on us. The stench of sweat and smoke and earth filled my nostrils. He tore Nakia away from me and tossed her aside. She skittered and slid across the sand and brush, collapsing into a heap.

"Nakia!"

She didn't move.

I turned to run after her, but the troll was faster. His claws tore into my neck and shoulder, then dragged down my arm as he tried to catch me. Jagged wounds split open in his talon's wake. Blood stained my gown, dribbled down the troll's wrist, but the sight only seemed to fuel him on. He shoved me to the ground, pinning my arms with his knees. I nearly passed out from the wounds, from the agony of his weight on my injured arm.

His laugh was deep and cruel as he lifted the sword. The tip pressed into my ribs. Hot tears ran down my cheeks, the pain sharp and growing every passing second.

"Please," I whispered. "You don't have to do this."

The troll smiled. One of his tusks had a ring through it, the gold hoop embedded with an emerald that glinted in the light. Another callous laugh rolled through him. His blade dug in deeper. I screamed.

But then the blade lifted; the pain ceased. Something barreled into him. The troll and his sword flew backward.

I clutched at my ribs and neck, trying to put pressure on the wounds. Connak had taught me that. I couldn't do much for my arm, not now.

Nakia still lay unmoving. I scrambled for her as snarls filled the air. She blinked up at me when I reached her, confused, but I didn't give her time to think. I yanked her to her feet, ignoring how she gaped at the blood I left on her arm. Then we were off and moving before the troll could process our escape.

But I couldn't resist shooting a glance over my shoulder as we fled. I took in the troll, pinned to the ground, his sword glinting in the dirt just out of reach. And, for a moment, I caught the furious stare of the massive black wolf who held him down.

The wolf growled, snapping his teeth at us.

I didn't look back again.

1

I woke with a gasp. My hand unconsciously wrapped around the rough, mangled scars that scaled my left arm and crept along my neck. Phantom pains ached along the marks beneath my fingers, the raised scars lingering remnants of the old wound.

Nakia and I were attacked one hundred and eighty-seven years ago.

Nearly to the day.

I took a long, slow breath, exhaling gradually. After the troll attack, the fae had tightened security around our city. Eldoris had always utilized protections of its own, but the northern and southern entrances now had a permanent rotation of fae guardians. I wasn't sure if they actually helped, but troll sightings were few and far between.

No one knew why the fae were so willing to guard the elves either, especially when their own people were nearly extinct. Maybe some guilt remained over stealing most of our land and nearly draining us of all resources. But the Ninth War had taken its toll on all of us—Numeryon, our continent, had never really recovered, not even almost a hundred and fifty years later. For all that the fae had lost, we had lost more. More people. Land. Resources. There was so little left on Numeryon.

But that was what the trolls wanted. They had come from an unknown land, far to the north of Numeryon, to conquer, to steal, to murder or enslave anyone in their path. In many ways, we were lucky the fae survived as long as they did. That we survived at all was a testament to what they had laid down to keep Numeryon safe.

If only it had worked, and we weren't scraping to survive *while* trying to keep the trolls from regaining their former strength.

"Another nightmare?"

I glanced across the small room to the tiny bed Nakia sat on. Her green eyes caught the light of the candle that flickered on her bedside table. Warm light softly glowed across her brown skin.

"As always," I murmured.

Nakia nodded. When we were much younger, our nightmares were few and far between. They were petty, the worries of children—a favorite toy lost to a devastating accident or a bogeyman in the shadows.

No one ever tells children what to do when the bogeyman is real.

My nightmares since that day were violent, brutal, and so unbearably real. I could still taste the salt of the sea air, could still feel my skin relent as the troll's claws ripped through it, could still hear the warning in the wolf's growl.

A shiver ran the length of my spine. Nakia was lucky to not be haunted by that night. At least, not as I was.

I inhaled deeply, blowing off the lingering fear holding my chest tight. I focused on the walls of our shared room—at the embroidery projects that we had hung next to our charcoal sketches on scraps of parchment—and grounded myself. A dream. Just a dream. I was home, safe, with my family, and in the room Nakia and I had shared since we were small, when my parents had basically adopted my friend because she practically lived with us already.

Safe.

The attack had happened so long ago . . . And no trolls had been seen anywhere near Eldoris since. Still. I couldn't seem to shake the fear.

Only a dream.

"Breakfast will help," Nakia offered. "There's nothing in the world good food can't cure."

I offered her a soft smile, running my fingers through the hair that fell just past my waist. Food *was* an acceptable balm for night terrors. Maybe it didn't cure them or heal the ache that lingered in my bones after, but it certainly helped.

And though Mama couldn't bake to save her life, her ability to cook savory meals was nearly magical. When she had a mind to dress her scrambled eggs, they became the most delicious food I had ever eaten.

I lowered my fingers from the scars and untangled myself from my blanket. The knitted fabric was worn but cozy. Mama had made the blanket for me two years before, for Snowdream. The winter holiday was one of the only times we exchanged gifts, but they were so much more meaningful that way. Snowdream celebrated quiet reflection, rest, and promoted caring for oneself. Winter was the only season we didn't scramble to plant and harvest; the one time of the year Papa was home from the fishing boats for more than a few days at a time.

Unfortunately, right now, we were in the Hearthfall Equinox and Papa was out at sea—a fact that I was jarringly reminded of when baby Siyna began wailing from the room beside mine. The next sound was as predictable as the sun.

"Sabrena! Your sister, please!"

I heaved a heavy sigh. Siyna was only a few months old, but it had been many years since a baby had last been in our home. Truth be told, I wasn't sure why Mama and Papa thought we needed another mouth to feed. Siyna was the eighth member of our huge family.

"I'll find her food," Nakia volunteered as I eased from the bed.

The cobblestone floor was cold beneath my feet. I looped my blanket around my shoulders, pulling it tight when a shudder wracked my frame. The walls were thin and the fireplace didn't warm our home well. Only the living room was truly warm, and only if one of my brothers remembered to stoke the fire throughout the night.

I took Siyna there, to the rug before the hearth, settling her on my lap so I could feed her the mashed carrots Nakia eventually brought her from the kitchen. My baby sister didn't look much like me. It was Mama's bright blue eyes that stared up at me and Papa's dark curls on her head. Then again, of all six children, I was the only one who had Mama's hair—a blond so light it was nearly white.

No one was sure where my eyes came from. Papa's eyes were the color of fresh honey, and even combined with Mama's, they didn't equal mine—a dark blue green the color of the angry sea. They were unique though, unlike any of my siblings.

It seemed like all around I was simply some kind of strange anomaly.

Mald Magicae, indeed.

I sang to Siyna under my breath as she ate. Her tiny, pointed ears wiggled as she chewed, her little mouth coated with globs of orange mush. Nakia disappeared into the kitchen again, only to reappear minutes later behind Mama. Their arms were laden with plates full of steaming food. Sliced potatoes, fluffy eggs, thin cuts of meat . . . We didn't have much, but once a day we sat down as a family and enjoyed a meal together. I was grateful for that—grateful that we all respected the shared meal as an important part of our day, grateful that Mama cooked it, grateful that Papa worked tirelessly to provide for his family, no matter how much we missed him when he was away.

"Sabrena, hush," Mama said, gripping my arm. "Your sister

needs to eat before she naps again."

I blinked, glancing down at my little sister. Her eyes had begun to droop, her little jaw moving more slowly. I stopped singing with a laugh, running my fingers over her little feet until she giggled and cooed with more alertness.

"What smells so divine?" asked Rhett. My brother's voice was deep and rich, a familiar balm on the worst days. He was the sibling I had always been closest to, older than me but younger than our eldest brother Connak. Rhett leaned down as he passed me, brushing a kiss to my cheek. His blond hair, several shades darker than mine, fell around his shoulders before he straightened. "Good morning, Brena. Thank you for helping with Siyna."

I grinned up at him as he unloaded Mama's arms before setting plates around the single table in the living room. "I wasn't aware I had a choice in the matter."

"You didn't," he admitted with a smile of his own, "but it's appreciated nonetheless."

"Rhett and I went out hunting last night," Connak added from the doorway. "We saw something."

The fear from my nightmares returned in a wave of nausea. Mama paused, glancing at my expression, then looked back to Connak. "After breakfast, then."

Connak nodded. "Aleksei and Kirsi can play in the garden."

Mama muttered a soft agreement, shoving a plate into my eldest brother's hands. Rhett dropped to my side, poking Siyna's small belly until she giggled. Nakia ate quietly across from me, watching Connak with an intensity that made me squirm. My brothers reported sightings of all kinds of things in the woods—bears, big cats, griffins . . . Nothing that got too close to Eldoris or stood much of a threat to us. We never let my sisters hear their reports, though. They were young and unburdened. We wanted them to have that as long as they were able.

But Nakia could read people, better than anyone I had ever met. And the way she was studying my brother . . .

I glanced up at Connak, past the chestnut hair that brushed his cheekbones, to the way his eyes flitted nervously around the room. He was watching the doors, the windows, with a strange alertness.

What had they found last night?

I scarfed my breakfast down in record time, despite the knot in my throat. Mama took my younger sisters to the back garden as soon as we finished, telling them to gather all the prettiest flowers for the supper table. Rhett laid Siyna down for a nap, and Nakia stole the blanket from around my shoulders to lay across our laps before she leaned into my side. Connak stoked the fire.

When we had all resettled, Mama fixed a pointed stare on her eldest son. He cleared his throat.

"It may be nothing," he began, and my heart plummeted at the shallow reassurance. "But Rhett and I spotted a contingent of fae patrolling Castyr Lake's northern shore."

"Trolls?" Nakia asked. Her voice was hushed. Our minds were locked onto the same memory. Phantom pains shivered along the scars on my arm, neck, and ribs.

Rhett shook his head. "I don't think so. If there are trolls around, we didn't see any sign of them. No footprints, no animal carcasses. None of their usual tells."

"Or smells," Connak said, wrinkling his nose. "The odor they carry is impossible to miss."

I remembered that too. Vividly. Blood, sweat, earth.

Nakia squeezed my arm.

"Why is there a contingent of fae this close to Eldoris, then?" I asked.

My brothers exchanged a look that said they were just as confused as me. A beat of silence fell over the room.

The fae mostly stayed north in Lytharius and Zandamoor, and at the prince's great estate. All well above the Aldmir Divide. A divide, I imagined, that was a massive wall spanning the length of our kingdoms, or a fence, maybe. Some massive tribute to the two kingdoms. No one really talked about what it actually was, physically speaking. Regardless, that territorial line was drawn between the elves and fae after the Ninth War— when the trolls had arrived and pressed the fae so far south that they had nearly extinguished our kind. We wanted the fae out of our lands—and we only tolerated their guardians because they were shields that might actually help defend our cities. Like it or no, the trolls were a threat to us all. But their selfish actions had created a rift, and none of the fae had ever truly apologized for it.

"Could another war be brewing?" Mama whispered.

Connak shrugged. "Anything is possible with the trolls. But I don't think Numeryon would survive it."

He was right. The elves had missed a lot of the onslaught during the Ninth War. But when the fae started to run out of resources, they took from the elves without remorse. Their failure to stop the trolls after doing so had nearly toppled two great races and almost took a third had the humans not fled before they became too involved. No one knew if death or prosperity awaited the mortals on the other side of the Renian Sea.

But I often wished the elves had thought to do the same thing.

"Was the prince among the patrols?" Nakia asked.

Rhett cast an amused look at our eldest brother. "No, but I wish he had been. I have some questions for him."

"He would be one more distraction you don't need," Connak scoffed, rolling his eyes. "They were too far to make out, anyway. A nondescript group of fae on horseback. That's all we know."

The prince.

He was the only remaining royal of the fae, and the sole reason the Ninth War had ended. He had struck an accord with the leader of the trolls, a powerful High Sorceress who had wiped out entire towns with the flick of her wrist. Or so the stories said. I knew if Connak had the chance, he would ask the prince what deal existed between them. Not that the prince ever left his estate *to* be asked. But the arrangement was a closely guarded secret and, really, all that mattered was how the trolls had ceased their attacks.

Mostly.

They left the fae a dying race who were barely able to sustain themselves and with one ruling dignitary to moderate the needs of their people. A cruel man, the prince, as rumors go. But the fae still existed, a testament to his capability for survival and for militarizing his people. And somewhere along the way, he had sent men and women to each of the elven villages to act as guardians and protectors—and likely spies, if he were half as clever as I believed him to be.

"I think you should stay closer to the town tonight," Mama murmured. She looked up, and a crease along her brow deepened as she added more loudly, "I don't trust them. I'll never trust them."

Connak dipped his head in silent understanding. She and Papa had never been able to forgive that a troll had gotten so far south he had nearly killed their daughter. No troll should have been anywhere near the southern shore. And none had been seen since. Add in that our impoverished lives had begun because of the war and my family was filled with loathing for the fae.

I had been younger than Siyna when the Ninth War started, but elven memories were long. I remembered the gradual decline of our lives. Our roof hadn't leaked continuously then. Our beds had been warm, our food plentiful. Mama hadn't been quite so slender, nor had her hair held quite so many strands of silver.

Nakia's fingers looped through mine, squeezing lightly. I glanced up, not realizing that the others stared at me expectantly.

"Sorry," I muttered. "I was thinking."

"About a boy, I presume," Rhett said with a wink. "Or maybe one of those strapping fae warrioresses."

"No. About our lives. And how the fae have changed us."

His smile slipped at that. Mama's expression darkened. Papa was a good fisherman. Once, he had made substantial money off the massive hauls he brought in from offshore. Now, if he charged a fair amount for each catch, none of the townsfolk could afford to buy the fish. No one had money these days. Papa knew it, too, and so he charged far less than he could really afford to.

I had only asked why once.

"Because kindness is more rewarding than coin," he had said. *"Our bellies are not entirely empty. Some of theirs are. We can do this for our neighbors."*

"I miss him too," Mama admitted. It was a lot for her to confess, and she blinked away the emotions she felt as quickly as she expressed them. As though she, as a mother, wasn't worthy of the emotions she carried because she had children to tend to. I opened my mouth to say something, to offer her comfort, but she leaned forward and picked up her yarn basket. My chance was gone. I shut my mouth.

"Can you run to the market today?" she asked offhandedly. "I need to finish knitting a blanket for Siyna and I'm almost out of material. The months are only going to get colder."

"Yes, Mama," I said.

"Make sure you take Nakia. I don't like it when you go alone into town." Her hands paused; her needles stilled. "You're safer with someone else. You both are."

"I know, Mama. And while I'm out—"

A thunderous knock boomed from the front door. We all froze. Siyna's sudden wailing filled the air. Mama hurried after her, and Rhett vanished out the back to fetch our younger sisters. Nakia's grip tightened around my hand.

Connak grabbed his sword belt, looping it around his waist as he walked. His bare feet were silent on the floor, though the rest of us crept along behind him. Another more insistent knock urged Connak forward. My sisters, Aleksei and Kirsi, clung to Rhett's legs tightly as Connak released the bolt and yanked the door open.

A fist nearly collided with his face.

My elder brother reached up and gripped the man's wrist with ease, but the man was free with one swift motion.

Connak's stature grew larger, more imposing. The man raised his hands in surrender.

"I'm not here for violence. I was going to knock again. My apologies. I wasn't trying to aim for your face."

I stepped closer to my brother, examining the fae who stood in our doorway. His hair was dark, nearly black but for the smattering of short, sun kissed brown curls scattered throughout. A dark beard framed his bronze complexion. His ears were pointed, like ours, though much longer. But it was his bright amber eyes that drew my attention—eyes that were scanning, seeking, looking for something beyond my brother.

"What are you here for?" Connak asked, planting himself more firmly in front of the door, his hand tight around the hilt of his sword.

A smirk tilted the fae's lips. But then those honied eyes locked onto me as I inched another foot closer, and his smile slipped. "I've been looking for someone," he said. His stare was intense. Searing. "Her."

2

Silence fell. The tension around us was so weighted, I could feel it pressing down on my lungs.

Me?

I had never seen this fae before. Seven hells, I had never seen *any* fae up close before, aside from the guards that patrolled Eldoris.

Connak's sword slipped from its sheath with a scrape. He lifted it until the point was aimed at the fae's chest. Echoes of my brother's magic danced along the blade, shimmering waves of silver power. "I think you should leave."

The fae tutted softly, before he smiled once more.

"I'm not here to pillage your home and steal your finery. I'm not a *troll*." He extended a hand. "I'm Bleiz. Personal assistant to His Highness, Prince Kiran Devayne of Garenwrynn. He sent me to your little city in hopes of brokering an agreement of cooperation, but . . ."

Bleiz's eyes returned to my face. His expression lifted with curiosity and a glint I wasn't quite sure I liked—almost predatory. Rhett straightened at that, coaxing my sisters toward my mother. When they were firmly latched onto her skirts, he stepped forward to stand with our brother until the two of them formed a barrier between the fae and the rest of our family. Connak didn't budge, but I was surprised when he conceded his name.

Bleiz dipped his head appreciatively. "Again, my sincerest apologies for the intrusion, but I have a strange . . . *request.*"

My brothers inched forward, unhappy with his emphasis of the word. The tip of Connak's sword dug deeper into Bleiz's leathers.

"If this request has anything to do with my little sister, the answer is a resounding *no,*" Rhett snarled. I recoiled. I had never heard so much aggression in his voice.

Bleiz appeared to sense it too; the arch of his brow hinted that he understood my brothers weren't likely to hear him out. After a couple of long, tense heartbeats, he lifted his hands in surrender. "I mean none of you any harm. My companions are at the inn. I came only with my sword."

"A sword of ebonsteel," Connak stated bluntly. The magic on his sword brightened in a warning.

Ebonsteel was rare and expensive. It could cut through nearly anything as easily as a hot knife through butter. Bleiz might be alone but, against our weapons, Bleiz had my brothers more than outmatched. All he needed was that one sword.

"I'll leave my blade outside. I want to talk, that's all. I have a proposition for you all, and if you decline, I won't bother you again."

Connak considered for a long moment, glancing over his shoulder to where we all stood to seek approval from Mama. When he got it, he lowered his sword and gestured to a shrub along the front wall. "Hide it under there or it'll be gone before you get up the stairs."

Bleiz nodded his agreement, moving to tuck the sword deep into the leaves for more secure concealment. He scanned the street, but it was too early for most of our neighbors. I wondered if that was why he had chosen now to come.

When he stepped into the central room, his gaze skimmed across the aged furniture, the barren rugs, the doorway leading into the kitchen with its crooked frame. I could feel his judgment. And it sent fury seething under my skin. Nakia rested a restraining hand on my shoulder as Rhett offered the stranger a seat at the living room table, close to the fireplace. Bleiz nodded with barely smothered reluctance, and the flood of anger I felt rose. He stared at the weathered edges of our table runner and my jaws ached with how tightly I clenched my teeth together. Better that than wailing him in the face.

Mama lingered near the kitchen door, my sisters clutched tight to her, and Connak leaned against the fireplace mantel with his sword still in hand. But the rest of us sat around the table: myself at the end directly opposite the fae, Nakia to my right, and Rhett a firm warden at Bleiz's side.

But Bleiz's eyes were back on me, undaunted by my watchful brothers. "I imagine you're all very curious about the nature of my proposition, so I'll get right to it. I have two kingdoms in need of some reparation. Of peace. Mutual cooperation, at the very least. In front of me, I see the most interesting elven girl I've been in the presence of in a long age. And, more importantly, I have a prince back home"—he leaned back, grinning as he folded his hands behind his head—"in need of a bride."

The room exploded into a frenzy of chaotic chatter. Nakia's hand gripped my forearm, tightening so much I could feel the bruises forming. Bleiz simply looked amused, taking in the faces of my infuriated family, of my mother who nudged my sisters back a step.

Then he cleared his throat.

When the room didn't quiet, he cleared his throat again, and my family drifted into slow silence.

"Why her?" Nakia asked softly, not allowing him the chance to speak. I knew her well enough to hear the fear that laced her voice, but Bleiz didn't seem to notice.

"I don't know."

My eyes lifted at that. A muscle ticked in Rhett's jaw, and I saw the words forming on his lips even before he opened his mouth. But I shook my head and he hesitated.

"If I'm to go with you, I want an answer to her question. Because in a village filled with beautiful women, Nakia included, it makes no sense that you would choose me."

Bleiz's expression was stoic as he said, "Truly, I don't know. When I look at you, I see a kindred spirit to my prince. A soul drifting through a world it wasn't quite made for. I think a kind heart would be a welcome change in the Devayne Estate."

"That's it?" Connak snarled. "That's your answer? 'I don't know.' You're going to have to do better than that."

"The creepy answer, then," Bleiz muttered, then sighed. "This isn't my first visit to Eldoris. I've been, once before, and I saw your fair sister. I was drawn to her in a way I've only felt with my prince. And as I've watched him fall into himself over the years, I couldn't stop thinking about this beautiful elven girl who might be exactly the balm my prince needs to pull himself back onto his feet."

My brothers looked at me, Nakia's brows rose, but I shook my head and shrugged. If he had seen me, I had never seen him before. I didn't recognize him at all, and I didn't imagine this particular fae would be easy to forget.

"You're right, that is creepy," Rhett said finally, grimacing. "Do you often stalk young girls for years at a time?"

"No stalking," Bleiz said, raising his hands again in surrender. "One trip. One fateful crossing of paths. And a feeling I haven't been able to shake all those years since."

"I think you should leave," Connak said.

"But I hadn't quite reached the part about the proposition," Bleiz said, mischief edging into his wide smile. He lifted a finger as Connak started to speak again. "Ah-ah. I really think you should hear me out."

His gaze circled the room, landing on each member of my family. But this time when he spoke, it was not to them but directly to me. "I can ensure they live in comfort for the rest of their days. The prince has the power to do that, and the financial means."

"And Nakia?" I asked without hesitation.

Nakia started to protest, but I put my hand over hers and silenced her argument. If I could give my family a better life, simply by sacrificing my dream of marrying someone I loved . . .

This plan wasn't ideal. It wasn't the life of love and happiness I had wanted for myself.

But I could do this. Maybe.

I could give my family a better life.

Bleiz eyed my friend for a moment, then nodded. "And Nakia."

"You can't seriously be considering this," Rhett growled, glaring at me in a way he had never done before. "You have to know better. The fae always lie. You don't know what will happen if you leave here with him."

"Funny, I thought we could only tell the truth," Bleiz said with an arch of his brow. "Between your lot and the humans, I can't tell which path I'm supposed to follow. Guess I'll just have to make it up as I go." The grin on Bleiz's face was positively wicked, almost wolfish. It made my stomach curl. And I realized quickly that the fae were as able to lie or be honest as we were.

"The prince is a brutal, bloodthirsty man. As all fae are." Mama stared at me, tears welling in her eyes. She looked to Connak, her expression pleading.

My eldest brother, for once, looked lost for words. Calculating. Our minds were very similar, his and mine, and I knew he was thinking this all through the way I was. There was logic to this proposition. And had he been offered the deal in my place, he wouldn't have even hesitated this long.

"You can't want to marry that *monster*," Rhett tried again. My heart pounded in my ears.

Bleiz didn't bother defending the prince, pursing his lips instead. He looked all too amused by the chaos, and I realized how devilish the fae must truly be. The prince had lived through the Ninth War, after all. Perhaps he *was* more than I was ready for.

I studied Bleiz for a long moment before I asked, "What are the specific terms? I want them in writing."

He pulled a scroll from the bag at his hip, unrolling it before he retrieved a quill and inkwell.

"N-a-k-i-a, am I correct?" he asked. Nakia cast me an uneasy glance, then nodded her reluctant consent. Bleiz scribbled on the scroll, then passed it to me. "Take a look."

My family crowded around, reading over my shoulder as I carefully reviewed each line of his terms. They were clear cut and simple, surprisingly. I married the prince. My family—amended to include Nakia—lived prosperously and comfortably for the rest of their days. And given the length of elven lives, it was a generous offer. Once a moon cycle, when the guards at the gate changed, a fae would be sent to the house to see that their needs were being met and deliver a stipend.

"And what is expected of me, as his wife?" I asked.

Rhett hissed in frustration. Connak clapped a hand on his shoulder to silence him. He would let the decision be mine, and I appreciated that of him. Nakia leaned a bit back now, staring at me as though she was piecing together a puzzle. As though she saw every piece and couldn't decide how they fit together anymore.

"Not much, to be honest," Bleiz said with a shrug. "He has some staff and they care for the estate as well as they can. They'll prepare meals. You might have to attend a formal meeting or event, but that's unlikely. The prince tends to sulk around the palace more than anything these days."

I frowned. "And this is how you speak of him when trying to convince me to marry him?"

Bleiz leaned forward in his seat with another shrug.

"I'll be honest. I see you as an easy solution to a great many problems. You'll take a great weight off me if you say yes. But I'm not going to pretend the prince isn't moody and closed off and solitary, because he's exactly that."

"Brena," Mama said, inching closer while nudging my brothers out of the way. She dropped to her knees beside me, scooped my hands into hers, and squeezed them tightly. "My songbird, my baby." Her eyes flowed with tears now. "Our family is better off together and poor than separated and wealthy."

"But our family is always separated," I murmured. "Papa is always out to sea. Rhett and Connak are always seeking work, or toiling at hard jobs, or hunting for food to tide us over until father returns again. You know I've considered worse alternatives. And you know we're only getting poorer by the day. If I did this, you could all stay home. Together."

"And what about you, songbird?"

"She will live in the utmost luxury. She will have the finest things, the most beautiful rooms, an entire estate to explore." Bleiz smiled, more gently than he had thus far. "I don't offer your daughter a prison sentence. She will be treated far better than she would in any brothel in all Numeryon."

"Can I bring someone?" I glanced at Nakia, and she nodded her agreement subtly. "What about my friend?"

"No," Bleiz said. "The agreement was only for you, and Prince Kiran will have enough trouble adjusting to your presence."

I fixed my gaze on the parchment on the table, ignoring the heavy stares of my family. His proposition wasn't a hard question, even without bringing Nakia along. In fact, I really didn't even need to consider. My family would be taken care of. They would have three meals a day, instead of one. Nakia would have options. She could buy her own home, away from her parents, if she wanted. Had I ever desired anything more?

Mama let out an anguished sob when she saw the look on my face, then she released my hands to go gather up my sisters again.

She vanished into the kitchen without another word and my chest ached at the pain and betrayal I knew she was feeling.

"Brena," Rhett said quietly. "You can't—"

But I met his eyes, noting the exact moment when he registered the resolution Mama had already seen. There truly wasn't a question of what I would do. And with my defect, my magic-less blood, there was little to no chance I would find a better match in Eldoris. Flings and stolen kisses weren't love, and the one time I thought I had found more . . .

I squashed the thought. Maybe this was simply how my romantic life was destined to play out—loveless, but full in other ways.

Mald Magicae.

Cursed with the worst luck, in all the ways that mattered.

But maybe the love I had for my family, and that they held for me, was enough. Maybe I could salvage some part of the future for us all.

And maybe that wasn't so bad.

"All right, Bleiz. I'll marry your prince."

3

B leiz gave me two days.

Two days to pack my belongings and say goodbye to my family and to the dearest friend I had ever known. One more rise of the sun and I would be gone.

I tried to tamp down the nerves that churned through my stomach. I didn't know what waited at Devayne Estate, and Bleiz hadn't exactly been forthcoming with details. But I knew I was going north. Farther north than I had ever been.

Mama fussed over my clothing most of the morning. Connak and Rhett were strangely quiet, guiding Aleksei and Kirsi into the garden to play when Siyna settled for her nap. My sisters' wide eyes were filled with confusion—over the strange man who had entered our home, about the uproar that had followed. Siyna didn't understand at all, but Aleksei and Kirsi had been silently observant, their eyes tracking me all around the house as I packed my few belongings into a sack.

But they were young. If, for whatever reason, I didn't

return, their memories of me would be faint. A face in a dream, a whisper in their minds. They would be well loved by the family that was here, and their lives would be improved so much because I was leaving.

That's what I kept telling myself, anyway.

Nakia's silence worried me the most. She followed behind Mama like a shadow, gently folding anything she could get her hands on, and reminding me of knick-knacks I might want to take. But Nakia had never withheld her feelings from me before, and the tension between us was a weight I couldn't stand to leave carrying. So, when Mama paused her fussing to make lunch, I grabbed Nakia's arm and pulled her back into the room we had so often shared. I pushed the door shut behind her, then released my hold, crossing my arms over my chest as I leaned against the door.

"What's wrong?"

Nakia frowned deeply, toying with a lock of the wavy black hair that fell to her waist. "You really think that's the best question right now?"

"Yes. You're clearly upset. I want to hear your thoughts."

"You already know what's wrong," she said, rolling her eyes. Her jaw tightened, like she was withholding more, and it was my turn to frown.

"You know I'll do what I have to for my family," I said slowly. "Bleiz wasn't wrong, you know. Observant, if anything. You already knew I planned to speak to Mistress Selene at the end of the moon cycle."

"Mistress Selene treats her girls well, and they're all paid handsomely."

"Paid as handsomely as she can afford, which still isn't much," I reminded her, tightening the grip I had on myself. "All for the lowest dredges of Eldoris to paw them and touch them and hiss dirty words in their ears until their five seconds of glory are over."

"You would judge those women?"

"No," I said gently. "Their work is honest, even if for many it's born of desperation. But it's not what I wanted for myself. I wanted . . . I wanted love, and adventure, and a stable home. Two out of three isn't so bad."

"There are other options."

"Not for me, Nakia." I sighed. "Any trade position would require at least basic magic. And that's assuming I could be hired at all, given that most of the town is wary of me."

"You're really so willing to marry a prince? A *fae* prince, whom you know little to nothing about? That's just . . . that's . . ." Nakia growled under her breath. "I don't know what you're thinking, to be honest."

I tossed my hands in the air with a groan. "I'm thinking I'm tired of watching Mama split my little sister's food, so there's enough that I only skip a full meal for her every few days instead of every day." I ran my hands across my face, sighing heavily. "I'm thinking that if my brothers didn't feed themselves with berries and mushrooms when they hunt, we wouldn't be able to help you at all. I'm thinking that you don't deserve to go hungry as often as you do, and if your parents cared for you even an inkling as much as we do, you wouldn't."

Nakia lowered her head in shame, and a pang of guilt touched my chest.

"You know we don't count you as a burden," I added. "But you eat less than all of us *because* we can only do so much. Your parents drink every penny they have. They neglect themselves and you, and they've left you absolutely nothing to survive on. I can change that. None of us will have to suffer. Don't you see why I have to do this?"

"I don't want to," she whispered. She looked up at me from under lashes brushed with tears and I stepped forward, scooping her into a crushing hug. Her natural curves had thinned out over the years, the lack of food letting her ribs rub against my arms. The feel of her bones only strengthened my resolve.

"Let me take care of you and my family. I can do this."

"What if he hurts you?"

I hesitated, loosening my hold on her. "You know I'd like to say he won't, but I don't know him. It's a risk I'm willing to take."

"If he lays a hand on you, I'll kill him myself," Rhett said, rapping his knuckles against the door. "Let me in."

"How long have you been listening?" I reprimanded, pulling the door open.

My brother shot me a smile, but it was halfhearted. "Not long." He dropped onto my bed, propping his legs up before he said, "Connak or I should be doing this, you know."

I rolled my eyes. "That's archaic."

"See, you're assuming I mean that we have a duty as the men of the house. Truth is, we're just prettier. Clearly, Bleiz is blind."

A laugh slipped from my lips, a snort tearing from my nose, and Rhett's eyes widened in surprised delight. "Ahh the wee piggy Brena has returned. I wondered where she went."

I clapped a hand over my nose and mouth, trying to restrain the sound even as I fought to breathe through my laughter. Nakia collapsed on the bed beside Rhett, lost to gasped giggles.

"Hate you," I muttered, tossing my blanket over them both.

"**S**top flinching."

"Stop hitting me with a stick!" I protested, glaring at Rhett.

Connak grinned. "I thought you were good at this?"

I swung my long, smoothed stick at him. The end nearly made contact with his chest, but he dipped to the side at the last second. He laughed, swinging his own stick at me with a flourish. I grunted as his makeshift weapon slapped my stomach. We had never been able to afford swords for all of us, but we made do.

Kind of.

At the very least, I didn't feel as helpless and unprepared as I had all those years ago. I never wanted to feel that helpless again. My brothers vehemently agreed.

"We've been training you for how long? And you can't

even dodge our basic attacks?" Rhett's smile slipped, and real concern entered his voice when he added, "What if you get into trouble out there? I'm not confident in your ability to defend yourself when you can't guard your stomach. How am I supposed to simply let you go?"

Connak lowered his stripped branch and cleared his throat, murmuring something about water. He disappeared into the house, and I was left to the thick silence that followed Rhett's revelation. His questions.

"I'm not helpless," I said finally.

"You have no magic, and you've never quite mastered combat. In any form."

I knew he meant well. I knew he was trying to look out for me. But the words stung, mostly because they rang true. If I had magic, maybe I wouldn't be covered in scars. Then again, even Nakia had faltered that night. Maybe it didn't matter how prepared you were. And that sometimes you were faced with things beyond what you knew how to handle until you had to.

"I'll be fine," I murmured.

A low growl of frustration rolled up Rhett's throat. "What are you going to do? Sing them into submission?"

"Who's this 'them' that you're so worried about?" When my brother wouldn't meet my stare, I stepped closer and gripped his arm. "The fae?"

He exhaled, jabbing the ground with his stick. "The fae, the trolls. Does it matter?"

"Speak your mind."

His hazel eyes shimmered when they met mine and I moved without thinking, wrapping my arms tightly around his waist. His own circled my shoulders, pulling me tight to his chest. For a moment, he simply held me, the staggering motion of his chest my only confirmation that he was crying.

"What if something happens to you?" he managed, finally. "What if you don't even make it to the estate? What if—"

"I can't live my life in fear of 'what ifs,'" I said gently.

Rhett pulled back a bit, studying my face with his red-lined eyes. Then he nodded, slowly. "I know. You're right." I hesitantly released my grip on him as he stepped backward, picking up his branch again. "Okay. You're going to do this. And I'm going to tell you everything I know before you do."

"Well, that won't take long," I quipped.

He smiled then, finally, and my heart lightened. "Fae are simple enough. They fight and die much the same as we do, though they can hear quite a bit better with those longer ears of theirs. But they only have one critical weakness." I raised a brow and he said, "Their tattoos."

"Art that's been inked on their skin is their weakness?"

"Their tattoos aren't like elven or human tattoos, Brena. They channel their magic."

I considered the fae that stood watch near the gates, their skin bare as far as I could see. If they had tattoos, I couldn't see them. "So, if they're covered by armor, I'm screwed?"

"I mean, yes. Maybe. But if you can break their tattoos, you'll disrupt their magic. They won't be able to cast."

He whipped an attack at me, so quick that I barely managed to duck out of the way. I narrowed my eyes on him, then considered what he said. "Cutting their tattoos? That sounds too simple."

"I mean . . ." His attention slipped to our sisters, where they danced together among the garden flowers, and he sighed. "I mean, that's what I've been told. I've never tried it."

"Foolproof then, got it."

My brother lifted a shoulder. "Elven magic has limits, but we can do basically anything we need to as long as our powers aren't drained. Conjuring drains a lot of magic, and we can't shift, but that's why we're not fae."

"Sounds like they have the cooler abilities, then."

Rhett sighed again, more heavily this time, ignoring my comment. "Okay. Trolls."

"We've gone over trolls before."

"I don't care. You're leaving so you're going to hear it again. They have two weaknesses, and you have to exploit them whenever available. First—" His stick raised, jabbing into the hollow of my throat. I sputtered, trying to bat it away, but he shook his head. "Trolls have thick skin. It will be really hard for you to land a killing blow on them, especially given that they usually guard their weak spots well. But for some reason, it seems as though most trolls forget about their necks. They probably believe no one will ever get that close. But if you can hit them, aim for their throat. It's a quick death and one of the softest spots on their bodies."

I nodded. "Makes sense."

"As to the other." Rhett lowered his makeshift weapon. "Trolls are greedy. If you can show them something with enough value, you might be able to bargain your way free. They hoard worse than any other creature, worse than the goblins or drakes even. But the pieces they collect are unique. Priceless, even."

I glanced at my clothing, at the tattered pants and oversized hand-me-down shirt. "Well, I think that's out of the question."

Rhett stepped closer. "You're about to marry into the wealthiest home in Numeryon. Do not underestimate how much a trinket belonging to the prince might be worth to the trolls."

I hesitated, trying to read my brother's face. "Are you suggesting I betray the prince? Before I've even met him?"

His stare was intense, his mouth a thin line, when he murmured, "I'm suggesting you do everything you need to stay alive."

4

Eldoris's central square was little more than a grouping of small shops jumbled around a broken excuse for a cobblestone path. No face was unknown, no door unopened to the other residents. The streets smelled of baked bread that mingled with the woodsmoke from the smithy's forge. Ours was a town of peace, of collective camaraderie—mostly.

It was hard to believe that tomorrow morning Eldoris would be my home no longer. My steps faltered at the thought. Home. I was leaving my home. Was I ready for that?

Another part of me leapt at the idea of adventure. At being away from the people that had taunted me in quiet whispers since I was old enough to present magic—since I was four years old. My stomach churned at the memories that welled up. But I pushed them down, as I always did, and tried to pretend they didn't rot me from the inside.

I had known this city since I was small, but that didn't mean they accepted me. A fact I was roughly reminded of as a hard shoulder slammed into mine and rocked my balance. Nakia grabbed my arm to steady me.

"Oh hey, gremlin."

Donovan. My biggest tormentor from childhood on. He was the son of the local blacksmith, all brawn and very little brain. But that didn't stop him from making my life miserable or encouraging others to do so. It was worse that they joined in so easily.

"Go away," Nakia said evenly.

Donovan smiled, running fingers through his short-cropped black hair. He was handsome enough, with a smile that dimpled his sun-tanned cheeks. But his soul was rotten, if our interactions were any indication.

It was that smile he adorned now and I braced for impact. "You've never been able to stop me before, and you certainly don't stand any chance now." His grin widened. "You know, Nakia, you might actually be able to scrape yourself from the bottom of the barrel if you stopped hanging around someone like her." Brown eyes turned in my direction. "Sabrena's like the putrid filth at the bottom of an old vegetable barrel. Disgusting to look at and useless to boot."

I dropped his gaze. I never knew what to say to Donovan.

Nakia's nails dug into my arm. "You're just jealous you never had a chance with her."

"Isn't that the point?" he said. "*No one* wants her. Even Maryna wised up." He leaned closer to me. "Hope you like the spinster life. Maybe you could get a couple cats. I've heard they aren't super discriminating about their companions."

"Go *away*, Donovan," I said finally, the hurt fading into anger.

"Aw, did I strike a nerve?" Donovan laughed. "I'm sorry you're going to die alone and unwanted."

"Tell that to her husband," Nakia snapped.

I froze. So did Donovan, his eyes widening for a fraction of a second, betraying his surprise before he could conceal it.

Then he said, "Oh, wow, did you find another gremlin to breed with?"

Nakia opened her mouth to rip into him, but Donovan's father yelled for him. He waved to us as his son turned to leave, but I saw the way his eyes lingered on me. I didn't want to know the things that family said about me behind closed doors.

But then, I probably knew enough of it. Some of the elves weren't subtle about their feelings on me. I tried not to let it hurt. I never succeeded.

With Donovan gone, I gritted my teeth and moved for the well that sat in the center of the town square. The stone edges were rough under my fingertips. The air was permeated with a damp scent from the underground spring water that fed into the well. A wooden bucket hung from a rope, swinging gently with the wind.

And the weight of what I was doing pressed down on my chest.

Tomorrow, nothing would be familiar. Not even the company.

After another encounter with Donovan, I was starting to warm to the idea. My jaw relaxed a notch.

"You all right?" Nakia's hand warmed my shoulder.

I lifted my own, resting my fingers on hers. "It's strange to think that tomorrow I won't be here."

I turned in time to see Nakia's eyes skim the villagers nearby. None seemed interested in our conversation, but an air of tension surrounded the city that I couldn't quite place. As far as I could tell, there were only a handful of fae around—the ones guarding Eldoris, and the few who had come with Bleiz—and none were in eyesight.

"Is there anything I can do?" Nakia's grip tightened. "What do you need?"

"Sabrena, Nakia." My attention shifted to the interruption. Maryna, the tailor's daughter, nodded to us mildly as she slipped to my side and reached for the draw bucket. Her long chestnut hair fell in waves around her generous curves, her amber skin glowing in the morning light. Maryna had the kind of beauty that sent the men of Eldoris to their knees and the women into frenzied, shallow whispers—none of which a woman with such a good soul deserved.

Nakia withdrew her hand, sending me a look. It wasn't necessary, though. Maryna and I had been nothing for a long time. I certainly didn't intend to try to change things on my way out.

Besides, I'm betrothed.

My stomach flipped at that, at the thought that a husband now waited for me. Or, a fiancé.

"Is it true, then?" Maryna asked. She didn't look at me and focused on the rope she was unfurling.

I kept my tone casual. "Is what true?"

"One of those fae visited your house?"

Of course, the neighbors had seen Bleiz. Nothing went unnoticed in this town. There was no denying it. "And if one did?"

"What did he want?" Maryna looked up, finally.

I had always been drawn to her eyes. You could learn so much about a person through their eyes. Lies, truths, hesitations, confidences. The things that bring them joy. And the things that bring them sorrow. But Maryna's ever-shifting hazel eyes were somehow more. One glance at her eyes and you could see her spirit. The very depth of her person. Her eyes, to me, had always simply been *more*.

I shook myself. Maryna was older than me, and she had made it very clear she wasn't interested in my "shenanigans" anymore. My adventures with Nakia down the coastlines, dancing in the rain until our skirts clung to our legs, or our long swims in Castyr Lake. Nakia and I had wandering souls. Maryna did not.

But I often wondered if her reasons were genuine. I knew my lack of magic made me a tainted match in Eldoris; I was more aware of that fact than anyone. But Maryna hadn't seemed to mind the whispers that followed me. We were so different, and yet, we seemed to work.

Then one day, we didn't. Or so she said.

"He had a proposition," Nakia said finally, nudging my arm to jar me back to the present. Maryna lifted a brow.

"I think my father should know before the rest of the village." I cleared my throat, turning my attention to the well, to the clatter and splash that meant Maryna's bucket was rising. "That's all I can say for now."

"Boo," Maryna said softly. She sidled closer, pressing into my arm. I almost stepped away, uneasy at the familiar contact. "The inn is full of them, you know."

"Them?" I asked, reaching out to help catch the water bucket.

Maryna nodded. "Fae. The prince's personal entourage, if the cocky one is to be believed."

She had to mean Bleiz.

"How long are they staying, have they said?" Nakia asked.

"No idea." Maryna held her jug, filling it with the crystalline spring water. She studied my face for a moment, as though she could discern my secrets. When she came up with nothing, she dipped her head toward Nakia and me. "Have a nice day, ladies."

I kept my eyes on the well as she left, trying not to think of the sway of her hips, or the way her skirts swirled around her long legs. She was the past, and the past was best left there.

Nakia sighed. "Well, that was . . ."

My fingers trailed the rough stone of the well, then fell to my side. "Yeah."

Nakia frowned but didn't press. Instead, she said, "So. What do you need before you leave?"

"I'm not sure," I admitted. "From the sounds of it, nothing more than what I already own. But I wouldn't mind doing another pass of the city before I go."

Nakia looped her arm through mine. "Then that's what we'll do."

And we did. We spent the afternoon visiting each of the shops, chatting with the shop owners and listening to the whispers about the fae visiting the inn. Apparently, they said they were checking Eldoris on rumors of troll sightings, but no one seemed to believe them. Especially since Bleiz had visited our home

And *only* ours.

The right hand of the prince, the elves said. More powerful than any of the men he had with him. And he had come into our home. Rumors were swirling that our father had angered the fae. Stolen a prized catch or passed too far north into darker waters.

I wondered what they would say tomorrow morning when the fae left and I vanished with them? Not that it mattered. Whispers and rumors were nothing more than a fool's pastime.

Nakia's family home was on the far side of the village from my own. We passed it in silence. Her parents had always been terrible, their affection for her always laden with self-serving purpose. But there was one day, one singular event that had sent Nakia fleeing to be free of them—an event she rarely discussed. I was glad we were able to give her somewhere to flee to.

Our path eventually led us to the mystic's shop. Neither of us visited here often, but the inside was warm and comforting and smelled of herbs and spices. Dazzling crystals sparkled in the windows, splashing rainbows across the shop counter. The owner, a matronly woman with soft gray and white curls, smiled at us from the corner where she stood arranging books.

"Good afternoon, ladies," Astra said. Her quiet voice barely reached the front of the room. "What may I do for you?"

"Nothing specific, Astra. We're wandering the village a bit today," Nakia said, dipping into a respectful bow. The older woman returned the gesture, a symbol of the faith they both followed. Their deity was a woman of grace and strength, kindness, and compassion.

I still didn't know what I believed about the universe, or the powers it held.

"Let me read your cards," Astra said, holding out her hands.

"I read my own this morning, thank you," Nakia declined.

But Astra's eyes weren't on my friend, and I hesitated before I relented a small smile. Astra's readings were expensive, and she only rarely offered them freely. If she thought the cards would reveal something of interest though . . .

With the rumors floating around Eldoris, I could understand her curiosity.

"I would like that," I said. "Thank you."

The woman reached out, gripping my fingers in her soft, warm hand. I swallowed the unease that followed me into her back room, a small space draped with soft curtains and overflowing with vibrant green plants. She moved a potted fern from a circular table in the center, gesturing me into one of the thin chairs, and lit a bundle of incense that released shimmering smoke into the air.

Nakia stood near the door, her expression unreadable, watching Astra's every move as the woman gathered a small kettle and filled it with water. She hung it in the massive fireplace that took up most of the far wall of the room. A small blaze sprang to life below her down-turned palm.

"Tea first. Then I shall read your cards."

Astra pulled a deck from one of the cabinets above her head, stacking the cards on the table before she moved on to the next thing. Tea leaves were gathered, and herbs, and finally cinnamon sticks that she reverently laid into each teacup. When the water had boiled and poured into each cup, Astra passed a cup to each of us. Then she sat across from me, leveling her steely blue eyes on my face.

"You're holding a deep secret, young Sabrena." When I didn't deny or confirm, she smiled knowingly. "Never fear. The cards will reveal all, but I have no interest in the affairs of gossip."

Her hands moved swiftly—so smoothly that I almost missed the gestures—until two cards sat flipped before her. Their black faces had silvered illustrations on them, patterns I didn't recognize. She didn't comment on those she pulled, simply read them, then muttered to herself and pulled more. I sipped at my tea, unsure if I was supposed to do anything else, and savored the balance she had struck between the spices and sweeter notes.

"You're to embark on an adventure," Astra murmured finally. She waved her hands over the deck. The cards responded, sliding into a fan, then back into a full deck. Deftly, she pulled another. "And you will be far from home."

Those blue eyes looked up again. When I nodded reluctantly, she turned her attention back to what she was doing. I shot a glance toward Nakia, but my best friend seemed to be hardly breathing, watching with rapt attention at each card Astra drew forth. She would understand better than I what each of the mystic's small gestures meant, what each card symbolized.

Then, abruptly, Astra stopped.

"I can read no more," she said, and the glance she exchanged with Nakia had my stomach writhing.

Astra stared at my face a moment longer than was comfortable. Then she shook her head slowly. "Your future is more solid than most I've seen. Every card I pull points you in the same direction. No matter how many variables I add."

She stood without explaining further, moving for an ancient-looking trunk in the rear corner of the room. Clangs and dings and loud clatters came from the box as she searched. When she finally returned to the table, her hand was tightly balled, but when she extended it to me, her hand was palm up.

"Take it," Astra said. "There will come a time when you need this. You will know when it has come to pass."

The gem she held out was round and as clear as water, embedded with tiny pink flower buds. They seemed to twine toward the center of the stone, around a small, round chamber of deep red, identified as a liquid only by the small bubble that slowly trailed back and forth as the stone moved.

I swallowed hard. "Is it?—"

"Blood?" Astra nodded. "Guard that dropstone with your life. In the wrong hands, it's a powerful magical ingredient. In the right hands, it could save us all."

"And you trust me with this?"

Astra shrugged noncommittally. "The decision isn't mine. It is the way of things." She hesitated, then shook her head as if changing her mind. "So much weight is to rest on your shoulders, Sabrena. May Cytherea guide you through the trials ahead."

5

I was awake long before Bleiz's fist thudded against the wooden door of our home. The prospect of traveling north, across the Aldmir Divide, kept me far from peaceful slumber. No one of elven descent had crossed that line in eons. Or if they had, they hadn't returned. And no wonder, with the threat of both fae and trolls awaiting them. The fae may be kind to the elves in our lands—the Kingdom of Vallenwood—but they were under no such obligation in their own lands.

"We don't have all day," Bleiz called through the door. Then, more gently, he added, "I know this isn't easy. But Devayne Estate is several days' ride north. We have to go."

I sat huddled with Nakia and Rhett next to the fireplace, sharing a blanket. They exchanged a glance, filled with a remorse that, for the first time, made me question my resolve. But then Rhett stood and crossed the room, flinging open the door.

Bleiz stood waiting, clad in a thick wool cloak, a bundle gripped tight in his arms. "You'll need this." He didn't wait for my brother to move out of his way; rather, he simply strode past him and held the rolled cloth out to me. "It'll only get colder the further we go, especially at night."

I accepted the gift reluctantly, but Nakia snatched it away and unrolled the bundle before I could. A set of new fur-lined leathers tumbled into her lap, wrapped tightly in a matching cloak. My jaw slid open.

"You can't mean for me to wear these?" I looked up at the fae. "I can't take something so valuable."

Bleiz rolled his eyes, crossing his arms over his chest. "Wasn't the entire point of this bargain ensuring that you and your family were well cared for?" He paused, a grin spreading across his face. "If some basic leathers and a cloak make you this uneasy, I'm eager to see how you react to your new home."

I swallowed hard, pulling the clothing bundle closer. The dark furs were thick and inviting, soft beneath my fingers. I couldn't fathom the kind of animal that possessed such dark material, nor who had crafted it so finely. But the suit was stiff and unlined, the newest leather. Silver roses twined with vines and leaves were stamped along the bottom of the chest piece, and on the right side, a dragon crest was etched alongside.

"They're beautiful," I murmured finally. "Thank you."

"Get them on, then. We need to go."

My breath caught in my chest, nerves tightening my throat. But I didn't argue. I picked up the heavy pile and slipped between my younger siblings, trying my best to avoid glancing at Mama's tear-streaked cheeks. She had spent much of the previous evening attempting to convince me to decline the offer, but I couldn't do it. Even if any of her arguments had managed to sway me, I had already signed the agreement. The deal was done.

I barely shut the door behind me before it sprang open again, Nakia close at my heel. She eased in the crack, sealing the room again, and stared for a moment at the clothing in my hands.

"So, this is it?" she asked, her voice a soft whisper.

I nodded slowly, forcing down the lump in my throat. "I guess so."

She didn't answer, only inclined her head slightly. I hesitated in the silence, waiting for her words, her accusations, the probing questions I was so used to. But nothing. I waited, but the words never came. My eyes pricked with tears of regret, of concern, of fear, but I blinked them away and laid the new clothing out on the bed. I stripped down to my underthings. Nakia busied herself tossing who knew what into a small drawstring bag while I slipped the clothing on.

The furs were a luxury against my skin, so unlike the cotton I was used to wearing. Each piece fit as though it had been tailored to my body. I didn't know how it could—Bleiz hadn't taken my measurements.

Magic, maybe.

I was so used to not having it . . .

With so much going on, for one moment I had forgotten about my defect. It was strange, the wave of realization that swept over me. I hadn't felt the lack so keenly since I was younger, when we all underwent our testing. Out of the entire group of children, *I* had been the one to fail.

And now I was headed straight to one of the most powerful magic wielders in Numeryon.

To become his *bride*.

My fingers stilled over the threading on my wrist guards. So much could change in what felt like the blink of an eye. Maybe I shouldn't be letting my apprehension carry me away.

"You all right?"

Nakia's voice was a gentle balm to the thunderous beat of my heart. I hadn't noticed the steady pounding in my ears until she spoke, until the quiet broke through the chaos. She had always been that for me—the calm to my storm, the joy to my sorrow. And I had always been that for her.

Who would we turn to now?

"I'll be fine," I said. Nakia had fears enough of her own. She didn't need to know how worried I really was. How much fear I shoved down deep beneath the surface.

I pulled the leather strips through my wrist guards and tied them tight. "I'm wondering what he'll be like. That's all."

Nakia eyed me as though she could see through the lie. Maybe she could. She didn't comment; instead, she silently helped me lace up the sides of the chest piece. When she finished, I latched the small silver clasp of the cloak at my throat, then lifted the bag filled with all the possessions I had deemed most important. It wasn't very large. I hadn't taken much clothing; I didn't own much to begin with. But I had my blanket, my most beloved belonging, and that would have to be enough. That would have to tide me over when I inevitably grew homesick.

"Well," I whispered, reaching for the door. Before my fingers could reach the handle, Nakia threw her arms around my neck. The bag fell from my hands and I clung to her, letting the wellspring of emotions I had tamped down erupt into soft sobs. Her scent filled my senses, the soft floral notes of jasmine and lavender and violets that were Nakia, and hers alone.

"I'll be here, in Eldoris," she murmured, brushing away her own tears as she stepped back. "I'll stay here until you can return, or send word, or—"

"Don't hold yourself back from better things," I said, reaching out to squeeze her fingers. "You deserve the finest things. The best that life has to offer. I'll be okay."

Nakia didn't argue. She dried off her cheeks. I wiped at my own. And we stepped from the room, both acutely aware of the heavy weight that slid into place as we closed the door behind us.

Bleiz waited inside the door now, an ominous sentinel who was surprisingly silent. There was no judgment in his eyes today, no sarcasm. He simply gestured to my family and waited.

Connak stepped forward immediately to grip my shoulder. My eldest brother stared at me, hard, with his sapphire eyes. A beat of silence passed, then another. He warred with his emotions, as well as putting them to words, just as he always had. But finally, he said, "We'll be here. If you need us, you have only to ask. We'll be at your side."

"I know." I placed my hand over his. "I appreciate you, brother."

Rhett took my bag and placed it near the door. My little sisters stared at me, wide eyed, and I saw the moment their young minds processed what was happening. Kirsi and Aleksei couldn't fully understand. And the confusion in their eyes broke my heart.

"Brena—" Aleksei said with a soft whimper.

"You'll be okay," I assured, moving closer. She only stood to about my stomach, her little pointed ears framed by neat blond curls. I pushed one back, brushing a kiss to her cheek. "I'll come visit when I can."

"What about you?" Kirsi asked.

"I'm going to live with a *prince,*" I said, careful to infuse my voice with the same magical tone I used when I told them bedtime stories.

Kirsi's eyes widened. "A real-life prince?"

"A real-life prince."

My younger sisters launched themselves at me. I teetered under the force of their hugs. Their tears trailed down their cheeks in small cascades that left dark smears on my leather pants. I pulled them both tight into my arms, holding them against me until their scents mingled into a strange, bright mix of flowers and cinnamon that I would never forget as long as I lived.

"I promise. This isn't goodbye, it's a long 'see you later.'"

Connak stepped forward, scooping our sisters into his arms and carrying them back so Rhett could pull me into an embrace of his own.

"Remember what I said, and be careful," he whispered. "Please."

"I will."

"And if you die, I'll find your ghost and send it beyond myself."

"You won't have to find me." I grinned. "I fully intend to haunt you."

Rhett smirked. "Thanks for saving me a step." But his teasing expression slipped and he squeezed me tightly once more. "I love you, sis."

"Love you too, Ree-ree."

"You would," he murmured, mock scowling at the nickname. I laughed until he stepped away and Mama and Nakia were the final two.

Mama couldn't stifle her sobs long enough to get out much more than a choked reminder of how much she loved me. The words were heartfelt, no matter how broken, and I knew she carried the weight of my sacrifice almost as heavily as I did.

"Tell Papa to enjoy life," I said to her. "He'll have the time now."

Mama nodded slowly. "And you?"

"I will too."

She stared intensely at me for a moment, lifting her hand to brush her fingers over my cheek. "My beautiful daughter. My precious songbird. Don't let your voice fade, my love. I've always told you that you don't use it enough." I nodded, and she said, "I love you."

Bleiz threw my bag over his shoulder then. He hadn't interrupted my goodbyes, but he was impatient, his eyes flicking back and forth between the members of my family and the door. I wasn't sure what his worry was exactly, but then, I didn't really know what waited for us north of the divide.

When Nakia moved to hug me, Bleiz released a heavy sigh. He didn't protest though while I clung to the girl who was the closest thing I had ever had to an elder sister. She didn't speak, but she held out her hand, waiting for me to do our secret handshake—two pinky promises, because we would always be friends, a clawed hand, because we were untouchable, and finally a handshake sealed with a glob of our own spit in our palms.

Because I knew no one as well as I knew Nakia, and no one knew me as well as she.

"All done, then?" Bleiz asked.

I looked around the room, taking slow steps toward the door before I nodded. Bleiz flung the door open, revealing the small contingent of fae on horseback that waited outside our home. I knew the neighbors would be talking about that for months to come.

But if my family lived in comfort, I didn't care.

"Take me to your prince."

6

Eldoris was surrounded by large, woven wrought iron walls. Bars surrounded us with curved arches along the base. A cage, some said, albeit a metaphorically gilded one. The truth was that eons back, long before the Ninth War or the trolls, the iron protected us from the very fae who now guarded our borders. I could laugh at the irony of the trolls nearly obliterating their race, but the truth was, there was no humor in it.

Nothing was funny about the Ninth War, or the impact it had on our lands.

We passed the levers that controlled the massive gate at the front of the city, wrought of the same metal and hooked to a system of pulleys. They were covered with vines now and caked with flaking rust. Eldoris hadn't closed the gates since the Ninth War ended. After Prince Kiran struck a bargain with the trolls, we simply left the gates open. Besides my own attack, the trolls hadn't bothered us because of their accord, so we simply didn't bother. There were no curfews, no boundaries.

We could come and go as we pleased and the fae guardians did as well. Why keep out the fae if they might be the first line of protection against being murdered in our sleep by bloodthirsty trolls?

My gaze lingered on the decrepit guardhouse, where elves used to stand watch through the night. Now, only a single fae was posted nearby. He lifted his hand in salute to the group that surrounded me on all sides.

Bleiz rode to my left. The horse he had given me was a sweet animal, a gentle girl with a steady gait. Her eyes were bright, young, her mane a pale yellow that glittered in the sun.

I ran my hand over her soft brown neck, more to reassure myself than her. Bleiz had confirmed that the contingent around me was a majority of the prince's personal guard, but he didn't say why so many of them had ventured so far south. Did they really feel I would be in so much danger above the divide?

The group eyed me with curiosity, but Bleiz was the only one who spoke to me. I hoped this wasn't to be a new normal—a prince's bride, left in solitude even by the prince himself.

"Don't be afraid to ask if you need anything," Bleiz said, interrupting my thoughts as though he could read them. Maybe he could. I still didn't know much about the fae, or their abilities. "The trip north will take a few days. I don't bite. Usually."

"And the rest of them?" I gestured to the stoic men and women around us.

"Trained to not associate themselves with fae royalty unless permitted. Prince Kiran's wife-to-be fits that role."

"Oh." I frowned. "Well, then, whatever order keeps them silent, remove it. I want those around me comfortable. The silence is making my stomach even more uneasy."

Bleiz lifted a shoulder with a small smile, then said, "At ease, friends."

The immediate shift in energy was palpable. Shoulders loosened. Audible exhales whispered around me.

"Hi." The bright voice that spoke came from my right, a cloaked fae that sat astride a dappled mare. "Name's Damara."

"It's nice to meet you," I said.

Damara's hood fell back and I fought to keep my expression even. She was one of the most beautiful people I had ever seen—fae, elven, or otherwise. Her eyes were as blue as the sunlit ocean, her bright copper hair falling in loose waves around her waist. Soft freckles scattered across her ivory skin like constellations, expanding up to even dust her long, pointed ears.

"Is it?" Damara teased. "Are you sure you *want* to be with us?"

I hesitated, and the small beat of silence was all it took for Bleiz to speak up. "Prince Kiran will murder us both if he finds out you left the palace."

"Prince Kiran doesn't notice his staff's presence any more than he notices anything he's not personally invested in," she said, "and you can't convince me otherwise."

My gaze flitted between the two of them. Bleiz wore a deep frown, one that had me concerned that the woman to my right was in for a heavy reprimand when we arrived at Devayne Estate. But her teasing eyes, locked onto Bleiz, held a challenge.

Her lips quirked into a smile. "You won't tell him."

"Even if I don't—" He didn't finish, glancing at the party around us.

Damara lifted an unconcerned shoulder. "I've had my share of stern talkings-to. I'm sure I can handle another." The fae woman looked at me with a gentler smile. "You don't have to worry. Prince Kiran isn't some monster who's going to lash me for leaving the estate. He has his reasons for being concerned for my safety."

"Yes, he does," Bleiz said. His tone was laced with agitation. "He doesn't want to lose you. And neither do I."

Damara ignored him. "What Kiran doesn't know won't kill him, and if he honestly thought he could send Bleiz to the elven lands without him getting into some kind of trouble . . . I mean, *you* weren't in the plans and he dragged you along."

"I was sent to broker peace. Prince Kiran didn't specify *how* I had to do so."

"No, but I don't think he intended for you to bring him an elven bride." Damara grinned. "What's your name?"

"Sabrena," I murmured.

Damara repeated my name, rolling it on her tongue like a fine wine. Then she nodded. "I like it."

I wasn't sure what to say. Murmurs of conversation had begun to travel through the group around us and, for a while, I simply listened, letting their voices wash over me. Bleiz said something more to Damara but, for the moment, I tuned them out.

The road before us was little more than compacted dirt, winding off into a distance I couldn't see the end of. Papa had given me a map of Numeryon the day I turned ten, and I had memorized every inch . . . navigating the wide fields and sprawling forests with the tip of my finger, planning an adventure I would probably never go on.

Funny how so much had changed in the span of a few days.

Around midday, Castyr Lake was replaced by Sedryn Lake. For lakes separated by only a slender cut of land, they couldn't be more different—while Castyr had crystalline water, Sedryn was nearly swampland. Castyr Lake allowed us to feed our families at least small fares when the richer catches of the sea failed. Sedryn was dark and teemed with the creatures of nightmares. The life in that lake had festered, and even from a dozen feet away, the area didn't *feel* right. I couldn't help thinking of Nakia when I passed by this lake. She had literal nightmares of this place, and I wouldn't trade my own for hers for anything in the world. I pulled my horse a few paces farther away.

"It's strange, isn't it?"

I jumped at Damara's voice. She had slipped farther back in the procession for a while, but now she rode at my side again, making herself a barrier between myself and the lake. Even if she didn't realize her positioning, I was grateful for it.

"The lake?" I asked. "We tend to stay away from it."

"As well you should," Bleiz remarked, adjusting the reins he held. "Sedryn Lake isn't full of anything you would want to deal with."

I frowned at the slight emphasis he placed on the word 'you'. "Me, specifically, or my people?"

"Both. If you think the trolls are fearsome, don't ask what lives in the lake."

A shiver chased the length of my spine. I resisted the urge to touch my shoulder, to trace the scars that lingered there. Damara's gaze dipped to my neck, and I nonchalantly moved white strands of hair over the marks. She didn't comment, but I saw the glint in her eyes—the understanding.

"We'll make camp when we hit Eldynstone Forest, around Sinythell. The trees will provide cover, though the trolls know those woods as well as anywhere else." Bleiz's hand slipped to the hilt of his sword. I wondered what horrors someone like him had dealt with? I wondered how old he was and how he knew the prince? But I didn't vocalize any of it, and he didn't give me any clues when he continued. "Our goal is to cross the Aldmir Divide as quickly as possible."

"Where our journey will become significantly more dangerous," one of the men said. I shifted my attention to him, to the soft brown curls that hung around his long, pointed ears. His gray eyes scanned mine. Then he extended a hand. Wispy silvered tattoos circled his wrist. "I'm Oryn."

I shook it, offering my own name. "Are the trolls much worse, to the north?"

Oryn nodded, but it was Damara who said, "Especially for one like you."

"An elf?" I frowned.

She smiled, but there was no teasing in the expression. Her voice was low, barely a whisper, when she said, "No. I think you know what I'm talking about."

My brow pinched together as I considered. Then shot straight up as I realized. Did she know I didn't have magic? My eyes widened.

"Only I know," she murmured, glancing at Oryn, whose attention had strayed when Damara interrupted. "For now. I can sense auras."

A sinking feeling grew in my stomach. "Anyone who can read auras can tell I don't have magic?"

Damara looked around. Bleiz was deep in conversation with Oryn and a tall fae woman. Damara nudged her horse so close to mine that her leg nearly brushed my own. Then she whispered, "My talents are unique. There are very few, if any, in Numeryon who could read your aura as I can. But yes, I can tell you're without elven magic. Elves have swirling currents in their auras, and yours is as still as a calmed lake. I can also tell that you have some kind of trinket that is important to your aura. But that is all I see."

I hesitated. If she knew about the dropstone, it might be in danger. "What do you know of this . . . trinket?"

"Just that your aura is more complete with it around. I don't know what it is, or what purpose it serves."

"Ah," I said, releasing a sigh of relief. "So, the trolls can tell I'm without magic?"

"They can sense magic, they gravitate to it," she said gently. "Magic is rare among their people. It's why the Sorceress took control of them so easily. But, without magic, you're vulnerable to them and they can sense that too. I've never met a non-magic wielder who survived an encounter with the trolls before."

My fingertips brushed the scars on my neck. "You can tell?"

"There aren't a lot of creatures that can make scars that dense." She shrugged. "And I'm not unfamiliar with the troll attack that occurred in the south all those years ago. The prince was livid that one had slipped past our guard." Her throat bobbed, her eyes lowering. "I'm glad you survived. We've lost too many to the trolls."

"You're not bothered that I don't have magic?"

"No," she said, "but you're going to have to tell Prince Kiran. If you don't, I will. He needs to know."

I winced at the thought of having to tell the Prince of the Fae that not only was he marrying an elf, and a poor commoner, but one without magic to boot. Even by thinking the words I realized how little I offered this marriage.

He couldn't possibly want this.

"He doesn't know about it," Damara said, and I realized I had spoken the words aloud. "The marriage, I mean. Bleiz decided this impulsively because Prince Kiran told him to create a bridge of peace between our people. What better way to bridge an imbalance between our people than to unite them?"

I frowned. "Won't Prince Kiran be angry? What if he doesn't want to marry me?"

"He may be angry. If he is, it will be directed at Bleiz, not you." She paused, then sighed. "And honestly, I doubt he'll argue. The prince is desperate to improve relations between our people, and every idea he's tried so far hasn't really seemed to help."

The gnawing discomfort in my stomach grew. I fidgeted with the reins in my hands. "I'll tell him," I said finally. Bleiz's proposition had taken what little control I had over my life, but this . . . this I could still do at my own pace. Maybe if I eased the prince into my failings, my defect . . .

He would know I was poor and an elf immediately, he could see my disfiguring scars with his own eyes. But if he could accept me with those, maybe my lack of magic wouldn't bother him.

I didn't know why it mattered. Why I cared if he hated me. I didn't even know the prince. But for some reason, maybe because I was marrying him, I at least wanted him to *like* me.

Trees dotted the horizon line shortly before the sun fell from the afternoon sky. I hummed softly, ignoring the curious glances of the fae around me. We guided our horses carefully through the branches, over foliage and rotting tree trunks, until the soft sounds of a nearby stream chattered in my ears. Bleiz didn't speak as the water came into view, he just simply waved a hand. The band around him dismounted, then collected the horses to take for water.

Damara passed her mare to another fae woman—Faleen, if I was remembering right—before she offered me her hand while I slipped from the saddle. Standing, Damara was slightly taller than me, slender, but with gentle curves that her traveling leathers did nothing to conceal. She was stunning. I had a feeling that if Nakia were here, the three of us would be thick as thieves.

My heart twinged. I wasn't even a day away but the ache in my chest was a deep-seated pain. I tried to ignore it. In a strange way, it helped that my legs and hips were stiff from riding. My sore muscles were a welcome distraction. I rubbed at them, and at the aching pressure in my tailbone, trying to loosen the strain.

"First time on a horse?" Damara asked.

"No, but it's been a while."

She grinned, the dimples in her cheeks appearing. "You're going to be really sore by the time we reach the estate, then."

"Great," I murmured sarcastically.

But she shoved a waterskin into my hands and, while I greedily drained the contents, my own pains were forgotten for a moment. Instead, I found myself grateful. This fae woman seemed to have taken a liking to me for no real reason. I could use a friend.

When the waterskin was nearly drained, Damara shoved a fat, pink fruit into my hands. I stared at it curiously for a moment, blinking at the familiar shape in such an unfamiliar color, as though the fruit would explain itself. It did not.

"They don't grow this far south," Bleiz said. Juice dribbled onto his chin as he bit into a blush-colored fruit of his own.

"Good goddess, can you not eat like a savage?" one of the nearby fae taunted.

Bleiz grinned. "Oh come on, Galryn. Don't be coy. We know you're not one to shy away from juices on your chin."

I spluttered awkwardly, choking back a laugh even as the fae around us broke into raucous laughter of their own. They jeered good-naturedly at a now very red-faced Galryn.

"They're Sunset Pears," Damara interjected, rolling her eyes. She sank her teeth into a pink fruit, turning it so I could see the inside. The glistening flesh faded between pinks and reds, dripping with a pale juice. "Better than any of their cousins by far, but so hard to tend. Even the gardener at the estate usually kills a tree or two every harvest."

Gardener? I tried to picture the estate, but every image I conjured seemed far too vast or too intimidating for me to linger on.

I sniffed the pear gingerly. A faint, earthy scent lingered around it, softened by notes of sweet sugar. I took a timid bite, relieved when my mouth flooded with flavor—the familiar nectar of our native pears, but with an undertone of something else. Honey, maybe, but richer than any honey I had ever had.

The fae were right, though. The Sunset Pear was possibly the most delicious fruit I had ever eaten.

"She'll adapt to our kingdom quickly," Bleiz snickered, approval in his eyes as I inhaled two of the pink pears.

"Can't imagine why," Faleen said. "Eldoris is a right pisshole, if I've ever seen one."

I balked at the description. "It's really not *so* bad."

"No? Is it wealth and health, then, that most of the citizens are slowly starving to death? Or that the buildings are in such a state of disrepair that I question their survival throughout the winter without further aid?" Faleen frowned. "You may love your home rightly, but it's not without flaws. Your family didn't deserve the fate they were suffering."

"No one should starve to death," I said quietly. "My family or anyone else's."

"And now they don't have to," Damara interrupted, placing

a gentle hand on my arm. "Because you were willing to sacrifice everything for them. Don't think we don't recognize the courage that took. Prince Kiran will see it too."

I frowned, still not sure I should care what Prince Kiran thought. Or these people, if I were being totally honest. But a quiet part of my mind niggled forward, prodding at my common sense. I did care, and there was no helping it. Maybe I would always care. It was the side of me that kept me awake at night, obsessing over the scars that damaged my skin.

Before I curled into the sleep sack Bleiz had provided, I rinsed my face and arms in the stream. Then I crawled between the soft furs and huddled down, the ground hard against my back. I didn't get much sleep that night, despite how exhausted I was from traveling. Not when I looked up and saw towering, leafy canopies spread above my head.

Not when I couldn't see the stars.

7

A long, slow hiss tickled at my ear. I started to bat at the sound, annoyed because I wanted to go back to sleep, when something caught my wrist. No. *Someone.* Their scent—sage and lavender—was too close, too strong.

"Don't move," Bleiz whispered. "Maybe don't even open your eyes."

Fear was a lance that speared into my heart. I barely dared breathe as a soft caress passed over my neck, curling up into my hair. A tickle spread down my ear, to my cheek. The horses nickered and whinnied. Their hooves tapped a nervous beat on the earth. I resisted a shudder as a smooth form slid across my face, and the tiny press of nails bit into my lips and forehead.

"Not yet," Bleiz said, still holding tight to my wrist. "Any sudden movement and the rest of the trip is going to be really painful. So stay still."

I slowed my breathing, carefully measuring each inhale as the weight shifted, lowering to my chest and then down to my stomach. The thick leathers Bleiz had given me kept the nails from digging in, but the slow-moving creature took its time scaling over me.

Then the weight was gone.

"Steady," Oryn warned, his voice sounding from off to my left. "The mellek is almost gone."

Mellek? My heart stopped, then restarted, and I shoved down a burst of panicked laughter. Mellek were creatures from myth and legend, or so I had thought. Long, scaled lizard-like animals with four legs and a long, spike-tipped tail. Illustrated sketches of the creatures haunted the pages of children's books, a warning to keep us from wandering too far into their forests. Their tails were venomous. One jab, and they could end an elven life without thought. Fae were fortunate; they had natural immunities that meant at worst the mellek venom would make them violently ill.

But they weren't supposed to be *real*.

"Why is a mellek this far south?" Damara asked, as casually as though the creature they were discussing was a robin or a squirrel. It took all of my will power to remain still.

"I don't know," Bleiz admitted. A moment passed, then he said, "Sit up, Sabrena. You should be safe."

My eyes flew open. I pushed myself up. The fae around me were alert, hands on their weapons, attention focused on the trees around us. I scanned the clearing for any sign of the mellek, but the grass didn't so much as rustle. Under the panic, the fear, I wondered vaguely if the mellek looked like the illustrations had portrayed it. I glanced up to find Bleiz studying my face intently.

"You all right?"

"I mean, that's not the way I prefer to be woken up," I said. He chuckled. I pulled my knees up, looking around again. "Are we sure it's gone?"

"No," Damara said. "But I'm more worried about why a mellek is here to begin with. They're creatures under the dominion of the fae. Prince Kiran placed specific wards and traps between the kingdoms to ensure they can't easily cross the Aldmir Divide. And he always has small patrols along the crossing too, looking for trolls or creatures that could be of extreme harm to the elves."

I considered that small insight to the prince. If true, it meant he had taken more steps than required toward protecting my people. And I couldn't help the small swell of gratitude I felt at the thought.

"It's unlikely the mellek's presence here, especially in this specific clearing, was coincidental," Bleiz murmured, lips quirking up at the side. "I don't like the implications of that."

Damara turned, eyeing Bleiz carefully. "You think a fae would—"

"No," Bleiz interrupted. "Our relationship with the elves is precarious enough and Prince Kiran has issued strict punishments against any fae who even speaks against an elf unjustly. No fae would risk angering the prince. So no. Not a fae."

A shudder ran through the collective group.

One of the women leaned toward me, briefly introducing herself as Ren before she passed me a waterskin. I took a long swig, listening to the others discuss troll sightings on the borderline.

"Why would the trolls come after me?" I asked Damara quietly. "I'm no one. Literally, no one."

Damara frowned. "It's unlikely the trolls would know you're intended for Prince Kiran. But you're an elf outside the safety of your cities. To them, that could be enticing enough."

"You don't think it was specific to me, then?" When Damara shook her head, I added, "But I'm surrounded by fae. Did none of you sense them?"

"No, we didn't," Bleiz admitted reluctantly. "The trolls are more powerful than even we would like to admit. And they've only grown more so in the last decade, which is why an alliance with the elves is becoming all the more imperative."

"And it would take too long to incapacitate an entire party of fae," Oryn said. "Killing one elf would cause nine circles of problems, and the trolls know we would be the first the elves would blame."

"Because I left with you?"

Ren shook her head. "Do you know any elves who easily trust the fae?"

No. I didn't. Even I was wary of my place and destination, even if the fae had been nothing but amicable. But maybe it was true. Maybe, if the troll threat was so much greater than the elves realized, if we stood any chance of surviving, we had to work together.

When I didn't answer, Ren smiled knowingly. "Didn't think so."

"And the mellek . . . they're willing to work with trolls? In our lore, they're creatures of legend. It's hard to imagine them bowing to another race."

"They don't always have a choice." Faleen's voice was nearly a growl, thick with frustration. "As Bleiz said, the trolls have grown stronger. Mental manipulation isn't outside their skill sets now with the sorceress training them. The less sentient a being is, the more easily they're controlled. Animals, especially a self-serving creature like the mellek, are fodder for them."

Silence fell. The contingent began to move, collecting bed rolls and weapons, calming the skittish horses. Bleiz reached out a hand to pull me to my feet, one so rough with calluses that, for a moment, I was reminded of my father.

That I hadn't been able to say goodbye to him weighed more heavily on me with every step we took forward. I wondered if I would ever have that chance.

"You're not off to a prison," Bleiz said softly. I wondered again if he was reading my thoughts. "Prince Kiran won't stop you from visiting your family."

I exhaled slowly. The ache in my chest eased. "Are you a mind-reader?"

Bleiz laughed, a bright, infectious sound. "No. But I am gifted at reading people in general. And I recognize that look in your eyes, the one that said you're somewhere else. The logical connection was your family."

"Well, you're right," I admitted. "I miss them a great deal already."

"You're all very close." He wasn't asking.

"Yes. Very. When your family is on the brink of starvation, it can bring you together or tear you apart. Nakia's family is barely worthy of the title. But mine was never like that. Every struggle only made us realize how much more we needed each other."

"Hardship builds character," Damara said, grinning playfully. She jerked her chin toward the mare I had been riding. "She's ready. We should go."

"**W**hat's he like?"

Damara's blue eyes turned my way. "Who, Prince Kiran?"

I nodded.

"Hmm." She considered my question, absently stroking the neck of her horse. "He's very serious, but he's always been that way. He was always the child that worried more about his studies and his upcoming title than playing in the mud or exploring the wilds. He was strange that way."

"You've known him long?"

Damara smiled. "Very. I had more than six hundred years on him when he and I first met, and he was young at the time. Maybe fifty."

"And now?"

"Kiran is three-hundred and fifty years old."

I paused on that for a moment. If he was three-hundred and fifty, that made him one hundred and fifty years older than me. Not much, when the lives of our people were as long as they were. And that made Damara . . .

Over nine hundred years old. I didn't dare ask for confirmation.

"Prince Kiran was in the war, you know."

I glanced up at that. Damara wasn't looking at me, though, her eyes locked on her hands. They were twined around the reins of her horse, twisting nervously.

"He was young," she continued. "Too young to be seeing the things he saw. Far too young to watch—"

"I think that should be the prince's story to tell, not yours," Bleiz interrupted, pulling his horse even with my right flank. "Can't give away all his secrets, after all."

Damara lifted a shoulder, then looked at me again. "Prince Kiran is a reserved man. But he should . . . no, he *needs* to talk about his past."

My thoughts raced as we pressed forward. Our horses navigated Eldynstone Forest without difficulty. The plan was to reach the Aldmir Divide by nightfall on the fourth day but, while that offered a measure of safety, it also presented a new danger—trolls. Not that they weren't a concern below the divide, but in the north they had much more reign. There weren't enough fae to control the entire northern region, and the only reason they left the fae be, and were forbidden to go south of the divide, was the prince's treaty. But me? The elves had no such deal with the trolls, and above the divide I was fair game.

And that put a large target on this entire group.

Despite my swirl of anxieties, the forest was quiet around us, broken only by the occasional chatter of birdsong or the rustling of small animals. The fae didn't speak much, instead more alert after the appearance of the mellek. But the silence wasn't uncomfortable.

I wondered if father had returned home, then realized how silly that thought was. How skewed my sense of time had become already. I wondered if anything had changed since I left. Bleiz hadn't given my family any coin that I had seen. But the thought that they might all have three meals a day in their stomachs . . . My family would thrive. Possibilities would open to them that had only been dreams before. Connak could train more. Rhett could pursue his love of literature. My younger siblings wouldn't be limited by the station of their birth.

This was the right choice. Deep within, my very soul sang at the thought.

Even though, as I studied the darkening trees around me, unease leadened in my stomach. Anything could lurk in these woods. I had never been so far from home. If melleks were real and trolls were targeting elves again, anything was possible.

I sucked in a breath, trying to steady the nervous tremor that tickled up my spine. Connak had told me years ago that I should start carrying a dagger with me, and I had always refused, saying that Eldoris was safe enough. Even after the troll attack, I couldn't bring myself to part with the idea that we were safe in our homes. One time, in so many years, had to be a fluke.

My fingers trailed up the leathers that covered the scars on my shoulder, climbing until I brushed the scars that climbed my neck, barely concealed by my hair.

A fluke.

I wasn't sure I believed that, but I still hadn't taken the dagger.

And as an owl's hoot echoed around us, I regretted that decision.

I thought I knew so much of the world. I was so confident, so sure.

But the reality was, I knew nothing.

Nothing at all.

8

Four days after we left Eldoris, we finally crossed the Aldmir Divide. I didn't even realize we were actually at the divide until one of the fae pointed it out. No massive gate greeted us, no stone wall, no gaping crack in the earth. Instead, there was nothing. Disappointingly nothing. The forest simply fell away, unveiling the mountains that rose to our west and a stretch of open field before us. A field that was flat, empty, and ominously silent.

Ahead, on the rugged path of trodden grass we followed, a small post stood. A red ribbon was tied to its top, fluttering in the light breeze. That was their marker, their indicator of the great divide—and a complete let down.

"It's almost as quiet as *Achmyn Morternos,*" Damara murmured to me. At the bewildered expression on my face, she added, "The Isle of Death, in common tongue."

I met her stare. "What language was the first?"

"Draconic."

"And it's very quiet there?"

"Nothing stirs there, anymore," Oryn said, voice low. "Once upon a time, *Achmyn Morternos* was a land of legend, filled with creatures that are now only dreams, even to the fae. And to the dragons as well. The Isle of Death used to be their sanctuary, their haven in a world that saw them only as beasts, even though they were more intelligent than many of the bipedal races."

"And then?"

"And then the trolls," Damara murmured.

I frowned. "Are the dragons gone, then?"

An amused smile flitted over Bleiz's lips, but it was gone so quickly I wasn't sure what it meant. "There was a line of fae, once, who shared kinship with the dragons. The trolls went for their families first."

"That's so sad." I frowned, thinking of the majestic creatures I had seen painted in the borders of one of my favorite texts. "They must have been powerful, if the trolls viewed them as such a threat."

Damara nodded. "One doesn't hold the power of dragons without a target on their back."

I considered that. Then wondered how, if the whole family held those powers, they had been taken out so efficiently. And how, if a force like that had existed, we were to stop them again should they attempt to take Numeryon once more.

"And the Isle of Death?" I asked instead. "It can't have always had such an ominous name."

"No." Bleiz cleared his throat. "We changed it after the war. Trolls used the island as a base of operations, but we don't actually know where they came from."

"We do at least know where their Sorceress hides," Damara said. "A realm, outside of Numeryon."

Bleiz nodded. "True. Madrion."

Even the way he said the name held an ominous tone. I skimmed the mental image I had of the map of Numeryon, but I didn't remember seeing the place marked.

Apparently, Bleiz could see the questions in my eyes. "Madrion is on no map that we can find. No storyteller can pinpoint its location."

"Prince Kiran has spent more than a decade trying to find it," Damara said, her voice so low I almost didn't hear her. "He's been so sure that the Isle of Death was the key, because the first time we saw the trolls, they came from the north. But he spent so much time combing that nightmare of a place and he never found a portal or key or any sign of how to get to Madrion. When Kiran returned from the war, he renamed the island *Achmyn Morternos*. The Isle of Death. He knew the landscape better than anyone . . . and he never wants to go back."

"The blood spilled there stained the soil red for ages," Ren said. "It's only just become somewhat inhabited again, but not many people want to live on an island filled with the bones of the deceased."

"Literally filled." Bleiz winced. "The ground is littered as far as the eye can see."

"All the people who died there were left behind? No burials or . . . or last rights?" I stumbled over my words, uncertain of the religious views of the fae around me. Regardless, the deceased deserved at least that much respect. I would give Nakia, or my mother, the last rights called for by their deities.

Damara's shoulders lifted delicately. "There were too many bodies and, of those, most were beyond identification. The island has become a graveyard in its own right. A sacred ground. Most don't want to or dare tread on *Achmyn Morternos*."

My mare stumbled and I glanced down. The ground was jagged and uneven, and I pitied my poor horse. We had been pushing them so hard for so many days. They were likely beyond exhausted. I hoped we would stop soon, if for nothing else than their sake.

I frowned when the mare stumbled again. I didn't know what I had expected the Aldmir Divide to feel like, but I knew I had expected it to feel . . . magical. *More.* But instead, it was nothing. Vast emptiness. Land and more land, without even the relief of grass or flowers to lighten the heavy atmosphere.

"I hate how exposed we are," Damara muttered. She gestured around. "We're far too easy to see here."

"You mean far too easy to attack?" I asked. When she nodded, I asked, "But Lytharius isn't far, right?"

Some of the fae around us exchanged uneasy glances. Even the horses seemed to hear the name of the city to our north and recoil.

"*Her* spies roam the streets of Lytharius," Bleiz muttered. "You can never be sure where you're actually safe."

My brow drew together. "Her?"

"The Sorceress," Oryn whispered. The tension in the group rose at the words, shoulders tightening, hands sliding to weapons.

Bleiz clenched his jaw. "No more mention of her. Not till we're home."

Fear settled in my stomach, a coiled viper waiting to spring at the first sign of danger. I knew of the Sorceress only by reputation. But the men and women around me were afraid, tense. And they all worked for the one man who had managed to reign her in, even for a time. They flinched at any small mention of the Sorceress.

And names only wielded power if matched by the person holding them.

Zandamoor rose to our right, an intimidating city of cold stone buildings. Bleiz explained, briefly, that the fae had built Zandamoor as a military base—a defensive position to guard the Aldmir Divide. Now it sat largely empty, host to stray fae families and the trolls who tormented them.

The city sat in ominous silence as we passed. Bleiz insisted we kept moving past, even though the horses' hooves were laden with thick mud and their steps had begun to drag. This was the north. And trolls were never far.

"Our goal is to get home safely," Bleiz had said. "And that means all of us in one piece."

But the sun slowly slipped down the horizon and darkness fell. Numeryon fell silent around us. And as the light vanished, safety seemed very far away.

I missed Connak, right then, and his sword. Rhett, and his unfailing aim. Both of their endless bravery. I was glad, though, that my family was safe and hopefully reaping the benefits of this strange arrangement.

Sleep tugged at my eyes and my shoulders sagged forward as we pushed the horses on. We rested at water sources, mostly at small streams that trickled from the mountains and ran between twisting tree roots. Even though the horses needed the breaks, Bleiz paced anxiously the entire time we were still.

I helped clean the horses' hooves, then fed them apples and treats. When sweat gathered on their flanks, we wiped them down with rags. And every time I mounted my poor mare, I murmured soft words of encouragement to her. Promises of rest, and safety, and troughs full of oats and alfalfa.

When morning light began to tease the sky with vibrant strokes of color, Bleiz slowed his horse.

"We're almost to the edge of their territory," he said. "Once we get to Kiran's land, we'll be safe enough to stop for a real rest."

"As long as it doesn't snow," Damara interjected.

"As long as it doesn't snow," Bleiz agreed. He cast a glance toward me. "Winters hit hard and fast this far north. We have more snow than not, and we've already seen flurries on and off for the last fortnight. The temperatures will probably fully drop in a moon cycle."

A shiver ran down my spine. Winters had never been particularly easy for my family, but we also didn't see near-constant snow. I hated the cold, the way it seeped into my very bones and made my body ache. Even my stomach tightened at the thought of winter, at the evenings when food was scarce among too many mouths.

Bleiz and Damara stared at me, concern in their eyes at whatever they saw on my face. I swallowed, composing myself. "And the prince enjoys the snow?"

"Prince Kiran has had his preferences disregarded most of his life," Bleiz said warily. "Including the location of his home."

"That's kind of sad," I admitted.

Bleiz nodded. "But he doesn't suffer for it."

"Much," Damara disagreed. The look Bleiz gave her told me this was a long-standing debate between the two. Maybe Bleiz didn't understand how having no choices, or your choices disregarded completely, could affect you.

"How much longer till we reach the estate?" I asked hesitantly.

"Nervous?" Damara grinned. All tension from the previous conversation melted away. "Another day to a day and a half. We'll camp as soon as we've safely passed into Kiran's lands, then be on to the estate by the end of the following afternoon at the latest."

I nodded and considered her response, but my stare was locked onto the elegant stitch work on the saddle horn.

A day. Maybe two. And I was to meet him.

Prince Kiran.

My *husband-to-be.*

The words sat heavier with each step forward. And that day, there were many. We hardly stopped at all. But as night began to fall, Bleiz gestured far to his right. The sparse ground melted into lush grass. A wooden pillar stood toward the edge, a few dozen feet ahead of us, wrapped with vines. At the post's top, a slender banner fluttered gently in the breeze—a cloth dyed in the palest, moon-white silver and a blue the color of a cloudless sky.

"Prince Kiran's colors." Bleiz glanced around at the group. "We'll set camp at the first creek and be set to move by late morning. I know we're all desperate for some rest."

Murmurs of appreciation broke the silence.

And something else.

A chorus of snarls and the soft, steady beat of drums.

"They wouldn't dare," Damara said, eyes wild.

Bleiz drew his sword in answer, the fae around him pulling their own weapons in a whoosh of smooth metal. Furious snarls sounded in response, but I still didn't see the trolls. Damara nudged my arm, pointing toward the trees that led into the mountains.

"There," she whispered. "They're trying to bait us toward them, I think."

"Quiet," Bleiz shushed, eyes scanning the grassland. "We need to—"

Creatures covered with slick, shining silver scales and bright white fur burst from the ground in a shower of rock and dirt. Three of the beasts, ten feet in length apiece, landed hard in sprays of earth. I covered my face with my hands. The motion cost me; my sweet mare reared back, and I wasn't fast enough to grab her reins again before she threw me to the ground. I landed beside the silver-plated creatures.

"Vyrshal! Pets of the trolls, vermin of the worst kind." Bleiz yelled as he grabbed my arm and yanked me to my feet. "Run! Get past the borderline of Kiran's territory. They can't follow you there. Hide in the trees."

"We can't fight these," Oryn argued.

"No," Bleiz agreed, "but we need to hold them so as many of us as possible can get to safety."

Panic coursed through my veins as Bleiz shoved me behind him. The vyrshal rose on their hind legs, staring out of sunken eyes that glowed icy blue in their sockets. Their massive underbellies were lined with more of those silver scales. Thick white fur covered their legs and paws and split the center of their backs.

"Go," Bleiz snapped. Bright amber magic flickered around his hands, swarming down the edge of his ebonsteel blade.

I turned on my heel and ran, bolting for the safety of the borderline. But loud, pounding footsteps shook the ground and a clawed paw slammed into my chest. I flew backward, tumbling into Faleen and Oryn and two others I didn't quite know. The air whooshed from my lungs as hands and strands of colorful magic scrambled to catch me, but the vyrshal's blow had been too strong, too fast. We fell in a tangle of limbs, all magic collapsing into the ground as though a weapon knocked from its wielder's hands. The vyrshal let out a loud bellow. One of the others mimicked the sound, followed by the third.

Bleiz yelled a command from my left. We scrambled across the ground on hands and knees, ignoring our wounds and aching limbs, racing for the banner that heralded safety. A vyrshal snarled, bounding after us, narrowly missing Damara's leg with a snap of its powerful jaws.

My face hit the ground. A heavy paw pinned me down, scraping the bits of my legs and arms exposed by tears in my leathers. My cheek pressed into the dirt, rocks biting into my skin. A scream of pain rose in my throat, but I shoved the sound back down. Instead, I twisted against the weight that held me captive, refusing, *refusing* to be a victim over and over again for the rest of my life. If this were how it was to end, I was going to fight back, not cower.

Not this time.

I shoved at the white furred paw, ignoring the scrape of the sharp claw tips against my neck. The terror that rose inside me tried to freeze me, to inhibit my senses, to overwhelm the courage I gripped in desperation.

But I would not be that girl the troll marred. I had worked too hard, come too far, to be her again. Even if the claws pressing down on me were suffocating me. Even if the corners of my vision were slowly darkening into black.

A roar shook the field, larger than all three of the vyrshal combined. Around me the earth trembled in its wake and the trees shook. The claws pressed down harder; the lingering air shoved violently from my lungs.

Then they were gone, and I was free.

I didn't pause to think about why. I just jolted to my feet, ready to run.

And then stopped dead in my tracks.

Dragon.

I thought Bleiz had said the dragons were gone. But there before me, shredding through the Vyrshal's fur in a spray of crimson blood, was a dragon as white as newly fallen snow.

He tore into the vyrshal that had pinned me down, brandishing claws and teeth as he snarled at Bleiz and the other fae. His icy blue eyes were filled with fury, and it wasn't until he lowered that furious stare on me that I noticed that his left eye was brown on the inner quarter. The dragon released a low, rumbling growl.

"*Move.*"

Damara grabbed my arm and yanked, dragging me toward the borderline. She paused every few moments to toss bolts of what looked to be blue lightning over her shoulder. But I couldn't seem to tear my eyes from the dragon, from the elegant white horns that arched backward over his neck, to be sure he was real. He loosed another bone-shaking roar as he caught one of the vyrshal between his jaws. Blood poured over his chin, flesh hanging from between his teeth. My stomach recoiled. I knew he was saving us, yet . . .

The drumbeats grew louder. Two more vyrshal rushed toward us from the trees. Damara tugged my arm with more force, leading us forward. A weight slammed into me; sharp pain seared down my right arm.

Then I was tumbling, rolling over the grass with speed. Rocks and branches jabbed into my hands as I raised them to protect my face. One of the creatures barreled after me. I sought Damara but she was laying in the grass, still as death. My heart clenched. I tried to lift myself to my feet, but my right arm collapsed under my weight. Blood coated the grass under my hand and I winced when I looked down. Lacerations spanned the length of my arm, deep gashes that reminded me of another time, another attack.

I took a deep breath, trying to steady myself, to keep focus. To be courageous again. But the vyrshal was closing in. I shut my eyes, braced for the pain.

But it never came.

My eyes sprang open in time to see the white dragon charge over at the last second, his massive claws tearing into the earth and shaking the ground around me. I looked up at his scaled belly, looming above me, his long tail flicking in agitation as he batted the vyrshal away. Bleiz dipped between the dragon's legs, scooping me into his arms, murmuring soft reassurances as he bolted for the borderline. The dragon followed closely, holding the beasts at bay.

We didn't make it to the prince's territory before the drumbeats faded away. Before everything around me faded into black.

9

*L**emon.*
    I inhaled again, slowly, taking in the scent. Definitely
lemon. I tensed. Lemons weren't easily found in Eldoris. The
bright fruits had to be imported in their seasons, from lands far to
the south, and they were so expensive that most of us considered
them a luxury. When we did get one, Mama would squeeze out
every bit of juice, and each time—even though she knew they
wouldn't take—she tried to plant the seeds. If we were lucky,
sometimes she could spare some of the juice and would make
sweetened lemon water.

    My mouth watered at the memory of summers spent
sipping at the treat. I took another deep breath, letting the
familiar scent fill my nose. Then my mind fully caught up to my
senses.

    It was too late in the year for lemons in Eldoris.

    I shot upright, ignoring the spinning behind my eyes as
I tried to figure out where I was. Aching pain spread through

my body and I glanced down. New scars ran the length of my arm, but they were soft pink like they had been healed for years. I wondered vaguely how long I had been out. Days? Weeks?

My fingers gripped soft, white fur blankets, spread over a bed that was bigger than any I had ever seen. Wispy curtains of gauzy blue fabric circled me on all sides. I leaned against the pile of down pillows behind me and inhaled a soothing breath to calm the nausea that tumbled through me. Then I reached out to push one of the curtains aside.

"Oh, good, you're awake. The mistress will want to know."

I jumped at the voice and scanned the room. A fae woman stood nearby, setting down what looked to be knitting needles and yarn, only to turn back and stoop into a bow. Her hair, a silver gray at the roots that faded into dull blue, fell loose around her shoulders. When she straightened, I took in her face, all soft angles that made me think she couldn't be much older than me.

"I'm Niserie, ma'am," she said, her voice bright and friendly. Her blue eyes were vibrant against her pale skin. Soft fae lights sparkled from the locks of her hair, and her gown was simple blue cotton with an equally modest white apron tied at her slender waist. "Mistress Damara has been asking about you. Shall I get her?"

"That would be fine, thank you," I murmured. The lemon scent was still strong, disorienting. Or maybe it was the strange room, the overly fluffy bed, the unfamiliar woman I hadn't expected to be waiting for me when I woke up.

Niserie bowed again, then moved for the door. I pushed myself to my feet, searching the room as I steadied myself on the small bedside table. The chair Niserie had been sitting on was large, plush, and seemed to have been dragged from in front of a massive fireplace where its mate waited. Opposite them was a wall of tall windows. Lured by the thought of the crisp morning air, I moved for those first.

A pair of tall doors blended in with the windows except for a pair of handles that sat at about waist height. At first, they resisted, the hinges tinged with rust that sharply contrasted the clean shine of the rest of the room. After a moment they released and I was able to step out onto the balcony.

Devayne Estate was massive, nearly a palace in its own right.

I was only a few floors up, but the building rose far above me. Flower gardens sprawled across the lawns below, trapped somewhere between meticulous care and a state of utter neglect. The beds weren't too overgrown, but the paths were cracked and littered with weeds, and the one fountain I could see was barren. I frowned, examining the estate around me. Once, the stone walls had clearly been white. Now they were aged, flecked, and stained with browns and yellows. Ivy and vines twisted the balcony railing, peeping over and threatening to grow across the windows.

How had a prince, a fae prince, with all the wealth and resources of his position, let his home fall into such disrepair?

"The estate was beautiful, once," Damara said, stepping out onto the balcony.

"You're all right?" I asked. The image of her, unmoving on the ground, flashed in my mind and I barely suppressed a shudder.

Damara grinned. Her thick red hair fell forward in a long braid. "Just a bump. An embarrassing one, sure, but I'm fine. No lasting damage." She stepped closer and reached out to grab my wrist. Her eyes lingered at the new scars as she rotated my arm, then her gaze slid upward, to the older scars that climbed from the collar of my nightdress up my throat.

Wait.

I gasped. Who had undressed me? Dressed me? I hastily crossed my arms over my chest.

Damara laughed, the sound more relaxed here at the estate. "Niserie and I tended to you. Not Bleiz."

Not Kiran, she left unsaid.

"Thank you."

"How are *you* feeling?"

I shrugged, taking in my surroundings again. Distantly, well past the gardens and an unkempt lawn, a line of trees rose dark and ominous in the morning sun. "How long was I out?"

"Not as long as you might think. The rest of yesterday and last night."

"Then how—" I gestured to the new scars on my arm.

"Magic." Damara moved closer, leaning against the balcony railing. Her brow furrowed in the middle as she eyed me warily. "I forget you don't have it."

"I don't," I murmured bitterly.

Damara's face softened apologetically. "I didn't mean—"

"Is he angry?" I asked, by way of changing the subject. "You said Bleiz brought me here without him knowing."

"I'm not sure," she admitted. "He never returned to the estate with us. Bleiz went out to find him last night but returned alone. He said wherever Kiran was, he didn't want to be found."

The prince's territory must be vast, if Bleiz couldn't find him. Or he kept haunts that not even his most trusted knew about. I wondered what that meant for me—if he would ever trust me, or if our marriage was only to ever be symbolic.

Damara must have read the curiosity and confusion on my face—she shifted uneasily and adjusted the laced tunic that hugged her form. Sheaths were tight around her left thigh, daggers tucked neatly within. "I could take you on a tour of the estate if you want. Not much else for us to do until Kiran returns and we can formally introduce you."

My expression must have told her how uncomfortable I was at that prospect because she giggled, her eyes glinting with mischief. "Come on. Let's get you dressed. And don't worry about the prince. Truly. He's not so bad."

By the time I was dressed, I knew the names of the primary serving staff I would be interacting with—Niserie, Luca, and Eero—and Damara had confirmed that they used a mixture of lemon, water, and herbs to clean the estate. I wasn't sure why that knowledge, or the lingering citrus scent in the air, were so comforting. But when my nerves raised, I took a deep breath. The familiar tang reigned in the heavy thoughts of Mama, Papa, and my siblings.

I missed my family so much.

And I missed Nakia. When Damara pressed the dropstone into my palm, because it had fallen from my clothing, and told me to keep it close, tears welled in my eyes. I blinked them away before she could comment, but Damara seemed to sense my changing moods. Maybe she was simply reading my aura, if it could tell her such things. I didn't know.

But I followed her through the estate, along chilled stone hallways laden with art—paintings and tapestries and sculptures of all sizes and styles—into rooms she thought might interest me.

Devayne Estate was beyond anything I could have ever imagined.

Damara pointed out a library, a music room, rooms for almost every kind of art in the known world. She didn't say if Kiran took interest in the different crafts, or if the rooms had been built for others. Maybe those who came before Kiran and his family. But a thin layer of dust covered many of the rooms and I found questions beginning to circle my mind, all revolving around this fae prince.

Like why the pristine piano had been immaculately polished, in a room where many of the other instruments were clearly falling into abandoned disrepair.

I didn't dare ask, though.

Damara was kind, and generous with her information, but I could tell that certain topics were off limits. A secret, or maybe many, weighed heavily on these halls. And I couldn't stop myself from searching every room to figure out what those secrets might be while carefully considering her every word.

My curiosity peaked when she led me outside through the paths that lined the gardens. Cobbled gray stone ran between the beds of flowers and herbs, cracked and tickled with weeds. The whole area was enclosed with rough stone walls that rose to about the height of my head. And toward the back, I found my first hint to all the secrets that lingered in the shadows.

A door—closed, padlocked, and covered in chains now overgrown with thorny vines.

"We don't go in there," Damara said softly, stepping firmly between me and the door.

I stared at the heavy lock, debating the merits of trying to swoop around the fae woman. But the thought of her blue lightning restrained me, and I asked instead, "What's in there?"

She shifted uncomfortably. "Not much. Not anymore."

"So, what *was* in there?" I persisted.

Her gaze fell to the ground. When she looked up again, sadness lay where moments before there had been joy. "Hope."

I didn't press further, though her answer only added to the swarm of questions circling around my head. She led me back inside, the light in her eyes returning at the mention of the kitchens and lunch. We were almost to the foyer when thundering footsteps brought her chatter to a halt. Damara pulled me into an alcove with a finger over her lips. When I raised an eyebrow, curious, she tapped her ear. *Listen.*

A second pair of steps joined those booming ones. The voice that spoke was soft, persuasive, almost pleading in its insistence. I recognized the tone immediately: Bleiz.

"*How dare you!*" the second voice growled. I recoiled as the sound echoed through my mind, projected as loudly as though the speaker was yelling in my face.

Clicking filled the silence and I glanced at Damara in confusion.

Talons, she mouthed.

Talons? As in—

I jerked my head back and forth between Damara and the foyer ahead so fast it nearly made me dizzy. Damara had to restrain a laugh, pulling me closer to her and deeper into the shadows before she murmured, "Yes. The dragon. You'll see."

I didn't know what that meant. Did that white dragon live here? *In* the estate? That would explain the high ceilings and wide door arches. I shook myself and focused back on the male voices. Their angry conversation continued, part of it echoing in my mind and the other part Bleiz's voice.

"*You went against my direct orders,*" snarled the dragon.

"She needs you as much as you need her," Bleiz argued. "Her family lives in squalor. And damnit, Kiran, you deserve to be happy."

Kiran? I stilled completely, my blood icing through my veins. Kiran was the white dragon?

I was to marry a dragon? *An actual dragon?*

Damara's grip tightened on my arm. I barely felt it.

"*You think she doesn't deserve to be happy?*" Kiran continued. "*This poor, innocent girl, whom you dragged from her friends and family? From her home?*"

"You can give this *woman* things they cannot."

"*I cannot give her a proper husband!*" The prince spat, his voice blaring in my mind. "*Did you tell her that, when you stole her future?*"

"No, your highness. You know I don't believe that's true."

Flame lit the shadows, heating even the space where we stood hidden. Kiran huffed angrily as the light extinguished. "It doesn't matter what you believe. *You've damned that girl to a miserable life.*"

"But if—"

"*I'll be keeping my distance, Bleiz.*"

"But sir—"

"*No. You can explain to her why she's betrothed to a dragon.*"

"It doesn't have to be that way." Bleiz paused. When he spoke again, his tone was soft. "Kiran, she's beautiful. I know you're going to love her."

A beat of silence passed, then the prince said in a low, pained voice, "*Then you've damned us all.*"

10

Damara held me still several moments past when the foyer went silent. The loud steps that marked Kiran's presence faded far into the estate, and though Bleiz lingered behind, it wasn't long before even he left, back through the front doors.

"I wish you hadn't found out like this," Damara murmured, leaning against the wall behind her.

"That I wouldn't have found out what, exactly?" I asked. I turned on my heel, pacing a few steps away. A dragon. I was to marry a *dragon*. I wrung my hands, twisting my fingers together until they ached. "I can't be . . . he can't be . . ."

"A dragon?" Damara heaved a sigh, crossing her arms over her chest. "There's a lot to it. More than I could explain in a few moments. And it's not really my story to tell. But yes, Kiran is the white dragon. He's always the white dragon by day."

"And by night?"

"He returns to his fae form, unable to shift back to his dragon even if he tried."

I frowned. "So, he has no control over his powers?"

"No." Damara winced. "Not really."

"That sounds—" I couldn't decide. The fae prince not being able to control his powers put him in a danger I couldn't fathom. Was this part of his bargain? My brow drew together. "That sounds risky."

"It is," she agreed. "And it's not an arrangement he would have chosen for himself, if he felt he'd had an option. But, again, this isn't my story to tell. You'll meet Kiran tonight. You can ask him the questions I'm sure you're eager to ask."

I nodded. "I have a few, yes."

I wasn't so sure I would be able to ask them of the fae prince, though.

Damara seemed to sense my reluctance. "For now, let's worry about lunch."

She crossed the foyer and I followed, somewhat reluctantly. Soft scratch lines were etched along some of the stones, the marks uneven and so shallow I was certain they could be easily scrubbed away.

"It's been harder with limited staff," Damara said, pointing to the marks. "Not as many of us to clean up in general."

"Us?" I didn't know what I assumed Damara was, but I hadn't pictured her working under the dragon.

"Bleiz and I are more like . . . part of Kiran's court, rather than staff. But we've all had to help around the estate after—"

"You wouldn't be revealing our secrets in less than a day, would you?"

I turned at Bleiz's voice, and my shoulders loosened at the casual grin on his face.

"We're touring the estate," Damara said.

"And we're about to find lunch," I added.

Bleiz's smile widened. "My favorite part of the tour. Mind if I join you?"

Damara turned with a shrug. "Try to keep up."

She led us through a small hallway and into a kitchen stocked with more cutlery than I had ever seen in my life. Cabinets lined the upper parts of several walls, though one wall was dedicated to the massive stone hearth that was currently pouring heat into the room. A woman rushed around the counter, stopping to bow deeply as we entered.

"My lady," she said softly, reaching up to push a silvered curl off her forehead. I glanced at Damara, but she nudged me forward a step. "It's an honor to meet you. I'm Nythal. At your service, day or night."

"That—I—" I stammered, glancing at the two behind me. Bleiz bit down on his lip, barely restraining an outburst of laughter. I narrowed my eyes at him and took a steadying breath. "Thank you. I'm Sabrena, it's nice to meet you."

"It's been a long time since there's been a *real* lady around the house," Nythal went on, seemingly unaware of my complete lack of grace.

Damara huffed. "All right, well that's just insulting."

Nythal's cheeks bloomed pink. But she shuffled back to the counter without a word, pulled out a long knife and began slicing up a small mountain of potatoes. "I'll have a fruit salad brought to the dining hall if you want. I need a bit longer to finish lunch. I had to get the stew on for supper."

"Sounds fine with us." Bleiz shot Nythal a smile that had her flushing all over again.

Damara grabbed my arm with a roll of her eyes that made the corner of my mouth quirk. She steered me from the kitchen into a massive dining hall and steadied me when I stumbled to a halt.

The dining hall was the same pale stone as the rest of the estate, but the walls danced with rainbow light from the three long, stained-glass windows scaling one side. Farthest from where we stood was a crest, what I assumed to be the crest of Kiran's family—a shield, etched with a rose, circled by the moon, and crowned with stars. A dragon was draped over the shield, its wings draped protectively over the edges. Closest to us was a vine of roses, pink with purple-edged petals, that twined from the bottom of the pane to the very top.

And in the middle, a mural of shimmering glass dragons.

Across the top, wings spread wide, a crimson dragon breathed flame into the blue sky. Right below, an emerald dragon looped up toward the first. And all the way at the bottom was a white dragon with iridescent scales.

I knew that dragon, remembered those icy blue eyes and how the left one was spotted with brown. A shudder ran up my spine. The raw warning that had been in those eyes . . .

And he was to be my husband?

Even if he didn't seem thrilled about it . . .

Damara steered me away from the windows to the long table, gently nudging me into a cushioned chair. The dragon window drew my gaze again, and I frowned.

I turned a hard glare on Bleiz. "I thought you said the dragons were gone."

"No." He smiled. "I said there was a line of fae with dragon lineage."

"*Once,*" I pointed out. "You said once, and that the trolls went for their families first."

Bleiz dropped into the seat across from me, Damara to my right. He lifted his feet, propping them up in the chair beside him. His smile faded, though, as he considered his response. "Kiran has lost a lot. He is possibly the last remaining fae within the bloodline."

"Possibly?"

He lifted a shoulder. "It was never confirmed that his family was the only line of dragons. They were simply the only ones we were aware of."

"And the trolls respect him enough to leave him alone?"

"No," Damara said. Bleiz shot her a warning glance and she shook her head sadly. "I'm not going to say more. We can't. We're forbidden. Even if we wanted to, there are magical binds in place."

I considered her words as Nythal brought out plates loaded

with sliced up fruits. It did explain why everyone seemed so . . . vague. No one really answered my deepest questions, and I still didn't know the details of his bargain. Just that he was a dragon by day, and since Damara had been able to speak those words, it seemed as though they weren't the trigger for whatever curse gripped these halls with fear.

After I picked at the plate with my fork, eating a few bites, I asked, "Is this my life now, then? Being tracked by you two and doing . . . whatever I please?"

Bleiz laughed. "No. For one, we have better things to do."

"Rude," Damara said, rolling her eyes. "We have duties and responsibilities. Unless we or Kiran have need of you, you're free to do whatever you wish."

"I wander? Around?" I set my fork aside and glanced around the massive dining hall. "I'm not sure I'll know what to do with myself."

"You've never had a day with nothing to do? No chores, no responsibilities?" Bleiz asked. When I shook my head, he frowned. "Maybe we can find something for you to do, if that would help you regain some normalcy?"

I thought back across our day, to every room I had seen. So many of them had caught my interest.

But winter was coming, and I realized I wanted to take advantage of the last days of nice weather. And so I said, "What about the gardens? They seem to need more hands than they're getting."

Damara glanced at Bleiz, hesitant. I wondered at it for all of a moment before Damara said, "That would probably be fine. As long as you don't pass through the door we saw. We can ask Kiran later tonight."

"Yeah," I murmured. "Tonight . . ."

When I would meet him face to face for the first time. The thunderous rhythm of my heart grew loud in my ears.

Bleiz snickered at the look on my face. "Don't be so nervous. The prince really doesn't bite."

"Well. There *is* one exception to that," Damara said gently. "One rule, that must never be broken." When my eyebrow rose, she said, "Unless he's in dragon form, never, *ever,* touch Prince Kiran."

11

Don't touch the prince . . .

Damara's cryptic warning lingered in my mind long past lunch. I couldn't stop turning it over in my mind, trying to find a meaning. I knew Damara and Bleiz were trying to help me, to give me clues as to what was going on, but I wasn't putting anything together. Wasn't the point of our marriage that I would *have* to touch the prince?

My mind wouldn't stop swirling through the clues. Would touching the prince stick him in his dragon form forever? Would it undo their bargain?

Damara didn't seem to want to let me dwell on the thoughts, even when I tried to ask her questions. She spent the better part of the early evening dressing and fluffing me until I was what they deemed ready. But now that they had finally given me a moment's peace, and I stood before the reflective glass, I wasn't sure what to make of what I saw.

"*Who is that?*" I murmured to myself.

Unconsciously, my fingers raised and brushed against the smooth pane I stood before. I didn't recognize myself. A soft pink gown draped my shoulders, the sheer, gossamer fabric shimmering around me. Delicate silver embroidery climbed the skirt of the dress, sparkling with roses and vines. Niserie had procured a soft white rope that now looped my waist, holding the gown more snugly to my hips. Both she and Damara had found silver rings and bracelets that now sat on my wrists and fingers. A matching necklace hung at my throat.

But it wasn't only the clothing—they had tied some of my hair back into elegant braids, but loose tendrils were left free, lightly framing my face. Damara had pinched my cheeks into a soft blush. Even my eyes looked brighter against the pinks and silvers.

I truly didn't know who I was.

"You look beautiful," Damara said, squeezing my shoulder. "Are you ready to meet your husband-to-be?"

I tried to restrain my wince, but part of it must have slipped through because Damara grinned. She handed me a pair of silver-embroidered satin slippers, and I stared at them for a long moment before I slid them on. When I looked up, Damara's eyebrow was lifted, as if confused.

"I've never seen anything so fine, let alone imagined walking in them," I admitted, apprehensive as I took a few steps. The silken fabric was soft against my feet, the leather bottoms sturdy against the stone floors. I spun in a half circle. My skirt rose, fluttering gently back into place.

When I couldn't find another reason to stall, I sighed. "Let's do this, then."

"It's not a death sentence."

I didn't answer. No, this wasn't a death sentence. It wasn't even the worst arrangement I had ever considered. But my mind was full of images of that white dragon, jaws drenched in blood, eyes lit with rage. They scared me. *He* scared me.

And I hadn't even met him yet.

Prince Kiran was to meet us in his formal study, a room on

the second level of the estate, on the western side. Damara led me through with the self-assured confidence of a woman who knew where she was going, and the walk breezed past in a blur of art and nervous heartbeats.

Bleiz waited outside the large, ornately carved wooden doors to the study. Instead of his usual carefree smile, his expression was tight, his shoulders tense. But he forced a grin as we approached, then tapped on the wooden door.

"Here we go," he said to me under his breath, as he pulled one of the brass handles.

I took a deep breath, suddenly aware of how much the soft gown I wore left exposed. Heat flushed my cheeks at the thought of the prince seeing my scars, the ones laid so exposed by the thin material that tied above my shoulders.

But then I was being unceremoniously shoved into the prince's study and the doors closed behind me with a click. I turned to them, like I would flee, but a light cough made me freeze. Panic swarmed my senses. *Dragon* kept replaying in my mind.

I couldn't let him know my fear, though. Not more than he probably already did. Inhaling a deep, steadying breath, I willed steel into my spine and spun around.

The air caught in my lungs. A knot climbed my throat that I tried to shove back down.

Prince Kiran was *stunning*.

Not in the way I was used to. He wasn't like Maryna, all soft curves and lithe beauty. The prince was tall, with dense muscle that pulled at his shirt as he crossed his arms over his chest. His hair was golden brown, pulled back into a loose bun. Light scruff grazed his angular jaw, and those icy blue eyes, the left broken with that singular spot of brown, narrowed on me.

"I um. I—" The prince lifted a brow at my stammering and I tried again. "I'm Sabrena, Your Highness."

"I'm aware," he said dismissively. He moved a step closer, and it was then that I noticed the thick leather gloves that he wore.

Never, ever, touch Prince Kiran.

"It's a pleasure to meet you."

"Is it?" The prince took another step forward. "Because you look more likely to jump out my window than to enjoy this conversation."

"I—"

His brow lifted again, a knowing look crossing his face. I couldn't even find the words to deny it. The prince's expression shifted into casual neutrality, but curiosity sparked in the corners of his eyes—the interest was dim, so hard to see that I nearly missed it.

"You're to be my wife?" he asked finally.

"Yes, Prince Kiran."

"Kiran," he said, waving a gloved hand at me. He leaned against a heavy wooden desk, those piercing eyes still locked onto me. "And do you want that? Marriage to a man you've never met?"

"I've met you now."

I could have sworn the corner of his lips twitched, but as fast as I thought so the expression was gone. "Yes, but not when you accepted Bleiz's ridiculous offer."

"No, that's true." I dropped my gaze, staring at my twisting hands for a moment before I added quietly, "But if you could change your family's lives for the better, would you not do anything? Take any opportunity given to you?"

Kiran was silent long enough that I glanced up. It was with more emotion than he had allowed himself to show thus far that he said, "I would do anything to change my family's lives."

He didn't elaborate and silence fell. A soft ticking caught my ear, and then a gentle melody I hadn't heard in many moons. I sought the source with my eyes, drawn to a wall lined with books—but I couldn't find what made that lovely song. Without thinking I gave voice to the tune, humming softly along until the tinkling music fell silent and I turned to find Kiran staring at me once more, his expression a bald blend of emotions for several seconds before they fell away again.

"You know that song?"

I nodded, curiosity pulling my attention back to the shelves. "My papa used to sing it to me, after he was gone to sea for long periods. He'd rock me to sleep and sing that song."

"And where is he now?"

"At sea again," I sighed, desperately trying to ignore the homesick ache in my chest. "Where did it come from?"

"It's an old fae lullaby. I hadn't realized it had traveled so far south." When he caught sight of my drawn brow, he said, "Oh. You meant—"

Kiran stepped around me to shuffle aside a few trinkets. He pulled out a little silver box. The top was etched with roses and had a circle with twelve numbers. Two arms sat inside the ring of numbers, both still then, without warning, one moved slightly to the right.

"It tells the time of day," Kiran explained, pointing to the numbers. "A clock. But inside . . ."

He lifted the lid. Beneath was a series of tiny gears, all working together to turn the little arms of the clock. Below that was a small cylinder with little metal nibs.

"Every time the clock reaches an hour mark, the music box is triggered by these gears. It'll play the song, then stop."

I stared at the device, fascinated. "An hour mark?"

"Every minute is sixty seconds, every hour sixty minutes," Kiran explained patiently. I looked up, realizing again who I was addressing. And how absolutely naive I must sound.

"I've just never seen—"

"Most haven't," he said. He clicked the box closed and slid it back onto a shelf. "Seconds, minutes, hours . . . It's all a made-up construct. Only the sun and moon can really control the cycles of our lives. A clock is simply a means of personal control. And I must confess . . . it can be nice to set a routine to it."

"I like the stars," I said quietly, dully. The instant the words were out I wondered if he thought me completely stupid.

But then he smiled, a small, tight-lipped expression that

only lasted a few seconds. Too few. I found myself immediately wanting to find a way to make him smile again, but I didn't know how.

His face had become carefully neutral by the time he said, "Let me show you *my* stars."

I raised a confused eyebrow. Kiran clapped his hands together and a light blue glow seemed to emanate from the skin beneath his long sleeves. I gasped when the room fell dark, all the candles flickering out in unison. He adjusted his right glove, pulling it free, then turned his back to me. Another soft glow appeared and lit the shelves. Then he stepped away and tugged his glove back into place.

"Watch," he whispered.

Another clicking rhythm joined the tick of the clock. The steady sound went on for only a handful of beats when small pricks of light began to brighten across the top of the silver box. Kiran gestured to the ceiling of the room, bright with dancing, twinkling specs of light projected from the tiny clock box.

The little lights had formed our night sky, down to the most recognizable patterns.

"Stars," I whispered.

"Of a kind." He pointed to the brightest spot, a star in the middle of the other constellations. "The Star of Elysian."

The central star. Always in the northern sky. I nodded, then pointed to another one. "I'm not familiar with that one."

Kiran examined the diamond shaped constellation, then said, "See the small tail? Fortuna Nanti."

"The fortune swimmer?"

He nodded. "Only visible every fifty years, and so rare that many of the fae revere it as a symbol of luck."

I nodded. Kiran stared at me for an unnerving amount of time. His lips moved, as though he was going to say something. Then, like he thought better of it, he clapped his hands together. The stars vanished and the candles relit. He distanced himself, moving to lean against his desk again.

"I have a question for you," he said, crossing his arms over his chest once more. I frowned at the return of distance but gestured him to proceed. "You don't have magic?"

Heat welled up my neck and shoulders, scorching me with my own shame. Did I have a wax seal on my forehead that said 'magicless?' Almost as immediately, I mourned the loss of the only control I had retained in this entire situation.

"Damara said she wouldn't tell you, so I could." I sighed. "No, I have no magic."

"She never said a word."

I hesitated. "Then how can you tell?"

"The vyrshal," he admitted. "You were completely off guard and off balance, but never once did you reach for any kind of magic to defend yourself. No wielder would have let things get so out of hand without trying their powers."

Guilt, regret, and embarrassment flooded through me. I dropped my gaze to the floor, ignoring the heat that bloomed in my cheeks and the weight that pressed on my chest. "I'm so sorry."

I didn't dare look up during the beat of silence that passed, or even after, when he asked, "For what?"

"For being . . . for having . . ." I wanted to cry. I knew how much of a flaw it was to not have magic. Not only because I was virtually defenseless, but because my lack could pass to any children I might bear. If I chose to bear them, anyway. I heaved in a shuddering breath, fighting to restrain myself, and finished with, "I'm sorry for having this *defect.*"

Kiran crossed the room, so quickly and quietly that I didn't realize he was beside me until the scent of him overwhelmed me— sandalwood, a subtle, sweet citrus, and another layer I didn't quite recognize. A gloved hand cupped my chin, tilting my face up, until Kiran's was mere inches away.

And there was an unidentifiable emotion in his eyes that sent chills the length of my spine. "You were born exactly the way you were meant to be. Your lack of magic isn't a defect, or a flaw. It's simply who you are. We'll work around it."

I sucked in a breath, not sure what to say, but he retreated before I could utter a sound. I couldn't remember the last time anyone outside my family had been kind to me about my lack of magic. My last encounter with Donovan popped into my mind and I winced at how uncontrolled the hurt that rose in me became.

Kiran faced away from me, staring at his bookshelves. When he spoke again, his voice was measured, back to the tone of cool indifference he had been using before. As though nothing said in the last moment had even happened.

"Do you have a weapon? I noticed you didn't reach for anything."

"No," I admitted.

"And you think that's wise?" Kiran spun around, moving two steps closer. He pulled open a drawer of his desk, reaching for an article inside. Then he held a sheathed dagger out to me, his eyes lingering a bit too long on the scars that climbed my neck and arm. "Let's not add to that collection, shall we?"

"Thank you," I said, and took the weapon without argument. The weight was much more substantial than the sticks my brothers had trained with, and my arm wavered.

Kiran didn't miss the tiny tremble.

"We'll work on that, then."

I didn't know what to say. Kiran had evaluated me, in some way, and had decided that my flaws weren't shortcomings? Merely things to work on?

So why didn't I feel better about them?

"You should go," he said, breaking my thoughts. I looked up, confused. After another pause, he added, "It's been nice meeting you."

I hesitated. Things had been going so well, or mostly, I had thought. And then . . . dismissed? In the seconds it took me to process the rejection, Kiran crossed the room, opening the door and holding it wide. I dipped into a stiff bow.

"Your Highness."

He scoffed, a rough sound from the back of his throat, before he said, "Kiran."

And closed the door behind me.

12

"I mean, you lasted longer than I thought you would," Damara said, biting a strawberry in half. "You were in his office for quite a while. I was expecting him to give you his name and boot you out."

"Is he that callous?" I asked. "He didn't seem *so* bad."

We sat in the gardens, surrounded by the sweet scents of flowers and herbs. Damara had offered to join me for my first day tending to the beds, and I was grateful for the help; the gardens were immense, the paths long and twisting and broken. I didn't mind the work, but I would certainly mind getting lost.

"Kiran is . . . *Kiran*. His motivations have always been his own." She finished the strawberry and tossed the leafy nub aside. "He's been through a lot and has a kingdom on his shoulders. A kingdom he never wanted, from a war he only ever wanted to fight and be done with."

"He wanted to fight?"

She shrugged. "Loyalty is ingrained into fae from childhood. We take care of our own. Kiran is no different. When the trolls started pushing, we wanted to push back. Kiran fought that war for too long. And when he came back, when everything started to fall, he was a ghost of who he was. He's still not quite the same. Probably never will be."

I wondered if the Kiran who had shown me his stars was a glimpse into the before. Or if he would always simply be the after.

"But he has his territory, right? The trolls don't come here?"

"Honestly, we don't have enough patrols to ensure they don't *ever* come here," Damara admitted. "But they don't hit the central lines, usually. I can't tell you the cost of securing even a small section of land, but it was high. Too high."

I frowned. Mentally, I tried to picture Numeryon, but seeing a map was vastly different than traveling the land. Living it, working it. Before, I had believed the fae didn't know the hardships we did. It was easy to think that, to not understand the strife and struggles of anyone outside my own people when I had never been outside my home. Even easier when I had on the blinders of my own hardships.

"I'm going to leave you for a bit," Damara said finally, as most of our meal vanished with a flick of her wrist. "I need to check in, make sure there hasn't been any news. Will you be all right out here, or should I send a guard out to follow you around?"

"I'll be fine, thank you."

We gathered the remnants of our lunch into the basket Damara carried. When she headed back inside, I resumed my task—pulling weeds from between the cracked stone walkways.

My knees were achy, red, and imprinted by the uneven stone when night began to fall. A pile of weeds sat to one side, but behind me the walk already seemed improved. Healthier even. The familiar work was comforting.

And the task had kept my mind off the gnawing ache that filled my chest every time I thought of my family.

I skimmed the gardens around me. Bleiz had been

absent all day; Damara hadn't seemed to know why when I asked earlier in the morning. No guards lingered around the walls or corners; no eyes ensured I was doing anything in particular. I hadn't heard or seen anything of Kiran.

The forbidden door taunted my thoughts. I wondered what was inside that, in an otherwise open estate, I wasn't allowed near.

I paced, weighing my options. Opening the door would be a betrayal of trust, trust that they had given me too easily. But I yearned for some control over my life, for a piece of the puzzle that lay broken before me.

And looking . . . just a peek wasn't *really* breaking the rule, right?

Before I could rethink it, my feet carried me across the gardens.

I ran my fingers over the thick chains on the door, wary of the thorns that grew around them. A strange tingling started at my fingertips, trailing up my arms. Reflexively, I started humming a nervous tune, a sound that was little more than air. I didn't have magic, but the sensation flowing through me was what I imagined power might feel like: a warm, buzzing sensation that climbed into one's body as though it simply existed to be there. As soon as I withdrew my hand, the feeling went away.

"Didn't Damara tell you to stay away from this door?"

I jumped at the voice, withdrawing my hand. The heat grew in my cheeks. "Sorry. I couldn't help myself."

"I think you could," Bleiz said with an easy grin. "*I* think you didn't want to."

"Sorry," I murmured again.

He casually looped his arm through mine, tugging me away from the door. I still had questions. I still wanted to know what was so forbidden in the *gardens* of all places.

But now, freshly caught breaking the one rule, wasn't the time to worry about that. I turned my attention to another matter.

"What does magic feel like?"

Bleiz's steps faltered, then resumed. "What do you mean?"

"I don't have it." Bleiz didn't look surprised at that. I wondered if Kiran had told him. But I asked again, "What does it feel like?"

"Well." He hesitated, and I didn't understand why. What could telling me hurt? It wasn't like I could wield anything. Finally, he said, "It's different for everyone, and I obviously can't speak for differences with elven magic. But for us it's a buzzing, or heat, or trickle through the veins. It feels as much a part of us as our skin, and we know when we've been cast on because the magic is foreign and unwelcome in our systems. For the fae, the only painful or uncomfortable part comes from the shift."

"The shift? Is that why Kiran is a dragon?"

Bleiz nodded. "In part. Every fae has an animal form, though. If not for magic the pain would be intolerable."

We passed through the garden gates, moving toward the main estate. The grounds were silent except for the melody of birdsong, twining with the soft shuffle of a breeze that skittered through the leaves. I considered Bleiz's words, and if I would be asking too much, but curiosity won out.

"How does that work? Your shifts?"

"Hmm, asking for fae secrets now. Have you turned spy on us?" He smiled though, and I relaxed. "Every fae receives their animal form when they come of age. We go to a tattooist, one who has been imbued with the magic to see form, and they go into a kind of trance. When they're done, we're inked with our own symbols. To any passerby, they would have no meaning, if the symbols were even seen. But the size of the tattoo can tell you a lot about the size of the form the fae can take; Kiran's upper body, for instance, is nearly covered in inked strokes."

"Because he's a dragon."

"Indeed." He grinned at the hesitation he heard in my voice. "You still don't quite believe it, I see."

"That the man who stood before me last night grows to the size of that massive white dragon? That he *is* a dragon? It's a bit hard to take in for one like me."

"Fair point." Bleiz paused. "He wants to meet with you again this evening."

I winced at that. "And your tattoo?"

"Is sizable enough." He winked, reaching in front of me to pull open the front doors. "Don't you worry about that."

13

My days fell into a steady routine. Mornings spent in the gardens, lunch with Damara or Nythal in the kitchens. Afternoons in the gardens. Rainy days were spent inside, cleaning off statues or paintings or shelves upon shelves of books.

Forgetting was easier, then, when I was busy with tasks around the estate. When I wasn't left to the silence that filled my thoughts with Nakia and Rhett and Connak and all the other family I had left behind. Damara offered to send them letters for me. But given that the guards between Eldoris and Devayne Estate only swapped once a moon cycle, the wait for a reply was long and my own letters piled up. The promised correspondence wasn't much of a balm against the ache in my heart.

Even my nights were filled, each one spent with Kiran in awk-ward, stilted meetings. He didn't seem to want friendship or to get to know me beyond pleasantries and small talk. Our evenings felt like a chore, a task for him, where we asked each other menial questions like our favorite colors and vegetables, and I doubted he retained a fraction of my responses.

After that first night, I never saw him smile.

He didn't talk about the stars. The small hints of emotion I had gleaned from him were all but lost to the weight in his eyes. Somehow, he was even more guarded than before.

Even so, wedding preparations were underway. I had been measured for a gown, asked my color preferences a dozen times or more. The wedding was to be a small affair in the spring, but apparently the lingering staff were determined to make the most of the event—meaning that the preparations started now, to give them more than a season to find and gather resources from Lytharius. Fabrics would have to be woven and dyed. Decorations would have to be crafted. Bright flowers were brought in, and then rejected, only to be planted in the garden in random places. Any the staff thought might hold potential were taken to the estate conservatory, a room nearly as neglected as any of the others.

Niserie told me that she hoped by the time the gardens were blooming, Kiran and I wouldn't be such strangers. She said it with such gentle sincerity that I knew she meant that the awkward tension we carried would be gone. I didn't say I doubted that very much, I simply thanked her. With no progress in our nightly visits, I didn't see how it was possible.

And every day, without fail, I had to answer a million questions. Questions from the prince and anyone else who might snatch moments of my time.

As much as I could, I hid in the gardens. I bided my time, waiting for another opportunity to examine the forbidden door. Under my labor, the pathways slowly cleared. The flowers began to flourish without weeds weighing them down and blocking out the sun. I knew their lives were limited; the air at night grew chillier with every passing day, and the gardener had already begun to prepare the beds for the snow. He laboriously followed the trail I cleared. We didn't really speak, but

I could tell he was grateful for the help. He didn't even seem to mind my relentless humming.

Every day, we inched closer to that door.

And every day, Damara or Bleiz would come out to the gardens and peek in on me, bringing me snacks or water. I knew they were making sure I wasn't doing exactly what I most wanted to do. Their regular, spontaneous visits made sneaking around nearly impossible.

I began to think a full moon cycle would pass before I had another opportunity. By then the small flutters of snow might become full storms, and I would be crazy to leave the estate more than I had to.

In the back of my mind, I knew I should let it be. One rule, and I couldn't seem to respect it. But not knowing was killing me. Curiosity was flooding my sensibilities. Making no progress with Kiran only made me more desperate to get back to the door. I had to understand what kind of secret these fae would keep from me when they were so open with nearly everything else. What could be so bad, in the garden of all places? No one seemed to want to answer even the most innocent of questions that I asked about the enclosed area. I wasn't used to a home laced with secrets and deceit.

That door haunted my dreams.

But then, I found my chance. Early one afternoon, Bleiz visited with me for a shorter time than usual. When the gardener went inside for his lunch break, I moved.

I brushed my fingers tentatively over the vines that had overgrown the door. They were such a deep, poisonous-looking green, they felt wrong even in these neglected gardens. I scanned the gardens again. No one. A veritable silence.

I pulled my hair back into a leather tie and tested the strength of the chains. Rusted, but strong. The buzzing sensation returned as I poked at the door, at the wood that seemed to have resisted weathering. I didn't know what they were keeping in there, but the door was certainly protected—or strengthened—by magical means I didn't understand.

I circled the long way around the sector of garden, testing for weak spots in the wall. A few chipped niches held promise for hand and foot holds, but the walls were too high and the handholds too few. I frowned. They had thought of nearly everything.

Nearly.

A fruit tree leaned a touch too far over the enclosed edge. The branches peeped into the forbidden area to make the most of the morning sunlight that hit this section of the garden. The branches were too high for me to jump down from, but high enough that I might be able to at least catch a glimpse . . .

I slipped from a rear gate and snuck along the garden wall, till the base of the tree laid at my feet. It wasn't very large, and there weren't many places for me to hold onto, but I wasn't deterred.

"Thank you, Rhett and Connak," I muttered to myself, leaping up to grip the lowest branch.

Bark bit into my palms. I cursed the delicate slippers Damara had given me for the past several days, wondering vaguely if she had done so to prevent this exact situation. Unfortunately for her, my brothers had taught me to climb trees—in boots, cloth wraps, and barefoot. I was more used to not wearing shoes than wearing them.

I clambered to the end of a sturdy looking branch midway up the trunk. My heart pounded in my ears. But aside from the usual, natural sounds, there was nothing to give me pause. No footsteps, no yells. I leaned forward. My breath caught in my lungs.

And I frowned.

The area behind the locked door was as ugly and unkempt as any other part of the garden. Weeds grew rampantly over whatever plants had once grown here. The whole section was a gnarled, twisted mass of vine and leaf. The small segments of path were broken, but not from age like in the rest of the gardens. From a temper, if I had to guess. It looked as though the cobblestones had been torn from the ground, thrown against the walls to shatter into bits. Small, barren plants grew in squared off beds, but they were little more than dried twigs. A graveyard to whatever hope Damara claimed had lain here.

I leaned closer. Beneath me, the branch bent, groaning against my weight. But along the twiggy growths I thought I saw something, and if the little bumps were what I thought they were—

A loud crack interrupted my thoughts. The branch snapped. That dead, littered ground flew toward my face.

And then I was gripped, firmly but carefully, between massive jaws and yanked from danger. I fell onto my knees on the grass and sucked in the air that had left my lungs in a woosh. Dirt bit into my palms, my heart loud and terrified in my ears.

"What do you think you were doing?" A voice snarled, a growling rumble that echoed in my mind. I flinched at the sound, still not used to the shifted-fae way of communication. Then I sighed, and looked up, not quite recognizing the harsh, angry tone.

Kiran.

In full dragon form. Fury blazed in his eyes with such intensity that I almost cowed before them. But I swallowed, hard, and said, "Climbing a tree, what did it look like?"

"Climbing a tree." He huffed at that, a swirl of hot air that heated my skin and ruffled my hair. *"Climbing a tree in the one area you were expressly forbidden to go near."*

"And if I was?" I staggered to my feet, brushing dirt off my legs. "I'm to live here for the rest of my life, and I get no answers whatsoever about this big secret area in the garden? The one everyone whispers about and treats as though it's cursed? How am I supposed to contain my curiosity? Simply stay away?" I took a step forward, so close now I wouldn't even have to extend my hand to touch the scales on his massive nose. Those dragon eyes watched me, and if it weren't for the brown-dotted blue, I would have wondered if Kiran was inside at all. But I stood my ground. "If this is to be my home, I deserve to know."

"*You think I should just trust you?*" he snarled.

"I trusted *you*," I snapped back. "I left everything I've ever known and moved to this estate, days away from my home and family, to *be with you*. And you can't even trust me a *little?*"

"*I don't know you*," he yelled, his anger reverberating in my mind. "*How can I trust you?*"

"You can trust me because I'm here, against all my and my family's better judgment. You can trust me because I've never given you reason to believe I am a person unworthy of trust."

"*I didn't choose this*," he said. His tone was soft, but the words cut into a place he shouldn't have been able to touch. "*I didn't choose* you."

My breaths were laborious, my chest heaving with anger, with frustration, with a lot of emotions that I had been suppressing since I had arrived at the estate. But so many of those emotions were reflected in the eyes staring back at me. Something in my chest caved. I exhaled deeply, dropping my gaze to the ground.

"No more than I chose you," I reminded. I met his stare again. His anger had faded to apprehension, to an emotion that almost felt like concern. "You can trust me, nonetheless. Let me help you."

"*I don't need your help.*"

"Tell me why you're stuck as a dragon during the day. Tell me what was in that garden before."

"*No.*"

"Kiran, please," I pried gently. I stepped forward, running my fingers over the scales of his nose. Their smooth warmth was a contrast to the mild afternoon. For a moment he closed his eyes, and I thought he might bend. I pushed a little more. "You didn't know I was coming, and I left everything to be here. Please. Be my friend."

His eyes sprang open again, and another heavy, warm exhale blew from his nostrils. "*I don't . . . I can't . . .*"

I took a deep breath, crossing my arms over my chest,

plastering on a grin meant to lighten the thick tension rising between us. "Pretty dresses, hours spent humoring your seamstress, days and days of wedding planning. I'd say you owe me this much."

Too far. I knew the moment I finished that last sentence I had pushed too far.

"*Stay away from this section of the garden,*" he snarled, his temper returning. Those dragon eyes narrowed. "*And let's get one thing straight. You have a warm home, food, and clothing. You will want for nothing, and Bleiz has made arrangements to ensure your family will live in wealth and comfort for the rest of their days. I owe you nothing.*"

"Kiran wait," I spat, as his wings spread wide. I opened my mouth to reassure him that I was grateful, to tell him I didn't mean the words the way they came out. But with a shove of his wings and a massive gust of air, he took off into the mid-morning sky, ending all chances I had of uttering another word.

I stared at the dirt on my knees, then looked back into the sky. "Stubborn bastard."

14

A full fortnight had passed since I had last seen Kiran. After our argument, he didn't seem to have any interest in even entertaining our nightly . . . awkwardness.

I couldn't really blame him. But he was right, and I wanted to apologize.

He didn't owe me anything.

Kiran was, without consenting to the arrangement himself, now responsible for providing for my family. He was preparing for a wedding he obviously had no interest in. All for the favor of Bleiz, and the mysterious conversation they'd had in the foyer. And for the peace of two races. This was another life-altering deal brokered for his position and not for his personal interests.

A prince of endless sacrifice.

I wondered what he really gained from it all. He certainly seemed to hold little joy. Maybe he was hoping for an objection; marriages could be ended before they began with a few simple words of protest during the ceremony—words of protest by anyone in attendance.

But since he refused to see me, even when I had sent Damara to arrange a meeting, I had to sit on my apology. I at least stayed far away from the secret area of the garden. Kiran had been right about that too; I had been given really only one rule. Breaking it, with all he was doing, reluctantly or no, was disrespectful. I had known that and chose to ignore it. And if he hadn't intervened, I might have broken my neck.

I supposed I could understand, too, why he might not be so willing to trust me in a circumstance like that. Not that I could make any sense of why that sector of garden was so carefully watched. A grouping of dead, or nearly dead, plants meant nothing to me.

So, I spent my time in the gardens, trying to restore the beauty I knew they had once held, and ignored the growing guilt that gnawed at my stomach. The days were growing darker, colder, and I knew it was only a matter of time before I was stuck in the estate, watching all our hard work become buried beneath blankets of white.

Though, come spring, the gardens would be ripe for replanting, and we could begin replacing the cracked stones. They were already set to be removed. Pulling the weeds now gave us one less thing to worry about when the weather warmed. Visions filled my head of the potential, of how much work was yet to be done, but how glorious the gardens might be with an extra hand.

I sang softly as I trimmed a row of thorny briars off one of the multitude of statues that were littered throughout the gardens. This particular statue was tall, slender, dressed in an ambiguous clothing style I didn't quite recognize—all sharp lines and big buttons.

"Roux," Damara said from behind me, her footsteps so silent I barely heard them. I spun, but her eyes were locked onto the marble figure. "They're the embodiment of the West Wind."

"I've heard those folktales," I said. "The deities that guard our world, guiding us from the skies."

"They're not folktales." Damara crossed her arms over her chest. "And they're not deities. The Winds are a people of their own kind. Without each of the four, the balance of the world falls into chaos."

I glanced up at the tall figure in front of me, at their strong jaw and bright eyes, at the spiked hair that sat haphazardly atop their head. And I frowned. "Where were they when the trolls attacked? When the fae drained the elves of our resources, only to nearly lose your entire race and damn ours?"

Damara winced at the accusation in my voice. Regret was a cold chill that shuddered through me, but she cleared her throat and continued. "The Winds don't tend to involve themselves in the lives of mortals. Even those of us who have extended lifespans."

"So where are they now?"

"No one knows," Damara admitted. She paused to help me with a section of bramble, lifting it to a pile beyond us that we would burn later. "Well, no one but the Seers of Saryshna. And good luck finding them."

"Hmm." I gave Roux one final glance, staring into that marble face carved with such detail I thought they might come to life at any moment. Then I sighed heavily and returned to my task, unconsciously returning to my song.

Damara spent the afternoon with me. We cleared the courtyard around the figure of Roux, and Damara told me stories of the other three Winds—Avriel, of the north, Edric, of the south, and Hanelle, of the east. Each had their own courtyard in the gardens, each area filled with the flowers each Wind preferred. An offering, of kinds, but also a show of respect to the higher beings.

Bleiz joined us near dusk, to warn of dinner and to help us light the bonfire that would sweep away some of the excess weeds and decay that plagued the estate. He brought bars of chocolate, sweet, soft biscuits, and puffy balls of white fluff. He showed me how to char the white fluff in the fire, then laid them on the chocolate and smushed them between the biscuits. I had never eaten such a divine treat in my life. The sweet white fluff melted to a gooey consistency that mingled with the warmed chocolate, and I ate far more of them than any sweet I'd ever had in my life.

With all thoughts of supper completely spoiled, I stared into the fading flames and wondered what my family might have thought of the strangely delightful treat. Nakia would have hated the white fluff. Rhett would have loved them, openly and without care, as would my sisters. Connak would have tried to pretend he didn't enjoy them. Mama would have loved the chocolate, at least.

But it was Papa on whom my thoughts lingered. He would have made sure we all had our fill before he even tried a bite. The ache, the one in my chest that never quite lessened even after nearly a full moon cycle, spread wide. Before I could stop them, a few tears streaked down my cheeks. I tried to wipe them away quickly, but Bleiz caught the motion.

"You all right?" he asked. I dried my hands on the edge of my shirt, nodding shortly, but he lifted an eyebrow at me. "Don't lie. What's on your mind?"

Damara scooched across the paved stone and pushed into my side. "You can tell us. We won't say anything. Even if it's about Kiran," she said with a wink.

I laughed softly, trying to ignore the pang of guilt that the prince's name sent through me. Sighing heavily, I admitted, "I miss my family."

Damara's expression softened considerably. She leaned her head against my shoulder, and I nearly recoiled at the thought of this beautiful girl touching the ugly scars that lay beneath the thin cloth barrier that was my shirt. "Now that I understand."

"Maybe after the wedding you can visit them," Bleiz said quietly. "Once things are a bit safer."

"Safer?"

"Once Kiran has publicly accepted you as his bride, the threat to those who might harm you will be much clearer. No one with an ounce of brains would touch Kiran's chosen queen. Plus, traveling this near to winter isn't all that advisable."

"Makes sense," I muttered. For a moment, we all fell silent. Without thought, I started to sing again under my breath, the words to that lullaby my father had sung to me over and over again.

"Far along the forgotten waves, 'neath the Elysian star, along the shore the path doth wind, far and forever more." Damara's voice joined mine, soft and low. Her eyes were narrowed, though, and when I paused to ask why, she said, "How do you know that song?"

"Papa always sang it to me, when I was little."

Damara glanced at Bleiz, exchanging a look I didn't quite understand. A rasping click broke through the quiet of the gardens. Before I could blink, Bleiz drew his sword and was gone.

"Stay here, stay quiet," Damara whispered. She slunk off into the shadows behind him.

The two fae moved with such near silence that beneath the chirp of cricket song, I couldn't hear them moving about. My hands shook, but I reached for the dagger Kiran had given me that I kept strapped to my right thigh. I held the hilt tightly in my white-knuckled fist. Words filled my mind, in my brother's voices, reminding me relentlessly how to fight—dodge, jab, thrust, turn. Every move meticulous and focused on survival, even with a weapon that was too heavy for me to wield properly.

But when Damara and Bleiz returned, they were in no hurry. Nothing pursued them. Bleiz's sword had been returned to its sheath. No blood spotted their clothing.

"Sabrena. Where did your father hear that song?" Damara asked slowly. She held her right arm behind her back, shielding something from my view.

My brow pulled together. "Out at sea, that's all I know, why?"

"Because no one has sung that song in our lands in a very, very long time," Bleiz said. "And it seems that, for whatever reason, the estate responded to you."

"What does that mean?"

"Do you remember who your father learned it from? A crewmate? A friend?" Bleiz leaned toward me. "It might be imperative that we know why your father knows this song."

I shook my head. "He never said. I could ask, in my next letter?"

"Sabrena," Damara said slowly. "Have you been singing in the gardens every day since you arrived?"

"I'm not sure," I admitted. "I tend to hum, at least, kind of . . . subconsciously? So yes, probably, why?"

The two exchanged a nervous glance, then Damara brought her hand forward. A bright, faintly glowing rose was held between her fingers. In its center, the petals were bright pink, blooming out into a beautiful purple. The firelight made the rose sparkle like it was covered in thousands of diamond dew drops.

"What is that?" I whispered, moving closer. I reached out to touch the rose but pulled back at the last second when I caught Damara studying me curiously.

"You've never heard of the Eventide Rose?" When I shook my head, Bleiz said, "They're a symbol of hope to the fae. After the trolls' first attacks, they began to die. We haven't seen an Eventide Rose in bloom since before the Ninth War was finished."

"Over a hundred years?" I murmured. I returned my focus to the rose, to the soft glitters that sparkled across the petals.

He nodded. "But suddenly one blooms, in the estate gardens, at a point where Kiran—" Bleiz stretched his jaw awkwardly, like he was trying to force out words that simply refused to come. After a second, he clamped his mouth shut and a vein bulged in his throat. He grunted, as if annoyed. "Magic. I can't tell you, even if I wanted to."

"But . . ." Damara said.

Bleiz eyed me. "But the only change to the estate is your presence. And your singing in the gardens."

"They can't be related," I said, eyes widening. "I have no magic."

"And yet . . ." Damara twirled the rose between her fingers. A knot climbed in my throat, the growing silence heavy between us. Then Bleiz spoke again.

"Kiran needs to see this." He stared at me again with an intensity that made my skin crawl. "He needs to see what you've done."

PART TWO

15

I stared at the rose, clutched between Kiran's fingers as
delicately as though he held the finest silk. The petals
sparkled in the lights he had summoned into the garden
with a wave of his hand. No one had spoken since Bleiz finished
recounting what had happened; only the soft shuffle of Kiran's
pacing boots broke the silence. I couldn't read the prince's expression if I tried, but the tight lines of Bleiz and Damara's shoulders
held me still.

While I understood the basic idea of what the Eventide Rose was, and what it meant to the fae people, I couldn't
possibly relate to what they were feeling right now. The rose was
beautiful, maybe one of the most stunning flowers I had ever seen.
And I had seen many. But other than the glittering petals and
the split coloring, nothing about the rose seemed different to me.
The fae around me were visibly shaken. I didn't know what I had
done.

Or why Damara kept shooting me uneasy glances when she

thought I wasn't looking.

"I just don't understand," Kiran said finally, echoing my thoughts. "Why now? Why, when I'm so close—"

Kiran snapped his mouth shut, stifling the thought, his eyes darting to where I stood. He shoved the rose at Bleiz, the temper from the other day flaring in his eyes for the barest hint of a second. Then he stepped toward me.

"You have no powers, whatsoever?"

"None," I said. I moved backward, squirming under the intensity of his stare. "Not even the barest hint of any."

He took another step forward, the temper fading into mild curiosity. "Nothing strange has ever happened to or around you?"

I glanced around the room, at the three fae eyeing me, then rolled my eyes. "Well, there was one time. A fae showed up at my house and carried me away to marry a prince I had never met."

Damara snickered, and even Bleiz struggled to choke back a laugh. Kiran closed his eyes, inhaling deeply before he said, "*Magically.*"

"Oh, you should have specified." I raised a defiant brow. Kiran merely waited. "No, Your Highness, I have not had magic at any point in my life."

"And your singing . . . were you trained?"

My brow furrowed. "No. I liked to sing when I was very young, and I never really stopped. Why does that matter?"

"Because you were singing when the door opened," Damara said gently. "And while it might not be related, it's the only lead we have."

"My singing?" I laughed, a choked, harsh sound. Absurd. It was absolutely ridiculous to think my voice—my non-magical voice—could have anything to do with their rare flower showing up again.

"You'd be surprised," Kiran said. "Sometimes having no power allows you to see how much power you truly have."

I planted my hands on my hips, rolling my head backward until I could see the stars. "Okay, that makes no sense."

Bleiz shook his head. "He's right. Your family has been impoverished, starving, and probably for most of your life, yes?" When I nodded, he said, "To your knowledge, you've been utterly powerless. And yet, somehow a flower that has remained dormant for many, many years is responding to your presence." He gestured to the rose. "Power."

"You don't know that I have anything to do with the Eventide Rose blooming," I protested. "This is all speculation."

"Devayne Estate has been . . . *stagnant* for many years," Kiran said, his voice low and quiet. He wasn't looking at me anymore, rather at his hands and the gloves he never seemed to take off. "There has been nothing new, nothing bright, nothing at all for a very long time."

"What our prince is trying to say," Damara said with a kind smile, "is that you're a welcome change. But in a world filled with magic, you don't have to be magical to make an impact."

"Answer me this," I said tentatively. "You speak of all the magic and power that your people have. That mine have. How, if that's true, are there so many of *my* people starving and dying?"

Kiran didn't balk from the question, much to my surprise. "Magic has limits. Defensive magic is easy. It comes from our blood, and is the most similar to the elves. Shifting magic is channeled through our tattoos, but our tattoos react to any magic use. But even if I wanted to, it's not like we can conjure up regular feasts for your people. Conjuring magic requires an equal or greater sacrifice, much more than the fae can spare right now. You can't make something from nothing, and often the most sentimental sacrifices are the most valuable."

"So, my people are left to die?"

"We're trying," Kiran said, and his voice became a growl. Compassion sparked deep in my chest at the sincerity of his frustration, but it was gone a moment later when he said, "But if I don't save my own people the fae will go extinct. Then nothing will save you from the trolls. So be grateful we've done what we have thus far."

"Kiran," Bleiz warned.

"What?" The prince spun on his friend. "Should we sugarcoat things for her? Should we pretend that the majority of our people don't live in my lands, scrimping for survival, trying to weaken the trolls' forces, *and* trying to defend other races too? Should I pretend I'm the *savior* of Numeryon? That this deal, this *fucking* hundred year bargain—"

Kiran snapped his mouth shut as blue flared at the cuffs of his long sleeves. His hands balled into fists, his breath deep and shuddering. Damara rested her hand on his shoulder and he recoiled, taking several steps back.

"You're going to scare her," Damara said gently.

Kiran looked up at that. He seemed to regain control, calming the storm that raged within. His features relaxed, his hands unclenched. He took a long, deep breath.

But I wasn't afraid. I was intrigued. I was concerned. Kiran might be a man unwilling to accept help, but it seemed like there was much more beneath the surface. His rage, his fury, how much of it was from the weight of carrying a kingdom?

I wasn't scared of him; I wanted to help.

I wanted to ease the pain that crept into the corners of his eyes, hidden under what I was starting to realize was a facade of anger and distance. The weight on Kiran's shoulders was more than just casual responsibility. And the more I learned of the fae, the more I realized I didn't seem to know much of them at all. Not even the handful of stories that had been passed down to us.

If he was going to save his people, I was going to save mine.

I didn't know how much of what I was thinking showed on my face, but Kiran looked away abruptly. He turned his attention back to the rose Bleiz held tenderly in his hands. Glancing between me and the rose, Kiran's brow pinched together. His eyes narrowed.

"You know what this means, yes?" he asked, not waiting for a response. "I'll have to make a trip in the morning. I think it's time. And mother's talisman could be of use, I think."

"I can't go with you," Bleiz said warily. "I have to take a small force south to deal with a band of trolls that are killing off livestock."

"Did I ask you to come?"

Bleiz rolled his eyes. "If you're going *there,* you need someone to go with you. Don't go alone."

Kiran glanced at Damara, who shook her head. "I'm going to visit my mother tomorrow. I don't want to risk waiting much longer and having this war keep us apart more permanently."

He softened at that, again revealing a brief flicker of a man I was far more curious about than the facade.

And in the laden silence that followed, one I didn't entirely understand, I blurted, "I'll go with you."

Kiran's expression hardened in a blink. "No, thank you."

"What do you mean, no thank you? You need someone to go along, yes?"

"Yes, but not *you.*"

I bristled at that, looking to Damara and Bleiz whose attention was suddenly anywhere else. I took an angry step toward the prince. "What's that supposed to mean? Because I don't have magic, I'm not as good as you?"

Kiran's lips twitched. "No. Because you decided to travel across the continent without so much as a dagger to defend yourself."

"Well, I was under the impression your people could handle protection detail."

"You should never assume," Kiran said, crossing his arms over his chest. "Which is why I'm not taking you."

"You need someone to go with you. I have nothing to do. Why not me?"

Kiran eyed me for a moment, then shook his head. "Where I'm going, it's not safe. For anyone. I'm only going out of necessity, and I'm not willing to endanger anyone else."

Curiosity strengthened my resolve. I matched his posture, narrowing my eyes. "You're going in the morning?"

"Yes."

"You're going to need me."

Kiran's eyebrow lifted. "And why's that?"

"In the *morning?* When you're a *dragon?*" I leaned closer, grinning broadly. "Sounds to me like you could use someone with opposable thumbs."

Bleiz's eyes shot wide, his lips clamping tightly together to silence the laugh that rolled up his throat. Damara froze, her expression lit with panic.

But Kiran tilted his head, watching me like a predator that was sizing up its prey. He rubbed a gloved thumb over the hair on his chin. The silence was long, tense, and the smile slowly faded from my lips. I lifted my brow, forcing my expression to issue a challenge to the prince that I didn't really feel. He couldn't know that though—couldn't know that the way he stared at me made the breath catch in my lungs, or that the way his eyes raked over me, slow and accessing, sent flutters through my stomach. Sure, he was to be my future husband, but I didn't need to think of him like that. Not now, and certainly not when he had made his feelings on me abundantly clear.

Especially after he caught me in the gardens.

"Fine," he said, breaking the weighted silence. "You're coming with me. Be ready to leave by morning light. Dress warm."

Kiran turned on his heel, striding back for the Estate. Damara gripped my arm, her grin infectious. She waited until Bleiz had gone after Kiran to whisper, "I hope you're ready."

Confused, I asked, "For . . .?"

She smiled, but the expression was weak. "Kiran's taking you home."

16

Kiran was waiting in front of the estate the moment the sun broke the horizon. I only knew because Bleiz had begun banging on my door while the sky was still dark outside my windows. Damara and Niserie forced me through some semblance of a morning routine, pushing my sleepy self into a bath and nudging me awake every time I started to drift off in the warm water.

Now I stood, staring up at the iridescent white scales of Kiran's massive dragon form, waiting for instructions on what exactly I was meant to do. Bleiz stood near Kiran's head, and though neither of them spoke, they seemed to be sharing thoughts. I wondered how Kiran's dragon speech worked. Magic? Telepathy?

A bitter taste filled my mouth at the first. Magic seemed so useful, and I would never know.

"*But you do have those* thumbs," Kiran said in my mind.

I jumped at the sound. "Are you reading my thoughts?"

His head swung in my direction and it took every ounce of willpower I had not to back away. Those massive, angular dragon eyes held a glimpse into his humanity, even with their vertical pupils, but they were no less unsettling. It was the sheer size of him that made me want to balk away, though. One of his nostrils was easily the size of my head, if not larger. Waves of heat rolled off him, not unbearable, but warm enough that he made the chill morning air feel like a late summer afternoon.

"*I can hear your thoughts, yes.*" Something like amusement flicked across his bright eyes. "*You'll have to learn to control them if you don't want me to. But, it's only like this in dragon form. In my natural form, I cannot hear a thing.*"

"And my dreams? My memories?"

"*Safe, as long as you don't focus on them and turn them into thoughts.*"

I frowned at that, then glanced around. My pack was slung over my shoulders, a bag of food and waterskins. My dagger was strapped at my thigh, the only weapon I would agree to take. Maybe that was foolish, but looking at the beast in front of me, I doubted it.

"*No, you were right the first time. It's always foolish to go unarmed. Especially in our lands.*"

I rolled my eyes at Kiran's voice, loud in my mind, then asked, "What now?"

He jerked that big head toward his back. I stared, eyes wide. Bleiz laughed openly, pointing to a smooth spot between Kiran's wing joints.

"How else did you think you two were going to travel? I can't fit him into a wagon and none of the horses would ever agree to pull him." Bleiz smirked as Kiran snorted. "Have fun."

I started to protest as he walked away, heading for the estate. Part of me wanted to go after him, but since *I* had been the one who insisted I would go . . . I swallowed, hard.

But Kiran's voice rumbled through my mind again, tinged with an uneasy edge. "*I won't let you fall.*"

He didn't move, not even a twitch, just waited as I took in his dragon form. Thick scars cut through some of the otherwise pristine scales across his back. The scales shimmered with rainbow light, and I realized fairly quickly that I wasn't so distracted by his flaws next to his beauty. And it was hard not to get swept into the beauty; Kiran was graceful, elegant. The horns that flowed back over his neck were smooth white bone. Spines rose at even intervals down his back. His long tail laid in the grass, the brilliant scales a sharp contrast to the slowly browning lawn.

"*Are you afraid?*" Kiran asked. He tucked his membranous white wings closer, as though he could make himself a bit smaller and less intimidating.

I shook my head. Because I wasn't afraid, not of him at the very least. And I believed him when he said he wouldn't let me fall. But I couldn't seem to bring myself to step forward, to move closer to the massive dragon that loomed in front of me. It was the dragon that intimidated me, not the man inside.

He seemed to sense that, too. Maybe he was simply reading my thoughts. But his front legs bent, his wings tucked in close, and then his head rested in the grass. To put me at ease, the Prince of the Fae knelt before me. To allow me to climb on his back, he lowered himself to the ground.

And the flutters that battered my ribs then had nothing to do with fear.

Kiran snorted. A gust of warm air brushed over me. I shoved my hesitation—and that lingering other emotion—into the back of my mind and stepped forward. Taking a deep breath, I rested my palm on one of those iridescent scales. Kiran radiated warmth, but his scales didn't burn to the touch. I glanced around for a foothold, for any way to leverage myself against his smooth armor. Kiran huffed, then nudged me upward with one of his long taloned paws.

I practically flew onto his back, falling into a flat space between his wings. A spine sat in front of me, another behind, but I hesitated as I tried to find a hand hold.

"*You won't hurt me,*" Kiran said in my mind, his tone lightly amused.

I wrapped my hands around the spine, gripping tightly. A soft chuckle rumbled through my head and then, with a jolt and a mighty flap of wings, he pushed off.

My knuckles turned white, my hold was so tight. Kiran shook beneath me, each heave of his wings sending us up only to slowly drift a few inches back down. The motion repeated again, and again. My stomach clenched as the trees below us grew smaller, the branches becoming harder to make out as they turned into green masses far beneath where we flew.

Green masses I could fall into.

Vivid images filled my mind, of my body falling. Hitting every branch on the way down. Breaking each bone, one after another.

I clung to him more tightly. Another laugh rolled through my mind. I breathed through my nose, desperately trying to keep the food I had eaten firmly in my stomach.

"*Dropping my elven bride-to-be above a forest and letting her plummet to her death wouldn't work in my favor, if you're wondering.*" Kiran's voice was loud in my mind, and I winced at the sudden sound. "*I'm trying to placate the anger the elves feel toward us, not piss them off even more.*"

"Oh, and now I'm your bride-to-be?" I snarked, regretting opening my mouth almost instantly.

Kiran tossed his head, letting his scales catch rainbows from the sunlight. "*You've been. Even if I'm reluctant to accept Bleiz's plan for me. For us.*"

I wondered how he could hear me, over his wings. "And why is that?"

"*Because you deserve better.*"

"What does that mean?"

Kiran didn't answer, silently leaving me to speculate his words.

After the initial terror, flying wasn't so bad. The world looked different so high in the air, tucked between clouds and ground.

Animals paused in their day to day to stop and stare at the massive dragon that flew above them, but there didn't seem to be any threat to send them scurrying away. Which meant, wherever we were going, it must be in Kiran's territory.

When Kiran began to descend, the sun was high, beating down on my bare skin. I couldn't see much of where we were going, but through the dense foliage hints of the building below peeped out.

Kiran lowered us onto a patch of overgrown grass, alongside a forest line. A throaty growl rumbled through him. Silence fell. Even the birds quieted their song.

"Do you need help?"

I shook my head, then realized Kiran didn't see the gesture. "No."

I slid down his side. Every inch of me dripped with sweat, a thought that made me cringe given I had just been literally riding on Kiran's back. I wiped at my brow, then loosed the leather tie from my wrist and pulled my hair into a messy knot.

Then I looked around.

The grass was actually a lawn, I realized. One that might have been well manicured but had fallen into complete chaos. A massive steel fence rose before us, nearly hidden behind large trees, with a gate large enough that even Kiran could fit through. A gate woven with the forms of dragons, clenching massive jewels in their claws.

An overgrown path of gathered stone led deeper into the trees, but I could only see the barest hints of the building that lay within. The whole place seemed reclaimed by nature.

Still, I expected Kiran to stride forward with the confidence of someone who ruled his realm. I expected him to push through the gate and start grumbling commands.

But he hesitated.

The massive dragon faltered at the sight of a *gate*?

"It's not the gate, but what's inside." Even in my mind his tone was soft, wary.

I hesitated at that, glancing at the gate with new curiosity. "Should I go first?"

He considered a moment longer, scanning the area. Then he stepped forward, nudging the lock with his nose. The hinges were flecked with rust, but it busted with a little pressure. Still, the gate resisted. The metal squealed. Kiran pushed harder and finally the aging metal relented. Then he stepped aside, jerking his head toward the gate.

It was then that he spoke again, and I couldn't name the emotion that made his voice thick when he said, "*Welcome to my home.*"

17

"Your home? Isn't Devayne Estate your home?"

"*It is now,*" he said, his voice a soft caress in my head. "*But once, this was my home. And in many ways, it always will be. Now it's simply full of memories.*"

I stepped through the gate. Tentatively, I led us down the path. Gravel crunched beneath my boots. Birds chirped in the trees around us. It was clear this place had once been well loved and tended. The path was carefully laid, even if it was now overwhelmed with weeds. Once elaborate statues broke the greenery around us, made of purest marble. Now they lay in pieces, scattered ruins on the ground.

But none of the devastation of overgrowth and shattered artwork were nearly as heart wrenching as the building itself. If I thought Devayne Estate was neglected, it was nothing to this crumbling palace of a home.

"What is this place?" I murmured.

Kiran was quiet for such a long time I wasn't sure he was

going to answer. Then he said, "*Ingryst. Or, it was once.*"

I remembered the name. *The Ruins of Ingryst.* It was a pile of rubble on the Numeryon maps and had been since early into the Ninth War. I couldn't remember much about what it had been before. Nor could I remember what had happened here; I only vaguely recalled hearing that it was one of the greatest tragedies in fae history.

Kiran's steps thundered through the unnatural quiet. With every step we took, the birdsong faded. The bugs seemed to keep their distance. Even the light was dim, filtered through the branches of the heavily overgrown trees that had overtaken much of the property.

But then, this palace had been abandoned basically as long as I had been alive.

Nearly two hundred years.

The paths through the property were wide, large enough for Kiran to pass over them easily. I started to wonder at the sheer size of everything, and it took me an embarrassingly long time to realize his family *was* the line of dragons Bleiz had mentioned.

There was a line of fae once who shared kinship with the dragons. The trolls went for their families first.

Hearing my thoughts, Kiran confirmed them in my mind, "*My father had the palace designed to accommodate our shifter forms. Not all of us were dragons, but it allowed us to shift in case of danger.*" He paused for a moment, staring down at the shattered walkway beneath his talons. "*In the end, it didn't matter.*"

I wanted to press. I wanted to ask Kiran a dozen questions. But I held back. Maybe it was the sadness in his tone, or the sorrow in his eyes, but I couldn't bring myself to ask him to relive whatever had happened here.

"Why are we here?" I asked finally.

Kiran jerked as though I had startled him. Then he pawed the ground and shook his head. "*If the roses are blooming again, then things are being set into motion that aren't supposed to be happening yet. I need to find a talisman of my mother's.*"

"Can I help?"

"*We have to get to her wing, first.*"

"Her *wing?*" It was easy to forget how much wealth went into building a home like this when it lay ruined at our feet.

"*My father and mother had their own spaces. Their own hobbies and interests.*" He sighed, but the stare he leveled on the palace was wistful. "*They were in love, though. They didn't deserve their fate. No one deserves their fate.*"

I stepped closer to the dragon prince and rested my palm against one of his scales. He nearly recoiled from the touch and, instead, shivered while bracing himself, as though I would throw a blow. "Kiran. Let me help you. And if not for your sake, let me help for your peoples'."

"*Don't you hate the fae?*" He looked up at me, his fae side shining more brightly through those dragon eyes.

"I don't hate anyone," I admitted. "And I don't hate you."

Kiran huffed, then started walking without a response. I followed, perturbed, but then he said, "*My mother's wing was in the west. Most of the palace has collapsed. I would rather . . .*" He paused in his steps, then blew out a soft breath. "*I would rather you stay out here. You're so . . . fragile.*"

I scoffed at that. Sure, he was right about my not carrying a dagger before. And sure, I was completely out of my element, and in a place of legend to the elves. But I wasn't frail. I had brought my dagger. And climbing rubble certainly wasn't going to hurt me.

"*It's not climbing the rubble I'm worried about,*" he chastised softly. "*It's the collapsing walls. I don't know how much of what remains is stable. Anything could fall at any time. I would rather you not be under it.*"

I rolled the sleeves of my shirt back, checking that my hair was secure in its leather strap. "I'll be fine."

A low growl rolled up Kiran's throat but he didn't stop me as I walked around him, striding for the front doors. I wondered at the emotions revisiting this place must bring up for him. His former home in ruin, little more than a graveyard. We weren't far from the Isle of Death, either.

Then I realized. Ingryst must have been the place the trolls had made landfall.

My stomach clenched. Our first line of defense was the home of dragons, and they hadn't been able to stop them.

What kind of deal had Kiran struck that kept them at bay all this time? I wasn't sure I wanted to know. If Kiran heard the thought, he didn't comment. Maybe he was too magically bound to do so.

The doors were shattered, barely more than splinters that hung on their hinges in their elaborately carved frame. Another rumble of displeasure rolled through my mind as I shoved past the jagged edges and clambered into the palace. Kiran wasn't so elegant, shoving aside the old wood with talons that sent it crumbling to the marbled floor. He seemed uneasy, his gaze flitting around every corner of the dimly lit foyer.

His home had been destroyed, and yet the essence of beauty was still present. The main hall was dark, overgrown with weeds that had shoved their way through the gold veining in the shattered black marble floors. A thick layer of dust lingered on almost every surface, from the ground to the sconces, and up the sweeping staircase that took up most of the far wall.

But there was also an unseen weight here. A presence. As if all the sorrow and grief and death from these halls had never quite left.

As if the end had never really come for the people trapped inside.

Small footprints trailed my steps across the room as I delicately explored the lingering shelves, some still laden with elaborate vases. Decaying plants curled inside a few, little more than brittle remains. Kiran lingered by the entry, watching. Shifting uneasily from paw to paw.

I hesitated at that. The prince had never seemed so . . .

vulnerable. And given that he was a literal *dragon* that loomed several feet above my head, the fact that he seemed almost afraid gave me pause.

Kiran met my stare reluctantly. *"I had almost forgotten what it looked like."*

I couldn't imagine how that would feel. Your childhood home, a faint memory? "Do you remember your parents?"

"Not well," he admitted. *"Memories fade too fast in our lifetimes. I can remember that my mother smelled of the brightest flowers. And I remember my father's laugh. But as to much else..."*

"It's all dim whispers," I said quietly.

Kiran dipped his snout, the closest thing I could imagine to a dragon nodding. *"You sound like you speak from experience."*

"It's not quite the same." When he tilted his head curiously, I added, "Lost love doesn't compare to lost family."

"True," he murmured. *"But grief comes in many colors. It's always painful, no matter the shade."*

I moved closer to Kiran. He eyed me as warily as anything else around him, like I was a snake coiling to strike. But I rested a hand on the top of his nose, and said, "You know you can talk to me. About anything." My fingers roamed the sharp edges of his scales. "I may not understand what you've been through, but I'm willing to try."

"I appreciate that." Kiran hesitated. *"And I'll keep it in mind."*

We fell into silence, but it wasn't uncomfortable. I pulled my gaze from his after a long moment. "So. The west wing?"

Kiran grunted. *"I can go there on my own."*

"I'll just follow. Might as well let me go first."

A loud sigh carried through my mind. But he didn't fight. Simply led the way down the long corridor to our right. His massive taloned feet stirred the dust, and I sneezed until my nose ran and my eyes watered. But I kept following.

The marble floor extended throughout the palace. A

decaying rug splayed out beneath our feet. I worried the scuff of my heels would only rip through the fabric more, but Kiran seemed unphased at the punctures and tears his talons made in the thin material. Maybe he was beyond caring. Or maybe he simply realized this would never be his home again.

Half the corridor had collapsed in on itself, leaving barely enough room for Kiran to squeeze between. We made our way through, toward a staircase near the end that climbed upward in a broad spiral. I was surprised how nimbly the dragon before me climbed those stairs. His wings scraped the walls on either side of us, even as tightly as he had them tucked to his sides, but he kept climbing.

Kiran hesitated for a long moment on the second floor. When he finally moved, I saw why. The landing had caved in, so much so that none of the floor beyond was visible. Debris had spilled onto the stairs. I nearly slipped on the chunks but caught myself before Kiran's annoyed huff could reach me.

We passed another destroyed landing before Kiran finally stepped out onto the third floor. I marveled that the stairs climbed on without us. The sheer size of this home, this palace . . . even without having been constructed for dragons . . . it was enormous. My family's entire home could fit inside the foyer.

The third floor didn't seem safe, exactly, but there was enough space for Kiran to navigate. Every wall was speckled with art of some kind: paintings, tapestries, beautiful woven murals. Time hadn't been kind to any of them.

Nor had it been kind to the family that stared at me from a particularly large painting. Even in oils Kiran's eyes were the brightest blue, the left smudged with brown. But he was younger here. To his right sat a fae girl, younger still. Their parents were behind them, poised and perfect. Kiran looked like his mother. The frown was his father's, though.

"*Keep moving.*"

"Kiran . . . I think you should talk about this. About all of this.

I can't imagine being back here is easy for you."

He didn't respond.

I stumbled on an uneven spot of rug and Kiran shot me a glance that screamed "I told you it was too dangerous."

"I'm fine." I huffed.

But a scream shattered the quiet of the house, and a loud, pounding set of thuds hammered down the stairs behind us. Goosebumps sprang up across my skin. I raced for the railing, leaning over. A figure lay slumped on the stairs beneath.

"Kiran." His name came out of my lips sounding strangled. "Kiran, I didn't think there was anyone here."

"*There's not,*" he said roughly. "*Keep moving.*"

He moved farther down the hall, but I couldn't stop staring at the body laying below. Long hair was scattered across the stone, their face downturned and hidden in the shadows of the stairwell. I shifted between my feet, uneasy, but I couldn't just leave this person here. No matter what Kiran said. I *saw* them.

I couldn't have watched someone fall like that and not do anything about it.

So, I ignored Kiran's order to keep moving and darted down the stairs. The person wasn't terribly far down, but I didn't know which landing they had fallen from. I glanced up, toward the stairs that spiraled so high I couldn't see their ends—and swallowed. But I didn't stop.

Goosebumps skittered across my skin anew when I knelt next to the unmoving form. I reached out a hand to grip their shoulder, only to watch my fingers pass straight through. My eyes widened. I tried again. Straight through. The only indication that the figure was even there was the icy feeling that spread across my hand as it met the spot where we should have touched.

"*Why didn't you listen?*" Kiran asked.

I looked up to see him watching from the landing, and his eyes were filled with sorrow. With grief, pure and stark, and as painful as though whatever loss had happened here had only just happened.

"I had to help," I whispered, reaching for the figure's shoulder again. Cold, and nothing. Nothing solid. "I had to try."

"*You would help her? Most of the fae weren't so willing to help the elves. I understand why you resent us.*"

"Of course," I said. "She's fae, sure, but she needed help . . . I thought."

Kiran considered that. "*I don't understand you. Not one bit.*"

I hesitated, unsure how to answer that. Instead, I used the beat of silence to study the form before me. Her face was feminine, beautiful. She was young, not much older than myself. Her long, pointed ears cut through the elegant tresses that fell around her cheeks and obscured her features. But as I looked, I realized that she had a blue hue to her. Not just her hair, or her eyes, but her skin and her clothing. An aura, almost.

"Who was she?" I asked gently.

Kiran was silent, the air so thick with tension, I genuinely didn't believe I was going to get an answer. Then he inhaled a slow, shaky breath.

"*My sister,*" he said finally.

I spun where I knelt on the ground, seeking eyes that Kiran turned away from me. But the dragon seemed cowed by the admission. I looked back at the girl splayed at my knees. "Is she—?"

"*Yes. And if you wouldn't mind, I don't really want to get into her death at this very moment.*" Kiran paused. "*Besides. Reliving them here, out loud . . . it's asking for the energy here to follow us back to the estate. I'd rather not.*"

"I'm sorry."

Kiran turned away. "*Come on. Be careful. And don't forget that not everything you will see is as it seems.*"

"I see that now," I said. I murmured soft words of safe passage to whatever realm his sister believed in before I stood, climbing back up the steps. By the time I reached the landing again, Kiran's sister was gone. As though she had never been there to begin with.

"*She was the best of us.*" Kiran's voice was barely a whisper in my mind. "*We didn't deserve my sister. And she, of all of us, didn't deserve a fate so cruel.*"

I thought of my own family, then. What I would do for them, how far I would go. "I think you really would do anything for your family."

"*I would have,*" he said. "*But what kind of life is filled with woulds and coulds?*"

18

Finding anything around the devastation seemed impossible. Many of the rooms and halls were collapsed. Two levels above the specter of Kiran's sister, the staircase became little more than crumbled rock jutting from the wall. We could go no higher. Kiran wasn't deterred, though. With passages and staircases throughout the palace, he still had hope we could get to whatever remained of his mother's rooms.

He grumbled quietly in my mind as I picked my way through the ruin. It wasn't so bad though, clambering over fallen stone. The hardest part was knowing that this had been a home, his home, and that the tragedy that had come to them still lingered in these halls. Spirits, like his sister, wandered in meaningless paths around and sometimes through us. They didn't hear me when I spoke to them or react when I touched their arms. If they were here in any conscious way, they didn't show it. Kiran didn't seem to think they were a threat, which was a relief, but my shoulders wouldn't quite relax.

We followed a narrow hallway, one Kiran claimed had a stairway that would lead into his mother's rooms, when he paused in his steps. A low growl rumbled up his throat.

"*I can't go any farther.*"

Those were the last words I had expected from him. I turned around. "Why not?"

"*Look.*" He jerked his chin, motioning toward the passage to our right. The door frame had split and fallen into a pile of wooden debris. Without its support, the stone wall around it must have loosened, because the floor was littered with chunks of rock and dried mortar. A small gap remained, one which a slender form might slip through. But, if Kiran tried to shove through, he would likely collapse the entire wall.

"I can go."

Kiran growled again, softer this time. "*No. We'll have to figure out how to do this without mother's amulet. We don't need it.*"

"What does this amulet do, Kiran? Why is it so important?"

"*It can keep you safe when I can't.*"

I faltered at that. Why was Kiran afraid there would be a time he couldn't keep me safe? And why did he care? I cleared my throat. "We didn't come all this way to give up now." My words were laced with a kind of bravery I didn't feel, but I moved for the hole in the rubble. "What does it look like?"

"*Sabrena,*" Kiran said. Even in my mind I could hear the gentle plea in his voice. "*Let's go back. Forget it. I'll find another ward.*"

"I'll be careful."

The sharp, jagged opening scraped at my leathers, leaving faint marks along the knees. I pulled myself up, pausing for a moment as stone and mortar shook loose under my grasp, tumbling to the floor. Only a bit fell, though. I found solid purchase and pushed.

"*Sabrena, please,*" Kiran nearly begged, more desperately this time.

I slid through the gap, landing on a pile of rubble. Rock

skidded from beneath my boots. I took a moment to steady myself, peering back through at the white dragon that watched me with uneasy eyes.

"See? Perfect." I grinned broadly, then winked. "Guess these thumbs came in handy after all."

"*I don't think you should—*"

"What does the talisman look like, Kiran?"

He hesitated, then said, "*Silver, with a dragon and a black stone.*"

I could feel the agitation rolling off him, but I moved through the narrow passage ahead and tried to focus on not slipping. The air was different, on this side of the opening. Colder. The hair on the back of my neck stood on end and an invisible weight settled over my shoulders. I tried to ignore it, the sensation that something was very wrong. I almost turned back. But I could hear Kiran pacing anxiously behind me, his talons tapping and scraping across the floor. Even if the talisman were only symbolic, even if it had no powers at all, I would get it for him.

This house held so much grief. Maybe taking a token of his mother's would ease some of the pain Kiran carried with him.

Elaborate windows lined this hall, ones that let in the bright light above the trees outside. But afternoon was fading, and the colors of sunset crept in. I didn't know what would happen at night, in this place. Or if we should even be here. But I had to slow my pace as I picked my way down the hall. The open floor had narrowed, the walls around me little more than support beams. When the twisted spiral staircase rose before me, vanishing into the cracked ceiling, relief flooded through me.

Cold steel bit into my palm. Rust caked the once smooth metal railing, and the steel steps protested under my weight. But the palace was quiet—too silent, especially without Kiran nearby. If he could hear my thoughts at this distance, he didn't respond. But I kept climbing. And after a few moments, the stairs opened to the most ornate room I had ever seen.

Passing time had been a little kinder to this room. The elaborate rugs weren't so weathered, their golden threading sparkling under the fading sunlight that leaked in the fractured windows. Full bookshelves climbed a lot of the walls, much of their contents spilling to the floor. A massive wooden desk sat toward the left side, across the way from a small wooden door that was set into the wall.

And all along the ceiling, the shelves, and tucked into the bare wall spaces, hung beautiful cords loaded with precious gems. They dangled like raindrops on spider's webs, glistening in the brightest rainbow of colors.

Behind the desk, on the wall, was a massive painting of a woman with wavy, red-brown hair that dipped around her waist—the same woman I had seen on the portrait floors below. She cradled a tiny sleeping baby in her arms, wrapped in a blanket of silver and blue. Even through the painting, the affection she felt for her child was clear in her blue eyes. I didn't doubt, even for a second, that I was looking at Kiran and his mother.

I wondered then what had happened here. What had happened to each member of his family. Had his mother died violently, a victim of a war the fae seemed to want no part of? Where was his father in all of this?

And, again, I found myself thinking about his bargain. A bargain strong enough to hold the trolls at bay, a race fueled by bloodlust and the need to conquer.

But the sun dipped behind a cloud and I remembered why we were here—the talisman. If I didn't find it soon, we wouldn't have the light to continue.

I searched the office respectfully, checking each drawer and shelf, trying my best not to disturb more than I had to. Nothing stood out to me, though. There were notes and papers, immaculate blue and green quills, wax sticks and metal seal stamps. But no talisman, nothing that even vaguely resembled a magical artifact.

The little wooden door stuck when I tried to push it open.

I winced as I rammed my shoulder against it, unsure the wood wouldn't simply decay under the force. But it popped open, leading to a contrastingly simple bedroom. There was minimal furniture—a massive bed, an armoire, a chest of drawers with a mirror perched on top. A few pieces of clothing lay strewn across the bed, laden with dust and crumbling with age, and scattered about as though someone had grabbed them quickly in an attempt to flee.

But no one had survived the horrors that had fallen on these halls.

No one but Kiran.

I reached toward one of the gowns, brushing my fingertips against the still-soft ebony silk. Ragged lace trim scraped my palm.

"We shouldn't have wasted time on the gowns." I jumped at the soft, female voice. Before I could spin around, she added, "But Kayne insisted. He was so optimistic, until the very end."

The woman standing behind me was tall. Elegant. Her full figure was draped in a dress nearly as elegant as the one I still touched. Long, auburn waves of hair fell to her waist, parted over her lengthy pointed ears. It wasn't her ethereal beauty that caught my attention though.

Instead, I was distracted by the blue aura that clung heavily to her skin and clothing.

"But that's not why you're here, is it?" she asked, pulling my attention back to her face. Her eyes were an icy shade of blue. "No. That's not why you're here."

I shook my head, struggling to swallow the lump of fear that lodged in my throat. She waited patiently until I managed to choke out, "Who are you?"

Her brow lifted in amusement. "Me? I should be asking that of you, a stranger in my home." She leaned forward, taking a closer look at me. "An elf, no less. This should be some story."

I willed steel into my spine, straightening my posture and wishing calm into my voice. Then I tried again. "My name is

Sabrena. I'm here seeking a talisman. You must be Prince Kiran's mother?"

"Astute," she said, a smile tilting the corners of her mouth. "You can call me Aurelia."

"Pleased to meet you," I said hesitantly.

Her blue-tinged fingers brushed along the furniture, reverently. "I know what happened here. I remember every detail as though I lived it only yesterday." Aurelia turned her keen eyes to me again. "What I don't understand is why I'm here now. What changed?"

"I don't know," I admitted. "All I know is the roses bloomed, and now I'm here searching for a talisman that Kiran said might be of help."

Aurelia's head tilted to the side, as though she hadn't quite seen me before. "How do you know Kiran?"

A lump forced its way up my throat again. How to explain the circumstances we found ourselves in? Ours wasn't an ordinary union, even as far as arranged marriages go.

"We're to be married," I said finally.

"My Kiran? Marrying an elf?" Her expression softened, a small smile gracing her beautiful face. "That sounds like him." She paced the length of the room, her phantom skirts not disturbing the dust on the floor. "But I don't understand what talisman you could be searching for. I've only ever had two, and one—" Aurelia lifted her hand, touching a chain that disappeared beneath the neck of her gown. "When I died, it was destroyed. The trolls saw it for what it was."

"Kiran wasn't very specific. But when the roses bloomed, he said we needed to come here, and that he was looking for a silver talisman that could protect me. Could the other talisman have anything to do with the Eventide Rose?"

"The Eventide Roses *stopped* blooming?" Aurelia's eyes widened when I nodded. She considered, running her thumb across her chin. "That's unprecedented. I don't think my second talisman would be of any help."

Aurelia spun, moving for the armoire. She reached out, only for her fingers to pass through the door. Heaving a heavy sigh, she motioned for me.

I opened the door for her, then stepped aside. She gestured to an apron, hung loosely off the door, and specifically to a pocket on its front.

"I never left it behind. Not until that day. In all the panic, I never thought to grab it. I'll be honest, I'm surprised the trolls didn't pillage it. But theirs was a conquest of power, not one for treasure."

The apron was thick cotton and the pockets were deep. I fished around for a moment before I found what she indicated—the missing talisman, a shimmering silver pendant that dangled from a matching chain.

"It's a protective talisman. The metal was enchanted by the Seers of Saryshna, to guard its wearer from poisons and a multitude of malicious magics."

I stared at the etched dragon for a long moment, at the orb of black tourmaline inlaid in its paws. "But how does this help with the roses?"

Silence.

I looked up, scanning the room. There was no sign of Aurelia, no sign she had ever even been there. But behind me, a curtain rustled. The softest breeze flowed through a window near the bed. I sighed, moving to peer out the glass, wondering if that's where Kiran's mother had gone.

The wood flooring squeaked beneath my boots. I reached for the window. A floorboard groaned in protest as I tugged on the pane.

And then the board snapped.

19

The air whooshed from my lungs. I scrambled for grip as I slid through the hole, grasping at the decaying wood crumbling to dust between my fingers. The stone building—once a support beneath the boards—had been ripped away. Below my dangling feet, the floor was nothing more than a jagged wasteland of shattered stone. And I hung precariously, my knuckles whitening as I struggled to shove myself back into Aurelia's room.

I pulled myself partially up, gaining purchase, and a string of hope brightened within me. Sharp pain bit into my legs as I tried to use them as leverage, but I ignored it, clinging desperately to anything that gave me an extra inch.

But the board beneath me splintered and fell apart with a loud snap. Startled, I lost my grip. I slid down, back into the hole. A string of curses left my lips before my grip slipped farther and my breath caught in my throat.

So much for those opposable thumbs now.

I lost another inch. My eyes cinched closed. Images of my life flashed through my mind in a matter of seconds. A life overflowing with regrets and missed chances. Nearly two centuries worth of memories of being too afraid to do the things I wanted to do or to follow any of my dreams. It wasn't the joys of my life, the loves, the smiles that I remembered in my final seconds. Nor even the family whom I missed so desperately my chest had grown a permanent ache.

No, it was the pain. The loss. A list of things I hadn't done and would never do. The comments made by people who didn't even know me, who caused deep scars no one would ever see but I felt every day. My memories turned into a cycle of regrets, and the weight of each one was pulling me down, down, deep into the remains of the palace.

A strong, gloved hand caught my wrist, and Kiran's voice pushed away the nightmares. "I've got you. *Get off her.* Sabrena, I've got you, open your eyes."

My eyes snapped wide.

Kiran's sleeves glowed bright blue from the tattoos etched beneath. His jaw was tight in anger. A small crowd of ghosts were gathered around him, surging forward. More stood below, literally pulling on my legs, fighting Kiran's grasp. The magic in him pulsed brightly and he pulled hard. I stumbled to my feet. Blue light filled the room, and the ghosts wailed as the sudden brightness melted them into nothing.

I struggled to regain my balance. Every inch of me shook with adrenaline and lingering fear, and I couldn't decide which was stronger. Kiran's fingers tightened subtly, the seams of his gloves pressing into my hand.

"You all right?"

I nodded, looking up to meet his concerned gaze. He scanned every inch of me, and his jaw clenched faintly when he got to my knees. I glanced down.

Between the leather, my pants were torn and scuffed, stained with deep crimson streaks. I jerked my hand from Kiran's, smoothing my shirt, and glanced around as though somehow that would mend the wounds before he could comment on them. But his gaze was fixed, and when he met my eyes again, they were filled with that confusing muddle of emotions that I couldn't make sense of.

"You're hurt," he said finally. His voice was thick, but the confidence he usually held was gone. He finally dropped his hand, having held it awkwardly in place after I retreated.

"I'm fine," I said. But a wave of panic shivered through me. My hands were empty, the talisman lost. I turned around, kneeling near the edge of the hole, peering down into the semi-darkness below. "Or would be. Fuck. Kiran, I lost the talisman."

"It doesn't matter," Kiran said. His tone was still too rough, still too emotional for the controlled prince I was growing used to.

"How can you say that? It was your mother's." I crept around the edges of the hole, hoping for any glimpse of the necklace below. "I'll go down there. I can get it."

"We'll find another way," he murmured. "I can heal you. Let me heal you."

"I'm *fine*," I insisted again. I scrubbed my face with my hands, running them up across my forehead and into my hair. "I *had* it. And I *lost* it. I can't believe I lost your mother's talisman. She *trusted* me."

Kiran stilled at that. "She *what?*"

"She trusted me." I dropped my hands to my lap. Kiran was too silent and I turned. With a glance at his raised eyebrow, I realized how utterly insane I must have sounded. "Your mother was here. Or, her spirit? Like your sister, but she could move and talk . . ."

"My mother wasn't here, Sabrena," he said gently. "All that wanders these halls are ghosts. You've seen them. They're echoes of what was. Things that, to be honest, you shouldn't be able to see."

Beings I shouldn't be able to see. Roses I shouldn't be able to make bloom. For a *Mald Magicae* I was certainly causing a ripple. I frowned. "Then explain to me how she told me about you? How she said she had never forgotten that particular talisman before? How she told me where exactly it was?"

"And where was it?"

I pointed to the armoire. "An apron, in there."

Kiran didn't answer. He spun on his heel and moved for the armoire, then opened the door with the reverence of fond memories. His fingers skirted over the smooth fabric and I heard his soft intake of breath.

"Only our family knew that she never left that particular talisman behind," he admitted finally. "I wasn't even sure if we would find it, if I'm being truthful. But I don't know how she spoke to you. That's never happened before."

"Why did the spirits grab me?"

"I don't know," Kiran said. "All the palace has ever done is replay the events of what happened when it collapsed."

Chilled night air seeped in through the holes and crevices of the collapsing palace. I climbed to my feet and crossed my arms over my chest to hold back a shiver. "What did happen here, Kiran? You never *really* said."

Kiran took a deep breath and glanced around. Longing filled his eyes with each slow sweep of his gaze across his mother's room. His expression was full of regret. "I don't want to discuss their deaths here. The spirits could follow us if we do. Or worse."

"Apparently they're already acting out of character, if they're grabbing me and telling me about themselves." I moved closer, as close as I dared. "I'm not afraid, Kiran. Of you, of them. Of your past. I want to help, but how can I do that when all I know of your history has been tainted by the bias of my own people?"

I waited. Kiran was quiet for a long minute. He crossed the room to peer down into the gaping hole while fidgeting with crumbling bits of wood and stone. Then he said, "They came at first light. We weren't ready for them. Our watch barely spotted them crossing the fields, but we had no advance notice. They came in force, all their best covered with their finest armors . . .

"But it wasn't the gear," he continued, "or their stealth, or even the sheer numbers that won the fight for them. It was Amirah. Their leader. The Sorceress."

"What about her was so different?" I asked, my voice barely more than a whisper.

"She wields powers I've never seen. No one had. It's likely why the trolls follow her." Kiran shuddered. "Entire units would vanish before our eyes only to reappear flanking our people. They were so much faster, and their endurance much greater. We never stood a chance."

He fell silent for a long moment, then added softly, "Even a force of dragons couldn't stop them."

"And your family?"

Kiran shook his head. "Not here." He sighed, a heavy, weary sound. "We shouldn't linger, anyway."

I stared at the prince. At the clothing that covered nearly every inch of his skin, at the boots tight on his legs and the gloves that hugged his hands. "How are you dressed?"

"Magic," he said, and for the first time in a while I saw a hint of amusement touch his eyes. "I sacrificed a curtain to conjure them." But the emotion was gone in the span of a blink, as always. "We should go outside. There are other buildings—safer buildings—we can sleep in for the night."

"No dragon?"

Kiran shook his head again, tugging uneasily on his beard. "Not at night."

I didn't press. Maybe Nakia had rubbed off on me some after all, and I was getting better at reading other people. Or maybe I was starting to understand the quiet dragon prince. But he had shown a lot of vulnerability, and I appreciated that. I appreciated the glimpse into the world he kept bottled in his mind, and the sacrifice he made in sharing it with me.

Kiran extended a gloved hand and I let him take mine, the warm leather soft under my fingers. A soft blue glow spread from his wrists all the way up his arms, crossing his shoulders and down his back. Tingling magic pushed into my veins followed by two sharp pinches around my injured leg—the scrapes and cuts on my knees were healing.

"That really wasn't necessary."

"Funny way of saying thanks," he muttered, tugging my hand lightly. I followed him back through the hall, down the spiral stairs, and over the rubble and debris that clogged our path. My mind had become so fixated on his gloved hand around mine, around the blue glow that still lingered around his clothing, that it wasn't until we were back in the main foyer that my thoughts cleared.

"Your mother's talisman. We should have looked for it more."

Kiran reached into his pocket, holding out his other hand. Glimmering in the blue light was the silver talisman.

My brows drew together. "How?"

The dragon prince grinned, and for a moment I forgot to breathe, to think. If he was beautiful when he was miserable, he was the radiant sun when he smiled. My eyes widened, and I knew the second he noticed because that mask slipped back into place. The grin, the happiness, were gone.

"You didn't drop it all that far," he admitted. "It was caught on the side of the flooring."

But I barely heard his words, because I knew the second that I saw that joy on his face, I was in trouble. I would do anything to see him smile like that again, even for a moment. And I knew what dangerous territory that could be. What I would do, what I would sacrifice.

I pulled my hand from his, swallowing hard.

The building could collapse around us but somehow that smile was far more treacherous.

20

Kiran knew the grounds like the back of his hand, even now. The Ruins of Ingryst were extensive, stretching far beyond what I could see, but he led us unfalteringly. He knew every statue, every tree. I worried though, watching him move. Kiran's expression remained stoic. His gaze didn't wander over the crumbling ruin. And it was that, more than anything he said or any reactions he'd had, that made me realize how much he struggled with being here.

The property had everything Kiran's family could ever have needed. Besides the massive palace, various buildings were scattered across the lawn, some little more than cluttered ruin like the palace. A giant pile of scorched wood drew my eye for several seconds too long. Kiran noticed.

"Stables," he said. "Or, they were. I couldn't tell you what happened to the horses. Most of the staff fled as soon as we dismissed them. But there were a few—" He swallowed, his voice thick. "A few stayed behind, tried to free the horses. I don't know if they succeeded."

"I'm sorry," I murmured.

"There's nothing anyone could do. My family failed. If *my* family failed . . ." For the first time his steps faltered. But he kept moving. "If *my* family failed there wasn't anyone in all of Numeryon who could have saved us."

I started to reach for him, to offer comfort, but I held back. What could I say or do that would assuage decades of guilt? Maybe he didn't see the true value of the bargain he had struck with the High Sorceress.

"But you didn't fail. The trolls have stopped, or at least mostly."

Kiran's shoulder lifted. "For now. But if those roses are any indication, things are about to get a lot worse."

I frowned. "Explain the roses to me. Because I understand that they're important, but I don't really know why, or why their reappearance is such a big deal."

"Eventide Roses are a symbol of hope to the fae," Kiran said. He paused long enough to open the door to a small building on the farthest edge of the property, next to a wildly overgrown maze of shrubbery. "Gardeners shed. The trolls either didn't see it or didn't care. We should be safe in here tonight."

I stepped past him. The shed was cramped, filled with tools and sacks of fertilizer and seeds. Kiran dragged a few of the seed bags onto the floor, tamping them down with his hand.

"Beds. Kind of?" He dropped to sit on one.

"Back to the roses," I nudged gently.

Kiran sighed. "When the trolls first arrived, the Eventide Roses started to die. It was evident that the trolls were planning to cause trouble for our people, but we didn't realize they intended to conquer us. To wipe us out. But the roses persisted for a long time, into the beginning of the Ninth War."

He took a deep breath. "Until my family was slaughtered."

I reached out to grip his arm. The thick cotton of his sleeve was soft under my hand. Kiran visibly flinched, but I was surprised when he didn't pull away. A minute passed before he spoke again.

"When the dragons died, so did the Eventide Roses. We haven't seen one in all these years, not a single one . . . Until the other night. Until you."

"I don't understand," I admitted. "I don't even have magic to *make* them grow. Why me?"

"If I knew I would tell you." He paused, sprawling out on the makeshift bag-bed and stuffing his hands under his head. "But sometimes it's not about the magic you have, or don't. I believe the Universe has its course for us. Whether we're ready for it or no."

My brow scrunched in confusion. "And you think I was meant to be singing in the garden right when that rose bloomed?"

Kiran shrugged. "Everything happens for a reason."

I laid back on my own pile of seed bags and stared up at the ceiling for a few moments. This close, I noticed the slight scent that clung to Kiran—amber and sandalwood and a light citrus note. It was comforting, in a way that I couldn't quite explain. *He* was comforting, his presence reassuring, and in a way I couldn't have anticipated. I liked being around Kiran. He made me feel . . .

He made me feel *seen*.

Not just seen but seen beyond the scars. Beyond my lack of magic. Like he saw me as a person, a being, who was capable of functioning without the power everyone claimed I had to have.

Kiran gave me a feeling of belonging, and it was so foreign, so frightening.

"And do you think this happened for a reason?" I asked, gesturing between the two of us. I didn't dare look at him, though.

"Yes."

He didn't elaborate and I almost didn't ask. But curiosity got the better of me. I wanted to know if it was just me. If I was the only one who felt that something was growing between us, or if the emotions were all in my head. "And why is that?"

"Because you make me curious," he said simply and as though

that explained everything. When I didn't say anything, he added, "I haven't been curious in a long time."

I stared hard at the ceiling, afraid my expression might give away the feelings that sat timidly in my chest, wavering between acceptance and fear. "Curious about what?"

Kiran shuffled and I finally turned my head. He met my stare unwaveringly, propping his head on his hand. "About possibilities."

"Okay, prince cryptic."

The corner of his mouth twitched. "I haven't dreamed of possibilities in a very long time. You're like a splash of cool water. You make me feel awake." Kiran paused, his cheeks and neck flushing a vibrant shade of red. "You make me feel hopeful." He huffed out a half-laugh, a choked off sound that stirred something deep in my chest. "It's like you're my own personal Eventide Rose."

"Your own rose?" Heat swam up my neck and face. I had to look away from his eyes, but I could still feel it, the moment the air changed between us, and I knew something had shifted. We had stepped into a new level of this timid relationship and there was no going back. Only forward.

"My own personal rose," he said softly, with such reverence that it made warmth spread through my chest.

"Well, you have me surrounded by enough fertilizer," I said with a snort.

I looked up again, unwilling to miss the fleeting grin that graced his expression. And that warmth spread to the tips of my fingers and all of my toes.

"Tell me something," Kiran said, leaning toward me ever so slightly. "You said your grief didn't compare to mine. You know what I've been through, or at least some. Tell me about yours."

Instinct told me to be quiet. To make him work for information about me, instead of offering it freely. Trusting was hard. So hard. Every vulnerability I had was exposed to the world, and they had all been used against me in Eldoris. But I looked around the gardener's shed, to the abandoned supplies and the tangles of cobwebs in the corners, and realized how much he had shown me today. I had met his *mother,* even if she was an echo or ghost or whatever that manifestation was.

Kiran was doing his part. Now it was my turn.

And so, when I opened my mouth, I didn't try to stop the words that spilled out. He listened quietly as I told him about Eldoris—about the home and family I missed so dearly, about Nakia, and about the less positive things. The hunger, the poverty.

I mentioned my father, and how dedicated he had always been to not only filling our stomachs but those of our neighbors.

But it wasn't until I started to speak of my missing magic that he sat up, leaning toward me as though he would reach out to me. To comfort me? Maybe he could hear the pain in my voice. I recalled the mocking, the teasing. *Mald Magicae.* The term haunted my nightmares. It had gotten better as I grew older, but then the ridicule I had faced my whole life came out in new forms. Years of feeling lesser that all accumulated in the loss of Maryna. I told Kiran about her rejection and the ache that still lingered in my chest whenever she passed by. I told him about Donovan and the relentless taunting. Even though it made me squirm, I even shared some of his favorite nasty comments. The ones that hit deepest—that I would be alone, that no one could want me, that I was a failure, and a defect. I told Kiran everything.

"No magic and covered in scars," I said finally, my gaze locked on the ceiling. Kiran was close, so close I could feel the warmth of him against my arm, but I didn't dare meet his eyes. I didn't want to see the sympathy, the pity. And I knew it would be there. It always was.

"You're right," he said finally. "Your grief isn't like mine. But I can't imagine mourning the loss of a regular life every day. I'm sorry."

"Eh," I muttered, waving a hand at him. "Maryna was

the worst of it. Losing her showed me that I wasn't capable of being loved for who I was."

"Not in that judgmental town," Kiran scoffed.

I shrugged. "Who doesn't have magic? I'm broken. They literally created a term to remind us how abnormal we are. I am."

"You know, my sister used to think the same thing."

I glanced to my left. Kiran was staring at his gloved hands now. "Your sister?"

"She didn't have magic either." My eyes widened at the revelation, even as his hands balled into fists. "I'll never forgive myself for thinking she was safe in the palace."

"You couldn't have saved everyone," I said gently. "I'm sure she knew that. I know she couldn't possibly have thought less of you."

"I saved myself." His tone changed on that, became less emotional, more distant again. "You should get some rest."

I reached for him again, but he shook me off. I frowned. We had made so much progress, but he still couldn't see the threads between us. He still held back. I hated the way my heart twisted at the thought, at the way he retreated into himself. "Kiran—"

He withdrew completely, sprawling back out on the seed sacks. "Sleep. We've got a long day ahead of us."

But I didn't know how I would sleep. Not when my heart ached and my mind raced, and every facet of my being was focused on the man laying beside me.

Not when I knew he needed help and that he didn't know how to ask for it.

21

Before daybreak, when the midnight sky was beginning to soften into the earliest light, scraping, snarling sounds broke the silence. I woke first, my senses on high alert. The scars that lined my neck and arm tingled in anticipation of an attack, but the sounds around us were animal, not humanoid. I tried to push down my fear. *Animal.* Not humanoid.

Not troll.

"Kiran," I whispered, reaching out to grip his arm.

He shot upright, blinking rapidly as he reached for his swords. "What's wrong?"

"Listen."

The growling grew closer. Kiran tensed. "Do you have your dagger?"

I nodded, slipping it free of its sheath. In the seconds it took the prince to circle the shed, listening carefully, I focused on gripping my blade properly, preparing for the conflict ahead.

Kiran unsheathed his swords—slender, curved ebonsteel blades he wielded like extra limbs. "Stay here."

"Not a chance," I murmured.

He clenched his jaw, cursing under his breath, but he didn't say more. We crept toward the door, trying to be as silent as possible in the cramped space. But the area around us had gone quiet, the footsteps absent.

Like they, too, were listening.

Then there was a soft knocking. A scratching against the wooden walls that sent my heart into my throat. The growls and snarls weren't humanoid but the slow, tortuous sound of nails splintering wood definitely was.

My hands shook on the dagger. I tried to steady my breathing, but I knew it wasn't working when Kiran shot me a concerned glance over his shoulder.

"*I'm fine,*" I mouthed.

His brows narrowed and pulled together. "*Don't lie,*" he mouthed back.

I forced an optimistic smile onto my lips, but the prince relaxed his tense pose, just for a moment, to move closer to me. He gripped my arm, squeezing lightly. His voice was barely a whisper when he said, "No more scars for you. Not today."

"Scars *can* be sexy, though," I joked quietly. My voice was choked. At the sound, Kiran offered me a smile that was more sympathy than real laughter.

"Well, guess I better go collect a few, then." And he winked. That grumpy bastard had the audacity to wink.

But then he turned around, squared his shoulders, and I knew without explanation what he planned to do. "Kiran—"

Too late.

Kiran kicked open the door of the shed, startling one of the beings outside. I froze in horror.

They were like creatures out of mythology. Out of the legends Mama and Papa had told us when we were so little. These beings were like trees given life.

But their bodies were more muscular, more humanoid.

The long spike-nailed fingers they jabbed at Kiran were caked with dried blood, their gangly bodies covered in glowing red tattoos. Their skin was more like dried leather, their mouths gaping and filled with long, sharp teeth.

One swiped at Kiran, but he dodged the attack, swinging his sword to draw ebony blood from the creature's skin. It was then that another spotted me, turning his cat-like orange eyes onto my face. Dark feathers fluttered on its head as it lunged. The creature reached into the gardening shack and drew me from inside with ease. I kicked and stabbed at its lanky fingers. Nails dug into my sides and I dug my dagger into soft skin. A guttural screech came from the one holding me. My ears rang, and then I was falling, right into Kiran's open arms.

"Stay back," he insisted. He dropped me hastily to my feet and dove again at the monster before us.

I went with him. My dagger was nearly useless against the great beings, let alone three of them, but I slashed at every inch of skin that got too close to me. I aimed for what I assumed to be their knees. The creatures were awkward and tilted at angles that felt wrong.

"*Fuck*," Kiran yelled, and I froze in my attacks. "Fuck, not now. Not *now*."

I glanced up, meeting the prince's eyes.

"Run," he yelled.

My feet were moving before I could think, running toward the blinding morning light that peeked over the treetops. The lawn filled with an intense blue glow. I kept going until Kiran let out a grunt of pain. He needed me.

I spun in time to watch the dragon prince rise into the air, the intensity of the blue light sending the creatures wheeling away from him. A pop, and a bursting wave of sapphire, and an iridescent white dragon landed on the ground in front of me. His tail crushed the gardening shed. His feet left heavy impressions in the earth.

Kiran didn't hesitate, didn't falter even after such an intense change. His eyes scanned for the creatures—and stilled. He paused only for a half-beat of my galloping heart. Then he was striding after the beasts. Each thundering step louder than the hammering pulse pounding in my ears.

They were done in three hasty snaps.

Those sounds, the ones still echoing around us, would haunt my nightmares for eternity.

Dark splatters covered his snout. He moved toward me slowly, lowering his nose as though I might run away. Instead, I ripped off the left sleeve of my shirt and then gently wiped away the blood staining his scales.

"*You're not afraid?*" he asked in my mind.

"Should I be?"

"*You have been before.*"

I considered that. He wasn't wrong. "But I know you now."

Kiran snorted. "*You're beginning to.*"

"Why didn't you want to shift?" I asked, tucking the wasted sleeve into a pocket.

"*I didn't want to land on you,*" he admitted, staring guiltily at the destroyed shed. "*I can't always control how I fall. And I thought you'd be scared. And . . .*"

"And?"

"*And I remember how you looked at me, the first time you saw my dragon. I don't want to see that look on your face again.*" He closed his eyes, breathing in deeply. "*I never want you to think I would harm you.*"

I ran a hand over his nose, along the smooth scales there. He was warm, intensely so, like someone had built a fire beneath his skin. His eyes opened again, and he watched with interest as I studied his dragon. Really looked, taking in the small spikes that lined his jaw, and the way the morning light cast rainbows over each scale. Kiran lowered his head to the grass so I could run my hands along his curved ivory horns.

"*What are you thinking?*" he asked gently.

"Not stealing my thoughts?" I teased.

He shook his head. "*They're moving too fast, for once. I can't pull them apart.*"

"I'm thinking . . ." I withdrew my hand, crossing my arms tightly over my chest. I was thinking that he was beautiful. In every form. But I couldn't bring myself to say that. "What were those things?"

"*Ryntalen.*"

I recognized the name. "Are they really demons, as the legends say?"

"*No,*" he said. "*Achmyn Morternos used to be home to many creatures. When the High Sorceress came, she harnessed many of them to her own will. The beings that attacked us? They were under her power. Corrupted dryads, if you will. Of their own mind, their runes would have been green or blue.*"

"And how many other creatures of nightmare and legend live in your lands?"

Kiran grimaced. "*All of them.*" He cast a glance over his shoulder, toward the corpses staining the grass. "*I don't know why the ryntalen are here, and I don't particularly want to. We got the talisman. There's nothing more for us here. We should go.*"

I nodded my agreement. And tried not to think too much about how many creatures would love a fresh elven meal for supper.

We didn't wait to start the journey home. By early afternoon, we were over the mountains. And as we crested their highest peaks, Kiran began to circle lower, searching for something. It wasn't long before he found it: a plateau, not so high in the mountains that it was covered in snow, but not so low that the air wasn't chilled.

"*Stay close,*" he murmured as we landed. "*We won't be here long.*"

He led me toward an overhang, covered with long, hanging moss and ivy. When he nudged the greenery aside, a dark cave opened to greet us.

"*It's safe,*" Kiran assured, "*There's food inside. I needed the break anyway.*"

I slid past him into the darkness, feeling my way across the jagged stone floor. Bright lights lit the space the farther along I went. Fireflies. Magical fireflies in jars set to light up as I passed them. I had never seen such a thing. Nakia would love to learn that trick.

A lump of sorrow and longing rose in my throat. I *missed* my family. My steps faltered and I stumbled over rock debris on the ground. Without missing a beat, Kiran's voice was in my mind.

"*Are you all right? What happened?*"

"Fine." I grinned to myself. "Why, are you *worried?*"

Kiran huffed. "*No. Yes. You're my bartering chip, remember? I need those thumbs in one piece or the elves might get suspicious.*"

I rolled my eyes. But Kiran was trying to joke and that was a strangely warming thought.

The cave narrowed on a small stone table, draped with an aged runner. Elaborate silver threading ran the length of both sides. A small stream of mountain water trickled into a stone basin, slowly feeding back into the earthen floor below. But it was the food that drew my attention. Bowls of fruit, jars of preserves, something that looked suspiciously like stew, and tiny brown pods that smelled of yeast.

"*Bread beans,*" Kiran said in my mind, "E*verything is preserved with magic. The beans will grow into fresh loaves if you add water. And yes, that's likely stew.*"

"It's creepy that you hear what I'm thinking," I muttered.

But I emptied two of the stew jars into an aged pot and carried it back out of the cave. Kiran had lit the campfire outside, and I hung the pot above it, vanishing back inside to fill our waterskins and grab some bread beans and a bowl, ladle, and spoon. Kiran was right; when I sat by the fire and added a drop of water to a bread bean, it sparkled for a few moments before expanding into a warm, fresh loaf of bread.

"That's . . . useful," I admitted.

Kiran grunted in agreement, dropping his massive dragon into the grass beside me. *"Eat fast. I still have to get us home before nightfall."*

"Kiran . . ." I frowned, and he turned one of those dragon eyes on me. "Why, if you have these bread beans, couldn't some have been sent to the elves?"

"We did," he said. *"We sent them as much as we could spare. But preserving food is its own kind of magic and the trolls targeted those who presented it. They thought they could starve us out, if they couldn't beat us outright."*

"I've never seen these, though. Nor my family."

"It sounds like the higher-ranking elves may be keeping secrets of their own."

The thought sat heavy in my chest. We didn't have a ruling dignitary as the fae did; our leaders were voted in periodically, though some retained their positions for eons. Each city had three representatives. Between them, they retained the peace between the elven regions.

I hated to think that they would allow the elven people to starve to save themselves, but I knew how possible it was. Power was its own kind of addiction. And those who had it were going to want to do anything to keep it.

Could our own leaders be starving us to save themselves?

Or was there more to it? Could they be buying safety from the trolls? It was true that all of the elven leadership had survived the war and seemed relatively unharmed now. I had always assumed it was because of the bargain Kiran had struck. Maybe it was something more.

The thought made my head spin.

Then I glanced at Kiran. His watchful eye was trained on the woods around us. Kiran had more power than any of the fae, both magically and by position. And yet, he was willing to sacrifice his own comforts to save his people. Even enter into a cursed life. Dragon by day, fae by night.

Kiran was better than all of them, and he didn't even realize it.

I ladled stew into my bowl, then offered it to Kiran. He shook his head, then laid his nose in the grass and closed his eyes. I wondered what he was thinking. I wondered if he was wounded from the fight that morning. But I didn't ask any of that. Instead, I sipped at the warm stew and enjoyed the delicious flavors that danced on my tongue.

And when I got up the courage, I asked, "Can you tell me about your sister?"

Kiran inhaled sharply.

I was picking at the food in my bowl, worried that I was pushing too much, or too soon. That he didn't know me, so he had no reason to trust me. And to be fair, he didn't have to.

But then Kiran said, "*Elentya was the most beautiful soul I've ever met. She breathed kindness. I don't think I ever heard her utter a cross word to anyone, even to me, and trust me when I say I deserved them more than once.*" He opened his eyes then, his gaze distant. "*But Elentya didn't have magic. When she came of age, there was no tattoo for her. No power or magical instincts coursed through her veins.*

"*My parents hated it. I wouldn't go so far as to say they hated her, but they certainly made her feel that way on more than one occasion. A woman, born to the noble Devayne family, the last remaining family to have dragon in their blood . . . and she was without magic at all.*"

"I know how that can feel," I murmured.

A soft rumble rolled up his throat. "*And I'm sorry you ever have. Because it made Elentya an outcast to our people. To some. Others wanted her body, treated her like an exotic commodity they could partake in but not commit to. She deserved better. She should have had better.*"

"But . . ."

"*But our world isn't kind to those who are different.*" Kiran's voice grew thick with remorse. "*And when the trolls came, she . . . she . . .*"

I slid closer to the dragon prince, resting my hand on his warm nose. "You don't have to tell me."

Kiran sighed, warm air rolling from his nostrils. *"Memories are hard but my sister doesn't deserve to be forgotten."* He paused, lost to his thoughts for a moment. Then he said, *"The palace had hidden passages and an underground refuge. My father and I sent my mother and sister to retrieve a couple small heirlooms. Family valuables. Then they were to get out. And we fought with everything we had to ensure they could."*

I stirred my stew unconsciously, waiting with bated breath. Kiran's voice was thick with emotions. Grief, and sorrow, and equally as poisonous—anger.

Bitter, spiteful anger.

But I couldn't find it in myself to hold it against him. Not with all he had endured. Not with all his family had endured, simply trying to survive. I would do the same for my own family; I had proven I would do just about anything for my family. Wasn't that why I was here?

"Sorry," Kiran murmured.

"For?"

"I thought the years would make it easier, that with distance their memories would be easier to recall."

"But that's not how it is at all."

"No," he agreed. *"Time doesn't kill the grief, only makes it easier to bear."*

"You don't have to tell me about your family," I murmured. I understood the pain of recollection. It was why I still winced whenever Maryna came near.

"You need to know," Kiran said with resolve. *"You're in this now, even in some small part. You need to know as much as I can tell you in case . . ."*

"In case?"

"In case—" Kiran cut himself off, shaking his head lightly. *"It won't come to that."*

I raised a brow, concerned. "You're being cryptic again."

He huffed out another breath of warm air but didn't comment. Instead, he said, "*My mother and sister went after the heirlooms. Mother's talismans were only one of the things we needed to retrieve, and quickly. We didn't need them falling into troll hands. But they never made it that far.*

"*Father and I fought for a while, and when we didn't hear anything from mother and Elentya, I was sent to find them. I found Elentya first.*"

I moved closer, pressing the weight of my arm against his neck. When he didn't move away, I said gently, "Was she already gone?"

"No," he murmured. "*She fell from above as I climbed the stairs. I was a single flight below, and there was nothing I could do. The sound of it still haunts my nightmares. Her screams, the troll's laughter . . . the thump. The silence.*"

A lump pressed into my throat. I imagined myself in his position, if my littlest sisters, Aleksei or Kirsi, had been in Elentya's place. And something deep in my chest fractured for the pain the dragon prince must have felt. Still felt, if the distance in his eyes was any indication. I couldn't imagine getting past something like that.

"*My mother,*" he continued, voice thick, "*was a different story. I couldn't have saved her if I wanted to. I stopped to check Elentya, and I lingered too long, but by the time I got to Mother's chambers she had been long gone. The best I can guess is she tried to protect my sister. She was battered and bruised and beaten.*"

He blinked then, heavily, like he was fighting tears I wasn't even sure a dragon could cry. But another emotion sat in his eyes—pain. Raw and fully on display for everyone to see. On instinct I started to hum, like I did for Siyna, a soft lullaby that always calmed her tears. The song was barely more than a whisper of sound, but he seemed to hear it. His expression cleared, the tension that had tightened his massive form uncoiled. He sank deeper into the soft grass.

Kiran shook his head, as though clearing away the worst memories, and said, "*Father wouldn't let me retrieve their bodies. I wasn't even sure where they ended up, if they were buried or just left to fall into the decay of that building. But their spirits . . . If their spirits are trapped, their bodies must be too. Somewhere."*

I cleared my throat. "We could always go back. Try to free them."

"I appreciate the thought," Kiran said softly. *"And maybe someday we can. But for now, there's no going back. There simply isn't time."*

"Why not?" I frowned, absently running my fingers across his smooth scales.

"Because, my rose, there are things about this world I can't begin to explain. Not even to you."

22

Bleiz was waiting in front of the estate when we returned. Oryn, one of the guards from the escort that brought me north, stood beside him. His tousled curls were flat on his head, like he had run his fingers through them again and again.

"*What's the report?*" Kiran said, projecting his voice through all our minds.

"Your Highness?" Oryn asked, glancing at me warily.

Kiran snorted. "*She can hear. Speak.*"

I stared at him, at the hint of power in his voice that was a reflex to him and so foreign to me. Before I could think on it too long, Oryn had stepped forward. He dipped into a clipped bow.

"Your Highness. A small contingent of trolls was spotted moving south along the western coast. We don't know what their intentions are, and there was no sign of the Sorceress or her daughter."

Kiran didn't answer for a moment, his eyes trained on the lingering rays of sun that lit the horizon. "*If you'd excuse me for one moment,*" he said calmly.

Blue magic shimmered along the lines of his scales. It grew as the last of the light in the sky faded, then burst into a cerulean wave that filled the grounds. Kiran disappeared behind an arch covered in white roses. Another, softer flash of blue lit the roses and the prince strode around the archway fully dressed, his long hair pulled into a loose knot behind his head.

"Apologies," he murmured. "I thought my nudity might detract from the importance of your message."

The other two men smirked, glancing at me in a way that was full of assumptions. Untrue assumptions, about what the prince and I had been doing all day, or what I might think of a nude Kiran. I started to protest, but Oryn went on.

"We have a group tracking the trolls' movements. But given that we don't actually know what they're doing, it's hard to prepare. If they move to attack any of the elven communities, especially Beriene or Eldoris, we may have difficulty stopping them."

Kiran nodded slowly, rolling the sleeves of his shirt up. Blue tattoos swirled and spiked their way up his arms, glowing faintly in the dark, remnants of the magic left over from his shift. "Okay. And Damara?"

"In the patrol group," Bleiz said. His jaw tightened, his nostrils flaring lightly. "I don't understand why Oryn thought he should send *her* though."

"Damara is arguably one of my best," Kiran said.

"If anything happens to her—" Bleiz started.

"Nothing will happen to her."

"I've heard that before," Bleiz snapped. The glare he leveled on Kiran was venomous.

"You let your losses cloud your judgment," Kiran said evenly. "Every single one of us have lost someone, Bleiz. That doesn't mean we can simply hole up and stop doing our duty. Damara will be fine. Her fox form is discreet. I don't love the idea of her wandering Numeryon tracking a pack of trolls. But if anyone can keep up with them unseen, it will be her."

Bleiz growled. "Oh, so suddenly you're okay with her leaving the estate?"

"Are you questioning my judgment?" Kiran waited until Bleiz reluctantly shook his head. "I made a promise to her sister, but I did not agree to become her captor. If Damara is in danger, I will go myself to ensure her safety."

Promise to her sister? I looked at the prince inquisitively, but he keenly avoided my stare. Even Bleiz's face gave no hint of what they were talking about. I didn't pry. Not especially when Bleiz opened his mouth again.

"And your safety, highness? Who ensures that?"

"I do," Kiran said. "And the loyal fae who run missions like these and who guard the elven lands. I am in less danger than anyone in those trolls' paths, at least for the time being. Send word to Eldoris. Let them know trolls have been spotted moving south and that they might want to close the gates. You're both dismissed."

Bleiz and Oryn nodded, the latter slipping into another clipped bow. The two strode into the estate, not even daring to look back.

When they were gone, Kiran cleared his throat lightly, rubbing his gloved hands together. "You should probably get some rest."

"And you?"

He relented the smallest smile. "I'll be around the palace tonight, if that's what you're asking."

I frowned. "You need rest too."

"I know." His expression flattened, his eyes turning dull and distant. "I don't get a lot of sleep. I try but . . ." He blinked. "I'm used to it. Don't worry about me."

"But—"

Without reply, Kiran strode to the front door and opened it, waiting till I passed through to let it fall closed behind him. Before he climbed the foyer stairs, he dipped his head in quiet salute.

"Goodnight, sweet rose."

He disappeared down the corridor toward his study, but I stood for a moment, processing all that had happened in the last day. All that I had seen, all that I had learned. I wondered if now that we were back to the estate, Kiran would go back to being cold and aloof, those small, sweet sentiments forgotten.

The thought made my heart ache in a way I never thought it would again.

A soft whisper fluttered through my rooms, a caress of quiet sound so low that I barely caught it in my half-sleep stupor. But the sound shivered closer, and when the curtains around my bed began to tremble, I struggled to push myself upright, still heavy with exhaustion.

"Niserie?" I murmured. I didn't know why the fae would be in my chambers so late, but maybe I had called out in my sleep and she thought I needed something.

Silence.

I frowned, then rubbed at my eyes. The silence persisted, but I knew I hadn't imagined the sound. I reached out, yanking back the curtains to my right. Nothing.

My gaze lifted to the windows, to the balcony door. Closed, not even cracked enough for a breeze to get in. My pulse quickened. I froze, listening intently. A soft shuffle of sound brushed across the foot of my bed. A figure stepped into the moonlight, just enough that I could see their silhouette through the curtains—and that of the blade they held gripped in a striking position. My throat was tight, breathing was hard. I regretted that the dagger Kiran had given me was so far away, tucked into the drawer of my vanity. Focusing, I repeated Connak's words in my mind over and over, reminding myself that I knew a little about how to fight. It could be enough. All I needed to do was stay alive long enough to get help.

I slipped silently from beneath my covers, tucking the

blanket Mama had made me under the thick comforter to keep it safe. Then I adjusted myself until I was braced against my forearms. When the curtains slid open, I was ready.

I pressed the advantage fast, ramming the heels of my feet into the stomach of the darkly dressed figure. A grunt of frustration broke the near silence. But the person recovered quickly. Gripping my legs, they flipped me onto my stomach. I scrambled for purchase on the sheets, but my fingers slipped on the silken fabric. The shadow of their blade rose on the wall beside me. I flipped myself over, twisting against their firm hold of my ankles. I threw my hand up to brace the blade away. I sucked in a breath and screamed, as loud as I could muster, a sound that echoed around my chambers. The attacker panicked, releasing my ankles to try to cover my mouth. I seized the opening, rolled from under them, then bolted across the room.

For a split second, I was grateful for the soft nightclothes I had chosen—pants and a top, instead of a gown or something more exposing. But they were still thin, still no defense against the figure making their way toward me. They were dressed head-to-foot in black, as dark as the shadows, and only a slit of skin around their eyes was exposed to the slanted moonlight.

The attacker strode closer with bold, confident strides. I backed up, reaching toward the fireplace, waiting for my fingers to find the metal pokers that waited there. When I finally made contact, I pulled one free, clumsily. The rest clattered to the floor loudly, and I hoped the volume might be enough to wake someone.

Anyone.

Another dagger appeared from the figure's sword belt. They slowed as they closed in, careful, calculating, not wanting to risk me slipping from their grasp again. I brandished the poker like a sword, swinging out at the dark fabric that covered their stomach. A low, cruel chuckle filled my room.

The sound was distinctly male, but I didn't recognize it. I

wasn't comforted by the fact.

He swung out at me, one blade after another, nearly hitting my arm. I retreated another step and my back met a wall. Panic filled my chest, clogged my lungs. Had no one heard me? The estate *was* huge. My heart squeezed with fear.

Twin blades moved for me. I ducked, hearing the metal clatter against the stone wall just above my head. I dipped under my attacker's arms, spinning out behind him, and jabbed the end of the poker into his leg. He grunted in pain but simply rotated on the spot and jerked himself free.

Then he was on me. No more hesitation, no more cautiously meticulous motions. He attacked with ferocity, pinning me to the ground, and the terror that trembled through me froze me completely.

Because here I was, again, helpless on the ground.

His daggers glinted in the faint stream of moonlight as he tossed one to the floor beside him. One hand gripped my throat, tightening. That soft chuckle filled the room again. He squeezed and the edges of my vision darkened.

The sound of splintering wood cracked through my room and a furious roar echoed off the walls. For a moment, my attacker's hand tightened more and his blade lunged for my chest, but then I was thrown to the side. I slammed into one of the chairs nearby. Metal clattered as the man's blade was torn from his grasp and then he was laid out on the ground, clutching at his throat. Kiran stood over him, hand outstretched, his tattoos bright with blue light under a mostly unbuttoned white shirt.

"What the *fuck* do you think you're doing?" Kiran snarled. Fury trembled through his entire body. His fingers clenched into a fist and the man's breath cut off completely. He flailed on the floor, pleading with gestures for Kiran to release him.

"Kiran, stop," I said. If he heard, he didn't acknowledge me. I pulled myself off the ground, limping across the room. The man choked and gasped, the clasp of his cloak tightening around his throat. A glint of gold caught my eye from beneath his hood.

I reached out a hand, resting my fingers against the soft cotton of Kiran's shirt. He recoiled, all focus pulled from the intruder. The glowing light of his tattoos doused.

"Don't!" he snapped. His venomous anger turned on me and I sucked in a breath, retracting my hand as though he had burned me.

"Don't kill him," I tried again. The man laid on the ground, wheezing for air, clutching his throat. I couldn't watch this. I couldn't see this side of Kiran. "Please don't kill him."

Kiran's eyes softened a fraction. "He tried to kill you."

"And *you* saved me," I said gently. "Punish him some other way. Question him."

A low growl rumbled through Kiran's throat, closer to the dragon than the man. But he took a step away from me, adjusting his dark leather gloves before he bent to lift the intruder by the clasp of his cloak.

The man swung his fist, aiming for Kiran's face. A sliver of pale blue skin caught in the moonlight. *Troll.* Kiran caught his wrist and twisted until I heard a soft snap. He shot a look in my direction, taking in the grimace on my face as the troll howled in pain.

"What?" he said casually, lifting a shoulder. "I didn't kill him."

I sighed. "Technicalities."

The anger on Kiran's face faded for a brief moment, letting a glimmer of amusement shimmer through. Then it was gone, the rage settling in again as the troll in his grip flailed and moaned.

"I'll be right back," Kiran said. His voice was gruff, guarded. He dragged the troll from my room unceremoniously, heedless of the sounds of agony that seemed to grow louder the farther away they got. I wondered how rough Kiran was being, now that I wasn't in sight.

Niserie and Damara snuck into my room seconds later. I grabbed my robe from where it lay slumped over a chair and draped it around my shoulders, unable to shake the chill that ran through me.

"Are you okay?" Damara asked. Her fingers were dancing over the hilt of one of her daggers, ready to pull it free in a second's notice.

But I nodded. "Kiran arrived here in time. When did you get back?"

"I only just returned. Bleiz should have been here," Damara said with a frown. "He was on corridor patrol tonight."

"I didn't see him on my way here." Niserie paused where she had begun straightening the room, the fireplace pokers in her hands. "I'm surprised Kiran heard you. His rooms are on the other side of the estate."

Damara frowned, scanning the room uneasily. "Regardless, Bleiz will answer for this." She turned her eyes on me. "Can you tell me what happened?"

I spared no detail, but it wasn't until I told them that I had held Kiran back from murdering the intruder that Damara looked truly uneasy.

"It sets a precedent," she said at my confused expression. "If Kiran begins sparing intruders, especially trolls, we'll see more of these attacks. And I'm already unhappy that they went for you once."

"But who was it?" I murmured. "I don't understand who would come for me."

"Anyone who's worried about what your presence might mean for the prince's bargain with the trolls," Bleiz said, striding into the room. He gripped my shoulders, looking over my face and body with pained concern in his eyes. "Are you hurt?"

"Not much. I'm sore more than anything."

Damara shoved Bleiz's shoulder, a little more roughly than necessary. "And where in the nine circles were you? You were on watch duty tonight, were you not?"

"I swapped with Oryn." Bleiz looked at the floor, then met my eyes. "I'm sorry. Sincerely. If I'd have known something like this was going to happen . . ." He turned to Damara. "Truly. Oryn is needed in Lytharius for his sister's wedding tomorrow, and he was worried he wouldn't be back in time for his shift."

I frowned. There had been no sign of the fae guard and a sinking feeling grew in my stomach. What if the intruder had done something to Oryn? His sister's wedding . . .

Swallowing hard, I asked, "Has anyone seen him?"

The room fell silent. I knew what that meant. No, no one had seen him. I clutched the robe draping my shoulders tighter, trying to shake the cold chills shivering through me. If he died because he had been protecting me . . .

Damara gripped my shoulder. "If anything happened to Oryn, he knew the risks were there. So did his family. It wouldn't be your fault."

"We need to find him," I insisted. If Oryn was hurt, or worse . . . I couldn't accept it as easily as they had. Lost life was always a tragedy, worse still when the life lost was too young. And suddenly, in some small way, I understood the scale of what Kiran had been through. Not only having lost so many but having lost so many that were family. If the thought of Oryn dead, someone who was just a friend, or even a loose acquaintance, twisted my gut in such a way, I could only imagine what it would be like to lose one of my family. Let alone all of them.

"You're bleeding," Bleiz said.

I turned. He had moved behind me while I was lost in my train of thought. Strands of my hair were lifted between his fingers, the white locks smattered with crimson blood.

"We should get that cleaned up," Niserie said gently, peering over Bleiz's shoulder.

"I'll take care of it." None of us had heard Kiran's return, and he leaned against the door now with the calm confidence of a man in charge. He turned his head slightly, leveling an intense glare on Bleiz. "Where were you?"

When Bleiz explained, Kiran straightened, then held his hand toward the door dismissively. "I want Oryn found. Now."

"But, Your Highness," Niserie protested. "I should really clean that wound."

Kiran frowned. "I'm fully capable."

"Even with gloves?" Damara smirked.

"Yes," Kiran said. "Even with gloves. Now leave. All of you."

"But—"

"*Out.* Now."

Bleiz's mouth snapped shut, the muscle in his jaw tightening angrily. He spun on his heel and left the room, Damara and Niserie close behind.

Kiran watched them out, slipping the doors closed and snapping a deadbolt I hadn't noticed before into place. My brow drew together at that. He turned to face me, shoving the few loose buttons on his shirt together to cover his chest.

"How bad is it?" he asked.

"I didn't even notice," I admitted, brushing my fingertips over the wound. My head ached at the touch, and when I pulled my hand away dots of crimson were scattered along my skin. "Ow."

"Here, don't touch it." The soft leather of his gloves was warm as Kiran moved my hands away from the wound. He parted strands of my hair, pausing to clean blood from them. "This might hurt." Kiran pressed a damp cloth against the spot, gently, then held it in place. "You're still bleeding. Once that lightens, I can heal you more easily."

"You don't have to," I murmured.

He dropped to his knees beside me, still holding the cloth in place. "Are you all right?"

"Why, Kiran, this is the second time you've seemed concerned about me. You did come awfully close to losing your bargaining chip, I suppose." I smiled teasingly, but there was a softness to his expression I had seen so rarely it gave me pause. In that second, I knew without a doubt he wasn't worried about our deal. The marriage, the elves, the fae . . .

none of them were on his mind right now, not with his eyes brimming with raw concern like that. Warmth grew, bright and comforting in my chest, and it took every ounce of self-control I possessed not to reach out and pull him into my arms. "Are *you* okay?"

"I don't know who I can trust," he admitted softly. "This shouldn't have happened. You should have been safe here."

"I'm all right, though. Just a scrape."

Kiran shook his head. His hand fell to his lap, the damp cloth stained with blood. "If I had been another minute . . . Too many people have been lost when I was supposed to be protecting them. I trusted my people to protect the estate and they failed."

"There was a miscommunication, or someone was in the wrong place. Mistakes like that happen."

"Not in *my* estate they don't," Kiran snarled. He took a deep breath, calming the temper that clouded his eyes. "I'm sorry. I'm on edge."

I reached for his gloved hand, slowly lacing my fingers through his, then squeezed. His eyes were locked onto where our hands were joined, his shoulders tense, but I said, "You can't shut everyone out. That's no way to live."

"You're the only one here who doesn't know the terms of my agreement with the trolls. You're the only one I might . . ." He didn't lift his eyes, swallowing hard.

"Can't you trust Damara and Bleiz? Don't doubt your friends, your most trusted advisors, over one mistake."

"It might have cost you your life," he murmured, and his hold tightened around my hand.

"Kiran," I said softly. A breath of silence passed before he met my eyes, curious. "What do you need from me?"

"I need to trust you," he admitted. Pain crossed his eyes for the barest of seconds. "Bleiz and Damara have enough responsibility, more than they should for their positions. I need to find the kingdom of the trolls and put an end to them before they can put an end to us."

"But the bargain—"

"Will expire soon. And I don't know what they'll do when it does."

I squeezed his hand tighter without thought, fear dowsing the warmth his care had lit. "What are the terms of your bargain?"

Kiran opened his mouth, then closed it again. Frustration balled his free fist, and a muscle ticked along the line of his jaw. "I'm magically bound to silence. So are all those who were in my employ when the bargain was signed. I can only share some details. To prevent someone breaking the curse intentionally, I insisted on the binding. The risk was too high. But now . . ."

"Now it might cost you more."

The prince nodded. He pulled his hand free of mine, gently, almost reluctantly, and climbed to his feet. A wash basin sat on a vanity nearby and he moved for that, rinsing the soiled cloth before he returned and gently began cleaning the blood from my hair.

"I can tell you some. Not all. You already know I'm a dragon by day and myself by night. You know that the trolls aren't allowed to touch your people below the divide, or mine at all, because of the bargain." He stilled. "If the curse is triggered, I'll be pulled to the Sorceress. And, through marriage to her daughter, my kingdom will become hers."

The air caught in my lungs. What a horrifying future. Kiran had gone this long without triggering the curse, yet neither outcome seemed a win in the end. If the curse activated, he lost everything. If it didn't, he kept his throne but the war reignited. There was no victory for him. Only a purchase of time.

"What triggers the curse, Kiran?"

He closed his eyes, breathing deeply. Then he shook his head. "I can't tell you if I wanted to. I shouldn't have bound myself, but I was . . . afraid."

"Afraid?"

"People who want power will do anything to take it from those around them. I was afraid if I were captured, or fell into enemy hands somehow, they could use the curse against me. In hindsight, I wish I hadn't." Kiran's throat bobbed. "I wish I could tell you."

"Tell me what you need," I said gently.

"Help me find the trolls. Their kingdom is a land hidden from time, space, magic . . . I've searched for decades with no luck. But your mind is fresh. You might see a clue I didn't." Kiran paused, kneeling before me on the ground, gripping my hands between his gloved ones. "I'll beg if I must. I just need . . . I need . . ."

"You need help," I whispered. "You don't have to beg. Not me. I'll help you."

"No, my rose, you misunderstand," he said, matching my volume. His beautiful eyes raised, and the desperation on his face paled next to the longing I saw there. "I need *you*."

23

Kiran was nowhere to be found the next morning.
Or the next.

I started to question if the conversation we'd had was a hallucination from the healing wound that still ached near the top of my scalp. The only reassurance I had that any of it was real was the mess scattered about my room the next morning, that Niserie spent the better part of both days cleaning. Her magic sped the process, but I never saw a hint of her tattoo. I wondered what her form was. But I didn't dare ask. I still wasn't sure of fae etiquette and asking where a concealed tattoo was and what it allowed them to shift into felt too . . . personal.

But she spent the days cleaning, and I spent them sparring with Damara. After the attacks in Ingryst and my room, I was more determined than ever to learn how to defend myself. Thankfully Damara took on the task with fervor. I kept a dagger on hand at all times now, but I still didn't feel safe. Not really.

At least the sparring kept my mind off Kiran's absence. Mostly. On the evening of the third day, a knock sounded at my door. The Kiran that faced me on the other side made my heart sink. His eyes were hollow, dark circles curving beneath them. A stack of books were clutched to his chest. He had pulled his hair back, but the strands were messy and haphazard, more down then up.

"Have you slept? At all?" I asked gently, stepping aside to let him into my room.

"No." He blinked slowly, then walked past me. "Not much. Not since . . . it's not important. I need your help."

I went to reach for his arm, then pulled back, remembering the anger on his face the last time I had touched him. But even his steps were slow, languid, his shoulders slumped. I realized, then, that the shirt he wore was the same he had been wearing three days ago, though now the white fabric was covered in deep wrinkles.

Kiran dumped his books on a small table, then yanked the chairs from in front of the fireplace over beside it. He shot me a pointed look after he dropped into one, jerked his head at the other seat, and started flipping through books.

I moved nervously, timid around this frazzled version of the prince. Kiran was always so well put together, I couldn't imagine something like an attack on *me* could shake him this much. But he looked up again and the desperation, the frustration in his eyes, sent me forward.

Perching on the edge of the second chair, I asked, "What do you need?"

"I've been in my office, searching," he said. His tone was clipped, distracted. "And I think I've finally found a clue to where Madrion is."

"And you didn't come get me?"

"I planned to," he said, pausing long enough to meet my eyes. "Then I kind of rabbit-holed into my books and lost track of time."

The mania in his eyes, and the exhaustion, were enough for me not to push too hard. Asking for help was new to him. We could go at his pace. Even if I was worried that his pace might actually kill him—immortal or no.

Warily, I asked, "What did you find?"

He flipped open a book, turning the pages so quickly and roughly that I winced. When he found what he was looking for, he shoved the tome toward me and tapped an illustration on the page. "Mulier Venandi. The Huntress constellation to your people. I've never paid attention to where her arrow was aimed before."

"The Star of Elysian," I murmured. I glanced at Kiran. His eyes were wide, crazed, and fixated on the next book on the table. "Kiran, what exactly am I looking at?"

"They're all like this." He pointed to another image. "Fortis Pistris. The shark."

I shrugged. "The symbol of strength."

"Whose maw is pointed at—"

"—the Star of Elysian."

He ran gloved fingers through his hair and down over his short beard. "They have to be connected."

"Madrion? Has to be connected to the Star of Elysian?" I stared intensely at him, more concerned for his wellbeing with each passing minute. I softened my voice, wary of the tired prince. "I don't follow how this will help you find the Sorceress, Kiran."

"This has to be something," he said, staring at the pages as though they would simply show him the answer. "It has to be." His hand clenched into a fist. "I can't accept that it's not."

He stood and paced the length of the room. I tilted my head in confusion. Kiran wasn't erratic. He was stoic and solid and firm. But he paced and tugged at his hair, muttering under his breath, and worry became a flood that drowned my heart.

"Kiran. Come, sit down, let's look over everything."

"You don't understand," he said, stopping in place. "This has to be it." His shoulders slumped, and he dropped into the chair beside me again. Defeated. "I have to find her."

"You asked me to help you," I said carefully. "I'm going to help you."

"This is the closest thing I've found to a lead in ages, Sabrena. I don't know what to do if you can't see a pattern here, too."

"We'll figure it out."

"Do you understand the cost if we don't?" he asked. His voice rose an octave in terror.

"I do. She'll go back to slaughtering our people," I said, in barely more than a breathless whisper.

"And if she's feeling bold enough to send people into my own home, then she's certainly feeling bold enough to break our agreement."

Silence fell between us as I considered the gravity of his words. His fear was bleeding into my own emotions. Without thinking, I started to hum under my breath, trying to ease the tense lock of my shoulders, trying to comfort Kiran in the only way I knew how—without touching him and making him more uncomfortable.

Kiran stilled beside me. His shoulders loosened. "Why do you do that?"

"Do what?"

"Hum when you're uneasy."

"I don't—" I paused. "I don't know. Is it bad?"

"No," he said. He closed his eyes for a moment, sighing heavily. "No, your voice is lovely."

Warmth seeped into my skin at the compliment. But a moment later the heat turned cold as I realized what Kiran had been saying. I swallowed. "It's hard to believe this is the upside of your bargain."

Kiran didn't answer. His gaze was heavy and focused on the pages in front of him.

"Kiran," I said finally. "If we don't figure this out . . ."

He looked at me then. And his eyes were full of a deeper sorrow than I had ever thought possible. He closed them, his expression pained as he murmured, "Then we lose everything, Sabrena. *Everything.*"

We spent the night pouring over books, volumes that reeked of damp pages and neglect. We searched for any connection that might point the Star of Elysian toward Madrion. Closer to morning, we moved to the library near Kiran's office—it had been built to accommodate his dragon form, unlike the guest wing where my room was situated.

The crisp pages of my book turned idly beneath my fingers. I wasn't sure when I had stopped reading them. Probably around the time I had noticed Kiran's soft snores, rumbling through my back where I leaned against his massive, scaled form. I hadn't seen him this calm, this restful, maybe ever.

But now, splayed across the enormous balcony off his study, in the warm afternoon sun, he napped beside me. I took comfort in the near normalcy of it. As normal as being betrothed to a dragon prince could be, I supposed. I curled closer to his glistening scales. He needed the rest and researching in his dragon form would be near impossible anyway. The task fell to me and I was happy to take it.

I didn't know what we were going to do if we turned up nothing.

Kiran had shown me the map that stretched along a table in this library, weighted down with beautiful glass orbs that swirled with stars and magic I had never seen. Small figures dotted the surface, little fae carvings that marked patrol routes and little orcs that warned of danger. He had spent years studying every detail, looking for anything that could remotely indicate an access point to the troll's base of operations, but there was nothing. No portals, no doors, no magical caves that would whisk him into the Sorceress's home. He focused on *Achmyn Morternos*, on the Isle of Death, because he believed their strong presence had to indicate an entry point . . . but there was nothing.

Nothing.

In volume after volume of magic and riddle, we had come no closer to finding the troll sorceress. And time was running out. I could see it in the dark circles around Kiran's eyes, hear it when he argued with me about going to sleep for fear he would miss something. But in dragon form, he couldn't turn pages and peruse tomes.

A thunderous snore shivered through Kiran. He shifted slightly, nestling his head closer to where I sat. I reached out a hand and rested it on top of the smooth scales of his nose. My fingers vibrated where they sat. He was so warm. *So* warm. Inside and out.

I knew I wasn't supposed to fall in love. That it wasn't my destiny to be in love, or to be loved, especially if it cost the peace and security of my family. I knew that, as an elf, falling for the Prince of the Fae would be frowned upon.

But what did the elves know about the fae, really? And what did the fae know of us?

Anyone would be lucky to be under Kiran's protection. Even when he failed, his remorse was filled with so much heart. So much feeling.

I wasn't in love with him. But I could see it in my future. I could see him stealing my heart away. He made me want things I had never considered possible. A *future,* with love and security.

And he made me feel . . .

A tap sounded at the door. Kiran's eyes shot open, his head jerked up, and a low growl rumbled through his throat and down his chest. I pulled my hand back, following his gaze while turning my thoughts away from him now that he was awake.

"Calm down, you brute, it's me," Damara said. She pushed the door open with her shoulder and I jumped to help her with the tray of food and drink that she carried in. "I thought Sabrena might be hungry."

"*Are you?*" Kiran lifted his head farther, turning to scan my face. "*I'm sorry. I should have stayed awake with you, I—*"

"I'm fine," I interrupted, patting his neck. "Go back to sleep. I'll keep looking."

He grumbled, climbing to his feet and stretching his legs. *"Did you find anything?"*

I shook my head, realizing as he watched Damara lay out the tray that he had projected into both our minds.

"No," she said, "But I did catch a lead that points toward the Library of Estaria."

"For what?"

"Books, mostly." Damara gestured to the food, then to me. I sat, picking at a slice of sweet bread, too curious what she had found to have much of an appetite. When she saw that I was eating, she continued. "There's a few volumes on the Winds that might interest you. They're the only beings who have been alive long enough that might be able to detect where Madrion is."

"The beings who have statues in the gardens?" I asked. Damara nodded, and I continued. "But isn't finding them impossible?"

"Generally."

Damara rolled her eyes. "Bunch of pessimists, I swear. You sound like Bleiz. No, it's not impossible. They just can't be found if they don't want to be."

"And what makes you believe they would want to be found now?"

"I don't. But I think it's the only lead we've had in a long time."

I frowned, picking at the skin on a grape. "You didn't check this library already?"

"I did," Kiran said, *"But some of the volumes are restricted, even to me."*

"So, they're not really an option." I sighed.

"I didn't say that." A mischievous smirk spread over Damara's face. "We're just going to have to be clever about it."

"In case you've forgotten, I'm not really any help during the day."

Damara plucked a strawberry off a plate, taking a big bite before she said, "No, I haven't forgotten. But cover of darkness is better anyway. Less guards watch the library at night."

Kiran paced on the balcony and stared off into the distance. His tail flicked. *"What if this is just another dead end?"*

"You haven't found anything here," Damara said gently. "Could it really hurt?"

He didn't answer, but his steps stilled. I finished a piece of sweet bread, studying the two fae. Silent tension filled the room, but I didn't know what to say that could break it. Kiran had to make the decision. It was his fate that hung in the balance.

Then Kiran blew out a huff of air. *"Fine. If we leave in the morning, I can have us to Lytharius by mid-afternoon. Then what?"*

Damara smiled, and I didn't miss the relief that loosened her shoulders. "We steal some books."

24

I slunk along a shadowed alley, waiting for Damara to lead Kiran to me.

The three of us had flown into Lytharius in the late afternoon, under the pretense that Kiran was doing a regular scouting mission to check up on his territories. Kiran hadn't wanted me seen, worried that the more my face was known, the more of a target I would become. The troll who broken into his home had shaken Kiran more than even I could fathom. More so, because the troll hadn't talked. Nothing Kiran or any of his people had tried had earned them any answers as to why he had come into my room, or how he had breached the estate.

And then, three days in, the troll escaped.

None of us knew how, but Kiran was taking the security failures hard. Oryn hadn't been found either. I knew the guilt of his absence weighed on Kiran too. It weighed on me, and I hadn't been responsible for assigning a guard.

Bleiz was gone almost continuously on patrol runs; I still wasn't sure the prince had forgiven his right hand's absence that night, but he was certainly keeping him busy. When he wasn't on patrol, Bleiz was looking for leads on Oryn's absence. So far, there was nothing. No sign of struggle, no personal effects missing from his rooms.

He was simply gone.

I took a steadying breath. This wasn't the time to focus on things outside of my control. For now, I stuck to the shadows, in the dark clothing Damara had given me. But I was still having difficulty remaining concealed.

Lytharius was the central city of the remaining fae population, a utopia of white stone and sparkling magic. Power was a soft buzz in the air, so palpable that I could taste the salty-sweet tang of it on my tongue. The feeling was unsettling, unfamiliar. I tried not to think about why that was. How magic would never pour from my fingers, how my only defenses were the dagger strapped to my thigh and Kiran's mother's talisman tucked beneath my shirt.

I hummed under my breath while I waited, sinking deeper into the shadows as fae passed on their way home or on leisurely strolls through the city. Many of them slowed into a relaxed pace as they passed my hiding spot. Could they sense me? A city so thick with magic had to feel the anomaly in its midst, the *Mald Magicae* blemish hiding in the darkness.

Or maybe that was simply my paranoia. I was used to being the outlier. At this point, I probably noticed it more than most.

"Sabrena?"

I jumped at Damara's whispered voice, clutching at my chest as though I could keep my heart from leaping out. "Over here," I responded quietly.

Two figures slipped into the alley. Kiran crossed the space between us in moments. A small glow lit the gloved palm of his hand as his eyes scanned over my face. "You're well?"

The sincere concern in his voice gave me pause. I nodded

slowly. "Never better."

Kiran doused the light in his palm with a subtle flick of his wrist. His formal leathers vanished and, instead, black clothing hugged every inch of him. The belt at his waist exploded into fine powder that wafted away in the night air. A price, for his conjuring.

I tried not to stare at his arms as he moved, at the way they flexed and pushed at his shirt. For once, I was grateful he was in his fae form. I didn't need him hearing those thoughts. Or realizing that I was fighting with myself to look away.

Damara snickered and I glanced her way, flushing hotly when I realized she had noticed the object of my heated gaze. She didn't say anything, though, clutching a dark bundle tight to her chest. Kiran seemed mercifully oblivious.

I swallowed the hard knot in my throat. "What now?"

"We get to the library. Sneak in. Find the books." Damara shuffled the bundle in her arms to one side, then pulled a small scroll from the bag on her hip. A miniature map of Lytharius was sketched across the parchment face. "There's an entrance here"—she pointed to a spot off the main walkway—"and another here. Inside the main library there's a rotation of four guards. They circle the aisles of the library in quadrants. But as long as we're quiet, we should be able to dispatch them without notice."

I swallowed. "Dispatch?"

"Temporarily." Damara grinned. "They'll be off in dreamland long enough for us to peruse the shelves and get out. And by we, I mean me and Kiran. Your main focus needs to be searching for anything that might move us in the right direction."

Kiran grimaced. "I'm starting to regret going along with this."

"It won't be so bad," I said. "You have magic, right? This should be a breeze."

"Not in Lytharius." Kiran kept his voice low. His gaze dipped around the alley, then he said, "This is the one city the fae still pour time and magic into. Nearly everything is warded. There may be only a few guards, but their gear is enhanced. Our magic is limited and growing weaker with our race. Lytharius is the final stand for the fae people. And so, the ones that live here are pouring everything they have into keeping it safe."

I studied his face for a moment, then glanced around at what I could see of the city. "There's one thing I don't really understand," I said. "Why, if the fae and elves are so weak, would the trolls agree to this bargain? It bought the fae time to stand a chance against them, but the trolls don't really seem to have anything to lose by simply slaughtering us all."

"Because there aren't as many trolls as they'd like you to believe," Damara murmured. "The High Sorceress is powerful, but she divided her forces greatly to keep an eye on all of Numeryon. As much as it seems like it would be easy for her to slaughter all of the elves and fae in one go, she needed the time to recover her people and resources too. Plus, her magic is strong, but it's not limitless. The bargain is a stalemate. Everyone going in knew that the war would eventually resume."

"We just hoped we'd be able to find a solution before it got that far," Kiran said. "Lytharius is one of the best chances we have of standing in a united front."

"Didn't Bleiz say the city is filled with *her* spies, though?" I glanced around. "Isn't that why I need to be so cautious about hiding my identity here?"

Kiran sighed. "Corruption runs deep in Numeryon. There are traitors among even the most pious fae, those who value their own survival more than the lives of our people. And yes, they've allowed the trolls into the defenses of Lytharius. Unfortunately for us, their fae allies are as clever as they are talented. Bleiz, Damara, and I have only managed to find a few of the culprits in all the time the trolls have been here."

"Always higher up fae, always ones who had set wards or aided in guardianship," Damara said quietly. "The city has a face of security, but the shadows run deep."

"All this to say, magic or no, we have to be careful." Kiran's stare was intense on my face. I squirmed under his scrutiny, heat climbing my neck. He didn't look away.

"We should go," Damara whispered, finally breaking Kiran's focus. "We need all the time we can get. If Kiran becomes a dragon in the library, I'm fairly sure they'll catch onto us."

She pulled apart the bundle in her arms, freeing black cloaks for each of us. We fastened them at our throats, pulling up the hoods to cover our hair and ears.

"Ready?" Damara asked.

I nodded. Damara reached out, looping her arm through mine. Kiran fell into step behind us, the line of his shoulder rigid as we left the alley.

The main street of Lytharius was made of smoothed, silvery stone that reflected the moonlight and lit the city in a soft glow. Most of the buildings were carved from massive pieces of veined white marble draped in sheets of bright green ivy that grew wild down their sides. It was beautiful, but I couldn't shake the feeling that I was being watched. That eyes peered from even the empty windows.

"I feel it too," Damara whispered. I tilted my head at her, confused how she knew what I was thinking, and she murmured, "Your aura shifted. The facade of the city's safety is harder to believe in the dark."

I forgot she could see those. Heat poured into my cheeks as I thought about earlier when I had been watching Kiran. I wondered what she saw.

Damara laughed, a soft, hushed sound. "I don't share aura readings with others unless there's a serious reason. Like a security threat. Your secrets are safe with me."

"Thanks," I muttered.

Our steps were nearly silent as we traveled up the dark street. Kiran paused regularly, searching the city around us for prying eyes. But other than the small crowd that gathered outside a warmly-lit tavern, no one roamed the streets. Guards were posted at regular intervals, but they were as stoic and unmoving as the ones that had been stationed in Eldoris. They watched us closely, but we didn't seem to pose a threat to them; they averted their eyes quickly, searching for the next target.

Toward the center of the city rose a massive, tiered fountain. The water that flowed in it was crystalline, filled with sparkling magic that made the liquid shimmer like diamonds.

"Purifying magic," whispered Damara. "Reduces the chance of impurities getting into the city's central water supply. Or more sinister things."

"Like poison." Kiran's tone was ominous.

My eyes widened. I dared a look over my shoulder at the prince. "Would the trolls really do that?"

He gave a short nod. "Would and did."

Lytharius seemed heavier with that revelation. The glistening, pristine street felt tainted with the knowledge that the people here would allow themselves to be nearly murdered, then welcome their attempted murderers with open arms. I didn't understand. Or maybe, I had come from a place filled with so much peace I couldn't possibly. We may have been poor in Eldoris. Our homes may have been chilled with autumn air while freezing in the winters. Our stomachs may have ached and groaned with hunger . . . but we were safe.

Or mostly.

The troll that attacked Nakia and I was an outlier. I tried to remind myself of that. Papa would never have allowed that attack to happen had he been there. Mama would have tried her best. My brothers would have thrown themselves into the fray rather than let Nakia and I be hurt.

Even the meanest people in Eldoris, even Donovan, had never tried to kill me. It wasn't much consolation against the emotional damage they dealt, but I still felt a wave of gratitude for it. I was starting to realize there were terrible things happening all over our world. And while my pain was real, there was so much of it in Numeryon.

We all needed more kindness. More peace.

And maybe I could help make that happen. One step at a time for a better world.

But here and now . . .

Lytharius *felt* unsafe. And I was starting to feel a bit more brave, a bit more confident, but I was so used to having my family around to protect me. Being so far away from them made it easier to be afraid.

"What's wrong?"

Kiran's voice was gentle, but so close I felt his breath caress my ear. I jumped, then shook myself, trying to clear my thoughts.

"Nothing, why?"

"You stopped walking," he said.

I blinked, glancing around. He was right. I was stationary, in the middle of the street, Damara several dozen paces ahead with a look of concern on her face.

"I miss my family," I admitted softly. "I don't know who I am without them. Or how to navigate this world."

"I know how that feels," Kiran murmured. "Adjusting to a world without the people you love, the people you relied on . . . You were thrown into an entirely unfamiliar place, with unfamiliar people. And while I didn't have to adjust to all of that, I do know how empty I felt without my family around every corner. How unsafe the world suddenly felt." He stepped in front of me, gloved fingers gripping my arms, his eyes steady on mine. "You know I'll keep you safe, right? And once we've figured things out, once we get rid of the trolls, I'll take you home to see your family. I promise you. I won't keep you from them."

"I know." I dropped his piercing stare, peering over his shoulder at Damara who eyed us curiously from ahead. Then I sighed, heavily. "Thank you."

Kiran squeezed my arms, then stepped away. His absence left me chilled. I wanted to pull him back, keep him closer.

But he kept a respectful distance as we caught up to Damara. We passed the fountain, close enough that the glittering water splashed onto our skin and clothing. That buzz curled through my system again, the one I had experienced from touching the door. Damara shot me a puzzled glance, her eyes roving around me like she was reading my aura, but she didn't comment on what she saw. Instead, we made our way through the dark streets, climbing stairs and hills between tightly packed homes, all the way to the rear of Lytharius.

Sitting at the highest point, like a crown jewel, the Library of Estaria was built into the mountainside. It sprawled the width of the city, levels upon levels of towering white stone. The ivy I had seen in the city below grew wilder here. Every wall of the library was draped with it, all but the few windows that were lit by the soft glow of candles or lanterns within.

"The first entrance is to the rear. We're going to have to climb," Kiran whispered.

I nodded. With the thick leather boots Damara had given me, scaling stone and earth wouldn't be a problem at all. Easier than climbing a tree, in some ways. Kiran caught my eye and I knew he was thinking about catching me in the garden. From the way he looked at me, I knew he had no doubts that I could do this. His confidence hit an empty spot in my soul, filled it up. I was so full of uncertainty all the time, yet . . . I could do this. I was capable. And he let me see that he believed it too. The validation was invigorating.

Damara led us up to the main staircase that climbed to the library doors. Instead of following it, we dipped to the left. Damara led the way down a steep patch of grass, then directed us to a tiny door hidden behind a curtain of vines.

"Not well concealed or well guarded," she murmured, pushing the ivy aside. "But there are guards along the passages. We'll have to be careful."

I dipped my head in acknowledgment, but I hesitated when we tugged our hoods forward to ensure our faces were well and truly concealed. "What will happen if we're caught?"

"I'll probably be freed, likely with a fine that will gut my coffers," Kiran whispered.

"And us?"

I didn't need to see his face to know he winced at my question. But it was Damara who said, "The price for entering the restricted areas of the Library of Estaria, without formal consent, is death."

I inhaled, holding the breath for several long seconds before I released it. "Okay."

"You don't have to do this," Kiran said. "You can stay out here. It would be safer."

But I shook my head. "We need as many people searching as possible. It's a worthy risk if we might be able to stop the war from continuing."

Kiran didn't comment. Instead, he pried the door open then stood back, letting Damara and I slide past.

Inside, a narrow passageway met us with the scent of damp earth. Small torches were perched in grooves carved into the walls. The ground was uneven, compacted dirt rather than actual floor. Our boots barely made a sound as we trudged forward in a tight line. Then the path split—one path to our left, one to our right.

Damara turned slightly, referencing her map as she whispered over her shoulder, "The left leads to the main library. The places where the public can visit."

"Then why have a secret passage to it?" I asked softly.

"It's an escape route," Kiran murmured. I felt the warmth of him pressing up against my back before he pulled the cloak from my ear and added, voice quieter still, "If there were an attack on the Library, this passage could be used as a means of safety. But it hasn't been used that way in a long time."

"And the right?" I asked.

Kiran's breath was a soft caress across my cheek. I held myself still, trying fiercely to ignore the shiver that tried to tremble up my spine. "The restricted rooms."

"And where we need to go," Damara said. "All restricted, banned, and original religious material . . . it's all here."

Kiran released the hood of my cloak, letting it fall back into place. I frowned. "Wouldn't that make the library an awfully large target?"

Damara nodded, but it was Kiran who said, "And that's another reason the fae have poured so much of themselves into Lytharius. The very core of our people is in this city. Everything about who we are, where we came from. It's all guarded here."

"So tightly that not even their prince may access it?"

Kiran sighed. "Situationally, I might. But the guardians take their jobs very seriously. And in war, especially a war with a powerful magic wielder involved, no one can be trusted but those who have magically bound their lives to protect our greatest treasures and history. I don't fault them for their restrictions. They're just inconvenient."

The passage narrowed, squeezing against our shoulders and forcing us to shuffle sideways, but finally widened into a small, round room. A wooden door stood perched on the other side, at the top of a trio of stairs. Other than lanterns, the room was barren.

"Up the stairs, down another hall, and we'll enter into a guarded chamber," Damara said, sliding daggers from her thigh sheaths. "We have to dispatch them quickly, or they'll call the guardians. If they do that, we stand no chance. The guardians have some of the strongest magic in Numeryon, imbued to them by Kiran's family ages before he was even a thought."

"We'll be quick," Kiran murmured. His hands strayed to the ebonsteel swords on his hips. He cast a look in my direction. "Fight where you can. Stay back if you can't."

I didn't get a chance to answer, locked under the intensity of his gaze, before Damara tugged the door open. And gasped.

She faltered back a step. Kiran pushed me behind him

without a thought, unsheathing his swords and falling to Damara's side in the next breath.

"Tsk, tsk. Look who it is. The orphan prince. What would your people think if they knew you were sneaking around where you didn't belong?"

25

Kiran stepped backward, pressing his back into my chest. Trying to conceal me more, I realized, as he stood taller and expanded his chest to its full breadth.

"Pot, kettle, Amirah," he replied. His words were clipped.

Amirah? The High Sorceress of the Trolls.

I tried to peer around Kiran's arm at the woman. Amirah's voice was feminine, with a sultry gravel to it. But Kiran shifted, blocking my view—and likely hers, as well.

"Oh little orphan prince. I see your temperament hasn't dulled. Have you broken our deal?"

"You'd know if I had," he snapped. Damara slid sideways, gripping my arm and tugging me back a step. Trying to get me out of the little room. But it would never work.

Because Amirah moved closer, which I could tell when she spat, "get out of my way" at Kiran. He stood taller, but a moment later he was knocked nearly off his feet, stumbling into Damara. My friend's fingers slipped from my arm as she tried to regain her balance.

And I was left exposed.

Amirah was *tall*. Taller than I had expected, six feet or more easily. Her full, curvy figure was dotted with linear white tattoos. The scant bits of clothing she wore were made from dark leather that set off the bright blue of her skin. But it was her eyes that drew my attention. Not because they were a bright sunshine yellow, though that was unsettling. Nor that they were piercing and studied me as though they could see every inch of my soul.

No, it was that they held no emotion. No pity, no humor. Only cold, empty, chilled, nothingness.

"So, you're the one."

I frowned, confused. Amirah grinned, a sharp-toothed expression that bared her tusks menacingly. I started to take a wavering step back, only to feel Kiran press into my shoulder, the warm weight of his arm sending a wave of reassurance over me. But Amirah's smile grew and that warmth shuddered to ice.

"What do you want?" Damara asked, earning a glance from the troll sorceress. But in that same second, Amirah dismissed her. She didn't bother to answer Damara.

Instead, she turned the full force of her unfeeling gaze back to Kiran and me.

"It's only a matter of time, you know," she purred to Kiran. His jaw clenched, his stare unwavering. "The moon continues its revolutions and here you are, looking for *books*."

Kiran's hand tightened around the hilt of one of his swords. "Don't act like you don't know how much power books can contain."

"I do in fact," Amirah said. She moved closer to him. The bone necklaces around her throat clanked together. My stomach recoiled when I realized that the earrings dangling from her ears were tiny animal skulls. "But I'm right here, orphan prince." She traced a finger up his chest. Rage trembled through Kiran's shoulders, and something else—fear. He was afraid. And I didn't know exactly what made him so afraid of this woman, but I knew I would do anything to take that emotion from his eyes.

Without thought, I blurted, "Leave him alone."

Amirah turned, as quick as a viper who had been waiting to strike. Bait—I was the bait and this was a game to her. She smiled, leaning closer. I expected her to smell like the troll that had attacked me all that time ago, like sweat and blood, but her scent was sweet . . . vanilla, and what I was growing to recognize as magic: metallic and bitter.

Her nose brushed my cheek and I recoiled, but she gripped my chin tight, running her tongue from my chin to my cheekbones. I shuddered, resisting the urge to run that screamed through every inch of my being.

Kiran moved then, and Damara. Their blades threatened but didn't pierce, his to Amirah's throat and Damara's against the troll's ribs.

"Tsk," she murmured, withdrawing her face from mine an inch. She flicked her wrist, a brief glimmer of annoyance passing over her expression. Kiran and Damara were tossed into a heap against a wall, hitting it hard in the narrow space. When they didn't move, my heart leapt into a frenzy.

"It's just you and me now, little siren," Amirah whispered.

I froze, fully confused then. And more than a little afraid.

"I don't have—"

"Powers?" Amirah raised an amused eyebrow, a smirk creeping over her lips. "Oh, I know all about you. Apparently, I know *more* than you do."

Doubt trickled through me at the certainty in her voice. But I knew my parents. I had never known any others. "I'm elven. My parents are elven."

"Are they?" She leaned closer again, inhaling my scent. When I tried to squirm free, her nails dug into my chin. "Sing for me."

"What?"

"Sing for me," she repeated.

And I knew, then. Not because of the certainty in her

voice, or the slick patch that ran down my cheek where she had tasted me as though she could discern my identity from my skin. Maybe she could.

But it was in my memories. It was in all the times I had calmed Siyna's wailing long enough for Mama to feed her. It was Kiran's shoulders falling loose when I sang. Or the song that only Papa seemed to know, until I came here, until I met the fae and the trolls.

"What does it mean?" I whispered.

Amirah smiled. "For one such as you? Nothing. You are absolutely as powerless as you believe you are."

Kiran groaned from the floor. Relief that he was alive barreled through me, but Amirah still held me tight in her grasp. When the prince sat up, blinking his eyes, Amirah pressed her lips to my ear.

Her tusks brushed my skin as she whispered, "For him? It means the end. Freedom. Death. Call it what you will, but your prince is cursed and you'll be his undoing."

"Get away from her!" Kiran yelled. He brandished both swords, swinging for the troll sorceress.

But they whooshed through the air, blanketed in the thick, dark smoke she vanished into. We coughed, clearing the burn from our lungs. Damara sat up, gripping the back of her head.

"What did she say to you?" Kiran asked, insistent. He sheathed his swords and stepped closer, but I backed a step away. I didn't know what being a siren meant, or how it was even possible, but I knew she was right. It was as though pieces of a puzzle had been rattling around inside me, and her words had forced them together. I wasn't the curse that had been whispered behind me. I wasn't *Mald Magicae,* a broken elf with no future.

A siren.

Questions swirled my mind, filling it with an overwhelming fog. Too many, none of which I could easily find answers for. But I needed to find out exactly what this meant.

And if it meant I could, or would hurt Kiran?

I took another step back.

"Sabrena?" Kiran asked. Panic was thick in his voice. Gloved fingers reached for my arm, but I stepped around him, moving for the door Amirah had come through.

"We have to find those books before daylight," I said. I fiercely ignored the pain that flickered across Kiran's expression, the utter bewilderment on Damara's. "Let's move."

The Library of Estaria was vast, even in the forbidden rooms. The guards that had been there were unconscious, their breathing low and steady in a way that said they wouldn't wake for a very long time. Magic, Kiran guessed, deep magic that had saved their lives. Harming fae would have been against the terms of the bargain and would have freed Kiran. We all knew she didn't want that.

Around us, the walls were filled with shelves crammed with books. Tables for study sat in-between. Artifacts were cased in glass around the room, with handwritten notes that spelled out their uses, their dangers, and books that referenced them.

Exploring the shelves undisturbed should have been a dream.

Instead, I was trapped in my thoughts. The idea that I might have anything to do with harming Kiran . . . I wanted to run. To go home and see my family. And that was only the surface. I needed to ask my family about this new accusation.

A siren? Sirens were creatures of legend. They were few and far between and lured sailors to their deaths with the power of their voices. Why would they have interest in elves? Because I *was* elven, I was sure of that. Or at least in part. Had Mama been unfaithful? Or was one of my parents part siren too? Those were ideas I couldn't seem to bring myself to ponder. My parents had been in love all my life. They had shown each other nothing but respect and love and compassion. Loyalty.

But was all of that a product of an affair that had come before?

My fingers grazed volumes that claimed they were full of history, spells, the best cures for butt warts. And I couldn't even laugh at the latter because my mind was so full of chatter.

I could see how my distraction was affecting Kiran and Damara. They shot me looks of confusion, of concern. They had only been out moments, but in those few brief sentences Amirah had changed so many things . . .

And now I questioned if I should be marrying Kiran at all.

Or perhaps Amirah was making things up to get inside my head, and I was letting her win.

Maybe I didn't care if she won with me, if it meant Kiran would be safe.

We hurried through the shelves, skimming for anything that could possibly help us. Kiran and Damara both summoned their magic; waves of shimmering light poured from their fingertips and searched the volumes almost as eagerly as I did. Kiran's blue tattoos cast a soft glow over the shelves. A small hint of red light glowed through Damara's shirt, right above her left hip.

But the tomes and scrolls that mentioned Madrion only did so in passing and in fanciful recollection, like the place had only ever, and would only ever, live in legends and myths.

We knew that wasn't true, though.

And the more Amirah's words settled under my skin, the more questions that flooded my mind, the more determined I became to prove that she was wrong. What better way to do that than to find her home . . . and destroy it.

Nothing spoke to us in all the volumes we searched. No words about a spell or portal or magical staircase that would solve our problems.

But as morning drew near, I touched a tome that *sang* to me. It filled the hollowed spaces in my heart with a song so vibrant and alive I couldn't stop myself from lifting it. The aged leather creaked as I opened its cover, curious about the nondescript golden etchings that had lain on its cover. No title greeted me. No name of the scribe who had written in it. Only vivid images of creatures, and beings, and pages flooded with words that told of all their different races.

"We should go," Damara whispered as the darkness outside the long, stained-glass windows faded from black to gray. "The guard change will come soon and we won't stand any chance of escape if we don't leave now."

My gaze lingered on the book in my hands. My fingers tightened around it. I didn't know why I needed this book, why it called to me. But I had to have it. I had to read the words inside and learn about the history it contained. And maybe, somewhere deep within, I would find an answer to Kiran's problems.

Kiran eyed me warily. He could sense the change in me, I knew, and he didn't understand it. I had never been the type to keep my distance from him, or really anyone else. Friendliness was in my nature.

But so was protecting those I cared about.

He didn't ask about the book clutched in my hand. Neither did Damara, though they both gave it thorough glances. I wondered if they thought the answer to the change in me was in the book; if they perhaps suspected Amirah had sent me after it. I knew I should just tell them what she had said, but her words had felt so intimate. So final.

What if they were a curse all their own?

No one bothered us as we left the library, though the goosebumps across my arms didn't leave until we were free. Lytharius was beginning to wake as we left the city, concealed by our cloaks and purpose-driven strides. But others, too, kept their faces hidden, also dealing in shadow and secrets. No one so much as offered us a second glance. Not even a questioning peek at the bulk beneath my cloak. I wondered how many of fae we passed were Amirah's spies. And if one of them were the reason Amirah was in the library tonight. Maybe we weren't as careful as we thought we were. Or maybe she simply had too many eyes watching.

We were barely out of the city before the morning light

crested the horizon, and Kiran broke into a full-kilt sprint away from us. He was only a few yards away when his tattoos began to glow and then burst into dragon form. I felt his shame ripple through my mind, the embarrassment. And I didn't understand it, but I sympathized. Kiran wasn't in control, and his lack of control could easily hurt someone. Maybe even kill them.

And every time I looked at him, Amirah's words rang through my mind.

You'll be his undoing.

26

I stared at the moon from the estate's library window. A stack of books sat perched on the table beside me, the one I had taken from the Library of Estaria opened on my lap, and a steaming teacup between my hands. A constellation—Mulier Venandi, the Huntress—caught my eye. I wondered vaguely what it was like to venture freely among the stars. My gaze slid to Kiran, bent over his work, a strand of brown hair draping his cheek. Before the curse, he could change into a dragon at will. I tried to imagine how it felt to simply switch forms and fly away. But I couldn't fathom it.

"What is it like?"

Kiran stopped writing, quill poised above the page as he studied my face. His brow drew together. "What is what like?"

"Shifting. Becoming a dragon."

He considered. "The first few times are painful. Excruciating. It's a new experience for your body. But, after that, the change isn't so bad. My dragon form makes me feel powerful, untouchable." He frowned. "Or it did, once."

Before his dragon form became a prison. I regretted asking.

"I'm sorry she's trapped you like this," I said gently.

Kiran lifted a shoulder, turning his attention back to the parchment on his desk. "It is what it is."

I didn't believe him, but I didn't press. Some words were better left unspoken. With a sigh, I returned my attention to the book in front of me. I couldn't focus today. The words felt muddled and confusing, even though they weren't. Maybe that was simply because I was actually trying to read every page, to learn about all the creatures and races of our lands, when all I really wanted to read about was the sirens. I didn't believe Amirah. Not really.

Or that's what I kept telling myself. If it were the truth, I wouldn't have retreated from Kiran. I wouldn't have sparked another fire in his eyes, one that was keeping him in his library so much he barely ate. He was here *more* than he had been before. If that were possible . . .

My fingers ran along the edges of the book. The pages of this tome were delicate with age. I worried with each flip that the thin pieces might crumple and flutter away. The parchment was filled with neat lines of text and pages of golden-etched illustrations that shimmered in the moonlight. I sighed again, restarting the first paragraph once more.

"Why that book?" Kiran asked the question so softly I almost didn't hear him. I was actually surprised he hadn't asked the moment Damara had departed to go to bed. But Kiran hadn't pressed, and now . . .

Now I hesitated.

I should trust him. He had given me no reason not to. In fact, he trusted me against his very nature.

I glanced around his office. Other than the sound of the crackling fire, it was silent. No Bleiz, no Damara, no staff at all. Not even an errant owl crying into the night. If I were going to tell anyone what Amirah had said about me, it should be Kiran. And it should be now when we were well and truly alone.

His eyes were still steady on me, probably reading the emotions I'm sure flickered across my face. I inhaled slowly, steadying the fear that pulsed through me.

You'll be his undoing.

I didn't have to tell him that part. Because it wasn't going to be true.

"Amirah . . . said something to me."

"She did," Kiran said matter-of-factly. He stood from his desk, moving carefully toward me like I might run away.

I couldn't say the thought didn't cross my mind.

When he was only a few feet away I looked down at the page that sat open on my lap. *Milenworms. Excellent source of protein, but only if you remove the stingers from their rear sections and cook them thoroughly. Release them from their skin before consuming.*

I winced. Kiran knelt beside me.

"What happened?"

"She said . . ." I frowned at the golden illustration on the page, at the lumpy creature with its stringy antennas.

Gloved fingers gripped my chin, gently, nudging my face upward. I flinched at the touch, at the reminder of how Amirah had forced me to look at her. Kiran's eyes widened, and he released his hold, turning his grip into a soft caress that ran the length of my cheek. I met his stare and tried not to fixate on the brown strand that curled over the blue of his left eye.

"She said I'm part siren," I admitted. My voice cracked on the last word, like even considering it aloud was so vastly ridiculous that I shouldn't even be suggesting it.

But Kiran's brow pulled together. He dropped to the floor in front of me, fully attentive. "Do you believe her?"

"I don't know," I admitted. "It would explain some things . . . but my parents are in love. They've always been in love."

"Even the best people make foolhardy mistakes," he murmured. "It would explain why you've never presented elven magic. The two magics couldn't coexist together."

"No?"

Kiran shook his head. "It's not possible. The stronger bloodline would cancel the other in development, and if it didn't, the child would die soon after. Instinctually the magics would be too different. They would tear the host apart long before they could gain any kind of control over them. Siren magic tends to be more subtle than elven magic, or even fae, but it's stronger overall. With practice, a siren could sing an entire army to sleep with the softest lullaby. It could very easily override elven powers."

His words might have been meant as a comfort, but I only felt more lost. My whole life, I had been told I wasn't enough because I didn't have the magic I was supposed to. Because my elven family had such weak blood they couldn't even pass on their powers.

But I knew that wasn't true. My brothers were skilled with their magic. Even Siyna, only a few months old, had shown prowess. I had simply felt broken.

And now I was learning that I wasn't really broken, just different. It felt . . . strange. Confusing.

I really was an elven outcast.

My stomach churned at the thought. Instinctually, my hand lifted and rubbed at the scars on my throat. Was my siren blood the reason that troll had attacked me? Would I have been able to stop him if I had known?

"You're still the woman you've always believed you are," Kiran said.

I dropped his imploring stare, burying my face in my palms. "I've never known who I am."

"Then here's another piece."

"Did you know?" I asked. "Could you tell?"

"No," Kiran said. "But I can see the possibility. I've always thought your voice was beautiful and hypnotizing. Now I know why."

"You did?" I looked up at him.

He smiled, a half-curve of his lips that made my chest tighten. "I did. Now we just have to train you to use what you have, instead of focusing on what you think you've lost."

"Okay," I whispered, absorbed by his eyes. Kiran believed in me. He didn't think I was broken. And it eased something in my chest.

"Don't look at me like that."

I blinked, not lowering my gaze. "Like what?"

"Like this arrangement isn't damning you to a miserable life with a dragon instead of a proper husband. Like being around me doesn't keep you in danger every minute." Kiran studied my face for a long moment. "Don't fall in love with me, sweet rose. I can't give you what you deserve."

"Don't assume that no one could love you. Dragon and all."

Kiran turned away then, a flush climbing his neck and cheeks. He rubbed at the warmth, as though he could hide it, then sighed. "You didn't answer me, though. Why that book?"

I narrowed my eyes at him. He deserved as much affirmation as I did.

Maybe we were more alike than I realized.

"I . . . uh, it called to me." Kiran's eyebrow raised so I explained. "I felt it on the shelf. Like . . . magic. Like the lock in your gardens. When I touch it, I can feel the magic it holds."

"If you never had magic, you wouldn't have felt anything," he said gently. My turn to flush. But Kiran's tone wasn't unkind, simply trying to educate. He reached across, pulling the book from my lap. "But why *this* book?" He fanned the pages, skimming the entries and their elaborate illustrations. "Races of Numeryon?" Kiran glanced up. "Does it have a passage on sirens?"

"Yes." My cheeks heated. "But I hadn't gotten that far yet."

"You were reading the entire book?" When I nodded, he looked strangely impressed. "Maybe we should look at the siren entry first?"

"No, I—" I reached out, catching the book and stilling the pages. "I can't. I don't want the book to tell me. To confirm . . ."

"You want to hear it from your parents."

I took a deep breath. "The estate is great, Kiran . . . but I miss my family. Now more than ever."

"I know." His gaze dipped to the book, then rose to the moon glowing bright behind us. "We're running out of time. And I truly don't think I'm going to find Madrion."

"Kiran—"

He shrugged, his thumb absently flicking the corner of a page. "I'm being realistic. I don't have more than a fortnight until the curse is over, and I haven't been able to find her home in a hundred years. The advantage I hoped to gain? It's not there."

"You can't just give up."

"I'm not," he said. But his face reflected the exhaustion that weighed down his voice. Then he looked away from the moon, meeting my eyes. "Once the curse is over, Amirah will be a greater threat. Nothing will be holding her back." He paused, swallowing hard. "But I'm also not going to waste the time I have left."

"What can I do, Kiran? What do you need from me?"

He smiled gently, and my chest tightened. Once, a smile like this had been an effort for him. Now he offered it freely. And that did something to me.

Kiran made my heart feel seven times too big.

"Let's go visit your family," he said.

The warmth growing inside me combusted. Tears welled instantly, and I couldn't quite sort through the waves of emotion that threatened to drown me.

"Do you mean it?" I choked out.

"Of course." He reached out and brushed a tear from my cheek with a gloved thumb. "I didn't mean to make you cry, I'm so sorry."

"That's not it," I blubbered, the tears falling faster now, the initial surprise washed away by glowing excitement. "I'm ecstatic! I'm not crying because I'm sad. When can we go?"

Kiran considered. "I'll need Bleiz and Damara to accompany us. I'm not sure there's a stealthy way for a dragon to swoop into

Eldoris carrying two fae and an elf, though. I don't want to draw too many eyes to you."

"There's a beach—" I hesitated, brushing the scars on my neck with my fingertips. But with the three fae at my side, I could do this. I could face it again. And the thought of introducing Kiran to my family . . . Of *seeing* my family again . . . "There's a beach not far from my home. It's a little walk away, but it might give you privacy to land. The guards don't even patrol that far."

"They would know me, regardless," Kiran said with a gentle smile. But he nodded. "We'll do that, then. Land at the beach, then when night falls, I'll take you to your family. Can you be ready by morning?"

I jumped to my feet excitedly, all thoughts of the book slipping from my mind. "I'll go try to sleep now, so I'm rested for the trip."

Kiran didn't respond, merely gestured to the door. The expression on his face, though, the soft joy that shone so brightly from someone so pained . . .

I paused for a moment, drinking it in. Kiran truly was a beautiful soul. He was so much more than I could have ever expected. And even though he told me not to fall in love with him, I couldn't help but wonder at the way he made me feel. The warmth. The strength.

He was like no one I had ever met, and I wanted to keep him nearby forever.

With a soft smile, I murmured, "Thank you."

Before he could really respond, I hurried out the door. But as I closed it behind me, I thought I heard him say, "Anything. Anything for you."

27

Excitement jolted me awake the next morning, pushing me at top speed through the bath Niserie prepared for me, and through the meal Nythal laid out. Niserie barely got me dressed in heavy, fur-lined leathers and a thick white-fur cloak, before Damara knocked at the door.

"Time to meet the family?" she said with a grin. "I have to say, I was surprised when Kiran said he'd agreed to take you."

"So was I," I admitted. "But we have good reason."

Damara nodded. "Kiran wouldn't disclose. Said it was your information to share when you're ready." She reached into a fold of her black-furred cloak, pulling out a small bundle of cloth. "If we're going to be seen anywhere else, you should wear this."

She handed me the silken wad, and I pulled back the edges. Tucked neatly in the center was a small circlet of woven silver. Unadorned, simple. Beautiful. And worth more than anything I owned, for sure.

"I can't wear this," I murmured, running a finger over the

smooth metal. "What if I lose it?"

"Then it's a good thing you're not wearing your actual crown."

"My what now?"

Damara laughed. "This is small compared to what you'll have in the future. And the crown you'll wear to the wedding is much more . . ."

"Gaudy," Niserie said, so low I almost didn't hear her.

But Damara laughed again. "Gaudy is the word. You'll see. But for now, practice with this."

I held it out to her, laid flat on my palms. The wedding. My future. It was strange, after days of intense research, to hear Damara speak so casually of a future I knew even she wasn't certain of. The terrifying part was that of all of it—the wedding, Madrion, the trolls—I was most sure of Kiran himself. If you'd have told me, when Bleiz knocked at our door, that I might fall in love with the Prince of the Fae, I would have laughed myself hoarse. But now I knew him, and I saw how well we worked together. Our broken selves fit in a way I never expected, the shattered pieces of a future neither of us thought possible for ourselves.

And I was falling for him. Fast.

That was the thought that scared me most of all. More than the circlet in my hands, more than the wedding, or even the trolls. How Kiran made me feel things I had never felt before, and things I never thought I would feel again.

I was scared, because my one experience with feelings that intense had ended in heartbreak. Now that I had them back, I didn't want them to go.

I didn't want *him* to go.

Damara took the beautiful circlet from my hands and arranged it carefully in my hair. A small, knowing smile curving her lips. She situated the piece around the braids that held my hair back from my face.

"Perfect," she said, her expression glowing with admiration.

I glanced at my reflection in the vanity mirror, at the way the soft silver sat against my white hair, reminding me of moonlight. The person staring back at me wasn't someone I recognized. My cheeks were fuller, my eyes brighter. The sunken edges I had grown used to were softer. I saw joy reflected back at me, in the lack of dark circles and the smallest dimples I had never noticed. I couldn't remember the last time I felt so happy, or at peace.

And for the first time, I hadn't noticed my scars first. In fact, they were barely a lingering thought against a much bigger realization.

I felt beautiful, but not just on the outside. There was a glow to my face I had never seen before. I looked *healthy*.

"It's amazing what some food can do, huh?" Damara asked, squeezing my shoulder.

"I didn't realize . . ." I lost the words.

Damara squeezed again. "Your family was starving. *You* were starving."

"I can't wait to see them again," I murmured, swiping at a tear that slipped down my cheek.

"Soon," Damara said. She pulled me into a tight hug and I blinked away the wave of tears that rose up. As she stepped away, there was a tap at the door.

"Are you two ready? Kiran's in the foyer waiting." Bleiz pushed the door wide and shot me a warm smile. "The circlet suits you."

I moved toward him and gave him a hug. "Where have you been?"

"Prince Kiran has had me on patrol duties." He winced. "I still don't think he's completely forgiven me for swapping guard shifts when . . ."

"Any luck finding Oryn?"

A muscle twitched along Bleiz's jaw. "No. Not yet."

Silence fell, uncomfortably so, and after a moment, I said, "I forgive you, you know. Mistakes happen."

"Mistakes that almost cost us you," Bleiz said. "I won't make that mistake again." He glanced around the room, taking in Niserie cleaning off the hearthstones, and the warm clothing that Damara and I wore. "You're going to need this," he said finally, tugging on my cloak. "Just wait until you see."

My brow scrunched in confusion, but he merely jerked his head toward the door. Damara and I followed him all the way down to the foyer, where Kiran stood waiting, shifting uncomfortably between his four taloned claws.

"Did you sleep well?" he asked. I wasn't so jarred by the sound of his voice in my mind anymore. The thought made my heart flutter.

"I slept fine, thank you," I said, patting his leg. "Ready to go?"

"Brace yourself." He nudged the massive wooden doors open.

I recoiled.

Cold air burst in around him. Thick, fluffy snowflakes swirled inside. The winter storms we had been waiting for had arrived in force.

I tugged the hood of my cloak up and stepped outside. Thick layers of snow crunched beneath my boots and sparkling frozen crystals clung to my lashes as they fell. I held out my hand, watching the flakes pile on the thick leather gloves Damara had given me.

"We can wait, if the journey will be too cold," Kiran offered.

I shook my head. "No. I need answers, and we don't have time. Besides, your scales are warm enough."

Kiran huffed out a cloud of hot air in response. Damara stepped up beside me, pulling the hood of her own cloak up over the red hair that spilled over her chest.

"It's like a scarf," she explained when she caught my glance. "A hair scarf." She lifted the ends of her hair and looped it around her throat.

I laughed, snorting softly, then clapped my hand over my mouth and nose in horror. Kiran's head turned at the sound. Even in dragon form I could see the delight in his eyes, the wonder. Heat rose in my neck and cheeks, but I pretended I didn't notice.

Instead, I turned to Bleiz, who tugged his own woolen cloak tight around his shoulders.

"Let's get on with it before we all freeze to death."

Another laugh from Damara and myself and then the three of us were climbing onto Kiran's knelt dragon form. His wings extended when we were all secure. He flapped once, twice, throwing showers of snow into the air.

And then we were off and the world felt . . .

Quiet.

Kiran's wings were the loudest sound, a steady whooshing rhythm at our sides that swirled the snowflakes around us into a frenzy. But otherwise, the only noise was the wind when it kicked up. Numeryon was quiet, beautiful, a sea of trees and grass and cities beneath us.

I eyed Lytharius warily as we passed. No word had come from them, no apparent notice of the book I had taken from the restricted rooms. Kiran seemed so distracted by the curse, by the fate of his people and our lands, that he didn't seem to consider that the missing volume might present its own problems.

"*Are you warm?*"

I smiled to myself, tugging my cloak tighter. Instead of answering, I rubbed my hand over his side, reassuring him as well as I could. Damara was hunkered down in front of me, her shoulders hunched in against the cold. Bleiz sat behind us.

And as Kiran flew, I started to hum to myself, trying to comfort the excitement and nerves that both fluttered through my stomach. I was going home.

Home.

I understood their hesitation in bringing me back here now, before the trolls were dealt with. They were willingly putting themselves in danger, removing themselves from their protected estate. From the guards who swore their lives to the protection of their prince and his home.

Secretly, I was grateful for the circumstances that were sending me home early. I could see Mama, and likely Papa too since the winter had set in. My brothers, my sisters. Nakia.

Tears stung my eyes, but I swiped them away. Joy, anticipation . . . fear.

"*You miss them a great deal,*" Kiran said. It wasn't a question.

"I do." He, more than anyone, knew what I had been feeling. I only wished I could offer him the same joy, the same chance to see his family once more.

"*Once, when I was younger, Elentya and I thought we'd be clever and sneak off to the kitchens between lessons,*" Kiran began. His voice, normally so much louder in my mind, was gentle. "*Nythal had made these delicate, flaky pastries that looked like flowers. Their middles were the sweetest strawberry preserves, and she made this sugared sauce to dribble over them . . .*"

He trailed off for a moment, lost to the memory, then said, "*We stole the entire platter. Hid in mother's rooms because we knew no one would dare enter without mother's permission. And we ate the entire thing. Two dozen pastries. We covered the floor in crumbs and flakes, our faces were covered with strawberry preserves . . . And we had just climbed into mother's bed to nap off our full stomachs when the door burst open. Our governess had found mother when she couldn't find us anywhere else.*"

"What happened?" I asked. My voice was low and I wasn't sure he could hear me; Damara and Bleiz certainly hadn't.

But he had. Somehow, he had. "*We each got two lashings and mother made us finish our lessons, even though they went into early evening. But after dinner she had Nythal make us another pastry each for dessert.*"

I tried to picture a little Kiran, full of joy and mischief. The image wasn't easy to conjure, but it was there, in the barest smiles he offered, in the hope that lingered in the corner of his eyes when he looked my way. I wondered what he would have been like, without the pain, without all the loss. But then, would he have been the same man trouncing through my thoughts like nothing else in the world mattered?

He shifted slightly beneath us, earning a grunt from Bleiz and the softest of pats from Damara. I realized I hadn't answered for longer than I realized and laughed under my breath.

"I'm trying to imagine it," I admitted, my voice barely louder than the wind. He probably already knew that, though. "Not that I'm not grateful, but why are you telling me this?"

"*Because not all of my memories are of pain and loss. There was a lot of good, once. A lot of pressure and responsibility, too, but not so much as there is now.*"

"And then you weren't so alone."

"*Unfortunately, that's also true. But I want you to remember going to your family today, that you have far more good memories than bad. Your family loves you. And though I sense the answers they'll give you may hurt or disappoint you, take the bad, feel it, then process it. But release it when you're done. Because if there were mistakes made, they were long ago. Let them have your forgiveness.*"

"Before it's too late."

Kiran didn't answer, but I knew that was what he meant. More questions rose in my mind about his life, his family. What hadn't he said that haunted him to this day?

I didn't get to ponder them long, though. The wind picked up, spluttering snow into our faces and necks. The three of us pressed closer together. Kiran's pace picked up, even though I could see from the strain in his shoulders that he grew tired.

Near evening, the snowstorm calmed to a flurry of spiraling flakes that nearly missed us but for the icy wind. My bones ached from the cold. Even Kiran's warmth was only a low buzz beneath the chill now. But he flew on and on, until he landed on the beach.

That beach.

I hadn't been back here since that day. One hundred and eighty-seven years ago. It felt like ages, but it was really only a blip in our long lives. Nakia and I had gone to other places to swim after the attack. Other pieces of shore far closer to home, or to Castyr Lake, slightly north of Eldoris.

Kiran scanned the beach warily, his massive talons sinking deep into the sand. Damara slid from his back first. In a flash of red-gold light she turned into a large red fox and scampered away to sniff the ground and patrol. My jaw fell open, so startled by her sudden change, by the fact that her shift was so much smoother than Kiran's.

"That's what happens when you're a smaller animal," Bleiz said with a laugh. "It's like water pouring into a glass."

I watched as he dropped from Kiran's back. He reached a hand up to me, and I accepted while asking, "What's your animal form?"

Bleiz grinned, then tapped his left thigh and hip. His concealed tattoo. "You'll find out someday." His eyes dipped to my neck. Unconsciously, I had begun to rub at the scars there. That grin faded and he took a step closer. "You know you're safe with us, right? That's why we're here."

"I know," I said quietly. But my eyes still ran the length of the beach, and I still found myself reaching out to touch Kiran's side. He didn't say anything, turning those unique eyes of his my way, but he stepped closer, huffing out a cloud of warm air that calmed the chill slinking down my spine.

"I don't sense any trolls. Neither does Damara. Or any other danger, for that matter."

"Good," I replied.

"Are you all right? Your hand is trembling."

I pulled my hand back, tucking it into my cloak. "I'm fine." He tilted his head. "I'm nervous."

"As is to be expected." He turned his head upward, toward the sky. Glittering beams of sun peeked through the dense snow clouds, nearly at the horizon line. *"Almost night. Are you ready, my rose?"*

My heart caught in my chest. Nervous flutters resounded through my stomach.

But I was ready.

So, when night finally fell and Kiran's blue light lit the beach, when he took my hand into his own and squeezed my fingers tight, I led him to the people who meant the most to me in the entire world.

My family.

28

I n the moon cycles since I left, Eldoris had changed.

We passed through the enormous iron gates into the city; the guards dipping to their knees in salute to Kiran. Their eyes locked with mine briefly and I tried to focus on the city ahead, on the warmth of Kiran's gloved fingers entangled with my own, instead of the circlet that sat on my brow. But the truth was, I had accepted Bleiz's deal. I was to be Kiran's princess, his bride. Eventually his *queen*.

I would have to get used to the open stares.

And to the newly repaired cobblestone streets that lined the city. Eldoris was so different. Homes and shops had been repaired, with new roofs and windows and walls. Elven lights, glittering magic trapped inside of orbs of glass, hung around the city and cast all of Eldoris in a glow that made everything seem that much newer and more welcoming.

When we got toward the edge of the city, toward my familial home, I paused. I could see it. Steps away. I knew it was my home because I could see the gardens that spread out the back. But it was a different house. In a few moon cycles they had added an entire floor. The roof was new, the walls made of stone. Our ramshackle fencing had been replaced with solid, carved bits of driftwood that stood straight in their spots like tiny wooden soldiers. Elven lights lined the walk and sparkled from the gardens.

It was my home.

And not.

"They've done a lot with what they've been given," Bleiz said, crossing his arms over his chest. "They're good people, Sabrena. All of Eldoris has benefited from your agreement."

I didn't know what to say. Kiran squeezed my fingers, a gentle reassurance. I knew the money would do them some good, and I knew they would help our neighbors if they could. But they had done *so* much. I was willing to bet even our sister cities had seen financing, given the materials that would have needed to be brought in. I was proud—of my family, my city, my former friends, and neighbors.

But a question lingered in the back of my mind.

"How can you afford to give so much to my family now and not to the elves before? When we were starving?" I asked Kiran. I needed to know. Did they let us starve, so that when they swooped in to save us the impact would be that much greater? I didn't want to believe that of him. But I had to know.

"The money your family was given was the last remains of my family's estate," Kiran said softly. I squeezed his hand at that, at the stark grief that darkened his eyes. "We tried to stretch it out, as much as we could, between both our races. But in truth, it wasn't as much as it seems."

"We were desperate for a change in the tides," Bleiz said. "I don't regret the decision when it seems you were fated to play a role in all of this. Especially not when it seems to have gone much farther in helping your people because it went to *your* family. You *should* be proud of them."

I was. I was very proud of them. And also very scared to confront them about my being a siren. The distance between us felt twice as long right here in front of the house.

Kiran tightened his grip again, more pointedly, and I glanced up. He dipped his head slowly. Encouraging me. My heart thundered between my ribs, the thumping so loud I could hardly focus. I released Kiran's hand and walked down the walkway.

Rapped my knuckles against the door.

Connak flung the door open, his sword at the ready. And faltered. His eyes widened. The sword clattered to the floor. "Sabrena?"

I smiled at him tentatively. My hands practically vibrated at my sides; they were shaking so hard. I could feel the tears welling in my eyes, but I didn't really notice them until Kiran's gloved fingers brushed the back of my arm in concern. Connak's eyes narrowed on him.

But before anyone could speak further, Connak was shoved aside and a blur of bright color flew at me. I wasn't able to catch myself before I fell backward into the grass, the full weight of Nakia pressing down on me. Her arms looped my neck, squeezing tight. My tears spilled over.

And then we were laughing. Crying and laughing and hugging each other so tightly I thought our ribs might shatter. I tried to fight the intrusive snorts that broke my laughter, but the sound only made us start all over again. The jasmine and lavender and violet scent that was so very Nakia, and so very comforting against the waves of emotions crashing through me, overwhelmed my senses.

"I missed you so much," Nakia choked out. She rolled herself to a sit, grabbing my arms and yanking me up beside her. Then she swatted my arm. "Why didn't you tell us you were coming? Why haven't you *written* to me?"

"It's a long story." I wiped at my cheeks, then wrapped Nakia in another tight hug. "But I missed you too. So much. And I penned you letters! I just . . . kept forgetting to send them with the guards before changes."

"Typical," Nakia said, swiping the tears from her cheeks. "So typical."

"Does your family get to be in on this little love fest or is it best friend exclusive?"

The tears in my eyes renewed as I met Rhett's hazel gaze. A wide smile curved his lips. He reached out a hand, tugging me to my feet and against his chest. I squeezed him, hard, before I murmured, "I missed you too, Ree-ree."

"Well, I know that. I just didn't want the *rest* of the family to think you'd forgotten them."

I laughed, a choked, joyful sound, before I looked at the door. Mama stood in the front, crying silent tears into a beautifully embroidered handkerchief, Connak's hand protectively on her shoulder. My sisters peered out around her skirts. I searched the group for Papa. Mama noted my curiosity.

"He's inside with Siyna, sweet girl."

And with her words a kind of frenzy came over me. A need to see my Papa, whom I hadn't seen in months and months; a need to see his face and try to figure out our secrets for myself. But most of all, the need of a daughter to be held by her father in a world that suddenly felt so big.

I pressed kisses to Mama's cheeks, squeezed Connak's arm. I tickled my younger sisters, brushing my lips to each of their foreheads. Then I pressed past them all, into an unfamiliar house, only to find the most familiar face smiling gently my way.

"Papa," I said softly.

Two swift motions and Siyna was curled in Mama's arms and Papa had me in his. And a feeling pulled deep in my stomach, a gnawing ache that his strong hold couldn't quash. I breathed in his scent, salty sea brine that never seemed to leave him and the soft odor of tobacco smoke. He was a solid weight, a rock. He always had been. But I knew Amirah was right. In my heart, in my soul, I could feel it. Maybe it was whatever magic *did* flow in my veins.

Papa was my Papa.

But he wasn't my father.

I didn't know how I was going to ask what I needed to ask. He was going to be hurt. Even if the wound had healed, I was about to pick at the scab. And that . . . that shattered every piece of my soul.

"Are you going to introduce your friends, songbird?" Papa asked gently.

Heat slithered up my neck and blossomed across my cheeks. I had forgotten the fae in my haste . . . I pulled back from him reluctantly, pressing my face into my hands. Then I hurried to the door, gesturing my friends inside.

"Mama, Papa, my dearest siblings . . . I would like you to meet my friends, Damara and Bleiz." The two fae greeted my family as though they were equal to Kiran, and gratitude flowed through me. But then came the impossible, and I swallowed hard before I said, "And this, this is my soon-to-be husband, Kiran Devayne."

"Your Highness," Papa said, dipping to a knee. The rest of my family followed suit and my jaw slipped. It was easy to forget Kiran was actually a prince sometimes. He was so . . . so not what I expected of a ruling fae.

Kiran winced at his title and my family's reaction, but quickly smoothed his expression to some mix of formal greeting and caution. "The pleasure is mine. Please, rise. Honorifics aren't necessary if we're to be family. Call me Kiran."

My family seemed as wary as he was, but they were respectful. The beautiful home around them was thanks to him, after all, and their ability to help Eldoris had come from his wallet. Even if they felt he had stolen me away, the results of our agreement were evident in every corner of the village. And I . . . I was grateful. To Bleiz, for offering me the chance. To Damara, who had treated me like a friend from the very beginning.

And to Kiran. For being so much more than I had ever imagined he could be. For showing me, and my family, kindness when we needed it most. Bleiz had arranged our marriage. Kiran could have said no. But he didn't. And here, in this moment, I was so grateful.

"Let me get you all some tea. This snowstorm is right from the ninth circle," Mama said, vanishing down a hallway. "Follow me, songbird, I have some dry clothing for you."

I did. The ornate hallways twisted far past where we stopped—a guest room with full, beautiful furnishings. I tried not to gape at how much our home had changed. Mama offered me a warm, thick dress and I slid into it, draping my cloak around my shoulders again for extra warmth. Then I returned to the main foyer.

Papa was there, waiting. He gestured to his left, into a sitting room adorned in plush chairs that circled a broad fireplace. Nakia and I flopped onto a broad loveseat. My family scattered themselves around the room, Rhett disappearing to put Siyna in her crib for the night. My younger sisters curled up in a pile of furs in front of the fireplace, pulling knitting needles from a nearby bag and occupying themselves with their craft.

"Why the unexpected visit?" Connak asked. Never one to beat around the bush.

"Don't chase our guests off with the heavy talk," Mama said. Her arms were laden with a tea tray, loaded to teetering with cups of the finest porcelain and small sandwiches.

She didn't even have to ask Connak and he was on his feet taking the whole lot from her. He passed teacups to each of us, as Mama followed along filling them. Bleiz and Damara muttered words of thanks as they went. The two of them had fallen into plush chairs near the fireplace, likely warming up from the cold of the trip.

But Kiran lingered behind me, leaning against the back of my seat. His shoulders were curved, his head dipped. He was trying to make himself smaller. To make himself fit into the group around him. He was trying to draw less attention to who he was, the unshakeable title, the bloodline that sent fear through the elven people.

Kiran didn't need to do that, though. Not now. I *knew* him. And I would fight my own people, my own family, to give him a chance at being known for who he really was.

No matter how much he tried to shrink himself, my family's eyes followed his every move—when his gloved hands flexed, or his hair dipped around a pointed ear, or he murmured a soft, sincere thanks for the tea—stares tracked everything he did.

Clearing my throat, I looked at Mama when she settled on the arm of Papa's chair, his arm falling lightly around her waist. "How have things been? Since I left?"

"We've missed you," Mama said, as though softening a blow to come. "But I can't lie. Things have been so much easier, on everyone. And with your Papa home, we were able to expand and renovate the house . . ."

"Which desperately needed done," I admitted, taking a swallow of my tea. Light spice and sweet citrus danced across my tongue. I had only had tea so fine at the estate; I was glad my family could experience it too.

Mama nodded. "You changed so many lives, songbird. I hope you know that." She glanced at the fae in the room, before asking, "And you?"

"I'm well, Mama. The estate is beautiful."

Kiran cleared his throat softly. "I think we should give you all some space, since it's been so long. We can see ourselves out." He gestured to Bleiz and Damara, who stood immediately. The three laid their empty cups on the tea tray, Damara and Bleiz moving for the door, before Kiran paused, leveling an even stare on me. "If you need anything—"

"I'll find you."

"I won't be too far." His voice was steady, but the way he hesitated to break my gaze betrayed his concern.

Deep in my chest, warmth swelled at the sight. At his care. At him, at Kiran, for being exactly who he was.

"I'll be fine," I murmured.

He didn't speak another word, nodding politely to Mama before he saw himself out.

A whoosh of release flowed over the room. Postures slumped, Mama uncrossed her legs. But Papa's eyes were still trained on my face.

"Has he been kind to you?"

"Yes, of course. Why—"

"Does it look like he's hurt her?" Mama interrupted. Her attention fell to my face, to the circlet that sat at my brow. "She's positively glowing."

"And do you see the way he looked at her?" Nakia said with a giggle, digging her elbow into my side. "Maryna never looked at you like that."

"It's not a competition," I muttered. I felt the flush creeping up my cheeks before Rhett pointed at the red.

"Little sister, are you *blushing?* Over this fae prince? What haven't you told us yet?"

"Kiran's . . . *nice,*" I said uncomfortably.

Rhett positively giggled. "Nice? *Nice?* You're on a casual first-name basis with *the* Prince Kiran of Garenwrynn, and he looks at you like *that,* and all you can say is he's nice?"

"He's . . ." I considered. "Kiran's everything people say about him and nothing like that at all. He's stoic and serious and focused, but kind and considerate, too."

"See Mama," Rhett said with a smirk. "Sabrena's not suffering at all."

Mama frowned. "That's not the point, Rhett Feryn."

"I'm fine, Mama," I said softly. Not for long, though. Not with what I had to bring up. I swallowed, bracing myself. "But I do need to speak to you and Papa. Alone, if the rest of you don't mind?"

Nakia's eyes narrowed. "I'm staying."

I patted her arm gently, glad she wanted to stay. And grateful for the reassurance her presence brought. "Yes, you can stay, fine."

"If you think Nakia's getting to stay and I'm not, you have another think coming," Connak said. He crossed his arms over his chest, challenging me to move him. "We've never been a family of secrets."

I squirmed uncomfortably in my seat, glancing at my two youngest sisters. They looked engrossed in their work, but I knew them too well. People tended to underestimate the young. But they were always listening. And, when my potential abilities were still tender, and with Kiran's position in the world so precarious, I didn't need them blabbing my secret all over Eldoris.

Let alone the potential shame my parents would face, if the situation were as bad as I thought it might be.

"I'll take the girls to their room," Rhett offered. I caught his eye and he gave a knowing smile, but then he said, "But you better wait until I get back."

I sipped at my tea, answering vague questions about my life and the estate until Rhett returned. Mama coaxed a bit more out of me—descriptions of Kiran's gardens and what I spent my days doing, mostly.

And then a tense quiet fell over the sitting room. I set my tea down on the low table in front of me and laced my fingers together, trying to calm the nerves that shook my hands. This was one conversation I had never planned to have, and the idea that my parents, my loving, supportive parents, might not be everything they appeared . . . it shook something deep inside me. My world felt a little less secure.

I was worried that, when I had the answers, it would completely tilt over.

The heaviness of my silence weighed on the room. I cleared my throat, all too aware of the five sets of eyes that watched my every movement. And then, I began.

I told them about the Eventide Rose. What it meant to the fae people, that it hadn't bloomed in years. I mentioned all the small moments through my life, when I noticed that I hadn't quite fit in with my own people. And then I mentioned my song. How I loved singing and did it more on instinct than with conscious thought.

Mama's eyes were wide when I paused to gauge the room. My brothers looked confused. But Papa stared stoically into the fireplace.

Inhaling deeply, I caught Mama's eyes. And asked the question I so deeply wanted answered, as much as I dreaded the response. "How is it that I have siren magic?"

Rhett and Connak's eyes widened at that. Their gazes flitted between our parents, trying to see if it was true.

It was.

I could see it in the flexing muscle along Papa's jaw. Or in the flush and shame that poured over Mama's expression and posture. She shifted subtly in her seat, staring steadily at her hands.

"We shouldn't speak of past mistakes," Mama said finally. Before I could protest, she added, "But if we must, perhaps you were right. We should speak alone."

My brother's attention's affixed on Mama. She still wouldn't meet their eyes, or anyone else's.

Connak shook his head stubbornly. "We are a family. Good and bad."

Mama sighed and a weight settled on her shoulders, one I had never seen, even in all our years of poverty and struggle.

But Papa shrugged, his expression resolved. "You might as well tell them."

We waited in silence while Mama gathered her thoughts. She ran weathered hands through her hair, jabbed at the fire with an iron poker. Finally, she looked at me, though she still wouldn't quite meet my eyes.

"I need you to understand . . . I made a mistake . . . one mistake, one big mistake, in all the years I've loved your father." Mama paused, as if waiting for my acceptance. I nodded slowly. Nakia reached out, grabbing my hand and squeezing tight. Then, Mama continued. "Your Papa is out to sea a lot . . . he's always been out to sea a lot. You know this. You all do. And Connak was young and I was tired and lonely and . . ."

Papa moved, coming to kneel beside Mama's chair. He gripped her hand and ran a loving caress over her cheek. "I forgave you years ago. Sabrena deserves to know."

Mama nodded, leaning into Papa's hand. The gesture was so soft, so tender, my mind slipped to Kiran. To the future we might have. Or that, if we couldn't find a way to stop the trolls, we might lose.

I shook the thought. This was not the time. My powers could be of help solving that problem, and I could only learn of them if I paid attention.

"A man wandered into Eldoris. He caught me at the well, trying to balance the water and carrying little Connak. He offered to help . . ." Mama swallowed hard. "His eyes were like yours, Sabrena. Like the clearest water on the brightest day. And one thing led to another . . ."

"Papa isn't Sabrena's father?" Rhett asked softly. His eyes were wide, his mouth agape in shock.

"No, he's not," Mama said. "I only ever saw her father once. That was all it took. I didn't know how to tell your father, but he wasn't home till many months later and I knew . . . I knew I couldn't hide the bump, or the child. What if she didn't look like him, or me? So, I told your father the minute he came home."

Papa nodded. "I left for a few days. Stayed in the inn. But inevitably I loved your mother more than I hated her for her mistake. It took time. Years. But I forgave her."

He made it sound so simple, forgiving Mama's transgression. But Papa had always been the best of us. Maybe the anger that had begun to dance in my chest was simply too loud.

"And we never regretted you," Mama said, finally meeting my heavy stare. "Not once."

"I never felt like you weren't my daughter," Papa agreed,

"Even though you weren't really mine, I raised you. For me, that was enough."

Mama reached out and gripped his arm. "A father is more than blood. And your Papa has been the greatest father all these years. Don't punish him for my mistake."

"I could never," I said. "Papa is my Papa. Regardless of who created me." I paused. A tide of emotions was flowing over me: sadness, for Papa and how he must have felt. Joy, that he raised me as his own, so much so that I never suspected I might be different.

And anger. The anger was a wild storm, spinning up through my center, growing with every second that I lingered in my thoughts.

"Why didn't you tell me?" I asked after a moment.

"We didn't want you to feel lesser than your siblings. We loved you all the same. It didn't matter where you came from," Mama said.

But I shook my head, that storm swirling higher. I pulled my hand from Nakia's, crossing my arms tight over my chest as though I could hold the rage inside. "Why didn't you tell me?"

Papa's voice was gentle when he said, "We didn't think it mattered."

"Didn't matter?" I snapped, the winds of fury blasting through me. "Didn't matter? You watched me get torn apart by our community for years. You watched me grieve a love that no one thought I was worthy of, including Maryna herself. You saw what Donovan did to me, over and over again. And all this time, I *was* different. I was being measured against a standard I could never have met. And you didn't think I should know?"

"Brena, love—"

"No. I want to know. Why didn't you tell me?"

Mama's eyes welled with tears. "I couldn't bear the shame of admitting what I had done. Not to the whole community, where I would be judged for my worst mistake."

"So, you let your worst mistake take the judgment for you?" I spat. "You saw what I suffered. And you still thought it was okay to keep your silence?"

"Yes," Mama said quietly. "I did. And I'm sorry."

I was speechless. The words had been torn from my throat and the anger that trembled through every inch of my being threatened to lash out and destroy their beautiful home. I was willing to sacrifice everything for them, and they couldn't even be *honest* with me?

Mama's apology was going to take time. I needed to absorb this. I had expected to be told I was a siren, and even that Mama had made a mistake. But to hear that she had let me suffer for her mistake? Willingly? That . . . I needed time with that.

"I should go."

"Sabrena, wait," Mama called.

But I had climbed to my feet, tugging my cloak tight around my shoulders.

And without another word, I left. I let the tempest that raged inside me carry me outside, to the frozen storm that pounded on the city around us.

Because I would rather turn to ice than face the shard of pain that pierced my chest.

29

Cold snow bit into my skin. My limbs were stiff, all but frozen in the icy air, and I had no inkling where I might be. Everything was white, and I had wandered too far. I didn't recognize anything around me, not even the lay of the trees.

Foolish. I'm so foolish.

I should have waited for Kiran to return. Mama's words had been a lance to my heart. That she had watched me be ridiculed and still didn't stand up for me . . . Pain twinged in my chest again. It didn't matter, not now. Not when I had walked and walked into a storm of blinding white. I really should have waited for Kiran to come for me. Wandering into the storm was foolish.

And now I was lost. Cold. I would freeze to death before morning.

As if it could hear my thoughts, a chill blast of wind swirled around me, spinning snowflakes into my hair. I stumbled then and fell into the deep drifts of white. My skirts quickly soaked through. I wished I had my leathers still. The gown was useless in this storm and the cold was a deep ache in the center of my bones. I was going to die here, alone, all because I hadn't stopped to consider the repercussions of my anger. Anger that, in retrospect, I should have handled better. Or at least handled well enough that I didn't go running off into this mess.

This cold, bone-numbing mess.

Minutes passed with only the soft shuffling dance of snow-flakes to keep me company. I managed to pull myself into a curved nest of tree roots, no more dry but certainly more sheltered. Tremors shook through me. I could no longer feel my fingers, or toes, and I was almost certain my lips had gone blue.

I had nearly given up hope when I heard heavy footsteps. The crisp crunch of new fallen snow was music to my ears. I clawed at the tree trunk with my numb fingers, clambering my way upright.

"Kiran?" I called into the frozen quiet. "Damara? Bleiz?"

The resounding snarls that shivered through the trees wasn't the response I had expected. I knew the sounds Kiran made, even as a dragon, and these were nothing like them.

A tree cracked and splintered, a whoosh of snow collapsing onto the earth a dozen feet from where I sat. I pressed myself deeper into the nested roots, sucking in slow, deep breaths so I didn't make too much sound.

Three massive trolls stepped into my eyeline, shoving branches out of their paths. The first, a tall female with pale blue skin, sniffed the air as though scenting her prey. I was suddenly conscious of all the scents that perfumed my family home, of all the ways they might now be lingering on my skin. She gnashed her teeth together, her long bottom tusks pressing lightly into her cheeks. Her red and orange hair was shaved along the sides, the length all tied into a long braid that ran down the center from her forehead down to her waist. The female grunted at her companions, two intimidatingly large males with greenish skin tones and blue hair. They seemed to answer to her, spreading out to search the trees to the left and right.

They had to hear my heartbeat thundering against my ribs. Or smell the lingering scent of tea or woodsmoke or flowers around me.

I restrained the whimper that curled on my lips, and slowly moved my hand for the dagger strapped to my thigh. I didn't kid myself; I couldn't beat three trolls. But I could fight them. And maybe I could wound them enough that I could run.

My fingers curled around the hilt. I slid the blade free, centimeter by centimeter, faster still when the bulkier of the two males got close enough that I could smell him. His scent was a mix of fowl earth and aging moss and my nose wrinkled in distaste.

"What have we here?" he rasped as his eyes landed on my trembling form. His companions turned immediately, all steady, firm attention directly onto me.

I clutched my dagger tighter, trying to remind myself of Rhett's words. I loosened the brooch of my cloak, letting the extra hindrance fall free.

And then I lunged.

He didn't expect me to move. I didn't think I still had the strength. My numb limbs were an impediment against smooth motion. I stumbled, wobbling, shaking with cold.

But I shoved through and plunged the blade deep into the soft skin right below his shoulder. I knew his exposed neck was a weakness. My best chance at survival lay in wounding him there. I yanked my blade free and tried again.

The troll roared in anger. He swiped out his mace before I could move, clubbing me hard in the gut. Fire lit along my stomach everywhere he made contact, where each point of the rounded-off spikes all along the weapon's face had hit me.

I clung to my dagger as I hit the ground rolling. A flurry of snow blasted into the air. My arm hit a rock, scraping the skin and leaving a smear of crimson through the snow. I stretched out my hand and reached for the dagger that had slipped from my fingers, but the troll stomped the blade deep into the snow. My ribs ached as I rolled, trying to put distance between myself and the three trolls who were bearing down fast. Blood dribbled down the chest plate of the one I had wounded, his green eyes livid with blood lust.

Breathing felt too hard, my limbs felt too heavy to move. I didn't know where Kiran was, or Damara, or Bleiz. I didn't know how to get help.

And then Amirah's taunts played in my head, and I thought that my death might not be so bad if it saved us from that future.

I slumped into the snow. The troll raised his mace above my head. I squeezed my eyes shut.

And a new set of snarls joined the grunting sounds the trolls were making. My eyes sprung open as a massive brown wolf leapt into the clearing, latching himself onto the troll I had wounded and ripping his throat out in one swift motion.

He seemed so familiar, this wolf. I met his eyes for the briefest of seconds, the smallest light of concern blazing bright, and the world turned dark.

I woke in a pile of snow, shivering from cold. My muscles ached. My very being ached. I wondered where the wolf had gone or how long I had been out.

Not long, if the freshly scattered snow in front of me was any indication.

I wondered where Kiran was.

I didn't have to wait long.

A soft huff broke the silence, then he was there.

My dragon.

I could see the relief I felt mirrored in his eyes, mingled with frustration.

I struggled to climb to my feet. He moved closer, offering the support of his snout, and I didn't even try to argue. For a moment, I simply leaned into the heady warmth that pulsed from his scales and let the tingling rush of warmth run over me.

"I'm sorry I made you worry," I murmured finally.

A soft burst of steam rolled from his nostrils. *"Not now, my rose. I just want to get you home."*

Home.

"How badly are you wounded?"

"Cut on my arm," I murmured. "Took a mace to the stomach, too. I'm not sure if anything broke, but I'm definitely bruised."

"We'll get you taken care of."

He nudged me gently and I accepted the direction, climbing onto his back. My skin nearly burned against his scales while the heat of him thawed my frozen body. I winced as he shifted his weight, trying to secure myself. He shot a concerned look over his shoulder, his eyes narrowing at the way I shivered.

"You're safe now. I promise. I'm so sorry I left you alone."

I gripped his scales with trembling fingers and he spread his wings. A flap, a shower of broken trees and snow, and we were airborne.

And I was lost to the world once more.

I woke to soft sheets and the comforting scent of lemons. Every muscle in my body clenched on waking, in anxious anticipation, but they relaxed at the feel of the warm fur blankets that meant I was in my bed. I avoided looking at the blanket Mama had made me, spread out on top. I didn't want to think right now.

Blinking to clear the lingering sleep, I took in the closed curtains that draped my bed. A slight shadow moved near the windows, the sound of knitting needles tapping together in steady rhythm. Niserie, then.

I sat bolt upright as angry voices echoed through the walls. My stomach ached at the motion and I jerked up my shirt. Deep purple bruises stretched across my skin.

". . . believe you left her to the cold."

My attention returned to the door.

"I didn't leave her to the cold," Kiran snarled. "She left her mother's house before she was supposed to and she didn't tell anyone where she was going."

A beat of silence passed, then Bleiz asked, "Do you know what her mother said?"

"No." Kiran admitted, sighing heavily. "But her friend said Sabrena had run out into the storm, upset. Apparently she tried to follow, but Sabrena was gone before the friend got her cloak on. I haven't known Sabrena to be so reckless."

"No, me either."

"I can't imagine what she was thinking. I'm glad you were able to find her so fast."

Kiran had found me. Hadn't he?

"I don't want to see her hurt any more than you do," Bleiz paused. "Hopefully I didn't scare her."

"I'll ask. I'm going to check in on her now. Tell Damara I want a meeting with everyone in the house as soon as possible."

The tread of boots on marble marked the end of the conversation. I slumped back against the pillows, feigning sleep, ignoring the click of my door opening. Kiran said something, so low I couldn't hear it. Niserie abandoned her post and left the room.

Then the curtains around me slid back. I blinked slowly.

"May I?" Kiran asked, gesturing to the bed. I nodded and he took a seat. "How are you feeling?"

"Sore," I said, but my voice was a hoarse croak.

Kiran reached for a glass on the table beside my bed and held it out. Sparkling water danced with candlelight, and I drained it in a few large gulps. My ribs ached at the effort of sitting upright.

"Better?"

I nodded. "How did you find me?"

"I didn't," he admitted softly. "Bleiz did."

"But I remember you, your dragon . . ."

"You don't remember the wolf?"

I froze, a flood of memories flickering through my mind. Three trolls bearing down. And a wolf. A wolf that looked so painstakingly familiar . . .

Another rush of memories.

A beach.

Nakia, unmoving.

A troll that smelled of sweat and smoke and earth.

Fear washed through me, like the waves on the sand that Nakia and I had been running on. Our innocence had been stolen away. Ripped apart, by that troll.

But it was the wolf. The wolf that stood out in my memories, who had stormed to my rescue now twice. *Bleiz*.

"It was Bleiz," I murmured. Kiran's brow narrowed with concern. "It was Bleiz, who saved Nakia and me all those years ago." My fingers traced the scars on my neck and shoulder. "He's the reason I escaped with only these."

His brows shot up. "He mentioned he'd seen you before. I didn't realize . . ."

"I didn't either," I admitted.

Kiran watched me for a moment, silent, giving me a moment to process. Then his gaze dipped to my forearm, to the bandages that wound the length.

"I need to check that. If you don't mind."

Kiran gave me a weak smile when I held my arm out. He unwound the bandages with ease, scanning the reddened skin. "You heal slowly, for my kind or yours. Even with magic. Then again, I don't know how sirens heal."

I balked at the subject. Kiran noticed the change in my expression, the slump of my shoulders. I didn't particularly want to think about my parentage, or my mother's shame, or the fact that her need to protect it had come at the cost of my wellbeing for so long. I had thought I was damaged because I was scarred, but the damage had come long before that.

Kiran's touch on my arm was featherlight as he healed the roughened area. I must have hit that rock harder than I thought.

But every time his gloved fingers brushed me, jolts of static burst across my skin. I drew in a sharp breath. Kiran lifted his gaze to mine, brow drawn in concern.

"I didn't mean to hurt you."

"You didn't," I murmured.

Confusion flickered across his face, but he set back to his task. I inhaled a deep, steadying breath and, as my senses were flooded with the soft scent of him, I was once again struck by how close he was. Amber and sandalwood and citrus.

Kiran never lingered this close.

He studied the wound, making sure he healed every inch, steady and careful in his movements. But when he finished, his hands lingered, light on my arm.

"Are you all right? Truly?" I nodded, watching him closely. He didn't lift his eyes from my arm. "I was afraid last night. We went back to your mother's house and they had no idea where you were . . . half the town was looking for you. I was worried that you were taken. I was worried I was going to be too late. And I didn't . . . I didn't . . ."

Kiran bit off the words on a soft exhale, withdrawing his hands. Chill air filled his absence and I frowned. I wanted him to stay near. I wanted him to look at me the way he just had, to hear the concern he felt for me, so thick in his voice. I wanted . . .

Things I couldn't have. Not now. Not yet.

"I'm not so easy to take, Kiran," I said, trying to bury the disappointment I was feeling.

A wry smile tilted the corner of his lips. "No. No you're not."

"How long was I out?"

"Only for the day," he said gently. "Damara sat with you until I could."

I frowned at that. At the thought that his dragon form was too large to come into this wing. "I'm sorry I made you worry."

"I'm glad I have someone to worry about," he said, his voice low and husky.

I shuffled the fur on my lap, trying to ignore the heat that rose in my cheeks. When I dared a timid glance, Kiran was watching me, carefully.

"What did she say, your mother?"

The recounting spilled out before I had a chance to think better of it. Every word, the anger that had risen inside me. The shame I felt now when our family had never left things so off kilter before.

"I sent Damara to tell them we found you," he said when I finished. "If that's any consolation."

"Thank you."

"Why do I feel like there's more you need to say?"

"I'm not even sure what to say, honestly." I picked at the fur blanket. "I'll never be powerful. Not like my family. I don't even have elven magic. I can never be what they expected me to be."

"Like *who* expects you to be? A generation so set in their own ways that they refuse to see you? Because I see you." Kiran brushed a strand of hair from my face. "Your power comes from deeper than your blood. It comes from your heart, your soul. You are capable of more than any magic." He hesitated, then added, "And far more beautiful."

I didn't know what to make of his words. They touched a shattered piece inside of me that had long been broken and nudged it, encouraging those remnants of myself to finally heal.

Silence fell between us, but he released one of my hands and ran a leather-clad finger down the length of my cheek. I studied him for a moment, sure of what I saw in his eyes before I leaned in, before I tried, without thinking, to kiss him.

Kiran caught my chin gently, his lips mere inches from my own. "Would that I could," he whispered softly. "I have never been so tempted from my fate as with you, little rose."

30

Sounds echoed through the dark estate. They were faint, distant, like the soft rumble of thunder on the horizon. But the estate walls trembled.

I clambered out of bed, lowering myself to the floor. My ribs were sore, but the healing magic Kiran and Niserie had used helped my healing time significantly. I could flex and move easily enough.

The door to my room let out a low groan as I pulled it open, dipping into the hall. Faleen patrolled the hall outside my room and nodded lightly in greeting when I waved at her.

"What is that sound?"

"Kiran," Faleen said. "He has . . . some nights are harder than others."

I glanced toward his wing. "Has he always had nightmares like this?"

"As long as I've known him."

"How often?"

Faleen shrugged. "Not very, lately. Once a moon cycle, at least. Bleiz usually wakes him up by now, but I'm not sure if he's here or if Kiran put him on the border patrol tonight."

I frowned at that.

But I squared my shoulders and moved. Kiran's fears about the future were pressing heavily on him, I knew, but to send Bleiz away knowing he might be the only thing standing between him and nights like these . . .

I could step in, though. I could help him.

Hopefully.

I crossed the estate with long, purposeful strides. The floors quavered; my balance became unsteady with each step closer to Kiran's wing. Blue light filled the halls to his room, growing brighter the closer I came. The glow emanated under his door, where it shivered in its frame. I pushed, hard, against the magic that struggled to keep the room closed.

Kiran was curled into a ball in the center of his bed. His sheets were twisted tightly around him, as though he had been rolling and thrashing. He was still for the moment, though. His hands were wrapped tightly in his hair, the tattoos across his arms and back blindingly bright.

I called his name softly, inching closer. He didn't move, didn't respond. But the light faded, shrinking to a soft blue glow. I kept saying his name, asking if he was okay, all the while stepping closer and closer.

When I reached the side of his bed he relaxed, collapsing to his stomach. Then he groaned, loudly, as though whatever he was dreaming was tearing his heart in two. He flipped over.

I tried not to stare. His shirt fell back, and left his chest bare, cast in the light from his tattoos, a plane of smooth, muscular rises and falls. Kiran was glorious. His arms flexed, his fists tightening around his sheets, and my attention snagged on the ripple of muscle that shivered up his arms. He twisted slightly and I noticed a gnarled scar that curved along his left hip, just above the pants he wore. I was tempted to reach out and touch it. To see if it felt like my own.

Another part of me was shocked that someone who I thought was so beautiful had a mark that marred him, too. My head spun with the how seeing that imperfection on him made me feel. Because on him, the scar didn't feel like a flaw. Why couldn't I see my own scars any other way?

Kiran shot upright and, for a moment, I thought he was awake. But his eyes were closed, his chest heaving as though he had been running or fighting. His tattoos began to brighten again. The room grew warmer.

Warmer.

Too warm. Sweat spread across my brow. The heat was rolling off Kiran, off his body which now trembled as tears streamed down his cheeks.

I moved. I didn't really think about what I was doing, I wasn't even sure I could help him, but I gripped his arm and cupped his cheek, tilting his face toward mine.

"Wake up, Kiran, wake up. You're safe. You're okay." He didn't move. I ran my thumb across his cheekbone, whispering again, "I'm here. Wake up. Come back."

Kiran's eyes shot wide, then fell to my hands, gripped around his arm and rested on his cheek. And he froze. Panic jolted across his expression. I glanced down, and then up, back and forth between my hands and the stark terror on his face.

And I realized.

I realized why he hadn't wanted me to touch him. It hadn't been his own discomfort, or a boundary he had from before. I couldn't believe I hadn't seen it sooner.

I had triggered the curse. I had touched Kiran's skin, with my own, and had triggered the curse. Confirmation was bright on his face.

The world froze and trembled into place all at once. Kiran's tattoos lit bright again, then dimmed completely, as if to tell me what I already knew. My hands began to tremble where they laid, and a muscle worked in Kiran's jaw as he stared at me, emotions flitting across his face so quickly I couldn't read them.

"It's okay," he whispered finally, urgently. His shoulders relaxed as he heaved a sigh. As though he were releasing a weight. Meanwhile, I felt heavy. Panicked. Amirah had said I would be his downfall, and I had triggered the curse. She was right. The tears came pouring forth before I could stop them.

Kiran's hands moved, slowly, till they were around mine, pulling them into his own. Marveling at them, as though he were seeing me for the first time all over again. "It's okay," he said again.

"Kiran—" His name came out choked, pained.

But the prince was distracted, fixated on where his thumb traced a gentle pattern over the back of my hand. "You're so soft," he murmured.

"Kiran?"

"Sabrena?" he asked back. He turned my hands over in his, releasing one only to run his fingers over my palm, to trace the lines.

I didn't understand why he wasn't terrified. Where was the Kiran I had seen for days? Had he so easily succumbed to his fate? "What happens now?"

He paused then. A frown deepened on his lips, then he stood, never quite relinquishing his hold on me as he did. "When morning light comes, instead of becoming a dragon, I'll be summoned away. I won't have a choice in the matter. The magic will simply take me."

Fresh tears spilled over. I didn't want him to go. My stubborn, kind, brilliant husband-to-be. He had sacrificed everything for his people. And now, because of me, he was about to sacrifice so much more.

Including his people, once the Sorceress had him. He was our shield all along, and now he was going to be gone.

"I'm so sorry," I sobbed.

"Don't be. Don't cry," Kiran said gently. He released his grip on me, raising his hands to cup my cheeks and wipe away the tears that slipped free. "This isn't the end. Simply a new beginning."

"Not for you." I wanted to curl inside of myself, to hide away. I did this. I ruined this. He shouldn't be looking at me as though I freed him. This was a death sentence.

"Yes, for me. We haven't been able to find Madrion on our own. Maybe I can take them down from the inside. I won't give up. Not while you're out here."

I looked up at him, noting the flush that spread up his neck and over his cheeks. "Me?"

"You," he murmured. "Do you think I wouldn't do anything to protect you? I would give you the world, my rose. If only it were mine to give."

"Don't leave me," I whispered, the sound choked and painful. "Please, Kiran."

"I don't have a choice. The magic will come and I'm bound to it by blood." He leaned forward, pressing his forehead against mine. "But we have tonight, Sabrena. Stay here with me, keep me company until I'm called away. Give me this?"

"Anything," I said. "Anything you want."

"Anything?" His voice was deep and rough when he asked, and shivers coursed down my spine.

"Anything," I murmured.

He leaned closer, his lips so close I could feel his breath caress them. The soft concern in his eyes turned hungry when he asked again, "*Anything?*"

My heart skipped a dozen beats. His hands were warm on my face, his lips so close, *so close.* His fingers were gentle, caressing slowly, his chest warm against my own. I knew he couldn't love me. He had said as much. But even if it wasn't love, I would take this. I would give him this moment and I would cherish it for the rest of my life. So I nodded, just the barest hint of a yes, and he moved.

His lips were warm, soft. Kiran kissed like a man starved, like he had waited half his life for this one simple connection. He slid a hand into my hair, pulling me closer, as though his very air depended on the gentle swirl of tongues, the clash of lips and teeth. Kiran held me to him like I might slip away, as though for a minute in time he had everything he could need to exist while I was right in his arms. And for a moment, his shirt clutched tight in my fist, his free hand gripping my thigh, I could believe the lie. I could believe he might love me as I knew I had begun to love him.

"You start to take it for granted, touch," he murmured against my lips. "You forget the smooth caress of silken skin against your palms"—he squeezed my leg gently—"and the delicate brush of fingers that send goosebumps rising up." He ran his fingertips over the back of my thigh. A shudder raced down my spine. "You forget how to show love that way, to accept it that way."

"You've been neglected for so long, Kiran," I whispered. "I only wish I had the time to make it up to you."

He dragged a line of kisses across my cheek, and I felt the moment a soft smile curved his lips. "I have this. I have tonight. And I have you. I could not want for more."

"Not even your freedom?"

"Not if it means I miss this."

His lips were a fraction of an inch from mine, his warm breath a soft caress, a promise of what awaited if I had the courage, the desire. I dared a glance at his eyes and found him already watching, waiting. The want was bald in his stare, his need so intense that goosebumps raised across my arms. Yet beneath the poise of the dragon prince, I saw his fear. I felt it too. Neither one of us was sure if we should leap so far.

But if this was falling, I wanted to fly.

"What do you want, Kiran?"

"You," he said without hesitation.

"What part of me?"

"All of you," he said, his voice thick. "I want that brilliant

mind keeping me in check. I want your music filling my halls. I want your flowers growing all across the estate." He lowered his voice farther, a deep sound that vibrated through my chest when he said, "And I want your beautiful body in my bed, where I can worship every inch of you as a *proper* fiancé should."

I giggled nervously at that, at Kiran finally admitting he could be everything I needed. At the look in his eyes that scorched me in the best way. As though he was seeing me, and everything he wanted laid me utterly bare. And it made me less afraid, knowing he saw me. He saw all of me, and he still wanted to be here. As long as he was able.

And that, that was the courage I needed.

I backed away from him. His grasp loosened and his brow narrowed in concern. Then I slipped my gown from my shoulders, letting it slither into a pile of soft fabric on the floor. Kiran swallowed, and if I thought his eyes were blazing before, they were now fully ignited. I pushed myself onto his bed, then smirked at him.

"Come on, then." I grinned. "*Dragon prince.*"

I didn't have to tell him twice.

Kiran's skin was silk beneath my fingers. I found my way to small scars, to marks that reminded me over and over who he was. Who he could be. A prince, a warrior, a fighter. But most of all—a survivor.

His own hands roamed freely, caressing, exploring, coaxing a soft moan from deep in my throat. He chuckled at that. The sound was low, husky.

His fingers dipped to the curve of my hips, where he squeezed gently. Reflexively I arched toward him. A soft growl entered his voice when he said, "Don't taunt me."

I smirked. "Wouldn't dream of it."

He tugged softly, pulling me fully against him. My soft curves fit perfectly against his hard edges, and he smiled softly. "*Ashyndah talehn.*" I lifted a brow and he murmured, "Love of my heart."

Love. He had said love. And deep inside the warmth I had

been feeling burst into a shower of hot embers. Love. *Love.* Any lingering uncertainty burned away.

"I wish I had come to you sooner," I whispered, "told you how I felt, found a way to keep you to myself."

"Everything happens for a reason," he murmured, his lips tracing a line down my throat. Each gentle brush of his mouth sent a wave of heat through me. "I'm glad we have this, *Ashyndah talehn.*"

Love of his heart.

And I loved him, too. I needed to tell him. What was I scared of? Why was I hesitating? We only had tonight. One night to share mountains of pent-up feelings and thoughts. How could that ever be enough? How could I tell him all he meant to me? What if I didn't find the right words?

Somehow communicating this way, his fingers dancing along my skin, felt more appropriate.

Maybe we didn't need words. Maybe he would understand.

I tilted his chin gently, pulling his lips to mine and claimed them with a ferocity that made him smile. He kissed me back, pressing his lips along the line of my jaw, up to my ear, where he paused for the faintest of moments.

"*Ashyndah talehn,*" he whispered. "My beautiful rose."

I moved to claim him again, to feel his mouth on mine once more, but he shook his head. He continued down the scars that lined my neck, his breath hot, his lips gentle. Warmth pooled low in my stomach. Every inch of me screamed in want of this man, and the pleasure that the solid weight of him above me promised.

When he kissed my lips again, his hand dipped low, lower, until his fingers slipped between my legs. They moved, eliciting sensations I hadn't felt in such a long time. I moaned, a deep sound of want that rose from my chest. Kiran grinned against my mouth, pleased with himself.

"What do you want, *Ashyndah talehn?*"

"You," I murmured.

"Are you sure? We can stop. You can stay with me, like this. I would cherish the moments no less."

"Why would you think I want to stop?"

Kiran's smile slipped and he nested against my throat, pressing a tender kiss to my collar bone. "Because in the morning I leave. And I don't want you to think this is all . . . I don't want you to think . . ."

"I'm sure, Kiran." *Say it, say it, say it* . . . But it was fear that held me back. Fear that kept the words locked to my tongue.

But the way he looked at me, the way he seemed to know what I thought without words . . .

I hoped that could be enough. For now, that would be enough.

Kiran's hands ran along my body, exploring, worshiping as though he was parched and had found his oasis. The length of him brushed against me and I arched my hips, encouraging and tempting him onward. Instead, he reached down again, dipping a finger between my legs and pushing it inside me. When he found how he made me feel, his chest expanded in a low, deep inhale of need.

"Kiran," I moaned, arching my hips against him again.

He withdrew his hand, pressing a deep, hungry kiss to my lips. I threaded my fingers into his soft hair, pulling him close, closer, wanting to feel every inch of him against my skin. I ground against him, teasing, taunting, until he sank into me. Slowly, patiently. Waiting as I adjusted to him. Then he moved, a steady rhythm that let us savor every sensation. I moved with him, gently matching his every thrust. My name was a curse and a prayer on the lips he pressed against my throat. He slowed to lazy, deliberate strokes and my body responded, a shiver of pleasure running the length of my spine.

Too soon the tension of climax began to rise. I gripped Kiran tighter, holding him deeper until the lightning sparks of release zipped through my veins. Kiran wasn't long behind, moaning my name into my shoulder.

For several moments, we didn't move, simply enjoying the feel of each other. Skin to skin, our lips joining in brief, loving kisses, and I couldn't imagine anything better.

I knew, then, I would never want anyone else. I would never find the feelings Kiran wrung out of me with such ease in anyone else.

I would fight for this man, who had spent too much of his life fighting for everyone else.

Kiran pulled me into his chest, holding me as though he was afraid I would float away. I rested my cheek against his chest, comforted by the rhythm of his heart. A song I would never forget, on a night I would commit to a most cherished memory.

For tonight, I wouldn't think of tomorrow. For tonight, I had this. I had us.

"Sleep, *Ashyndah talehn*," Kiran whispered in my ear. His arms tightened, and he pressed a light kiss into my hair. And, as I faded into sleep, I heard him say, "I will fight for you, my rose."

PART THREE

31

I woke feeling lighter than I had in . . . ever, maybe. My heart was full with love, with warmth.

And then I bolted upright.

The bed I was in wasn't Kiran's. Nor was it mine at the estate. I didn't have any idea where I was, actually.

And Kiran was gone. My chest tightened immediately, so much so that breathing became difficult. The night before came flooding back in an ocean of emotions: the highs like waves, weightless and wild, the lows the shoreline they came crashing down on.

I scanned the room, looking for anything familiar. The blanket Mama had made for me was sprawled across the bed, but the bedding beneath was all soft cotton. Across the room, on a soft, plush armchair, my leathers were folded neatly beneath my thick fur cloak. A dresser of dark wood sat beside me, and a bag was laid on top. No, not any bag. My bag. The bag I had first brought to the estate, filled with the little things I might need. I hadn't even needed to unpack it; I had been given so much . . .

I reached for the bag, pouring the contents out on my blanket, hoping that there was some remnant of Kiran lingering inside. In the pile, there was a smaller bag I didn't recognize, and my heart fluttered with nervous excitement. I pulled the drawstrings and peeked inside.

The first thing I saw was Kiran's little silver star box, the one etched with roses and topped by a mini clock face. I lifted the lid, to listen to the music it played, and found a note tucked inside.

Achmyn Morternos,

I knew I was in trouble the moment I laid eyes on you.

I knew I loved you when I found you freezing in the snow. In all my years, I have never felt so desperately lost as when I couldn't find you. The world felt dark in a way it hadn't in ages, and I was so determined to never feel that again. Not as long as you'd have me.

With that, I know how you must be feeling. Know that there is little hope of finding me, Sabrena, and I don't blame you if you can't. It's truly an impossible task. I would be all too happy if you managed to stay with your family, safe. I sacrificed a decade's worth of paintings to make sure you got home to them. Escape the continent, if you can.

I know you're stubborn though. My words may not matter. If you refuse to escape, to listen, be safe. I could not live with myself if I was, in any way, the cause of harm to you.

If you stand any chance, follow my stars. They're the only clue I've found in all my long years of searching.

And no matter what happens, remember this: I see you. I believe in you. Regardless of all that you've been through and all that will come, know that you are your own kind of magic.

Yours eternally,
Kiran

PS: Keep the dagger with you this time. Please.

Tears streamed down my cheeks. I swiped them away

aggressively, trying to not let them stain the page. I read the letter over and over until I nearly had every word memorized. And then I tucked it away, back into the silver box for safekeeping.

Beside the box was the dagger I had used at the estate. I strapped the leather sheath on my thighs immediately, tucked under the long skirt of the nightgown I wore. His mother's necklace was curled into a tiny swathe of fabric, and I hooked it around my neck before I peered back into the bag. Kiran had tucked the volume from Lytharian in here too, with a bookmark tucked into the siren pages, "*read them*" scrawled across it in his handwriting.

The last thing Kiran had packed in the smaller bag was a little journal, filled with notes he had taken about Madrion, the Winds, the Seers of Saryshna, the constellations—plus anything that might even be slightly relevant to the hunt for the troll kingdom. And tucked into the front was a little folded map of Numeryon, delicate and ornate and labeled with all the major cities and waterways.

I cried again, then. Heavy, thick tears that carried the weight of every emotion I was feeling. I tried to keep quiet but, once the gates opened, the flood of emotions flowed free. Even when Kiran knew his life was in danger, even when he knew our time together was precious and limited, he had thought to gather these things so that if I decided to try to find him, I wouldn't be going in blind. And it was that, more than anything, the thoughtfulness in such a small gesture, that broke my heart.

Kiran was better than the world had always believed him to be. I wasn't going to leave him to the fate I had laid out for him.

You'll be his undoing.

Maybe I was.

But Amirah had never said that I couldn't also be his salvation.

"Sabrena?"

I knew that voice.

I knew it better than I knew my own.

"Nakia?" A wave of new emotions rose in my chest—joy and relief and more pain. I clamped my arms around myself, holding tight like it could stop the shattered pieces from falling away. I was home, or home in that I was with my family.

But it didn't feel like home anymore. Not with all the changes. Not without Kiran.

A soft tap drew me back to the door, then, "Can I— Should I—"

She didn't have to finish the question. Nakia was always allowed in. The door opened seconds later and the surprise and the delight on her face faded immediately. I knew I was a sight. My eyes and lips were red and swollen from crying, my cheeks streaked, my hair disheveled.

Nakia didn't ask. And I didn't need to explain, not yet. She closed the door and crossed the room, shoving the contents of my bag aside before she scooped me into her arms. For long minutes, Nakia simply offered comfort, letting me pour out the remnants of my tears onto her shoulder.

But finally, when I began to still, she gently asked, "Why are you here? Where's Kiran?"

"When did I get here?"

Nakia's brow narrowed at my avoidance, but she said, "One of the fae city guards brought Mama a note shortly after daybreak. It didn't say much. Just that you were here and needed rest."

"Who was it from?"

"Kiran," Nakia murmured. "What *happened,* Sabrena?"

"I triggered the curse," I said. I saw the confusion in her green eyes. Kiran's bargain with the High Sorceress was common knowledge but the curse . . . I told Nakia everything. Everything until last night, that is. I hesitated there, and though I hadn't thought I had any tears left they filled my eyes again. Nakia didn't question why I broke off into silence after I explained what touching Kiran had meant . . . where he was now.

She didn't need extra words to understand the pain that raked through my chest at the confession.

Or the guilt.

The soul-crushing guilt that curled dark and unforgiving in my mind. I knew what I had to do. And Nakia saw it too.

"We should tell your family what you're planning. And, well, you should probably tell me too."

"Yeah." My thoughts drifted to Mama, and how I left things with her. And though I was still mad, though I still couldn't quite forgive her for what she had done, I didn't want to leave things as they were. If Kiran was right, and I had little doubt that he was, Numeryon was about to see more strife.

And I might be the only one who could release the strongest leader we had right now.

The thought lit a fire deep in my soul. My sorrow took on an edge and hardened into anger. Amirah had taken enough from us and all of our people.

I didn't know how to use my magic. I wasn't brave. I wasn't even particularly strong.

But I *could* be those things. If I believed in myself, even a fraction of the way Kiran did.

And I knew I could.

"Should we go?"

I pulled myself from my thoughts at Nakia's voice and nodded. I dressed, quickly, in a soft cotton dress that Nakia brought me from her own room; it was mind boggling that our home was big enough that she had her own room now. *Our home.* I got stuck on those two words. The estate had become so fully my home that now it felt more natural . . . but without Kiran, and even Bleiz and Damara, or Niserie and Nythal, it would no longer feel like home.

My fingers paused on the laces of my boots. Bleiz and Damara . . . I wondered what the Sorceress had done with them. The whole estate would have been condemned, or taken, or whatever it was the High Sorceress had planned to do. Were they safe? Were they alive?

What a mess. What a hellscape of a mess.

And I knew it was only going to get worse.

M ama had laid an extravagant dinner for us. In part I thought she might have been trying to apologize, again, for her mistakes. But mostly I thought she was celebrating my return.

I didn't feel much like celebrating though.

My attention kept drifting to the windows all around the dining room. It was a beautiful space—all rich wood and, in its center, an ornate table big enough for my entire family. A soft runner in bright yellows and whites ran the length of it, and a cabinet of sparkling glass sat in one corner. Mama pulled fine porcelain dishes from inside, from clear shelves that didn't look like they could hold the heavy plates and bowls.

But my eyes were fixed onto the windows.

On the snowflakes that swirled down outside, covering Eldoris with a thick coat of white.

I hadn't yet told my family that I was leaving. I wasn't even sure how to go about it. But Kiran was out there, and possibly Damara and Bleiz and the others. I couldn't leave them to their fates. Even if I wasn't quite sure where to go.

"I've never known you to be so interested in the snow," Rhett teased.

"The snow has never felt so cold," I muttered.

Connak shook his head, pouring a rich crimson wine into the glass in front of me. I eyed it curiously, but he said, "That seems . . . dramatic. What happened to you, anyway?"

I hadn't explained yet. When Mama saw me climbing down the stairs, she had gathered me up as though I had been gone years instead of days. She clutched me to her in a flurry of tears and apologies and I simply hadn't managed to spit out the entire tale for them.

Nakia gave me a knowing look. She would tell them if I could not. But I wasn't afraid of recounting the story. I was more afraid to tell them I was going to hunt down the High Sorceress, that I was determined to kill Amirah herself.

And, if I were being honest, the thought petrified me.

I had never been born to violence. My gardens let me tend to life, to nurture new growth into the world, and I enjoyed the peace they brought me.

But it was no longer a choice between my comfort and the lack of. I had to do what was right. Even if, in the end, it might mean me taking a life.

I took a long swig of the deep colored wine, savored it on my tongue. Sweet grapes lingered over my taste buds as well as spices I wasn't as familiar with, though the wine went down smooth. Another long draught and I opened my mouth.

The story spilled out.

This time, instead of becoming overwhelmed with grief, I felt determination in my words. The anger that rose before had returned, hardening my resolve. We had been wronged. All of us, but most especially those at the estate. And maybe I was only one person, but I had ideas. I had a place to start.

Connak picked up on the tone of my voice as I spoke. My family was silent as I finished, but he stared at me with knowing eyes, and before I could add anything else, he was nodding his head.

"Fine, I'm in."

My nose scrunched. "What do you mean?"

"I mean I'm in." Connak swirled the wine in his glass. "You're going after him, aren't you?"

"Yes but—"

"Then I'm going with you," he said. "You think I'm going to let my little sister go off into the snow, facing trolls and who knows what else, alone?"

"I'm going too," Nakia chimed in.

"And me," said Rhett.

I sank back into my chair, looking at the three of them. I hadn't expected any of them to want to come with me.

"But I don't really know what I'm doing," I said gently. "And if one of you were lost, or hurt . . ."

"She's right," Mama said, eyes wide. "All four of you should stay here."

"I can't do that Mama," I said. "I can't leave Kiran to his fate. Marriage to a troll? Conceding his holdings to the High Sorceress? He fought for years to protect Numeryon from the trolls, from Amirah. And now I'll fight for him."

Rhett raised his glass, filled to the brim with crystalline water. "Here, here. And we're going with you."

I stared at the three of them for a long moment, then cast a look around. Mama looked upset, but she was quiet. Papa didn't seem to want to speak and invoke her wrath, but there was a glint of pride in his eyes that I would recognize anywhere. My younger sisters didn't really understand, but their sweet giggles at the look on Mama's face only added fuel to my determination. Because it was their future, too, that we fought for.

And, I realized, I wasn't going to talk Connak or Rhett or even Nakia down. Not when they had made up their minds. Instead, I laid out my plan. And when I was done, they accepted it without much question at all.

"Tomorrow, then," I said, as we stood to go to our beds. "Tomorrow, we begin."

32

At first light, alarm bells sounded.

Normally, I would have run from the sound, the warning of an attack. I would have hidden away with my family. But not this time. Not anymore.

This time I slid into the leathers Kiran had left for me on a chair. I strapped my dagger to my thigh. And before my elder brothers could even register what I was doing, I strode for the gates into Eldoris.

A small contingent of trolls were assaulting the fae guardians. Several of Eldoris's leaders were fighting with the gears that controlled the gate, trying to chip off the rust and oil the gears. So far, they'd had no luck.

And the fae were faltering.

Fear sat deep in my stomach. But I leapt into the fray before I could think twice. My dagger sliced soft green and blue skin. I wasn't strong but I was quick. I ducked around the trolls' cumbersome attacks, drawing their eyes. The distraction was enough. I was a bee, stinging, irritating, while the fae guards quickly dispatched the trolls one by one.

When they had all fallen, the fae dropped to their knees.

I stared at them for a long moment before I realized what they were doing.

"Rise," I said, trying not to show how badly I squirmed within. "You don't bow to me, friends. Heal yourselves. And thank you."

One of the fae stepped closer, and I recognized Galryn. His close-cropped ebony hair was damp with sweat that trailed down his olive cheeks. I greeted him and he smiled, then said, "Kiran's been monitoring Amirah's people for several moon cycles. She's been moving them into strategic places, biding her time. I doubt this will be the last attack on your city."

"You've been able to prepare?"

"Yes," Galryn said, "But we haven't been able to get the gates in working order. They've been neglected for a long time. What would you have us do if they fail?"

"Has magic not worked?"

"No." Galryn offered me a small smile. "Iron. Our magic is useless."

I froze, trying to decide what he should do. I understood the position Galryn was in, and what I represented to the fae now. But I was no advisor, especially on matters of attack.

Thankfully, my eldest brother had spent all his life training for these kinds of situations, and he laid a hand on my shoulder as he arrived.

"Reinforce the guard as much as you can using able-bodied men from the village. Ask them to use their magic on the gears. See if they can loosen the decay," Connak said. "Teach them what you know about fighting trolls. Give them the best advantage possible. And hold as long as you can. If you fail, at least the women and children might be able to get to the coast."

Galryn looked to me for confirmation. I nodded.

"Treat my brother here as an advisor in my stead. When we

leave, I trust you with the decisions that need to be made."

The fae nodded slowly, swallowing hard. "It's an honor. I won't diminish your trust."

"I know you won't."

And I did. I trusted Galryn well enough, and I knew he would do his best to protect Eldoris. But I knew it wouldn't be enough. Not if I didn't stop Amirah and save my prince.

As soon as morning light had fully broken the sky, Nakia and I made our way into the town center. So much felt the same here, and it was a comfort after a night in that unfamiliar home. It was polished, repaired, but Eldoris was mostly the city I remembered. Whispers still tracked my steps as we passed through, but they weren't so malicious anymore. They were whispers of awe, of admiration. The girl who was to marry the fae prince, now home after so much time and work had been put into improving everyone's lives.

I squirmed under the attention.

My sacrifice was for my family. But in the end, there was no sacrifice at all. Not for me.

Only for Kiran and the people he held close.

"Hey. Sabrena."

I winced at that voice. His was the voice of my nightmares. But when I spun to face Donovan, it wasn't with the nervous fear that I had always felt before. I held my chin high, appraising him as though he was the dirt on the bottom of my shoe.

"What do you want, Donovan?" I asked.

Nakia leaned closer, brushing her arm to mine. I appreciated the reassurance, but I didn't need it. Not now. Because Kiran was right. People like Donovan had never even given me a chance. And that was their problem, not mine.

"I think . . ." Donovan's throat bobbed and he rubbed at his neck. "Look, I think I was wrong about you."

"You think?"

"I was wrong about you," he corrected. "Eldoris is doing so much better because of your marriage. It's more than most of us have ever done. And you did it all without magic."

I crossed my arms over my chest. "I did, yes."

Donovan squirmed under my stare, and a small part of me took joy in his discomfort. "And . . . I wanted to apologize. And to ask if you could forgive me?"

"If I forgive you, it will be for myself," I said quietly. "Not to make you feel better about the way you treated me, for years. No. You have to live with your behavior. You don't get a free pass from me."

And before he said another word I spun around and walked away. Nakia giggled at my side. It felt good to tell Donovan off. I only wished I had done it years earlier instead of cowering under his judgment.

Better late than never.

Fierce determination blazed in my steps as Nakia and I made our way across the main square, past the well, all the way to the mystic's shop. Hers was one of the few buildings that hadn't seemed to have changed much at all. Repairs had been made but the polish of the other stores, the new coats of paint, the window displays . . . Astra's shop had none of that, or at least no more than she'd had before.

She leaned casually against a shelf, waiting near the door in anticipation of our visit. Piercing blue eyes leveled on us before we even set foot inside. Her gray and white curls fell loose around her shoulders, but she pulled it back into a leather tie when I approached.

"You're ready for your cards."

It wasn't a question, and I wondered again how much she had seen when she had drawn them before. But the cards weren't what drew me to her this morning.

"I need your help," I said simply.

Astra simply waved her hand, gesturing us to follow as she led us into the same small room as before. I sat at her table, Nakia at my side, as she bustled around making tea. The cups she handed us this time were filled with a floral brew that reminded me of honeysuckle dew.

Then she sat down at the table, pulling her stack of cards out. "I shall read them again."

"Astra, with all due respect," I said, placing my cup in its tiny saucer, "I don't need my cards read again. I need your help with this."

I reached into my pocket, retrieving the dropstone she had given me the last time I had seen her: a clear stone, with tiny pink buds growing toward the center, surrounding a core of blood. I had nearly forgotten about the gift, but it had fallen onto my bed from my bag of things. And now, when hopes were thin and desperation was knocking, it was Astra's cards and this small, strange gem that might now be my only hope.

"I shall read the cards," Astra insisted. Something about the way she stared at me, at the way she lifted a brow in cool insistence, gave me pause.

"You've learned of your powers?" she asked, pulling a card from the pile. The shimmering illustration on the black paper was of ocean waves.

I frowned. "You knew?"

"But it wasn't time for you to know," she said simply. "Everything has its time."

"And what is this thing's time?" I nudged the dropstone forward.

Astra lifted a dismissive hand, fixated on the cards. I shot Nakia a curious glance, but she merely shrugged, as confused as me. After a moment, the elder woman pushed all the cards back together, stacked them, and tucked them away.

"What is it you seek?" Astra asked. She crossed her arms over her chest, leaning back as if she could see me better with the extra inch or so of space.

"You gave me this. You told me it was a powerful weapon. How do I wield it?"

She leaned forward again, studying me with those piercing blue eyes. "You're asking the wrong questions."

DAYLIGHT'S CURSE | 291

Nakia frowned. "What does that mean?"

"Exactly what I said." Astra paused, and then asked again, "What is it that you seek, rose of the fae?"

I froze. So many answers flooded my mind, things I wanted, things I needed. What did I seek? If only one thing? What did I seek? A way to end the troll's reign, a way to save my family. Peace for all of us. To save my friends.

"I want to save him," I whispered. A lump climbed my throat, all the emotion, all the want, a physical thing I couldn't get rid of. "He's fought for everything else that matters to me long before I knew him. And I don't know . . . I believe in him. I believe he's what Numeryon needs to recover. So help me Astra. Help me save him."

A tender smile curved the elder woman's lips. "Take the stone. Go to Sinythell. Find your way to the Winds. And that is how you will save your prince."

"That's pretty vague," Nakia said.

Astra grinned, the smile broad and mischievous. "I never said I could tell you everything."

"Why Sinythell?" I asked, recalling the map Kiran had given me. We would have to go northwest, deep into the forest.

"The elves in Sinythell have been there for a very long time. They have seen things you and I could only dream of."

I tapped the side of my teacup, trying to form a plan in my mind. "Who do we need to speak to?"

"The cards aren't so specific," Astra said. But she picked at her bottom lip thoughtfully, then said, "Rhadagan might be able to help you."

"Rhadagan," I repeated under my breath. "Thank you for your help, Astra."

She smiled. "Cytherea guide you in your journey." Her smile faded, turning into something darker, laden with concern. And fear. "Go now. Your time runs out."

I paced the room that had been designated for me, staring at the piles of things on my bed, trying to decide what to take on this trip. Panic was a deep-seated knot in my chest, venomous, spreading, threatening to pull me down from within. The lack of familiarity and comfort around me didn't help. This room was mine, but it wasn't. My family had designed it as a guest room, assuming I would never come back, and the few belongings I had left behind had been tucked into storage. I didn't bother to have them retrieved. We were leaving soon anyway.

My brothers and Nakia were packing their own bags as I paced. As I worried. As I thought about every possible situation Kiran could currently be in and felt the beat of my heart quicken little by little.

I hadn't even confessed that I loved him.

In the moment, I thought words weren't needed. That he knew. That each touch, each lingering kiss, would be enough. But now I wrestled with regret. Kiran had poured out his heart and I . . .

I knew we had so little time and I had withheld. Because love felt like a vulnerability and giving him the words felt like giving him the power. He could use them against me—if not then, later.

He could do what Maryna had and claim that all his sweet words had been meaningless. That the things he felt weren't real. That they were a means to an end.

But now I was realizing that Kiran would never have done that. Especially not in the lingering precious moments we reveled in that night. Kiran didn't care about tarnishing his reputation. He, of anyone, understood how hard it could be to be a magicless person in a land full of power. And he didn't care.

Resolve sparked strong and bright in my chest. I didn't know what I was doing. But I was going to save him. I was going to save him and tell him how much I loved him until the words could no longer spill from my lips, until my tongue would no longer form the sounds.

I checked that my leathers were secure and my dagger was tight on my thigh. Then I tucked Kiran's note into a miniature bottle and tied it with twine, making it into a necklace that I hid beneath my shirt, right next to the talisman we had retrieved from Ingryst.

Afterward, I tossed anything and everything into my bag. The journal Kiran had given me, the map, the star box, the creature tome, all the things that might potentially have been useful to us.

I slipped the stone Astra had given me into my pocket.

And there was a knock at my door.

I looked up when it cracked open without another sound, assuming it was Nakia coming to retrieve me, but no. Mama stared at me with cautious eyes.

"Come in," I murmured.

"Can we talk before you go?"

I turned fully, dropping myself onto the edge of the bed. "Sure."

"You're leaving and . . . I didn't want to leave things the way they were," Mama said. She perched on the bed a few feet away.

She was right. I didn't want to leave this rift between us either. Time wasn't promised, as I was learning. And even through Mama's failings, she loved me. That I would never question.

I sighed. "I forgive you."

Mama's eyes widened. "That's it? I haven't even apologized yet."

"I know," I said. "You hurt me, betrayed me. And while it's no excuse, I do understand why you were afraid. No one would willingly submit themselves to a life of judgment."

"But you're my love. My songbird. My eldest daughter." Mama's eyes brimmed with tears. "A parent's one job is to protect their child. I failed you in that."

"That's true. You did fail to protect me. But you've also made choices born of love and care, for me and all of us kids. Choices that have protected me. Us. I haven't forgotten those. We had a happy home, Mama, even when we were cold and hungry. Because of you." I offered a soft smile. "I know your love for me is genuine. And before we go out there, I want you to know I love you too. I forgive you."

Mama scooped me into her arms, crying gently. "I'm sorry, Sabrena. I'm so sorry."

I squeezed her tight. The anger I had felt toward her began to slowly fade. We couldn't change the past, but we could work toward a better future, especially when I knew she was sincerely sorry. I had finally made peace within myself. "I know, Mama. Really, I do."

Nakia knocked at my door, then. I pulled away from Mama, wiping the tears from my own cheeks.

They were ready. I wasn't. But it was time.

It was time to save my dragon.

33

We snuck out into the cover of darkness, trying to avoid prying eyes. The fae dropped to their knees as we passed through the gate, Galryn assuring me again he would lay down everything to protect my family. I thanked him profusely. Kiran might be absent, but the fae still respected his leadership. He was to be their king. They believed in him. My heart ached that he had been taken from them.

Freshly fallen snow obscured the remnants of this day's fighting, a deceptive layer of calm. Troll corpses littered the ground. Abandoned weapons glinted from beneath the blanket of white.

Nakia pulled her cloak tighter around her shoulders. She, Connak, and Rhett all wore new leathers and thick cloaks of softest fur. Connak had negotiated them from Mama, who was trying to hold onto coin in case the worst happened.

In case they had to flee the continent.

I wouldn't humor that thought. Kiran was going to be fine.

We were going to be fine.

Hopefully.

"Do you have any idea where we're going in this storm?" Nakia asked, her teeth chattering together.

I unrolled the map Kiran had given me, sheltering it from the snowflakes as much as I could. Nakia looked it over, then glanced at the sky.

"Well. Without the sun we're going to need some help."

She rolled a ball of snow between her hands, then flattened it slightly. I raised an eyebrow at the disc of snow, but she tsked me and closed her eyes. A second later her hands were clasped around a silver object, one she tilted toward me. The face held an arrow that spun and twisted.

"A compass will always point north."

"Smart," I admitted, eyeing the little device. It was so strange to see magic without cost again. I was growing so used to the fae way of things. And the little compass reminded me of Kiran's stars, of the way they had twinkled and shone across the ceiling of his office. A pang tightened my chest. He would see his stars again.

"We'll find him, Brena." Rhett gripped my arm, squeezing lightly.

Connak nodded his agreement. "But first, let's find our way to Sinythell." He glanced skyward. Tiny ice crystals clung to the jagged, dark hair that fell loose around his cheeks. "Before we freeze to death."

Our boots crunched through the snow, a solid, steady rhythm. The sound was calming, somehow. Maybe because it was the only sound beside the soft shuffling snowfall. Talking felt like too much energy when we were damp and our bodies ached from the bone-chilling wind. There was no Kiran to save me from the cold this time, only myself, and for once I truly believed that I was enough.

But I couldn't say I wasn't grateful for my brothers and Nakia coming along. They had always been a source of security, but this time . . . this time felt like so much more. I *needed* so much more from them. Emotionally and physically.

Especially with the trolls around.

By late afternoon, we reached the main river between Castyr Lake and Sedryn Lake. The snow had faded, little more than swirling crystals blown around in the winter wind. We set camp along the riverbed—one large tent that we would all sleep in to share body heat, with a campfire just warm enough to thaw our limbs.

Connak lifted a hand above the river, murmuring soft words. His fingers lit with a faint green light and the water beneath went from a murky mess to pure, crystalline, drinkable water.

"Drink, and then fill your waterskins," he said after a moment. "We might not have a way to refill them later."

I sat down next to the fire, letting the heat warm me and dry my cloak. I fished the silver box from my bag, turning it over in my hands. But there were no clues. Nothing more than what Kiran had already shown me.

"You know," Rhett said, dropping down beside me, "Mama used to tell us a story about these seers who worship the stars. Bet they'd be useful right about now."

Seers. The word triggered a deep, buried memory. I looked at my brother. "Can you tell me the story?"

"I don't remember all of it," he admitted. "But it was something about three seers who lived beside a lake and worshiped the stars. If one found these seers, they would grant you certain wishes. If you could obtain their favor, that is. But finding them was the real challenge; they could only be found using the Star of Elysian."

"Do you remember how?" I stared at the tiny silver box in my hands, trying desperately to remember where the Star of Elysian had shown up when Kiran lit the stars. "Was the Star above them?"

"I don't know."

"You don't believe that old wives' tale," Connak asked, passing me a chunk of dried meat. I took it from him as Nakia sat at my right, studying my face.

I tore the jerky in half. "I think stories are meant to hold truth. Even behind the fantasy."

"And some are just stories," Nakia said gently.

"Have you ever seen a mellek?" I asked her.

She shook her head. "More creatures of legend, Sabrena."

"But one woke me on the way to Devayne Estate." Her eyes widened at that and my brothers both froze where they sat. "Don't be so quick to dismiss what you haven't seen. Nothing about the last several moons makes sense to me. Not Bleiz's bargain, not the trolls, not falling for Kiran. I'm starting to believe the unbelievable."

"So do we even need to go to Sinythell?" Connak tugged at a stray lock of his hair.

"Yes," I said. "I still don't know where to find the Winds. Or the Seers. I remember them, vaguely. Damara and Kiran both mentioned them."

Nakia frowned. "And they didn't give you any details of where to find them?"

"I don't think any of us realized we would need to." I picked at a blade of grass. "None of us planned for the worst. Not really. And even though Kiran tried to give me as much information as he could, I don't think either of us were really worried about triggering the curse . . . we thought we had more time."

"You blame yourself," Nakia said quietly.

"Of course, I blame myself. *I* triggered it." And the guilt had been eating me alive since.

"But you didn't know. He physically couldn't even tell you." Rhett shrugged. "We're going to find him, Sabrena. We'll find all of your friends."

"I hope so," I murmured.

I didn't feel so optimistic, though.

Days passed. A journey that hadn't taken nearly as long on horseback took infinitely more time on foot. To our benefit, the snow had lightened.

Not soon enough, the woods began to thicken. The grassy land around us became dense forest, thick with the scent of moss and damp earth. My hands moved instinctively to the dagger on my thigh.

"Anyone else feel like we're being watched?" Nakia whispered.

Connak and Rhett nodded in nervous unison. The trees around us were quiet, but not silent. Birds chirped in soft song; small animals skittered through the underbrush. But there was an edge, a tension to the air that had goosebumps rising beneath my leathers.

"The Sinythell elves watch everything," Connak murmured. "That's why their woods are still considered safe territory."

"And why we don't generally allow unannounced company within our city," said a voice, followed by a soft thud on the forest floor. All four of us jumped at the sounds. A tall, curvy elven woman stood before us. Her skin was the shade of deepest midnight, her eyes a bright, piercing green that glittered in the elven lights she held in her palm. The leathers she wore were creased and stained with age. A bow strap wrapped her chest and a sword hung at her side. "Who are you?"

"We're friends," I said. Nerves filled my voice, causing the words to waver, but I cleared my throat and continued. "We come from Eldoris, to the south. Our city is being attacked by trolls. For the moment, the fae and our own people are holding. But we're not sure how long they have and we want to help them. Is there someone in your city we might speak to about the Seers of Saryshna?"

"The Seers?" The elven woman's brow narrowed. "Why them?"

"They might know where to find Madrion," Rhett said carefully.

"Madrion?" This time the elven woman tossed her head back and laughed. Her dark, chest length locs fell around her shoulders with the motion, and she brushed them away before she said, "You jest. No one *seeks* Amirah and her kind."

"Please," I said gently. Nakia reached out to grip my arm but I stepped forward, letting the elven lights shine fully on my face. "I am Sabrena. I come from Eldoris, but I was set to marry Prince Kiran."

Her nose scrunched in distaste. "The Prince of the Fae?"

"He's not . . . he's not what we've been told," I said. "He's done more for our people than we knew."

She huffed at that. "Regardless, what do your problems have to do with us in Sinythell?"

"We told you," Connak said. "If you're not willing to help then just say so and we'll be on our way. But if you have someone within your city who might be able to help us, please direct us their way."

Those green eyes narrowed on my brother, and I felt myself instinctively standing taller, ready to defend if needed. But her attention returned to me, and she held out a hand.

When I shook it, she said, "Lyriath. I'm the first guard of Sinythell, right hand to our leader, Paxus."

Connak, Rhett, and Nakia introduced themselves then. Lyriath greeted each of them briefly, then said, "Paxus will need to approve of you meeting anyone beyond him and myself. But if he does, you'll want to speak to our Elder. If anyone has the knowledge you seek, it's him."

"Thank you," I said. Relief flooded my chest.

"Don't thank me yet. I need your weapons."

Keep the dagger with you this time. Please.

Kiran's words were aggressive in my thoughts. I could hear his voice saying them as clearly as though he stood beside me. That splinter in my heart twisted. I ignored it, though. If giving up our weapons temporarily could get us the information we needed, I was willing to take the risk.

"You'll be returning them?" Nakia asked, echoing my thoughts.

"Of course," Lyriath said. "On your way out."

Connak shot me an uneasy look, but when I unstrapped my dagger, he followed suit. They had magic, if nothing else, and I had . . .

I could sing them to sleep?

I winced at the thought.

Lyriath snapped her fingers and another elf dropped from the trees to land beside her, a tall man with bronzed skin and chestnut hair that was pulled back into a leather strap. Between the two of them, they took all our weapons. Lyriath jerked her chin toward the trees behind her and the elves began to walk, leading us forward.

For several minutes we traveled in near silence. Our boots were loud against the forest floor, and neither Lyriath nor her companion spoke. I eyed the sheath of my dagger, clutched in Lyriath's hands. For the first time, the absence of its weight was looming in my mind.

Soon elven lights began to line our path, and twinkling chains filled with glowing gossamer filament wrapped themselves around tree trunks. I knew we had to be nearing the entrance of Sinythell. But I was still surprised when Lyriath turned with a smile, and said, "Look up."

Sinythell was so much more than I expected. The treetops were lined with wooden platforms, connected together by bridges that looked unstable as elves passed over them, yet they didn't even flex under the weight. Lyriath guided us toward a ladder and pointed.

"Go on up. We'll leave your gear with our Guard Commander and I'll meet you up there."

The ladder swayed as I climbed, but the wooden rungs were smooth beneath my hands. Connak followed close behind, then Nakia, then Rhett. I struggled to pull myself up onto the platform above, but I was shocked when it wasn't simply a flat of smooth wood; it was a porch, jutting out in front of a home that sat comfortably between the branches of the tree. The house had been built into the structure of the oak so carefully it was as though it had grown there. All around us, the whole city was like this; an entire world built into the canopy of the forest.

"We try to minimize how much we disrupt nature," Lyriath said. I jumped. I hadn't heard her climb the ladder behind us. "Some disturbance can't be helped if we want shelter from the elements. But we repay the earth for its generosity often. Cytherea blesses us for our returns."

"Your home is beautiful," I said. And it was. The elven city had a polished elegance that Eldoris lacked, with its twinkling lights and smooth wooden buildings.

"It is," Lyriath said. "Come on. Paxus has granted you limited visitor privileges. Rhadagan lives this way. He is our most knowledgeable—and most revered—Elder. You will speak only when spoken to. You will wait to speak until he is finished. Do you understand?"

I nodded, glancing over my shoulder to make sure the others did the same. We followed the woman through a small door, curtained with moss. The furnishings inside were simple, natural, as woven into the structure as they were into the trees. Lyriath led us through the building, and across an open bridge on the opposite side, before coming to a stop before a wooden door. An elaborate carving of their primary deity, Cytherea, was carved into the face, surrounded by roses and a variety of birds. Stones in a rainbow of shades adorned the goddess's hair.

Lyriath knocked on the doorframe, carefully avoiding the art. "Sorry for the interruption, revered one."

"Come in, children," came the voice from within. The Elder's tone was light, friendly, but he spoke in a cautious, measured monotone. "I have long expected you."

Lyriath pulled the door open, stepping aside so that we could pass. I went first, and as I crossed the threshold, Lyriath whispered, "Be respectful."

As if I would be anything else. I would never jeopardize our chances like that.

I couldn't fault her caution though.

"Never fear, Lyriath," Rhadagan soothed. "There is no danger on this day. I have already seen it."

The elven woman didn't argue, simply leaned into a deep bow and stepped away. Rhett pulled the door behind him. Rhadagan was nowhere to be seen. His home was furnished much like the one we had already passed through, with heavy emphasis on nature and simplicity. After a moment, a door on the back wall leaned open.

Rhadagan wasn't quite what I had imagined. He was tall and slender, as lithe and graceful as the branches of a willow tree. His long, silvery blue hair fell to his waist, the upper half pulled back into a leather tie to keep the locks from his face. Bright hazel eyes studied me as intently as I studied him, and after a moment he dipped his head in greeting.

"Welcome, friends. Let me call for tea and we shall begin."

He didn't wait for a reply. His hand moved for a silvered chain that hung from the ceiling, and when he tugged a bell rang out that shivered through the trees as if carried by the wind. Then he waved us to a table that seemed to have grown from the wall. The four of us sat, the room thick with nervous silence.

Another elf entered, a curvy woman with tight blond curls and vibrant green eyes. She sat bamboo cups before each of us, filling them to the brim with a dark amber tea, then dismissed herself before Rhadagan finally joined us. His curious gaze circled the table. He stared at each of us in turn, then took a long drink from his tea.

"So. You seek the Seers of Saryshna." He wasn't asking. This close I realized how youthful his face looked, and I wondered vaguely how old Rhadagan was to be so revered and knowledgeable but still look so young.

"We do," Connak offered stiffly.

"And you seek them only as a means to find the four Winds?"

I nodded. "If the Winds can help me find Madrion, I will do whatever I need to reach them."

"Because the Sorceress took your prince?" Rhadagan didn't wait for a reply. "Understand that the Seers only guard the portal to the land of the Winds. They cannot help you find the Guardians, and they cannot help you save Kiran of the Fae."

Nakia leaned forward in her seat. Her dark curls slipped forward, framing her cheeks. "But the Winds can help us defeat this Sorceress, correct?"

"Possibly." The elder elf rubbed his palms together, then steepled his fingers. "The Winds are the most ancient beings in Numeryon. If anyone is capable of defeating her, it will be them." He paused, and his hazel eyes swiveled in my direction. "But what will you do if the Winds tell you there is no way? Will you give up?"

I shook my head without hesitation. "Kiran wouldn't give up on me. He wouldn't leave Numeryon to the trolls. So, if he can't fight for us, I will."

A small smile touched the corner of Rhadagan's lips. He looked at each of my brothers, then Nakia. "And you share her sentiments?"

"Where Sabrena goes, we go," Nakia said. I reached for her hand under the table and squeezed hard. Those words had always been true, for both of us, but they had never held more weight than they did now.

"We would be horrible brothers to see her do this alone," Rhett said. Connak nodded his agreement. My oldest brother hadn't shifted his gaze from the Elder elf, and amusement danced in Rhadagan's eyes every time he glanced his way.

"Then I will tell you what you need to know. Pull out your star box, Sabrena, and your map." I did, placing them on the table in front of us. Rhadagan adjusted the two, moving the star box to the south side of the map. Then he waved his hands, dousing the room in darkness.

Rhadagan snapped his fingers. The star box lit up, casting its constellations on the walls and ceiling. I heard Nakia's intake of breath, could see the twinkling of awe in her eyes at the shimmering lights.

"Your prince suspected that the Star of Elysian would lead him to Madrion. He wasn't wrong that it marked something, but he *was* wrong as to what." Rhadagan tapped the map twice. The star box dimmed, all except the Star of Elysian, which shone brightly, casting its light down on the table. "What do you see, Sabrena?"

I stared at the map, trying to remember all that Kiran had told me. Trying not to bury my thoughts in questions about Rhadagan himself. And then I saw what the Elder elf was trying to show me.

"The Star of Elysian illuminates Spiritwood Lake," I murmured softly.

Rhadagan nodded, pleased. "The Seers live in the woods along its shore. Find them. They will give you what you need."

I jumped to my feet. We didn't have time to waste; that journey would take days, possibly weeks. "Thank you, Rhadagan."

"You're most welcome," he said, clapping his hands again. The star box dimmed and the lights of his home blazed back to life. "Are you sure you won't stay the evening?"

I shook my head and gathered my things from the table. "We need to go. But thank you. Thank you so much."

He smiled gently. "Collect your gear on your way out," he said, and then added, "And Sabrena? Don't forget that information from the Seers comes with a price. Make sure your prince is worth it."

34

"If you don't stop snoring, I swear . . ."

I barely registered Nakia's voice before her foot landed a swift kick to the back of my thigh. Before she could kick me again, I rolled over, smacking her with the rolled shirt I had been using as a pillow. "I don't snore. I've never snored. *You're* the one who sounds like a barnyard of pigs."

"You snore now," Nakia insisted. "All that luxurious sleep in a big fancy estate changed you."

I rolled my eyes, flopping fully over onto my back. "I could say the same about all three of you, living in that new house."

"It's not new," Rhett said. He didn't even lift his head from his own makeshift pillow, and his voice sounded muffled. "It's improved."

"And look at our spoiled asses now," Connak grumbled. He sat up, poking at the few glowing embers that lingered from our fire the night before. "Sleeping in a cold cave with rocks digging into our backs, arguing over snoring habits."

"For good reason," I said.

He grunted, a sound I took to be his agreement. Then he started digging through his pack, pulling out breakfast rations for each of us—dried meat and fruit, surplus that Mama had been storing for the winter.

I stared out of the cave as I chewed, watching the blustering snow that swirled past. And the lighthearted conversation floated away with the white flakes, as the weight of our journey settled back onto my shoulders.

We had spoken to Rhadagan nearly a fortnight before. Beriene, an elven fishing village, wasn't far. Connak guessed we would be there before the day's end. But with every step, with every day that passed, my fears for Kiran grew stronger. He was my waking thoughts. My concern for him filled every dream. And I knew that the longer we took to find him, the more likely it was that he was to be married off to Amirah's daughter.

I couldn't help wondering how she felt about the situation. If she was a willing pawn or if her mother controlled her the same way she controlled her own people. A few times, I wondered if peace with the trolls was possible. But then I remembered the merciless slaughter of our people and the scars that climbed across my own body.

And peace felt very far away.

"You're different," Nakia said gently. "I don't mean that in a bad way."

I turned in her direction, raising a brow. "Then how do you mean it?"

Nakia leaned toward me, resting her cheek on my shoulder. Her ebony curls were pulled back into a neat bun, letting her bright green eyes shine vibrant against her brown skin. "I mean, I've never seen you like this. So invested, so confident. So *brave*. It looks good on you."

"Seems like that fae prince was a good influence after all," Rhett joked.

But I shook my head slowly. "Kiran is amazing. But I've

always had support. I've always had family and friends who loved me, even when I couldn't love myself. He believed in me, but so did you." I paused, taking in a shaky breath. "The difference is now I believe in myself. My whole identity fell into question, but I'm still me. I'm still strong and capable. And now I have a chance to prove it, in a way that matters more than it ever has before."

Nakia reached for my hand, lacing her fingers through mine. "Absolutely. Because you are all of those things."

Connak nodded. "I'm proud of you, Sabrena." He climbed to his feet. "But, if we're going to reach Beriene before nightfall, we're going to need to get moving."

"Always the responsible one," Rhett grumbled. But he sat up, pulling his long blond hair back and started weaving it into a braid.

We shoved our makeshift pillows into our bags, checking the waterskins to make sure they would last the afternoon. Connak stashed away the food, carefully wrapping it all to keep it preserved.

And then we were off. Our boots sank into the snow to our ankles. We wrapped our faces with shirts to keep the bitter wind away. Hours passed. We struggled to track how many, with the sun blocked by the heavy snow clouds. By the time Beriene was on the horizon, the storm had subsided again.

The town was boarded up against the bitter cold. Smoke rose from a few of the chimneys, but the majority of Beriene seemed still. Too still, even for midwinter.

Connak's hand slid to the pommel of his sword as he moved for the door of what looked like a tavern. He drew his blade, using the point to scrape snow from the wooden sign that dangled from the porch: *Oligard Tavern.*

"Do we stay for the night or move on?" he asked us, his voice a soft murmur.

"Move on," I said immediately. "We can't waste the time."

"I know you're desperate to find your prince," Rhett said gently, dropping a heavy arm around my shoulders, "But we could all use a good night's rest and a warm meal. And look at the docks." He pointed toward the far end of town. "They're covered in snow. We're not getting a boat out of here tonight regardless."

I hated to admit he was right. We had been pushing a hard pace since Sinythell and, as much as I wanted to keep going . . . I glanced at my brothers, at Nakia. They were tired. They hadn't complained as I had encouraged them onward, but dark circles lined their eyes and their shoulders were slumped in exhaustion. I couldn't ask them to keep going without at least one night's undisturbed rest.

"Fine. We'll stay here tonight, then we move on tomorrow morning."

One more night wouldn't matter. Not really.

I hoped.

But when morning came, my concerns were outweighed by the lack of new bruises on my back and limbs. Sleeping on the hard ground had taken a toll on all of us. The tavern's owner was a kind, matronly woman who filled our stomachs with a hot dinner and didn't ask questions I wouldn't know how to answer.

She could tell us that they'd had news from Eldoris only two days before. The city was standing, but the people were growing disheartened. My fears for Mama and Papa and my sisters only added to the weight I carried. Beriene was worried about when the attack would shift to them; they weren't as well trained and geared as Sinythell, and they hadn't had Kiran's finances building them up in advance.

I ran my thumb over the dropstone in my pocket. The smooth gem was soothing in my hand, and I had taken to carrying it there as reassurance. It might be our only chance against Amirah, and I didn't want it far from me.

Kiran's note was still tied in a bottle around my neck, next to his mother's talisman. The weight of the glass and metal against my chest was calming in a different way entirely. Pieces of him:

words and feelings he had etched on paper, a valued heirloom. I tried not to reread the note too often. I didn't want to smudge the ink. But I thought of him daily, hourly. Minute by minute when nothing else held my focus.

I knew the others could see the distress I felt. Nakia had taken to holding my hand more than she ever had, and my brothers wasted hours rotating between casual bickering and jokes to distract my mind.

But it wasn't until we were on the boat, sailing north from Beriene, that I finally felt like we were making progress. Even arriving in Sinythell didn't make me feel like we were moving in the way that watching the land melt from view did.

We hired a small sailboat to take us north—sturdy enough to sail on the open ocean, small enough that we could easily manage it between the captain and the four of us. Below deck was nearly filled with fishing supplies: poles and lures, bait, rations for the fishermen. But there was space to sleep. For the days we would be at sea, it would be enough.

"It's late in the year to be sailing." Luther, the captain, had his hands on the ship wheel. His eyes were trained on the horizon, but the moment I had climbed up from below deck and made my way to the bow, he not-so-subtly side-eyed me.

He hadn't asked many questions when we had hired him. We offered a hefty sack of gold, and any sailor in their right mind wouldn't turn down that purse for a few days of sailing.

But the waters were dark, sloshing angrily against the boat. The air was chill. Even the dense fur cloak I wore didn't keep out the cold. I turned my attention to Luther, taking in his bronze skin, his long dark hair, and deep blue eyes. He raised an eyebrow at my scrutiny.

"The trolls have changed things," I said finally.

Luther tilted his head slightly, as though in thought. "You know that sailing north is only bringing you closer to their territory?"

I nodded. "But it's also bringing us closer to the Star of Elysian."

"The star's position is ever changing. Why would it matter?"

"Because there was a point where the star's position was captured," I said. I stared at the stars that twinkled above us, releasing a wistful sigh. "And its location at that time is important to where we need to go."

"Cryptic," he said. His lips quirked into a teasing smile. Luther had a relaxed way about him. I didn't think he was much older than Connak.

But his easy smile only made me miss Kiran more.

A low thud sounded on the deck behind us, and I turned to see my oldest brother striding toward me. I almost laughed at the idea that he had been summoned by my thoughts. Then I realized I was still thinking about Kiran and the heartache settled low and heavy once more.

"Couldn't sleep either?" Connak asked, coming to lean against the side with me.

"No. I keep dreaming about all the ways our trip could go wrong. Doesn't lend to restful sleep."

He draped an arm around my shoulders, leaning his head against mine. A strand of his dark hair fell into my eyes and I blew it away. Connak just squeezed me. He had never been the brother to show his affection easily. I knew the discomfort he was shoving down to hug me, and I appreciated him all the more for it.

"We haven't seen any trolls yet," he murmured. "Maybe they're so busy with Eldoris they don't care about a little party of elves."

"But why Eldoris?" I asked. The question was rhetorical though. I knew who they were looking for. And why.

How else would Amirah break Kiran? He had already shown immense resilience. Finding me . . . I didn't want to think about what she might do to me. And that was before my inevitable death.

"I don't know," Connak murmured. "But you don't have to be afraid. I'm not going to let her, or any other troll, anywhere near you."

"Maybe her finding me would make this faster. Maybe if she took me, I could save him. I can't say I haven't considered trying to get her attention," I admitted.

Connak frowned. "She's probably already watching. She has spies everywhere, isn't that what you said?"

I had. "Still. Maybe I should draw her out."

"That wouldn't be wise," Luther said, pulling both our attention. "The Sorceress did not come by her magic naturally. She stole it."

I narrowed my eyes on him. "What do you mean?"

Luther shrugged. "It's an old sailor's legend, perhaps. But it's said that the Sorceress of the trolls hails from a land across the sea, where she was once a great queen. But her husband fell in love with another and Amirah was stripped of all her titles. She had enough lingering support and influence to gather the trolls that fight for her today, but many of them don't serve because they want to, and Amirah knew that could breed disloyalty. In her journeys, she came across Syris, the goddess of the oceans. Amirah's pride was great, and when she met the goddess she asked for a boon, which she could use to set her home in a new world."

"How do the fae not know this?"

"They might," Luther admitted. "But most of the fae and elves met Amirah after she had power, not before. Her story only holds relevance to sailors because of what it meant for Syris, and even then a lot of sailors have stopped passing on the old ways and tales."

"So, we have Syris to blame that Amirah has become this powerful?" Connak asked.

"No," Luther said. "Syris denied her request. She read Amirah's aura and found darkness. And so, she refused to give her any aid, whatsoever."

My brows drew together. "Then how is Amirah as powerful as she is?"

"Amirah took the goddess's offense personally," Luther said. "And when she couldn't convince Syris to give her a gift, she took the goddess's power for herself."

"I can't imagine how one would accomplish that," Connak muttered. His grip on my shoulder tightened slightly.

Luther lifted a shoulder. He adjusted the ship wheel, then said, "There's only one way to steal the power from a goddess." His stoic eyes fixed on mine. "You kill her."

A dark, familiar laugh shivered over the water. Goosebumps raised across my arms and I spun from Connak's grasp, my hand falling to the dagger on my thigh.

"And I'd do it again," the feminine voice boomed, a cruel sound that carried on the winds.

"Amirah," I murmured. "Get the others." Connak hesitated. Luther's eyes were wide in fear. "Go," I insisted.

He moved, running for the deck hatch. Luther's hands tightened on the wheel, fighting against the sudden stormy currents of the sea. The wicked laughter flurried around us again. Sparkling purple swirled in the winds that tossed the sails. The magic began to thicken, condensing into a twirling funnel beside the ship.

Luther struggled to control the boat. As the winds picked up, so did the waves that swelled high, spilling over the sides and onto the deck. The swirling purple magic began to spread and solidify, taking form before us.

"T-T-The Kraken!" Luther stammered, backing away from the bow. He ran straight into Rhett and Nakia, who were climbing up from the lower deck. They caught him right as a sparkling purple tentacle crashed down on the bow of the ship. The wood creaked and snapped under the weight.

I grabbed a rope to gain purchase, but the massive, magical sea creature loomed above us. Cackling laughter swirled through the wind. I looked left and right, seeking any kind of help or solution. But there was nothing. We were at sea and at her mercy.

And Amirah knew it.

Her laughter filled my mind. I looked to my brothers. They, and Luther and Nakia, had begun stripping their heavy cloaks and any unnecessary pieces of their leathers from their bodies. Piles of fur and gauntlets slid across the deck to my feet.

But I realized that everything I had of value, with the exception of my dagger, necklaces, and dropstone, were below deck in my bag. Rations, books, maps, papers. Kiran's star box. All of it. And I didn't know if we could survive this assault, but I knew if we did, and I didn't have those, it wouldn't matter.

I scrambled for the hatch as two massive purple tentacles slammed down on either end of the boat. The deck cracked and split as I threw the hatch open, tumbling into the hole. My bag wasn't far, and I snatched it up, throwing the strap over my shoulder. I moved for the ladder.

"You were far easier to dispose of than I had hoped," Amirah taunted. Another laugh followed her words.

And the boat split beneath me.

I barely had time to suck in a gasp of air before I hit the cold water, my heavy cloak and bag weighing me down. My fingers struggled with the clasp of my cloak but, somehow, I managed to loosen it.

In the end, it didn't matter.

The swirling weight of the ship sucked me deeper into the ocean. I looked around, terrified, praying to find any glimpse of my friends in the chaos. A tentacle slashed through the water in front of me, pulling me down, down.

I tried to suck in air and choked on salty water. All was dark, wet, cold.

I really wasn't going to survive this.

Kiran wasn't going to be rescued.

The air left my lungs entirely. And just before the world went black, I thought I saw in the water before me eyes the color of

an angry sea . . .
And hair as white as new fallen snow.

35

I woke on my stomach, sprawled on a rocky shoreline, coughing so hard my lungs ached. Every inch of my body was sore, covered in bruises. My dagger pressed awkwardly into my thigh, but I was grateful I still had it. My necklaces hung heavy at my throat. I reached into my pocket. The dropstone was still there too. I had no idea where my bag was, though.

Releasing a sigh, I pulled myself upright, groaning at the ache that spread through my body at the effort. I scrambled to my feet anyway, ignoring my body's protests. I spotted Nakia a few feet away and I ran for her, checking for her pulse. Her heartbeat thudded strongly against my fingertips and I breathed a heavy sigh of relief. She wasn't responsive, but she was alive. It would have to be enough while I searched for my brothers and Luther.

Rhett was farther inland, nearly to the grass line that ended the shore. His long, blond hair had come undone, falling around his shoulders as he spluttered and coughed and tried to regain himself. The second he saw me coming, he leapt to his feet and caught me to him, hugging me so tightly I nearly couldn't breathe. I hugged him too, grateful he was alive, grateful we were alive and standing after Amirah's attack.

"How did we get here?" Rhett asked.

I didn't know. I couldn't tell him.

And I wasn't entirely sure what I had seen in my final seconds underwater had been real. I had never seen anyone with my eyes before, though. If it were real . . . if my father had saved us . . .

There were too many feelings involved in that possibility. Too many questions. And surely my father wasn't the only siren in the sea.

Rhett grabbed my hand, dragging me back toward Nakia. She was hacking up seawater and I ran for her, pulling her into a hug while she regulated her breathing.

"Where are we?" she rasped.

"We don't know," Rhett admitted. "We're not even sure how we got here."

"Where's Connak?" she asked, looking between us. When we confessed we didn't know, she said, "What about Luther?" I shook my head. Nakia ran her hands over her face, sighing heavily. "What do we do?"

"Find them," I said.

I scanned the beach. No sign of my bag met my eyes, nor either of the men we needed to find. Each second that Connak was missing my heartbeat ticked a little faster, my breath a little hard to catch. Tears tracked down my cheeks. I yelled his name, growing more frantic with every yell.

Nakia pulled me into a tight hug. "All hope isn't lost. Maybe I can help."

She waved her hands, pulling forth a bird of shimmering gold, which she sent into the sky. It launched itself away from us, fluttering into the clouds and dancing through the air. I watched with bated breath, calling for my brother all the while.

Several minutes later the bird returned, chirping loudly. We abandoned our search of the nearby shore and followed it. At first, we didn't know what the bird had found.

And then we heard the choked sobs. The air stuck in my lungs. Connak didn't cry. In fact, the last time he had cried we were very young, so young the sounds and images of the memory were faint and barely recallable.

"Connak?" I called. The sobs didn't stop. I chased the sound, Rhett and Nakia close on my heels.

We found him farther inland, sitting on the grass, his arms draped over his knees, head down. Every inch of his posture was so unlike him, so defeated, so weary. And it occurred to me, I had never worried about Connak, because he had never given me reason. But that didn't mean there were none.

"Are you okay?" I asked, dropping to the grass beside him. Wildflowers bowed beneath our weight. I put a hand on his arm, squeezing lightly. "Connak? Are you hurt?"

He shook his head. His head lifted, his blue eyes swollen and rimmed with red. And then he was on me, pulling me into a sturdier, more aggressive hug than any of our family had ever done. Even Rhett.

I squeezed him tight, letting him cry into my shoulders, sobbing as he did. I let him squeeze me and reassure himself that I was alive until he finally seemed to believe it. Then he did the same to Rhett, and Nakia.

"I'm glad you're alive," he said finally, his voice choked with tears.

"And us you," I said gently, drying my cheeks. "I love you, big brother."

"I love you too." He swiped his own tears away, straightening himself out, back to the Connak we knew once more. "We should move on."

"We still need to find Luther," I murmured. "Or at least try. And you need to explain what's going on."

Connak hesitated, sniffling gently. Then he said, "I've

always been so confident. When we left Eldoris, I was absolutely sure there was nothing I couldn't protect you from." He looked around to Rhett and Nakia. "All of you. I never thought I'd meet my match before we even found Madrion."

"She was hardly a fair match," Nakia said. "Amirah's powerful. We knew that going into this."

"Maybe I didn't realize how much so. Maybe I'm starting to think we don't have a chance at all and encouraging us into this was foolhardy."

Connak's words should have shaken me to the core, until I crumbled. Only months ago, they would have. I was still shaken, only a fool wouldn't be, but now . . . now I knew that there was strength in doubt. In fear. Because if you can conquer the things you fear the most, then what could possibly hold you back?

"What do we have to lose?" I asked with a trembling thread of anger lacing my voice. "If we stayed in Eldoris, we would fight until we were dead. We almost died doing the right thing, but that's the way I'd rather go." I met each of their eyes, fire blazing, my jaw clenched in unwavering determination. Clarity. "If Kiran taught me anything, it's that you have to fight for what you want. If that's life, if it's love, if it's family . . . you don't sit back and let some arrogant bully come and take it from you."

"And if that bully can take everything with a snap of their fingers?" Connak asked me.

"Then I'll go out with my dagger in my hand."

"Who are you?" Rhett asked with a smirk. "What did they do with my little sister in that fae kingdom?"

I considered his words for a moment. "They taught me to be brave."

We searched the shoreline late into the afternoon. Connak's bow and sword weren't far from where he had woken up. Rhett's sword had stayed at his side. A sealed barrel had washed ashore, and when we broke it open, we found piles of spare clothes. They weren't ideal, soft cotton clothing that wouldn't offer much protection. But they were dry and clean, and after stripping most of our leathers so they didn't weigh us down in the water, we didn't have a lot of options.

Hours later, we had still seen no sign of Luther. Admitting defeat took a toll on all of us, but we couldn't linger longer. Not especially if Amirah figured out we had survived her attack. I found my bag, waterlogged, and the contents spilled to the stones. Kiran's map dripped ink onto the earth when I lifted it. The pang I felt at that was irrational; it was a map, not Kiran himself.

But all of his papers were ruined as well. And the journal.

From my bag, all that had survived our immersion was the star box, and the book from Lytharius. I wanted to be angry at the tome. I wanted to throw it into the ocean, furious that its magic had protected it when nearly everything else Kiran had left me had been destroyed.

When Luther was lost, to us and the waves, simply for being generous enough to offer us transport on dangerous seas.

But I tucked the book and star box under my arm and checked my dagger. Reassured myself that the dropstone was in my pocket, and that Kiran's note was still safe in its bottle around my neck . . . and we pressed on.

Evening faded into night. Stars lit the sky, surrounded by swirls of blues and greens. We followed the rise of the moon, aiming ourselves north and hoping for the best. Nakia whispered prayers to Cytherea under her breath.

None of us wanted to stop for rest, not when we were in such an open area. But toward late afternoon of the following day, our luck changed. A line of trees stood tall and proud along the horizon, and the hope of sleep pushed our sore bodies onward a little bit faster.

We were almost to the first trees when Nakia grabbed my arm. "Do you see smoke?"

"No?" I scanned the forest. Sure enough, deeper in, swirls of gray escaped the treetops and drifted toward the clouds. "What is that?"

Connak's hand went reflexively to the hilt of his sword. "Could be a troll camp."

"We should sneak up and see," Rhett said. His eyes were on our elder brother.

But Connak hesitated. "If we're caught, that could be the end."

Nakia crossed her arms over her chest. "We can't very well stand here. We might as well scout the area."

"What about your bird?" I asked. "Can it scout for us?"

"If the trolls have any warding runes with them, we'd be given away immediately," Rhett said. "I've overheard the fae guards discussing how some of the troll scouting parties carry stones the Sorceress has imbued for them."

"Forward it is," I said. I slid my dagger free, gripping it tightly in my right hand.

Connak slipped past me, then gestured for us to move quietly. We dipped into the trees, using the trunks as cover, inching our way forward with cautious steps. The scent of earth around us took on the distinct odor of woodsmoke. But there was no noise ahead, only silence.

"I don't think it's trolls," Rhett admitted. He still looked skeptical, but the grip on his own weapon loosened. My brothers exchanged a glance. Magic twinkled at Nakia's fingertips. I adjusted the dagger in my hand.

Connak gestured for us to spread out. I pressed my back to a tree, crouching before I leaned around to look. He leaned over me, peering out. Nakia and Rhett did the same a few feet away.

And there, tucked in the trees, was a little wooden cabin.

36

The house was small, smaller even than our own home had been once. It sat by itself in a rounded clearing, smoke trailing lazily from the thin chimney that rose from its thatched roof. Wildflowers grew in a plethora of colors, mingling with the pine and earth scents in a way that made my heart ache for days spent in the garden. I knew it couldn't last, that the snow would hit them soon. But I would enjoy the nice weather while it was there.

"What do we do now?" Nakia whispered.

"Knock?" Rhett straightened his stature and rounded the tree.

Connak grabbed for his sleeve but missed, and so we chased after Rhett as quietly as we could. He strode with confidence toward the door, balling his fist. Three heavy knocks thudded through the quiet woods.

Silence.

Nakia's lips curved into a smirk. "It's going to be *so* awkward if no one's home."

"Just wait," Rhett said. "I have a sense about these things."

I lifted a brow, crossing my arms over my chest. "Since when?"

The door swung open.

"Since now," Rhett whispered under his breath.

A woman stood before us, beautiful and tall. Her hair was tied back, but strands of loose ebony curls fell free around her face.

"Who are you?" She demanded. Amber eyes narrowed on Rhett, then circled to each of us in turn. "Have you lost your companion?"

"Our companion?" Connak asked.

The woman stepped back, holding the door wider. A simple crystalline chandelier hung inside the front hall, casting glimmering rainbow lights across the woman's rich brown skin. But it was the person behind her, who greeted us with a broad smile that brought me a flutter of joy.

"Luther! You *did* survive!" Rhett exclaimed. He moved forward and pulled the sailor into a hug. "You're well, then?"

"Aye," Luther said with a nod. "I ended up pretty far inland, somehow, and went looking for you all. I found Rohana here instead."

Rohana tsked. "I prefer to introduce myself, *sailor.*"

"Apologies," Luther said. Then he turned to me. His dark blue eyes glittered with excitement. "I do have some good news for you, though." I raised an interested brow. "Rohana is a Seer."

"A Seer?" My attention snapped to the woman in front of me. "You're a Seer? Of Saryshna?"

"Again," Rohana drawled, "I would prefer to introduce myself."

Luther snapped his jaw shut. The look he gave Rohana though was full of teasing.

Rohana eyed him for a second, like she was waiting for him to speak again, then said, "Yes. I am Rohana, the first of the three Seers of Saryshna. But before we discuss anything further"—she gestured toward the inside of her house—"come in."

She led us past her simple dining room and down a hall. The walls were covered in beautiful, elaborate paintings of various parts of the world—some parts I had never seen, and probably never would.

We entered into a plush sitting room. Thickly cushioned chairs sat scattered over a thick fur rug of the deepest grays and blacks. A short table of polished onyx sat at an awkward angle in the center of the room, a vase of red flowers on its top.

"Sit," Rohana said bluntly. She dropped herself into a tall-backed armchair, almost more throne than chair. A wave of her hand and a steaming teapot, painted with bright pink flowers, replaced the vase on the table. Another gesture and six matching teacups joined it. Then she clapped her hands together, summoning a tray of biscuits and fruit. "Help yourselves. I always have a bit too much food around for one person."

I eyed her warily, and then the food, but my companions waited until I gripped the teapot and poured the honey-colored liquid into my cup before doing so themselves. Rohana watched each of our movements with curious patience. She wore a dress of simple white cotton, embroidered with shimmering beads that curled into intricate patterns that seemed to change depending on the amount of light that shone on them.

"Thank you," I offered gently, after taking a sip of the tea. I set the cup down on its saucer, then said, "As our friend insinuated, I have been looking for you."

"Hmmm." Rohana lifted a biscuit, picking at the chocolate that had been piped into the center. "And what is it you seek of the Seers?"

"I need to find Madrion."

Rohana stilled at my words. "Such information would come with a high price. And you would have to pay thrice. My peers would need their dues as well."

"What is the price?"

"As I said, there are three. To me, you must pay with a story. To Aldor, you must pay the pelt of a rare beast. To Sloane, you must offer a gift she does not already have."

"What kind of story?" Nakia asked.

Rohana leaned back in her chair, all interest in the biscuit in her hand lost. Her eyes took on a glint, a greed, and the friendly demeanor that had radiated off her vanished. Nakia's brows rose, but she waited. The Seer smiled.

"Well, to be quite honest, the magic you seek is quite expensive. The more valuable the story, the more I'll be able to assist you, and potentially the less you'll have to do to satisfy the other Seers." Rohana leaned forward in her seat. Strands of shimmering silver magic glistened in her hair, and her amber eyes had fallen into dark, fathomless black. Her smile was less gentle, more predatory.

"I could tell you about Kiran," I said cautiously.

"That story is not yours."

I considered. "What about my scars?"

"I've heard those tales before."

Fear and panic gripped my chest. Those were the tales I had that carried value. My past, my present. I didn't know what my future held. I looked at my brothers, but their lives hadn't been all that different from my own.

"I might have one," Nakia said softly. "I don't know how much value it would be to you, though."

Rohana's eyes sparked with interest. She lifted a brow and gestured for Nakia to continue.

I reached for my friend, lacing my fingers through hers. There were few stories Nakia had that held the weight Rohana seemed to want. But I knew one. And if Nakia was about to share it . . .

Her grip on my hand tightened and she stared hard at the skirt of her dress. "My parents have never been the present kind. They've spent most of their adult lives in the bottoms of bottles, or tankards, or passed out on whatever flat surface they've landed on." Nakia paused and clenched her jaw. "When I was three, they nearly killed me."

Connak tensed where he sat. Rhett's head jerked in her direction, and his braid fell over his shoulder. My brothers knew my parents took in Nakia, of course. They knew she came from deeper poverty than us. But even my parents didn't realize the full extent of what Nakia's parents were capable of. What they had done.

Or tried to do.

"My parents liked to go to Castyr Lake during the summer," Nakia continued softly. Her free hand worried the hem of her skirt, picking and digging and pulling threads loose. "I was so young. I didn't know the difference between lakes. I just knew that sometimes my parents loved me. And when they did, we went to the lake. We splashed along the shore, we had food . . . they drank themselves stupid. What I took as a fun adventure in sleeping outside was actually them passing out, far too intoxicated to get us home.

"One summer, when I was three, we went to the lake. I've always been very emotionally in tune, but that day something felt wrong. But my parents weren't acting any different than usual. They had our basket, full of bottles of wine and whiskey and ale, and a meat pie for me. The walk felt longer. My little legs could barely keep up, they were walking so quickly. Normally, we got to the lake fairly early in the morning. This day, we didn't hit the shore till nearly afternoon. And the whole time I couldn't shake the feeling that something was wrong."

Rohana leaned forward in her seat when Nakia hesitated. The magic in her hair was glowing brighter, her dark eyes spinning with specks of silver of their own. "Continue," she urged.

Nakia swallowed. "When we got to the lake, I had my lunch, played with my parents while they drank themselves numb, then fell asleep on the shore when I was ready to recharge with a nap. But I didn't wake up in the fading sunset like I usually did. My father didn't catch fireflies with me after dark.

"No, instead they threw me into Sedryn Lake while I was still fast asleep. We weren't supposed to be there. Looking back now, I understand why the walk felt so much longer. But if they didn't want me found by anyone, Sedryn Lake would be the place to go.

"I didn't know how to swim. Monsters lurk beneath that water. All I remember is panic and fear. I woke up screaming for help, swallowing mouthfuls of water, staring at an empty shore."

A tear trailed down Nakia's cheek. I reached up, wiping it away. Her hold on my fingers was so tight they ached, but I didn't move them.

"Keep going," Rohana urged. Silver starbursts had formed where her pupils had once been. Her voice took on an ethereal, echoing tone. "Share your greatest pain."

"They threw three-year-old me in that lake and left me to die." Tears streamed from Nakia's eyes. "I still don't know how I got out. My memories go black for a while, and then I remember being home. My parents to this day don't remember doing it. And they've never apologized."

"That was the day you stopped believing your parents loved you," Rohana said. "The day that almost broke your spirit and cast your very magic from you. A part of your very *soul* died."

Nakia winced. I pulled her into a tight hug and let her release the tears she didn't often cry.

"It doesn't matter," I whispered to her. "We're your family. We always will be."

Rohana's silvery magic swirled around her as Nakia slipped away from me. The Seer held out her hand. In Rohana's eyes the starbursts expanded until they matched her powers, sparkling and bright. A golden disc began to form on the palm of her hand. After a minute, it solidified and, in a blink, Rohana's powers flicked out.

"Here," Rohana said, holding the disc out to me. "The fruits of your gift."

I took it. The metal was warm in my hand, etched with the

stars and moon.

Rohana's gentle smile had returned. "A gift for the dreamers. The fighters. Who call on the stars when no one in all the world will listen." She climbed to her feet. "Go now. Aldor will be awaiting you."

I turned to Luther, who had been oddly quiet through all that had transpired. "And you?"

"I think I'll stick around for a bit. Learn what Rohana can teach me about the land."

The Seer didn't seem all too keen on the idea, but she didn't comment, guiding us back through her home. When we reached the door, she gestured to a small, stone path that trailed into the woods to our right.

"Follow that. Aldor will have your next task ready. When a piece of the key is given, the other Seers are alerted."

"But what do I do with this?" I asked cautiously.

Rohana smiled. "You will gain the other two keys from my peers. And then you shall be able to reach your Winds."

With that, she turned back inside and clicked the door shut. I blinked at the bluntness of the gesture, of the abrupt dismissal.

"Who shoved a stick up *her* ass?" Rhett grumbled.

"*I heard that,*" Rohana's voice boomed in our minds. I flinched at the loud sound, but my brothers merely laughed.

Nakia was unusually silent. I looped my arm through hers as we followed the path, leaning my head on her shoulder. We both stared at the golden disc in my hand, etched with symbols we didn't recognize. I tucked the first piece into my bag.

"I know what that took out of you," I said to Nakia. "I appreciate you sharing it."

For a moment, she was silent. Then she said, "She was right, you know. I haven't felt like my parents loved me a day since."

"I know it's not the same, but you know Mama and Papa love you. *We* love you."

"I know." She leaned her head on mine. "I don't know what I would do without you."

"Excuse me," Rhett said. He nudged his arm between us, looping it around Nakia's shoulders. "I need more appreciation in this conversation."

Nakia looped her arms around my brother and hugged him tightly. "Yes, you too Rhett. And you, Connak."

My eldest brother waved a hand. His focus was on the path and the trees around us, ever alert, ever cautious. We knew though, that of anyone, Connak would be the one to drop everything for each one of us. It made me want to protect my big brother, even if I knew he didn't often need it.

I glanced over my shoulder, toward Rohana's cabin. But it was gone. The clearing was as bare as though no one had ever been there at all.

"Luther?" I called out.

Nothing.

No answer from him, or Rohana, or even the wild animals in the forest around us. Just silence.

"Well, that's odd," Rhett admitted. He dropped his arm from Nakia's shoulders, moving to get a grip on his blade. "Stay close."

Before the words fell from Rhett's lips, Connak was holding up a hand in warning. A thin tendril of smoke was curling from the trees in front of us. My brow scrunched together.

Sure enough, the trees split open again into another small clearing. Here a pond, filled with fish that darted after insects at the surface, took up most of the space.

Rhett didn't have to knock this time.

The door of the cabin slammed open with gusto. A tall, broad man stepped out. His black-and-gray hair was neatly combed to the side, his beard carefully trimmed. A long, thin scar ran from his forehead down to his cheek on the right side, and small dings and scars broke his skin elsewhere too.

"Rohana implied you'd be taller," Aldor said. His voice was full of deep timber. He crossed his arms over his chest, ruffling the fur that sat above his thick armor. "So, you need the second key?"

"Yes," I said, stepping forward. "How can we earn it from you?"

Aldor smiled. "Brave, I see." The smile faltered. "Or maybe it's overconfidence in your abilities."

A lump rose in my throat, but I swallowed it—hard.

Connak stepped to my side. "I am confident we can meet your task, just as we accomplished Rohana's. She mentioned you would require the pelt of a rare beast. What do you wish for us to hunt?"

Aldor stepped closer to my brother, measuring him with his hazel eyes. "So confident."

"My brother and I have hunted the lands below the Aldmir Divide for a long time," Rhett said. The Seer's attention slid to him. "We might not be the most skilled hunters in Numeryon, but we know our way around the forest, and we're knowledgeable enough about our weapons."

"So be it," Aldor said. His eyes began to glow, as Rohana's had, but the starbursts that began to form in his eyes were bright green. He waved a hand and a glittering lizard burst from his fingertips. It reminded me of Kiran's dragon, a fact that sent a pang through my chest and caught the air in my lungs. But this creature was much smaller, faster, the size of a squirrel maybe. After a moment, its body settled from shimmering green into a coat of purest white and sparkling gold. Small, feathered wings rose from its back, and the tiny beast bared its pointed fangs at us in challenge.

Aldor grinned, the doubt clear in his voice when he said, "Off you go. Knock when you've done it."

And he vanished into a burst of shimmering green.

I exchanged glances with my brothers. "What is that?"

"Uhhh," Rhett glanced at each of us, then shrugged. "A fluffdragon?"

"What's a fluffdragon?" Connak frowned.

Rhett smirked. "Dunno, made it up."

"How about we catch it and kill it before it completely escapes, and our chances of getting to Madrion go with it?" Nakia asked. She was already slinking after the little beast, but it was too aware of her, too quick. Every time she extended a slow hand the animal blinked, vanishing into thin air only to reappear several feet away.

"Alright so we need to spread out," Connak said, taking command. He motioned each of us to a side of the clearing: me to the north, Nakia to the east, and Rhett to the west, while he faced south.

The little fluffdragon looked around in confusion. I genuinely believed that if he could laugh at the four of us, he would have. Instead, he eyed Connak, as though he could sense my eldest brother was where the greatest threat lay.

"Rhett," Connak whispered.

Rhett took a step forward while the small creature fixated on Connak.

But the moment he heard that footstep the animal turned and narrowed his wide emerald eyes. Rhett froze. A tiny pink tongue darted from between those sharp pointed teeth. Rhett dared another step and the fluffdragon blinked, reappearing nearer to Nakia.

Nakia didn't hesitate. She dove at the animal, brushing the feathers of its wings before it disappeared again. Connak drew his bow back, fixing an arrow on the fluffdragon.

He released.

The arrow cut through the air, faster than the little animal anticipated. It wouldn't be able to move out of the way. My heart thundered against my ribs. Those wide green eyes were dark with fear. I couldn't kill it. *We* couldn't kill it.

We would find another way.

"Stop! We can't. We can't hurt it. Not for this."

I knew it was too late, but the words fell from my lips. The arrow froze in midair, and my shock was audible. No magic shimmered in the air as it did with my family. No tattoos lit up along my skin.

But the arrow had stopped and, as I breathed a sigh of relief, it clattered to the ground.

Slow applause filled the air. All of us spun, including the little fluffdragon. Aldor stood behind us, clapping his hands.

"You know, in all my eight thousand and seventy-nine years, only one other person stopped themself before killing the mystarian beast. Usually, I have to intervene. These are rare creatures; less than five are known to exist in all Numeryon. Doodle, here, is the youngest of his family. When he is fully grown, he will be the size of a young cow."

"Does that mean we passed your test?" Connak asked. His hand was still around his bow, his gaze flitting back and forth between the Seer and the beast.

"Indeed," Aldor said. "It is a far greater soul that sacrifices a victory when the contest means overpowering a weaker being." He held out his hand and, like Rohana, the green starbursts filled his eyes and a golden disc appeared on his palm. "Take the second key. Follow the path. Good luck."

As soon as the second piece fell into my hand Aldor, the cabin, and the mystarian beast all vanished. Clearly the second Seer wasn't as subtle as Rohana. Where the home had stood, the path appeared, winding deeper into the trees.

This time the walk felt longer. We followed the uneven stones in near silence, the weight of the two keys heavy on all of us. Each step closer was a relief and a curse; another step nearer to saving Kiran, and my friends, but another step closer to facing Amirah.

Finally, the trees fell away and opened to the shore of a vast, glistening lake.

"Spiritwood Lake," Nakia whispered.

My siblings' magic danced along their skin, a sparkling, dancing power that looked like the reflection of water and seemed to respond to the presence of the lake.

And to the left, a cabin—again. Only this time, instead of simple wood, it was made of stone and, instead of a singular Seer, Rohana and Aldor sat on the porch sipping from teacups while the third Seer approached. Aldor's little beast, Doodle, lay stretched at his feet. Luther sat beside him.

This Seer was short, slender, with dark waves of chestnut hair that fell to her waist. She walked closer, circling me for a moment. This close, I could see the dark smattering of freckles that dusted her nose and cheeks.

"My name is Sloane," she introduced herself. Then she said, "Your task from me is simple. I wish for a gift."

"What kind of gift?" I asked.

"One that I don't already have." Sloane gestured at the cabin and the Seers who were behind her. "I have immortality. I have a home. All of my basic needs are fulfilled, and I have more unnecessary trinkets than I can count. I have friends."

Connak frowned. "Then what could we possibly offer you?"

Sloane didn't reply. Instead, she lifted a brow, smirking. "That is for you to decide."

I looked at my family, but they looked as lost as I felt. We had nothing. I wouldn't give her Kiran's star box . . . it held too much value to him. But what else was there? I reached into my bag and pulled out the book from the library of Lytharius, but Sloane shook her head.

"I have no use for that. I have been alive for hundreds of years."

My heart dropped. What could we offer this Seer? I tucked the book back in my bag. And for the first time since we left Eldoris, I felt myself losing hope.

Hope.

The one thing in all the world that no one could ever run out of, or have enough of, was *hope.*

I didn't know how I did it before. I hadn't known about my powers, and I still didn't know enough about them to use them. But I knelt in the grass, placing my palms into the earth. I ignored the confused gazes of those around me and closed my eyes, beginning to sing Papa's song low and soft.

And I pictured that rose: the Eventide Rose, with its lavender tips and pink heart, and its petals that glittered as though they were covered in sparkling water. I pictured the smile on Kiran's face when he called me his rose; I heard the sound of his voice gifting me his vulnerability.

A gasp sounded before I opened my eyes. When I did, a beautiful bloom grew in front of me, more beautiful even than the rose I had accidentally awoken at the estate.

Sloane fell to her knees before it, touching the petals as though she expected them to wilt and fall to dust.

"How?" she whispered. "I haven't seen an Eventide Rose in decades."

"I don't know," I admitted. "But this is the second time I've done it."

"The second time?" Nakia asked. Her eyes were wide with awe. I nodded, and she looked at me as though she had never seen me before.

Sloane didn't move, didn't take her eyes from the rose. Lavender starbursts expanded in her eyes and then she handed the third disc to me. I pulled all three from my bag, and then, as if drawn by magnetic force, they slid together.

The metal hummed as the discs settled. In my hands sat a round key etched with unfamiliar runes that shimmered in lavender and silver and green.

Sloane smiled. "It is time, young ones."

"Time for what?" Rhett asked.

"Time to go into the lake," Sloane said. Her eyes were kind, but glinted with concern when she added, "Time to meet the Winds."

37

I stared at the expanse of water before me. Nakia's hand was gripped in my right hand, my left arm looped through Rhett's. Connak seemed to be weighing our options.

But this was it.

We had to swim.

"It's not *that* far down," Rohana said. I glanced over my shoulder to where she stood closer to the cabin. Her arms were crossed over her chest, eyes glittering with mischief. "Only a couple hundred feet."

"*Only,*" Connak grumbled.

"We can help, a little," Sloane offered. She raised her hand, and the gear we carried grew featherlight. Our clothing felt as though it was as thin as air, even though it hung heavy and warm around us. "That should help you swim."

"Thank you," I said. I took the time to look at each Seer, at Luther. "Thank you all. We wouldn't have gotten this far without you."

"Just doing our jobs," Aldor said. But he winked, and I couldn't help smiling back.

"How are we supposed to breathe?" Rhett asked.

Nakia smiled. "Now *that* I can handle."

She waved her fingers in the air and glittering gold danced off her fingers. The magic swirled across myself and my brothers, shimmering along our skin, before settling like dust.

Then my air constricted and I gasped. Nakia pointed at the water, and I dove in, my bag and its contents tapping my side.

As soon as my face was below the water, I sucked in a huge gulp of air. Water breathing. Nakia had made us humanoid fish. Sirens? I wondered, vaguely, what my siren powers might mean here. If I met my father, could he tell me? Even though I wasn't entirely of his blood?

The thought that I might be more capable than I felt tore at me. I always felt one step behind, and it seemed with every step that life let me take forward, something else would always linger. Some doubt, some insecurity.

For once, I felt free of expectations. And full of possibility.

We followed Nakia deep into the lake. Her magic glowed brightly on each of us, giving us the ability to see a few feet ahead. Fish scrambled to get away from us, the intruders.

If I'd had to guess which of our group would have siren blood, I most definitely would have said Nakia. She had always been drawn to the water, even despite her parents. We had found solace playing together in the waves.

Maybe it was because we knew if anything happened to either of us, the other would be on top of it.

Nothing could ever stop us if we were together.

And maybe, I thought, as fish and lake plants swirled past, maybe together was *how* we survived this. Maybe there was more strength in love and unity than division. Than solitude.

Rhett tapped my arm and I jumped. He put his hands to his neck, miming gills, moving his mouth in the perfect imitation of a carp. I couldn't stop myself from laughing. It wasn't until I saw the smile on his face that I realized I hadn't really laughed in a long time. Definitely not on our journey.

I was so lost in my thoughts, I didn't catch myself before I swam smack into Nakia, who had stopped in front of me. She put her hand on my shoulder for a second, a sweet reassurance, then gestured ahead.

We were there.

A vast white stone temple sat on the lake bottom, spreading as far as we could see. Elven lights sparkled along a small path that led to massive front doors.

"*How does this work?*" Nakia mouthed to me.

I shrugged. We swam lower, until we rested on the stoop in front of the doors. A round notch sat in their center, a perfect fit for the key. I fished it from my bag, easy to find with its runes glowing in the dim underwater light.

"*Here goes nothing,*" I murmured, bubbles spewing from my lips.

I fitted the key into the notch—and waited. Nothing. Nakia raised her hand, casting some of her magic onto it. Still, the key didn't turn. Connak tried, then Rhett.

Finally, I raised my own hand, pressing it against the smooth golden surface. I didn't know what I was doing, but I whispered soft pleas to whatever magic I had to help us. At first, I thought it was for naught.

But then the key began to rotate. A click sounded.

A bubble of silver magic expanded outward, surrounding us, pushing the water outward and away. We gasped for air as the water vanished from around us and our feet fell on a white marble landing. Before Nakia could dismiss her magic, a wave of tingling power rolled over us, sending small static jolts across our skin. Her magic fell away, and so did Sloane's; we could breathe again, and our items fell heavy on us once more. We staggered for a moment, adjusting to the weight, as the doors swung wide. A swirl of warm air gusted over us. Our sopping wet clothing and hair were immediately dry.

"Welcome to our home," a feminine voice said. "Please, step inside."

I straightened my shirt, then tried to tame my wild hair. Nakia did the same, but my brothers seemed unbothered.

Then we stepped inside. And the doors sealed ominously behind us.

The temple was beautiful, more beautiful than I had expected; though fairly, I didn't have much expectation for any building underwater. We entered into a lobby, a vast circular room with walls of glass. The outside was lined with elven lights, casting a gentle glow on the fish that swam by.

"And who have we here?" that same feminine voice said.

Air curled through the room and a figure appeared before us, hovering slightly above the ground. The woman was incredibly beautiful. Her long ebony hair flowed in loose waves down to her waist, and the high-necked, golden-trimmed red gown she wore perfectly complemented her bronze skin. She turned brown eyes onto each of us, then refocused on me, offering a gentle smile.

"I am Avriel, of the North Wind. And you are?"

"Sabrena," I said, then introduced my family. We each dipped our heads respectfully after, waiting for her lead.

But when we had finished saying our names, three other swirls of air filled the room, the counterparts hovering next to Avriel. I recognized the Wind to her right: Roux, of the West Wind. They stood regally beside Avriel, their sandy blond hair shaved on the lower half and slightly longer on the top. The statue in Kiran's gardens had done Roux very little justice.

"I see the recognition on your face," Roux said, their gold and brown eyes narrowed in thought. "Have we met?"

"No," I admitted. A flush spread over my cheeks. "My betrothed has figures of each of you in his garden, and a friend of mine had told me about you."

"That I'm stunningly attractive, I hope." Roux laughed.

"Stunningly arrogant," the man to Avriel's left said. "I am Edric, of the South Wind."

The man's muscular, light brown chest was exposed by his shirt, his shoulders draped with thick, soft furs. His deep chestnut hair fell to his shoulders, the perfect match to his short beard. His brown eyes turned toward the final woman, to his own left, and added, "This is Hanelle, of the East."

"Thanks for the introduction," Hanelle said with a smirk. "So eloquent of you."

"Eloquent is what I do."

Hanelle's smile grew wider. She straightened the white gown she wore. All four of the Winds dropped to the ground, but even without the magical presentation the Winds were intimidating. Power thrummed off the air in their presence, and even the white marble beneath their feet seemed to tremor with trepidation beneath their steps.

"How can we help you?" Avriel asked.

"We need to stop Amirah," I said with confidence.

Edric looked impressed. "You seem assured you can do so."

"I'm not," I admitted. "But we have to try."

"I appreciate your honesty," Edric said.

Hanelle stepped closer, examining us with curiosity. Her green eyes were bright against her warm brown skin, her black hair shaved close to her head. "Do you understand what kind of undertaking this would be?"

"We do," Connak said, and it was Roux that eyed him with interest.

"And do you know what must happen for you to accomplish this task?" Roux asked.

"I need a sword." I reached into my pocket. "Imbued with this."

Avriel appeared beside me and I jumped backward, startled. Edric smirked with amusement, but the North Wind seemed unphased by my reaction. Instead, she eyed the stone. "It has Amirah's blood inside?"

"Yes."

"And you know this with absolute certainty?"

I faltered. I didn't, and I wasn't sure how that could even be tested. "No. The stone was a gift from Astra, in Eldoris."

"Eldoris holds meaning to you?" Hanelle asked.

"It's my home," I said. I gestured to my family. "*Our* home."

"Then it is even more unfortunate that the city has fallen," Avriel said with sadness.

My heart fell into my stomach.

"Wait, what?" Rhett said. He stepped up beside me and would have walked right up to the Winds if I hadn't grabbed his arm. "What do you mean Eldoris has fallen?"

"You haven't heard?" Avriel asked. "The trolls overtook the city a few days ago. They breached the gate. We do not know if any survivors escaped. We do know they took captives."

I wanted to sink into the floor. I wanted to vanish from the world and let the intense pain crush me until I simply stopped existing. Our mission had just grown a million times more crucial, and a million times heavier. For a moment, I couldn't breathe. The thought that I might never see the light in my little sister's eyes again . . . That pain was unreal. Unlike anything I had ever felt before.

Then I said, in a voice I didn't recognize, "Tell me how to kill her."

The smile on Eldric's face was one of vicious satisfaction. Roux raised a curious eyebrow. But Hanelle and Avriel exchanged a glance.

"If you're serious," Avriel said, "you'll have to get the sword."

"Tell us how." Rhett's tone matched mine. I glanced at my brothers. Their jawlines were set, their expressions focused. They looked so much alike in that moment that it almost made me smile.

"You'll have to accomplish four tasks," Hanelle said. "Each of us has a room. If you do what is asked of you, you'll gain our piece of the sword."

"And if you gain all four, I'll forge them together for you," Roux said. "And imbue the hilt with that gem, so it will be capable of destroying the Sorceress. Assuming it's actually Amirah's blood in that dropstone you hold."

"How can we tell?" I asked.

Hanelle held out her hand. Reluctantly, I passed her the dropstone. On her palm, the stone began to glow. The blood inside lit with a teal light that swirled with greens and pinks. Then, as abruptly as it had brightened, the dropstone went dark.

"It's the real stone," Hanelle confirmed. "I can trigger Syris's magic, but Amirah's won't let it go. No one else would have the goddess's magic locked up like that."

I frowned. "I'm glad it's hers, but how was it gained in the first place? Can you tell me that?"

Edric smiled. "Hanelle can't, but I can. It was gained by the hand of a dragon."

"Kiran?" My heart leapt.

"No. His father. While he was fighting her. He knew the cost of the battle, and that they might fail. He sealed drops of her blood in a vial, one he sent to the Seers before he fell. They created the stone. Sloane, specifically. If not for Kiran's father's foresight, there might not be any hope now."

"How do you know this?" Connak eyed Edric with suspicion.

"Sunday brunch," Edric said, grinning wide. My brother sighed in frustration.

"What's the first task?" Nakia asked.

"And why do I have to complete tasks? Can't I just . . . have the sword?" I glanced around. "We don't have much time."

Avriel smiled gently. "No. The sword was split so that it couldn't be easily stolen, because reforged, even by hands other than our own, it is a powerful weapon. We are the keepers not creators of this weapon, as well as many, many others. You have to prove your worth, in four different ways, to even be able to find all the pieces you will need. No amount of urgency can override the magical seals that have been put on these challenges. I'm sorry."

"Okay," I said, taking a deep breath. "We're ready."

"Are you sure?" Avriel asked. "The magic will only allow one chance."

I nodded. "We're sure."

"Then follow me."

All four of us turned to follow her, but Avriel paused with an apologetic smile. "Only Sabrena can undertake these challenges. She must wield the blade, for she was gifted the dropstone."

"I will take you to a study where you can relax until Sabrena has finished her attempts," Hanelle said.

My brothers eyed me warily, but it was Nakia who swooped me into a tight hug.

"You can do this," she whispered into my ear. "You are strong, resilient, and intelligent. I believe in you."

"Thank you," I murmured, squeezing her tightly.

I released her and turned on my heel. Avriel gave me a gentle, knowing smile, then gestured for me to follow her.

The North Wind led me up a small staircase to the right side of the room, one that wound and twisted up a narrow space that eventually opened into an enormous library. Even Lytharius's massive collection of knowledge had nothing on Avriel's. Shelves upon shelves lined the walls, books lay around the floor in haphazard stacks. The tables were scattered with open parchment, books, ink, and quills.

"Apologies," she said, "We got late notice of your arrival from the Seers and didn't have much time to straighten up." She stopped in the center of the massive room. "Welcome to my chambers. Along with my duties maintaining the northern winds, I also display the northern lights and manage our collections of knowledge. My libraries contain centuries of history, from every race that has ever walked the surface of Numeryon."

"Even the humans?"

"Even the humans. There are still some that linger, you know.

They simply keep themselves well hidden." Avriel twirled a strand of her dark hair around a finger stacked with golden rings. "In this room, you could find the answer to any question you could dream of. There is nothing my books do not contain."

Apprehension was an iron weight in my stomach. "What do I need to do?"

"I have a riddle for you. Solve it, and you will gain access to my fourth of the blade. Fail, and you will be asked to leave."

I nodded slowly, even as my trepidation grew. So much relied on my ability to accomplish these tasks. And as confident as I might be starting to feel, the emotion wavered easily.

"Okay," I said after a long minute. "How much time will I have?"

"One hour." Avriel flicked her wrist and a silver hourglass, whose frame was wrapped in jeweled roses, appeared in her hand. "You will have to take the clues you are given to identify what I'm speaking of. Are you ready for the riddle?"

I nodded again.

"Very well." Avriel stepped over to a table and pushed aside some of the books that sat there. She offered me a blank slip of parchment and a quill, then nudged an ink well closer. "You may write it down."

I took the quill, a beautiful blue and purple feather. And tried to steady my breathing as Avriel began. When she finished, I stared at the page, reading the words I had scrawled down.

"I have two faces, but show you one,
A tether to my lupine son,
By day, my power's out of sight,
But I will guide you through the night."

My heart sank. I had no ideas. Avriel flipped the hourglass.

"Good luck," she murmured. Then she exited back the way we had come.

And I was alone.

The beat of my heart was loud in my ears. What the hell could this rhyme possibly be about? Two faces? There were deities, in elven and human religions, that had two faces. But lupine . . . that implied wolves. And none of the gods or goddesses that I knew of had anything to do with wolves.

I began to pace. The heels of my boots were loud against the wooden library floor. I was only on the first trial and, already, I was completely lost.

By day, my power's out of sight . . .

That reminded me of a note I had seen in the book from Lytharius, that a siren's power was lesser at night. But that didn't tie back to lupine.

Along the far back wall, I found a wall full of drawers, all alphabetized, all filled with neatly filled slips of parchment that indexed every book and document inside the library's walls. I found the "L" section as quickly as possible, flipping through until I found a few books that mentioned lupine origins and histories.

Then I was off, climbing a ladder that slid across the shelves, which allowed me to reach books far above my head. I perched precariously, flipping pages, looking for anything that talked about two faces. But there was nothing.

In every page I turned, in every volume I pulled from the shelves, there was nothing.

And my breathing began to come in short, gasped pulls. I was failing already.

Failing.

The thoughts that had filled my mind all my life came flooding back. Every insecurity, every doubt. Every moment I had wondered if I was enough. And for a few seconds, I shut down completely. My overwhelming thoughts were so loud I couldn't hear, my heartbeat so fast I felt like I couldn't breathe.

I was used to feeling worthless. I was used to feeling different or like a failure—or like I wasn't worth the space I inhabited. But this wasn't like all of those times.

This was lives. This was my family. Eldoris was held by the trolls; my friends were held by the trolls . . .

The man who made me feel like I could believe in myself, like I could be just a little bit more, was held by the trolls.

I sucked in a deep breath.

Right now, I didn't have to believe in myself. But they did. Kiran, Nakia, my siblings, my parents. Damara. Bleiz.

And even if I didn't feel very strong right now, I would figure this out.

I pulled another tome from the wall of shelves. The pages were old, so crisp they barely bent as I turned them. They talked about lupine packs, their travels, their meals.

A passage caught my eye, one that reminded me of a page in the book from Lytharius. I ran to where I had left my bag, next to the hourglass, and yanked the book free. Flipping the pages, I searched until I fell upon an illustration.

And I knew the answer.

As the final grains of sand poured into the bottom of the hourglass basin, as the last of my time slipped away, I *knew* the answer.

Avriel opened the library doors, and when she saw the confidence I felt reflected on my face, she grinned broadly. "Do you know the answer then?"

"I do!" I said excitedly. I held up the book, showed her the illustration I had found. "It's the moon."

Avriel clapped slowly, her smile bright with pride. "Well done, Sabrena. You've earned the pommel. Shall we move on to the next task?"

I took a deep breath, steadying my shaking hands, and nodded. "Let's do it."

38

Roux looked delighted to have the chance to lead someone into their challenge room. When I asked about it, Roux simply smiled.

"It's been a long time since anyone had need of a weapon of our making."

"I hope we never need one again," I muttered.

Roux's smile slipped. "Intelligent races never seem to manage peace for long. As much as we all say we want peace, war and domination will always exist."

"So why then don't you interfere more? Or the deities that any one of the races believes in?"

"Because that isn't our job," Roux said. "We balance the winds. We guide the seasons. Some of us carry more specific duties. Avriel records and stores histories. I forge weapons worthy of those very gods. But we do not interfere unless the balance is so genuinely threatened that we are unsure the races will survive it."

"And Amirah qualifies as that level of threat."

Roux sighed, a deep and weary sound. "Amirah has power that does not belong to her. But yes, if left unchecked she will destroy all Numeryon, including her own people. Not all trolls are the savage beasts that her most loyal make them out to be. Many of them don't want this war any more than the fae or the elves."

Luther had mentioned that some of the trolls were unwilling. I had never really considered that trolls might not want to spend their lives ravaging the very land they were meant to live on, or the people who might help them acclimate to it.

Living in Eldoris all my life had limited my vision. The world was so much more vast than I could possibly imagine.

"My challenge for you is simple enough," Roux said, halting in front of a door. They opened it, nudging me inside. "Find the oasis. You have two hours."

Roux didn't bother to explain before shutting the door. I turned in surprise but found the wall had vanished and I was surrounded by desert. When I reached out, sure I would feel the door before me, there was nothing. Only air.

I spun around—sand as far as I could see. I was surrounded by shimmering golden sand.

And it was hot.

Sweat beaded on my brow. I didn't know where to go. Roux hadn't given me any direction. I had the dagger strapped to my thigh, but I didn't think there was any threat here. My bag sat heavy on my shoulder. I surveyed the landscape. It was just sand. Sand and more sand.

Find the oasis.

What did that mean?

How was I supposed to find *anything* in here?

Nakia would use her magic. My brothers would too. But I didn't know how to use mine. Did I? The Eventide Rose I had summoned for the Seers popped into my mind. I hadn't really known what I was doing, but I had put intention into my thoughts. And feeling.

Maybe I could do that again. There might be a risk to using

my magic unguided, but I wasn't going to learn how to use it any other way, not now especially.

I inhaled deeply, breathing out slowly as I closed my eyes and began to hum. Trails of sweat raced down my spine, my arms, my legs. I pushed the discomfort away.

All I really knew about oases was that they were like living havens of refuge in the middle of the desert—life-filled areas that had water. And water should call to my siren nature, or something. So, I reached out with my mind, searching for liquid in any form. At first, there was nothing. Dry, empty landscape. But I started walking, blindly, focusing every bit of my energy into finding water.

And there, at the edge of my consciousness, I felt it. A trickle of water, tiny droplets on the far horizon. They danced in my mind like strands of hair, swirling and twisting together. I turned the direction they called from and opened my eyes.

Then I started walking.

I knew I had only been walking for minutes when it began to feel like hours. The unchanging landscape didn't give me any sense of the passing of time, and the sand dragged at my legs, making each step heavy. My mouth was dry. A sunburn ached over my exposed skin. It would be easier to turn back, I knew. I could give up; I could be over this hurdle.

But no. This was not really harder than the riddle. It was taxing on my body. My clothing felt pasted to my skin. But it wasn't any harder than anything else I had been through before.

I continued to hum softly. The familiar music was a balm to my nerves, and it distracted me from the growing unease I felt when the oasis still didn't appear for what I guessed to be an hour in.

Still, I didn't give up. I sang to myself. Periodically I checked my magic, noting that the strains of blue that called to me were growing closer and closer.

Finally, a flash of green showed up on the horizon. I was

panting and drenched in sweat when I saw the palm tree that beckoned to me. And when the grass and brush tickled my boots, when the palm leaves danced in the air above me, I nearly cried with relief.

In the center of the oasis was a deep pool of crystalline water and I didn't hesitate before I leapt into its depths. The cool water was a relief against my aching skin, but when I broke the surface, paddling in place, Roux didn't appear. They had said to find the oasis, but that couldn't be it. Because I was here and I wasn't being recalled.

I scanned the oasis. The pool was surrounded by bright greenery. No animals milled about the water; no insects chirped around me. I spun around. Silence. I focused hard and pulled up my magic. The swirling strands of magic were a flood in my mind, a cluster so dense I couldn't make heads or tails of them. I wasn't convinced the answer was there.

My eyes snapped open. And I looked down. If there were anywhere in an oasis that might hold the answers, it was the water that gave the entire place life.

Sucking in lungfuls of air, I dove beneath the surface. The bottom of the pool was all rocks and dense foliage. At first, nothing stuck out to me.

Then I saw it.

A skeletal hand rose from the thick mud. Clenched tightly in its fingers was the hilt of a sword that glittered in the sunbeams that broke through the surface. I swam up, getting more air, then dove again. Warily, I pried the fingers off the hilt and swam away.

But I knew it couldn't be that simple.

I was almost to the surface when a sharp pain gripped my ankle. I spun to find the skeleton holding me, pulling me down, back into the depths. Its eyes glowed blue, its jaw clacking like it was trying to form words. A stream of bubbles escaped my lips as I nearly gasped in panic. I kicked at the skeletal fingers that had their hold on me, but its grip was tight.

"*Fuck*," I muttered, releasing more air.

I tried to hit the skeleton with the hilt. When that didn't work, I tried to just swim. My lungs ached for air. But none of our efforts would matter if I drowned.

Still, the skeleton wouldn't let go. I closed my eyes, stopped fighting, and focused. The blue threads spun in my mind in a confusing mess, but toward the bottom I could see a dark shape—the skeleton. I had no idea what I was doing, but I willed the chords of magic toward the shadowed figure. The strands surged downward, condensed, and ripped the shadow apart.

Suddenly, I was free, swimming. I glanced down to see a shower of loose bones falling to the bottom of the pond.

I broke the surface gasping for air. Roux stood at the side of the pool. They smiled.

"Well done. Onto part three."

39

Every inch of my body ached when Roux left me with Hanelle. The East Wind was gracious, offering me her own magic to heal my pain, but she couldn't touch the stress I felt. I tried to give myself credit; I had completed two tasks. I was halfway done with acquiring the sword.

But I wished Nakia and my brothers were with me. I knew they were only rooms away, but facing these challenges alone was worse than I had thought it would be. Not only because I had no one to waylay my doubts, but also because I felt so lost when I didn't know what to do.

And I realized I had never really spent any time alone. Not as a child, nor a teen. Not when I left for the estate, not *at* the estate, and certainly not during the journey this far.

I had never been left to solve my own problems for myself. Nor had I ever had to face them so head on. Even though the challenges were meant to show whatever skills the Winds thought I needed, they forced me to look within myself.

Maybe that was the point. Because if I was going to fight Amirah, even with help, I would need to be able to show strength regardless of those around me. And I had never been very good at that.

Hanelle studied me carefully as we stood outside the door to her chambers. Her room was down the hall from Roux's, on the same floor as the circular entryway.

"Two more to go," she said. "You're doing very well."

"I don't feel that way," I admitted. "I know I am but accepting it . . ."

"Your doubts don't make your victories any less valuable." Hanelle smiled, fidgeting with a tiny emerald charm that hung at her throat on a silver chain. "Are you ready for the next challenge?"

"Will I get more advice than 'find the oasis?'" I asked with a soft laugh.

"Yes," Hanelle said. "This room is a bit different than the first two. Your very heart will be tested." I winced at that, but Hanelle continued, "Follow your heart. Your mind will deceive you. Your heart will lead you true."

"That's terrible advice," I said.

Hanelle laughed, the sound loud and pleasant. "It is. But it is genuinely the best I can offer you."

She opened the door. I took a long, bracing breath, and stepped inside.

The room I entered was circular, made of dense, dark stone. A few flickering torches hung on the walls, but otherwise the light was dim. Metal bars lined the walls.

And from within those bars were familiar faces.

I choked back a sob. Everyone I loved stared at me from within small cages. Kiran, Nakia, all of my family, Bleiz, Damara . . . they were all here. I fell to my knees in the center of the room, utterly at a loss for how to save them. There were no doors, no locks, no windows. Just dark stone and metal bars.

"We're in your mind," Kiran said. The sound of his voice

was agony. I missed him so intensely, and it was only the moments that I was alone, that I wasn't distracted, that I felt his absence so keenly. But hearing his voice . . . "But you have to choose."

"Choose?"

"You can't save all of us," Nakia said. I spun to face her, then ran to where she stood behind those metal bars. "You might not even be able to save one of us."

"What do you mean?" I asked. "How do I free you?"

"You can't," Damara said. I turned. Her red curls were limp, dirty. I eyed my loved ones and realized they all looked that way: bedraggled, exhausted, unkempt. "Save your family, Sabrena. Save them and go."

The words were so very in character. I knew this was in my mind. I knew the Winds wouldn't capture innocents and use them to torment me, that Kiran was with Amirah, and that my brothers and Nakia were actually safe in another room. But their words were still misery, their faces still so beloved to me. I certainly couldn't bear to watch even an imitation die.

"I'm sorry, speak for yourself," Bleiz said. "I would like to keep my life. Even an imaginary one."

A loud click sounded. A buzz. And then a slow, steady clank. My heartbeat raced to full speed.

I didn't know what was happening, but I knew I didn't want to find out.

"*How* do I get you out?"

"You have to use your magic," Mama said. I moved closer to her. She and Papa were trapped together, with Aleksei and Kirsi and Siyna. Even as imitations, my sister's eyes were bright and wide. I could never leave them behind.

"I don't know how," I pleaded. "There has to be another way."

Mama gripped my fingers through the bars. "There is no other way. And you do not have the time to save us all."

I raked my fingers into my hair, turning away to pace the room. If I couldn't save them all, who could I possibly leave to die? Beside my parents and youngest siblings, everyone else was in their own cages. I would meticulously have to save each person. The rattling chains above were ominous, counting down the seconds. I peered between the bars, toward the ceiling. Spiked platforms sat high above us, crawling slowly downward.

"I don't know what to do," I sobbed.

"Your mother is right," Kiran said gently. He leaned against the bars that held him, his tattooed arms crossed over his chest. This Kiran was thin, nearly as starved as I had been when I came to his estate. I tried not to focus on him, on the longing I felt to touch his face and kiss him and reassure myself he was okay. Because this wasn't my Kiran and this situation wasn't normal. Kiran smiled gently, as though he could sense the war I was fighting. "Use your magic. Each bar is attuned to a different musical note. Use your magic to harmonize your voice to remove the bars holding a specific person."

That sounded hard. I was terrified. "I can't do that."

"You can," Kiran insisted. "I believe in you."

The words were a white-hot brand. I wanted to cry. I wanted to run. I wanted to not do this trial anymore, because I was struggling to differentiate between reality and magic.

Connak reached out from the bars, trying to grab my hand. "Sabrena. Save Mama and Papa, and our siblings. Then get your husband. You deserve happiness."

And that was so like Connak. He had always put the family above all else, even his own happiness, his own pursuits. I glanced at Rhett, who nodded his agreement, and then I started singing.

I ran scales, watching as each bar began to glow brilliant blue in response to the notes. If I held them long enough, the bar would shimmer and disappear. But I didn't know how to harmonize them. I couldn't sing like that. I wished for it, willed it, prayed to deities I didn't believe in. But nothing. I could only remove one single bar at a time, and those spikes were looming, pressing down. If I didn't figure this out, I would watch everyone I loved crushed to death in front of me instead of just a few. I couldn't take that.

I held a note, watching the magic dance along the bar it correlated with. Then I gripped the bar beside it, willing it to light up. It didn't. But when I went to sing the next note, the first note held. The music echoed around the room, two notes, two bars removed.

Two bars, a gap big enough for Mama and Papa and my littlest siblings to slip through. They were safe. *They were safe.* Mama and Papa pulled me into a crushing hug and I didn't know how I could feel them, or how even Aleksei and Kirsi smelled right as they gripped my legs. But they were safe. And now I had only minutes to try to save as many of the others as I could.

I went to Nakia next, humming softly until I found the notes that matched her bars. When she was free, I moved on . . . to Connak, to Rhett. I was working on Damara when the ceiling grew too low. She, Bleiz, and Kiran were crouched, buying time, but I wasn't going to make it. My scales were shaking with fear. I wasn't finding the notes I needed.

Damara grabbed my hands where they lingered on her bars. "It's okay, Sabrena. You tried. We won't forget that."

They would. Their real versions wouldn't know until I told them, and I would have to live with this. I would have to see them die because I didn't save them.

I failed, I failed, I failed.

"You did everything you could," Kiran said. I ran to where he was, across the room, and reached for his hand through the bars. He nudged my fingers away, out of the cage. The spikes had him pressed prone to the floor. "I'm proud of you."

I grabbed the bars of his cage, but it was too late. The ceiling fell and I watched him crushed, felt the spray of warm blood on my cheeks. I recoiled. Tears ran down my cheeks in streams and I screamed at the top of my lungs, all the agony and rage I felt pouring out.

Hanelle opened the door. The images of my family, the blood, the remains around me, all vanished with her appearance. "Sabrena. You're free."

"I don't feel free," I sobbed. "How could you do this to me?"

The East Wind moved to my side and pulled me into a tight hug. "You sacrificed your greatest love for a family you're struggling to connect to. There's strength there. And motive. Your loyalty lay with those who had loved you longest and love you still. Understand that we try the things we find most important before we give someone a weapon of this power: intelligence, endurance, heart, and soul."

"Soul?" I asked, wiping at my face. "What does that mean?"

"That's not for me to say," Hanelle said. "But it will be your hardest trial by far. Do you think you're up for trying it? If you succeed, you could be to Madrion by tomorrow afternoon."

And that . . . knowing that I potentially could save my actual family, my actual Kiran, tomorrow?

"Show me my soul," I murmured. "How much worse can it get?"

40

Edric was waiting for us at the top of an ominously dark flight of stairs. He inclined his head in greeting, then muttered a dismissive thanks to Hanelle. His attention turned to me as soon as the other Wind was out of sight.

"Your final challenge will be the hardest of all," he said.

"Testing my soul doesn't sound . . . easy," I admitted.

Edric dipped his head in agreement. "It's not. But it's not meant to be. Because when you finish this challenge, you will acquire the blade. Arguably the most important part of your sword, but also the deadliest. With it, and the magic the Winds are willing to imbue into the weapon itself, you will be able to stop Amirah. But such a blade cannot be possessed by one who cannot master themselves."

My brow scrunched in confusion. Edric didn't respond. Instead, he opened the door. Darkness stared out at us. I glanced at him, but he simply pointed into the room.

"There's no light," I said softly.

Edric shook his head. "You won't need it. Good luck."

I stepped into the room. Edric closed the door. And the darkness enveloped me completely.

"Hello?" I called.

Silence. I reached my arms out, feeling for walls or anything that might give me any idea what I was supposed to do. But I could walk endlessly. The floor was smooth beneath my feet. My boots were loud, echoing through the vast emptiness.

"Hello, Sabrena."

I spun around. I couldn't see anything, but that voice. That voice was more familiar to me than any other, but also a complete stranger in the same vein.

"Where are you?"

"No greeting?" The voice tsked. "That's no way to treat yourself."

"M—Myself?" I stammered.

A soft laugh came in reply. The being snapped their fingers, from somewhere to my right, and I spun just in time to see a light glow spread across their skin and fall into shimmering aqua webs that filled the room around us. No, not a being. *Me.* Or, a version of me.

This Sabrena had aqua hair, and pupils so wide, they covered even the whites of her eyes. Her scars were worse and more numerous, showing up on almost every inch of exposed skin. Slash marks marred her cheeks, her nose, her chin.

"They're horrific, aren't they?" Alternate me cackled. "To you, anyway. To me, they're tokens that show I've seen more of life than you ever will."

"You don't know that," I said. "You have no idea what I've been through."

"I do," she said. "Because I am you, had Bleiz not interfered with that troll's attack. If your father had saved you instead. If you had learned of your powers and never met Kiran."

"But I'm glad I met Kiran—"

"Are you?"

"—and I like the path I'm on."

"Do you?" She smiled, but it was a wicked, calculating expression. "Because I am far more powerful than you'll ever be." I didn't doubt that. She *looked* more powerful than me. This Sabrena had swords strapped to her back and daggers to her thigh. Her scars were battle wounds and she wore them with pride. Her siren's magic flowed around her with ease, the aqua strands around us shifting and changing to where she needed them to be, while not taking any of her focus from our conversation.

And maybe I wasn't as powerful as this version of myself. But maybe one day I could be, in my own way.

"I'm where I'm meant to be," I said with certainty. "I've never been so sure of anything in my life."

"Then it's time we fight," other Sabrena said. She reached behind her back, sliding her swords free, spinning them in her hands as though she didn't worry about the sharp edges they wielded.

I choked. "Fight?"

"You didn't think you'd get out of here without defeating me, did you?"

"I mean, I thought we could have a nice conversation, and then . . ." I swallowed. "And then I could take the blade?"

She laughed, a loud, joyful sound. I couldn't remember the last time I had laughed like that. "No. Because, see, I don't believe you. I don't believe you're capable of killing Amirah."

"I am."

"You've never killed a fly."

I rolled my eyes. "Why kill them? They're harmless."

Alternate me laughed again. "That's the point, though. You never hurt anyone if you can evade it. You avoid violence at all costs. You try to help. You rarely break the rules. Even when you had an entire village ridiculing you, you just let them." Sabrena's smirk was angry now, almost feral. "You let them mock us. Donovan should have been put in line years ago. You let Maryna publicly leave you because you didn't have powers. And you never bothered to correct them, even when you went home."

"But it never mattered what they thought," I argued. "Not really. Not enough to put my energy into. They didn't know me. All they did was try to hurt someone who was different, and they did, but I didn't have to sink to their level."

"If I were you, I would have slaughtered them all," other me spat. "I would never have let those insignificant beings let themselves think they were superior to me. Or to make me feel like less."

"You're right," I said. "I hated myself. I let them make me hate myself, for years and years. But you know what didn't matter? Their opinions. I knew why I got my scars. And those scars didn't make me ugly, they meant I survived. I survived an attack the likes of which had taken so many of our other people." I paused for a second. "But you know what doesn't matter? The opinion of people who don't know you at all. And I'm stronger than that. I'm stronger than them. And I don't have to kill anyone to feel secure in myself."

"You're *weak,*" Sabrena growled. She swung her sword, narrowly missing my chest as I stepped backward.

"No. I'm strong." And finally, I confidently believed it. My hand slipped to my thigh, loosening my dagger. Because it *was* true. I *was* strong. Maybe I wasn't the best fighter. Maybe I couldn't use my magic. But I would keep going, and there was strength in resilience, in survival. "I'm strong, and I'm going to beat you."

Sabrena swung again and this time I raised my dagger to meet the blow. Steel clashed. She swung again and I ducked the strike. I scrambled to remember what Connak and Rhett had taught me about fighting while watching her every move, guarding myself. Sabrena summoned her power, pulling the aqua webbing into herself and creating a shield she wielded with her left arm. Every blow I threw she blocked aggressively.

"*You're weak,*" she said again.

I didn't respond. She would tell me I was weak again or refute anything I said. But I didn't need words to prove my strength. And when she stepped too far forward, when I snuck a blade into her stomach, she gasped in surprise.

"*How?*"

"I know myself. And I know I never remember to protect my stomach," I said quietly.

Other Sabrena fell to the ground. She and her glowing aqua magic faded into the darkness.

The door opened. Edric smiled.

"I'm impressed," he said. "Let's go forge your blade."

M y reunion with my brothers and Nakia was fraught with tears. I held them all tightly, still not quite able to shake the images from Hanelle's challenge room. But the Winds were eager to repair the blade and Roux was waiting in the temple's forge with each piece.

Roux heated the metal, using silvery magic to secure the pieces together. I handed off the dropstone with its blood and flower petals. Each of the four Winds blessed the weapon with their own abilities, creating runes that danced along the blade.

And then I had it. A weapon capable of destroying a Sorceress who could eradicate all Numeryon with a few flicks of her wrist. The sword was heavy in my hands, but I could swing it and jab. And after the confrontation with myself, after the challenge of the South Wind, I felt more confident that I could defeat the Sorceress than ever before.

We rested the night in the temple. The Winds showed us to guest suites that had soft, plush beds and thick pillows. I slept better than I had since I left the estate.

But when morning light came, we were all ready to move on.

"We need to go," Avriel said as I examined the blade for the dozenth time. "Time is of the essence. We don't know how long the prince has."

"Agreed," I said, sliding the sword into the sheath Edric had given me. "I can't thank you enough for your help."

"I hope you're able to accomplish what you're setting out to do," Hanelle said softly. "For all our sake."

"Me too," I murmured.

Roux clasped my hand, offering me a small smile. "I don't know what deities have put you on this path, or why fate might have put that dropstone in your hands. But I wish you luck."

"Thank you," I said.

Avriel stepped forward, holding out her hands. "Hold on. There is only one way into Madrion, and we will have to be quick before the location moves again."

I gripped her hand and Nakia's. Rhett took Avriel's other hand and then Connak's. Then a swirling whoosh of wind twirled around us, lifting us, pulling us upward.

Bright white light flashed. And then we were there.

Achmyn Morternos. The Isle of the Dead.

"Don't look too closely," Avriel advised. "Come, we must find the right stone."

She led us to a cliff face, but I couldn't stop myself. I looked around.

The landscape of the Isle was dry, nothing more than red dirt and the slender remains of brown trees. Even from this distance, I could see the small glints of white on the ground that were abandoned bones. The whole place was barren, the air heavy with the smell of ash and metal. Off in the distance, an unidentified roar echoed across the land.

Achmyn Morternos was horrifying.

"Don't look," Avriel insisted. She tugged my hand harder.

Near the edge of the cliff face was a massive boulder tucked securely next to the crumbling remains of what I guessed to be a once-great tree.

Avriel gestured to the tree. "It's here."

I reached into the hole in the trunk she motioned to. Inside was a stone, carved in with a rune that was filled with a coppery colored paint.

No.

Not paint. Blood.

I swallowed.

Avriel released our hands. "Keep each other close. Keep that stone on you at all times. It will be your only means of escape. You get two uses: in and out. Don't waste them. Good luck."

And she was gone, in a swirl of wind that ruffled the dust-filled landscape. I looked at Connak, Rhett, and Nakia, wondering how they wanted to proceed.

"Are you sure we should go now? After everything you've been through?" Nakia asked. "Surely you could use more rest."

"I won't be able to. Not now, not this close." I stared at the stone in my hand, felt the weight of the sword across my back. "You could go home. You could find a way. I could do this alone."

"Not a chance," Connak said. I was grateful for him, for his resilience.

But I said, "If you keep going with me, you might die. You might all die. I don't know if I could live with that."

"And if you go alone, you almost definitely *will* die," Rhett said. "We go together."

"You're not getting rid of us," Nakia added.

"Okay. Okay," I said, taking a deep breath. "Then let's go to Madrion."

41

We slammed into the ground, harder than anticipated, and rolled several feet. Groans escaped each of us, but we smothered the sounds quickly. I ducked into a crouch, hiding myself behind a tree in case any trolls were nearby, and looked around.

Madrion was an *island*. I moved closer to the edge we seemed to be near. Not just an island, though. An island in the *sky*. And it was beautiful.

Everywhere I looked was lush, green grass. Beautiful trees, covered in pink and white blossoms, showered the ground with their petals. Birds chirped softly; butterflies flitted around on the wind.

Between the beauty, though, harsh black glass structures jutted into the air. They were like daggers, splitting the ambience and creating harsh silhouettes against the bright sky.

"We should get some height," I murmured to the others. I clambered into one of the trees nearby, pulling myself up into the branches. When I got to the top, I carefully peered out.

There.

On a hill in the near distance, an obsidian structure rose bigger than all the others. A palace of shimmering black glass that climbed into the clouds. Tiny, dot-sized figures moved in the windows, lumbering back and forth—guards.

Not nearly as many as I had expected, though. Unless there were dramatically more inside than we could see, the palace was far lower security than I expected with Kiran as her captive.

"I wonder where he is," I whispered. There seemed to be endless possibilities.

I climbed down from the tree, waiting while each of my brothers took the time to gain their bearings. Nakia conjured another bird and released it into the sky to do surveillance laps in the air high above us. So far it seemed that wherever the rune stone had sent us, we were not close to anyone.

But we all knew that could change in a moment.

"You should rest," Nakia said. She ran her fingers through her curls, trying to ease some of the knots, before tying it back into a bun. "Even the emotional weight of what you just went through—"

"No," I said. "I'm fine. We need to find out where Kiran is being held. There just isn't time for rest. Not now. No sleep I get would be restful anyway."

"But you're going to have to fight her." Nakia's eyes were wide with concern. "Like *physically* fight her. One night of good sleep isn't nearly enough."

I looked toward the glass palace. As much as I hated to admit it, Nakia was right. But we were *here*. We were minutes away from finding them. And I couldn't give up now.

"Fine. I'll rest," I said after a long moment of silence. Nakia released a relieved sigh. "*After* we scout enough to make a plan."

Nakia buried her face in her palms with another heavy sigh.

Then she nodded. "Fine. Fine. We'll see what we can learn. And then we're going to get some rest before we try to take on Amirah."

"I can agree to that," Rhett said. Connak simply nodded, fidgeting with the hilt of his blade.

"We're going to need your bird," I told Nakia. "Can you spell her to carry conversations to us?"

"No," Nakia said. "She can alert us to guards, or even scout for the people we're looking for. But she won't be able to communicate that information. Not in a sentient way, I mean."

Connak picked at the stubble on his chin, so unusual for my normally clean-shaven brother. "What if Amirah has warding against magic? Couldn't the bird set that off?"

"If she does, my bird will disintegrate immediately," Nakia said. "She's not traceable, so she won't lead them back to us. But that doesn't mean the trolls won't raise their guard if they see her."

"From what I could see from the tree, security does seem to be pretty loose right now," I admitted. "Maybe Amirah truly believed no one could get to her."

"Yes, but she also probably didn't anticipate the Winds stepping in," Rhett offered. "Deities, ancient beings . . . no one expects them to care about the affairs of mortals or lesser immortals."

Connak lifted a shoulder. "No one expects mortals to take the power of gods, either."

The thought sent a nervous shudder through me. I was going to face someone with the power of a goddess. Power she stole. Even the weight of the sword across my back wasn't as comforting as it was minutes ago.

"All right." I shifted the bag on my shoulder, checked that my blades were secure. "We need to get closer."

My family followed reluctantly. But we stuck to the shadows, keeping our eyes on the glass structures around us in case a guard glimpsed a sight of us. We were lucky, though. No one spotted us, and other than the few guards pacing the main palace, there seemed to be no one patrolling the land.

Instead, we crept into a walled in garden, heavy with the smell of herbs and lined with beds of vegetables.

"This is oddly . . . homey," Rhett whispered.

"She probably uses them to concoct potions and things," Nakia said softly, eyeing the strange flowers that lined the walls.

Rhett grinned. "Does that mean she has newts somewhere?" When I raised a confused brow, he let out an exaggerated sigh and whispered, "Tail of newt? Don't you read faerie tales?"

Connak lifted his finger to his lips. "You're all ridiculous."

I squeezed my eldest brother's arm. "But you love us."

"I do," he said, giving me an oddly tender glance. "But you've also decided to take on this impossible mission. So how about helping me keep you all alive by being a *little* quieter by the big scary palace, could you?"

"If you insist," Rhett drawled under his breath. "Where do you think that leads?"

He pointed to a small wooden door that led out into the garden. We crept closer, listening carefully. This close, voices carried on the wind. The sounds weren't near enough to make out, but the voices were rough, loud, distinctly troll.

I pressed my ear to the door. Silence. No footsteps shuffled on the other side; no voices filled the space.

"We'll just have to find out," I whispered.

Reaching out, I gripped the door handle. I twisted slowly, trying to make as little noise as possible as I pried the door open.

The room it opened into was small and dark. It was mostly shelves filled with cheese and butter, dried herbs in jars, bags of rice, barrels of vegetables. The floor was stone, an oddly rough contrast to the gleaming black glass walls.

"Should we try to go farther?" Connak whispered, pressing his ear to the next door. "I don't hear anyone."

"Might as well," I said. We didn't have anything to lose.

Except our lives.

A little thing.

Connak pushed the door open gently, just enough that he could peer through. When he deemed it safe, he shoved it all the way open. The little pantry led into a massive kitchen. A pair of dead, skinned rabbits hung above a table in the center, as though they were being drained for roasting. Above a small cooking fire, a pot bubbled, probably in preparation for the evening meal. Two doors sat on the far wall and we exchanged a glance, deliberating which one to go through.

But the decision was made for us when the rear one started to rattle. A soft swear came through and I realized the person was probably struggling with something in their arms, because they should have had the door open by now.

We moved as one, slipping through the closer door. The clatter of bone and steel rattled down the hall and we split up, hiding behind long tapestries that hung on the sleek black walls.

A small group of guards wandered past us, armed to the teeth. Their booted steps were heavy on the stone, the sound echoing through the corridors. I held my breath.

These were the first guards we had seen so close.

"Tomorrow," a feminine-sounding troll to the front said. "After Princess Brielle marries that fae prince, the Lady will have what she wants and we can be done with these cursed shifts."

"You think the Lady will stop with the marriage?" The troll that spoke snorted in disdain. "She's going to kill them all and wipe this continent. And then she's going to go back and seek revenge on her estranged husband."

"Guess he shouldn't have been caught with another woman," the feminine voice said. "Now the Lady's just insufferable with her demands."

"No kidding," said a third voice. The group stopped walking and lowered their voices farther. "I've seen Alyvia taking potions up to the prince every morning and night. Amirah doesn't want him coherent. She's too worried he'll try to escape or fight back."

"Any orders yet on what to do with the elves and fae she took prisoner?"

The feminine sounding troll shrugged. "No. But she'll probably force them into hard labor after the wedding."

After another moment of muttered conversation, the trolls moved on. I balled my hands into fists, trying to still the anger that coursed through me. My nails bit into my palms. The tapestry I hid behind trembled where it rested against my chest. I fought the urge to jump out and scream at them to take me to Kiran and release him immediately. Or to put me with the other elves and fae. I could conspire from within. But I knew that would only get me captured and my sword taken away, so I focused my breathing, calmed myself down, and tried to figure out how I could utilize the information we had inadvertently been given.

"Sabrena?"

I jumped at my whispered name. Peering around the edge of the tapestry, I noticed that the rest of my family had already climbed out of their hiding spots. I moved from my own, then grabbed Nakia's arm and dragged her down the hall. My brothers followed without question. I pressed my ear to each door we passed, and when I finally found one I was sure was empty, I dragged them all inside.

The room we snuck into was dark. Rhett flicked his wrist, creating an orb of light on his palm that gave us low visibility.

"You all heard them, right?" I asked. "Kiran is upward, somewhere."

"And there are definitely captive elves and fae here," Connak said. "Maybe some from Eldoris."

"So, what do we do?" Rhett asked.

Nakia chewed the ends of her nails for a moment, then said, "We should find Kiran first. Try to intercept that potion so he's lucid. We're going to need his help getting the others out of here."

"Agreed," Connak said. "The trolls we heard were disgruntled, but they're not all going to feel that way."

"One of us should find Kiran's room." Nakia considered. "And then bribe this Alyvia to skip his dosages."

Connak frowned. "And if she's loyal to Amirah?"

"That's why it needs to be only one of us."

I unslung the sword from my shoulders, passing it to Connak, along with my bag. "It has to be me."

He narrowed his eyes on me in confusion. "What are you doing?"

"I have to find him. And I can offer Alyvia . . . something. I'll pay her. I'll help her get out of here. I don't know. But it has to be me."

Rhett nodded his head slowly. "You're right. It has to be you."

"You don't have to give all of yourself all the time," Connak said gently.

"No," I agreed. "But this is my journey. I need you three still, but if anyone is going to get through to Alyvia, I feel like it will be me."

"And if this all goes south?" Nakia asked. "*You* have to swing the blade against Amirah."

I smiled faintly. "I have a plan . . ."

Climbing the glass tower alone turned out to be more challenging than I thought it would be. The higher I went, the more guards appeared. Alone, it wasn't too hard to avoid notice. I hid behind tapestries and statues and ducked into vacant rooms. Eventually I was in a tower that pierced the sky, searching each room for any sign of my prince.

Finally, the security tightened and I started to struggle to get to the highest rooms. I waited until sunset, hoping for a guard change, and thanking any deity who would listen when it came. In the chaos that ensued I slipped inside.

He was there.

The relief I felt seeing Kiran sprawled across a bed of ebony wood, on thick black furs, sent my heart thundering in my ears all over again. His chest rose and fell in a steady rhythm and, before

I could stop myself, I crossed the room and was cupping his face between my hands, kissing his nose, his cheeks, his lips, whispering his name, begging him to wake up.

But Kiran didn't move, didn't so much as flinch. After several minutes of trying, I finally gave up and inclined myself to wait. But watching Kiran sleep, knowing he was right there and couldn't see me, or feel me, was a new kind of pain I didn't know how to process.

I had so much to tell him. So much to share.

Instead, I paced and waited for Alyvia to arrive. On a desk against the far wall, I found a slip of parchment and scrawled out a note to Kiran. I tried as vaguely as possible to fill him in on what was happening and how he would need to act without the potions. When the ink dried, I folded it up, and resumed waiting.

Hours passed. The sun moved down the sky, the bright orange and purple sunset fading to dark through the window of Kiran's prison. Sure enough, when the sky turned black, the door opened and a small troll entered the room. Her hair was long and blond, tied into braids that fell past her waist. Her tusks were small, dainty, barely peeking out of her lips. And when her wide green eyes caught sight of me sitting in the corner, I had to move *fast* to keep her from screaming out.

"Shhh, shhh," I murmured, clamping my hand over her mouth. "I don't want to hurt you. I just want to talk. Can we talk?" She nodded reluctantly and I released her. "Good, thank you."

"Who are you?" Alyvia asked, eyeing me suspiciously.

"I'm Sabrena. I'm to be married to Prince Kiran."

"Ohhh," she said, her jaw falling wide. "You're the elf? The one who triggered his curse?"

"Yes." I winced. "Listen, I heard you've been giving him a sleeping draught. Is that true?"

Alyvia nodded shyly. "The Lady demands it. He must have one every night and every morning. It keeps him like this."

"Can you stop? Don't give him one tonight or in the

morning?"

Her eyes widened. "If the Lady finds out . . ."

"I plan to be around," I said. "But give him this. He'll know what to do with it."

I handed her the slip of parchment. Alyvia hesitated, then agreed.

"How can I repay you?" I asked.

"Free us. We don't all want a life of servitude and war. I want to see my family again. Free us, and we're even," she said gently. She tucked my note into her bodice, then dumped the evening's sleeping draught into a nearby plant. "I'll give him this in the morning, when he's more coherent."

"I appreciate it," I said.

"You should go." Alyvia tilted her head, as if listening. "The Lady is going to come check on her investment soon and you'll want to be gone."

"Thank you," I said again. Alyvia gave me a shy, gentle smile. She offered to call the guards away for a few minutes to buy me time to leave. I thanked her, and she was gone.

I moved for the door, quickly. When I heard the guards' steps fade away, I moved fast. I didn't know how long Alyvia would manage to keep them busy.

But, when I opened the door, the unexpected knocked the air from my lungs.

I was ready to leave, ready to begin my descent, when a familiar smile filled the doorway.

Seeing it, though, wasn't the joy I expected to feel.

"Leaving so soon?" he asked, and my heart sank at the wicked smirk on his lips. "You'll miss all the fun!"

"What are you doing here?" I rasped out. "Bleiz, what have you done?"

42

Bleiz's smile, once warm and familiar and comforting, felt like a plunge into ice cold water. Gone were the traces of friendship and humor in his eyes. He glared at me and, as I stared hard back, I saw nothing of the friend I had known.

Or thought I had known.

"Why are you here? Free?"

"Why do you think, elf?" he asked with a cruel grin. He reached out, shutting the door to Kiran's room behind me. A barrier, to keep Kiran and I apart again. I struggled against Bleiz as he grabbed my arm and jerked me forward. "Don't try to resist. I'm not above shoving you down the stairs. But I'm hoping the bride-to-be will enjoy tearing you apart as a wedding present for her new beloved."

My mind whirled, trying to catch up to what Bleiz was saying, what this could all possibly mean. I was so very confused as to why he was here, freely walking around, and . . .

And . . .

"Why, Bleiz? Why do this? Kiran loved you like a brother."

"He did, once," Bleiz spat. He kept pulling me, leading me farther and farther away from Kiran. My heart pounded in my ears. "But then he failed me and I've never forgiven him since."

"What is going *on?*" I insisted.

Bleiz nodded at troll guards as he passed. There were still so few in the actual corridors, but it was abundantly clear that the ones we saw knew him. And not just knew him, respected him. He dragged me through the palace at an excruciating pace. I scrambled to keep up with him.

Finally, after leading me down a dark staircase, we arrived.

Amirah's dungeons.

The bottommost floor of the palace, and it reeked of mold and water and rotting earth. Bleiz grabbed a key from the wall and unlocked a cell, tossing me roughly inside before he latched the door behind me.

He started to stride away when I called after him, "I deserve an explanation Bleiz. You were my friend."

The fae halted in his steps. Then he said, "You want the truth? Are you sure?"

"Of course, I am," I said. "How long have you been doing this to Kiran? What did you do, exactly?"

Bleiz laughed and leaned against a wall, spinning the key to my door around a finger. "I did everything. *Everything.*"

"Tell me."

Bleiz shrugged. "After tomorrow it won't really matter if you know, I suppose." He paused, lost in his mind for a moment while he gathered his thoughts, then said, "It all started when I went into Eldoris, looking for a bride for my prince. See, the bargain I made with you wasn't the first time I came to Eldoris. But it was the first time I spoke to you. I saw the way the others looked at you. *Mald Magicae* they said. Magicless." Bleiz laughed. "What a character flaw. But it was the perfect one. Because if you didn't have your magic, you were the least threatening woman I could possibly bring back to the estate. And it was the exact defect that had killed Kiran's own sister. It couldn't have been more perfect if I'd have asked the gods for you myself.

"But I needed time. Kiran wasn't convinced of the bride situation, and you were very young. Convincing your parents would have been too difficult. So, I decided to wait. And in the meantime, I sent a troll to follow you. To watch you. To test you.

"Because you see, I had to make sure you truly had no magic. And when my dear friend Mintric nearly killed you, and you hadn't summoned a single drop, I knew it was true. You were the one. And you now had scars to prove it."

My fingers climbed up the scars on my neck, my shoulder. "You did this?"

"No, Mintric did. I said that. I simply set him on you."

I shivered at the callous way Bleiz spoke. At the way he dismissed years of pain because he felt his purpose was greater.

"So, you see, I kept an eye on you. Made sure you were safe. That Mintric hadn't damaged you too greatly. Kiran spent so much gold on trying to help the elves . . . he's a fool. And a fool the Lady plans to dispose of as soon as his property is the legal territory of her daughter. Because once it's all hers, there is nothing in all Numeryon that can stop her from moving on with her plan for domination."

"Except me."

Bleiz laughed. "You? I've seen you fight. I've seen so much of you over the years. And all this time I planted little seeds. Bided my time. Waited. All because I knew that if Kiran met you, there wasn't a chance he wouldn't love you. A little elven girl he could protect and cherish? With a kind heart? Ha. Kindness is a weakness. It made you so soft you didn't even see me coming."

"Of course, you would think that," I said. "Kindness isn't weakness. Do you think that, in a world that encourages violence at every turn, it's not harder to stay your blade and love instead? Kindness is a strength. A gift you have to work for every day, but one that will repay you tenfold."

Bleiz shook his head. "Believe what you want. But our Lady wanted the curse triggered and you were the perfect one to do it. The Eventide Rose threw in some complications, though. I hadn't anticipated you showing signs of suppressed magic. So, I tried to push you two together faster.

"When you went home with Kiran, I sent allies of the trolls to attack you. I hoped they would wound you, and in panic, Kiran would touch you. But you held them off too long and he shifted. A perfect plan failed. So, I tried to attack you more directly when Oryn asked me to change shifts with him. Poor Oryn, coming to check in on me to make sure I had eaten that night. But he saw too much. I did what had to be done. And when Oryn was disposed of, I released my ally from Kiran's dungeons. Mintric has been such a loyal friend."

My stomach churned. I wanted to hurl. Months, years of my life had been orchestrated and manipulated by this man. Kiran's too.

"Why do this?" I asked softly. "Why do you hate him so much?"

"Because he killed the woman I loved," Bleiz snarled, the spiked rage so intense, I actually recoiled. But his voice cracked when he said, "Because he sent her out to do a patrol and she never came back."

"You know that's not his fault. They all know what they're signing up for."

"Do they?" Bleiz asked, standing straight now, hands clenched into fists. "Did she know she was going to die and leave me? Did she know she was going to leave her sister aching for her for the rest of her life? Because twins, they're magically bound. And Damara will feel the pain of her loss for the rest of her life, even if she doesn't want to."

Too many emotions flooded through me so quickly that instead of processing them I simply froze. Damara's sister . . .

had loved Bleiz? And had died in active duty? And all of this . . . years of false loyalty and manipulation . . . were all because he was angry that Kiran had given the order?

"Bleiz, you have to know Kiran wouldn't have let something like this happen intentionally. You know him better than that."

"But he knew the risk of sending her and he did it anyway!" Bleiz yelled. His face, all the way to the tips of his pointed ears, were flushed with anger.

"You've had your revenge though! Why keep going?"

Bleiz's laugh was clipped and bitter. "It won't be enough till Kiran is dead too. Until he's gone, just like her."

The words didn't make me sad. They made me angry. Not just because they were a threat to someone I loved, but because Bleiz had lost all sense of who he was on this mission for revenge.

"Would she have wanted this?" I whispered. "Would she have wanted you to kill him?"

"No. But she isn't here to stop me."

"You're right, she's not," I said. "So, you chose to honor her memory by working with the very trolls she died fighting against. Makes sense. I don't believe for one second that the twin of someone as kind and considerate and brave as Damara would *ever* work with the trolls. Or stay with someone who did." Bleiz faltered at that, and I pressed on. "And where is Damara? You were so mad Kiran didn't protect her. Where is she now?"

Bleiz winced. "I'm not going to let anything happen to her."

"And I don't believe you can guarantee that."

"The Lady wouldn't renege on a deal." But there was doubt in his eyes. "It doesn't matter. I've told you enough. I'm leaving."

"Run away," I yelled after him. The cold metal of the cell's bars bit into my palms as I gripped them. I slammed my fist against them, angrier than I had been in so very long. "Cowardly bastard!"

"Pssst. Wake up. Please wake up," a soft voice said.

I groaned, aching all over from the hard stone floor I had fallen asleep on. Green eyes peered at me through the bars, and I nearly jumped out of my skin until I realized it was Alyvia.

"Nine circles, please don't sneak up on me like that again," I breathed.

"Sorry," she whispered. "I brought you some food and water. I don't know if I was supposed to, but it is kind of my job."

She held out a brown paper package with bread and cheese and thinly sliced meat inside. And then she offered me a small waterskin.

"Thank you."

"They're not much, but they should help." Alyvia stood, brushing her hands off on the apron tied at her waist. A beam of moonlight shone in through the tiny window at the top of my cell, casting white light onto her blue skin. "They're planning to make a spectacle of you, you know. At the wedding tomorrow."

I nodded, pulling off a bite of bread. "I imagined as much."

"The prince will be there."

"I know." The bite in my mouth stuck in my throat when I tried to swallow it. "I'm not giving up yet."

"Please don't," she whispered.

I paused, studying Alyvia for a moment. "Why are you helping me? I mean, I know you want to be free of Amirah, but you haven't questioned me once."

"Because I remember a time when the trolls were like any other race. We didn't come from Numeryon, no. But we lived on our own continent, full of life and joy. The trolls were prosperous, and joyous. We had children and families and businesses.

"And then Amirah's husband found love here, in Numeryon. And everything changed. She took her rage out on an entire people. A lot of us just want to go back to the before, when we had peace."

"Makes sense," I said thoughtfully. I hadn't considered the trolls enough in all of this. I was glad Alyvia had opened my mind more. "I hope you get there."

"Me too," Alyvia murmured. "I gave him your note. He woke up a lot faster than I thought he would. You'll be okay."

"Here's hoping," I said back. She turned to leave and I called after her, quietly, "Thank you."

"Good luck."

43

After Alyvia left, I fell back into an uneasy slumber. It was hard to relax, not knowing who had access to me or when someone might come. Even stretching didn't ease the ache in my muscles. And wondering what my family was doing while I was trapped here was an agony of its own kind.

But we had a plan. We had made sure to consider that I might not make it out of the glass palace. If they managed to pull off their side, we might still do this. And I needed whatever strength I could find to prepare.

I was jerked rudely awake in the late morning by Bleiz, who grabbed my arms and slapped iron cuffs onto my wrists. Without meeting my eyes, he tied a gag around my mouth. His smirk was gone this morning. He seemed to simply be going through the motions, even when dragging me up the stairs and through the glass corridors.

The guards were heavier today. It seemed as though Amirah had called her entire contingent home to protect them during this wedding. I didn't know why it mattered. If she thought Kiran was drugged, she could simply take his resources. Maybe she hoped the fae would be complacent if their prince was tied to one of her own. Regardless, as we passed rows of trolls who sneered and cursed at me, I held my head high. I wasn't going to let them catch me with my chin down.

Bleiz didn't speak, not even when we entered the massive throne room. It was filled with trolls, and even some scattered fae, much to my disgust. Kiran was slumped in a throne, seemingly half coherent, but the second I entered the room I noticed the slight shift in his shoulders, the stiffness of his frame. His eyes locked onto mine and for a moment, I faltered. But Bleiz simply shoved me forward.

Beside him, on another throne, sat a female troll with soft emerald skin and long black hair. Her gown was floor-length, made of shimmering silken material in a bright blue. Jewelry of bones and beads hung at her throat and ears. She looked as uncomfortable as I felt, even before Amirah strode into the room.

The High Sorceress was dressed to pull eyes. Her black gown made the blue of her skin brighter, and she showed a lot of it between the shimmering cuts of fabric.

"Ahh, darlings, we have a guest," Amirah said, looking toward the thrones. Her eyes lingered on Kiran as Bleiz shoved me to the ground. Kiran didn't move, didn't so much as respond, pretending to be in his drugged state. But the second her attention turned back to me his eyes widened imperceptibly and I noticed the subtle clench of his jaw.

The troll beside him didn't react either and I wondered at her. If this was the troll princess, was she also drugged and pushed into this? Or was she simply so used to the abuse, she just went within herself every time her mother was near?

Because it was written all over her face that she didn't want to be here.

Off to the side, I heard the sounds of struggle and turned my head.

Damara. Bound, gagged, and held by two trolls that eyed her in a predatory way that sent my blood boiling. The ropes on her arms were tight, so tight she could barely move, but she was trying. One of her guards pressed a knife to her throat and she stilled.

"I'm so pleased you could join us, Sabrena. This is going to be the event of a lifetime, after all," Amirah said. Her smile widened as she looked around at the gathered guests. "Friends. Allies. I welcome you. Today is going to be life changing, for all of us."

Amirah dramatically took the steps down from the throne, her gown swirling around her. The procession of people bowed their heads, but not me. Not Damara. Even Bleiz, who now stood closer to the thrones, dipped his head.

I wondered vaguely what Kiran thought of that.

"My friends, today we embark on a major step toward accomplishing all that we have wanted from this life. Today, we unite the trolls and fae in a momentous way." She flicked her wrists and soft black flower petals began to rain slowly down from the ceiling. "But let me not take any more attention from our new bride and groom. Let the ceremony begin!"

I started pushing at the gag in my mouth, slowly. Bleiz had thrown me in the center of the room, on the main walkway to the thrones. The perfect view to watch as I lost Kiran.

And the perfect place for me to start the plan my family and I had concocted the day before.

As the cloth grew damp with my spit, it began to flex. I pushed gently, subtly, as a cleric stepped out, adorned in beautiful traditional clothing—a long, elegant robe decorated with bones and beading, and a head piece of braided feathers and jewels. The cleric began to speak, reading the rites of marriage. I had the gag nearly free.

Then the cleric asked the question I had been waiting for.

"Does anyone in attendance, other than the groom himself, object to this ceremony?"

Most of the room was silent. No one would dare defy the Sorceress or ruin this moment for her.

No one but me.

I climbed awkwardly to my feet, spat my gag from my mouth, and yelled, "I do."

Amirah's rage was instant. She spun around so quickly the skirt of her gown tore. The gasps that filled the room were a river of sound.

For if anyone, anyone at all, objected to the rites of marriage, the cleric couldn't proceed until their objections were resolved. The magical binding was as old as the rites themselves. And Amirah, in all her confidence, had never thought I could do anything with a gag in my mouth and my arms tied behind me.

"How *dare* you?" Amirah snarled.

I smirked, painting on a confident face. "It's too late to stop me."

"I was going to give you to Brielle," Amirah said, stalking closer. "I was going to let her do away with you however she saw fit. Maybe she would have even shown you mercy." She grabbed me by the throat, her taloned fingernails digging into my skin. "But *fuck you*," she snarled. "I'll kill you myself."

Her nails burned like hot metal, digging into my skin. I could feel the thrum of her magic building. She was going to kill me, right here, right now. But if it bought my family time . . .

Then her power flickered and faltered. Her eyes widened. The talisman beneath my shirt warmed, pulsing out protective waves that rendered Amirah's spell useless. She snarled at me, lip curling, reaching for the chain at my throat

The doors to the chamber burst open behind me. Amirah's yellow eyes lifted, and then I was being tossed aside. A group of trolls in the audience half caught me as they scrambled to get out of the way.

My brothers were silhouetted in the doorway, their weapons drawn, their clothing sprayed with blood. I hoped it wasn't theirs.

Nakia lifted her hands, casting sparkling nets of golden light that draped the crowd and trapped them beneath.

"Are you okay?" A voice asked in my ear.

I spun. *Alyvia*. She waved a small silver key where I could see it, then shoved it into the cuffs on my wrists.

"Thank you," I murmured.

With a small nod and wave, she vanished back into some secret crevice I doubted the Sorceress knew about. I looked around. Just in time to see Bleiz lunging for me, trying to make sure I didn't escape. Ever loyal to his *Lady*.

Disgusting.

But before he could touch me Kiran was there. The prince's fist connected, hard, with the other fae's jaw.

"How *dare* you touch her!" Kiran snarled. He slammed another blow to Kiran's cheek. "You fucking traitorous bastard."

"Did you think I would forget Fiore?" Bleiz asked, throwing a punch into Kiran's ribs.

Kiran blocked another hit from Bleiz and twisted around him. "No. I never did. Is she what this is about?"

"Of course it is," Bleiz snarled. He spun, trying to punch Kiran any way he could. "I will *never* forgive you for losing her."

Kiran faltered, the pain in his eyes nearly bringing me to my knees. "But you were a brother to me."

"And she was my *everything*," Bleiz screamed. He landed two sharp blows to Kiran's head before Kiran reacted again, dodging more hard strikes.

I spun away from them, knowing there was nothing more I could do, and raced for Damara. I helped free her from her bonds as my brothers played games with Amirah. They bobbed and ducked around her, breaking her line of sight so she couldn't cast defensive magic easily. Connak loosed arrows at her. She clenched her fist and the arrows turned to shimmering purple dust.

Once Damara was free, I ran. Rhett had my sword, and he threw it to me as soon as I was close. I pulled it from its sheath.

The runes glittered bright, the magic in the blade responding to Amirah's presence.

"How dare you," she shrieked at me, her attention fully drawn by the sword. "How dare you come into my home and threaten me like this!"

She grabbed my arm. Yanking the sword from my hand, she screamed in rage when the blade burned and disintegrated her flesh. She threw it aside and I watched, helpless, as it clattered to the ground. Then she grabbed my throat again—roughly. I felt the blood trickling down my shoulders, my neck, my chest. The air in my throat was choked off. I punched her with my fists, trying to break her hold, or her focus, and accomplished neither.

Then I heard my name, from a voice I would have picked out of a hundred others.

"Sabrena, catch!"

I barely saw Kiran throw the sword before I reached up, grabbing the hilt as it flew past. Amirah hesitated in surprise and, in that second, I plunged the blade into her stomach as hard as I could.

For a moment, all the fighting around us stopped. Nakia held her nets, so the audience couldn't intervene. Bleiz had shifted, and my brothers and Kiran wrestled his wolf to the ground while fighting off guards who remained loyal to Amirah.

Swirling rainbows of magic surrounded me, Amirah, and the sword. The Sorceress's screams of rage were buried under the gargling blood that filled her throat. She fell. The rainbow colors extinguished the moment her body hit the ground. The magic . . . it had died.

Because she was dead.

Amirah was *dead*.

And then the clapping started. It wasn't a fae or even a random troll.

It was Brielle herself. The princess, the daughter to the Sorceress, clapped at her mother's death.

"I knew it was only a matter of time," Brielle said. "Someone had to be strong enough to defeat her. I never was."

I stared at the troll princess in shock. "What?"

Brielle offered a gentle smile. She lifted a shoulder. "Once upon a time, my mother was loving. Kind. My father broke her. And she became so fixated on revenge she lost sight of everything that she was." Brielle stared at her mother's body, and the sadness I had expected finally began to shine through. "Most of us knew she was in the wrong. But Father had fallen for an elf, you see. An elf from this very land. And so, mother thought she could simply take it all, and that would be enough. That by hurting his lover, she could hurt my father.

"But that was never enough. It would never *be* enough. She became obsessed with the power. The control. And when she took that goddess's magic . . . I thought it would never end. *We* thought it would never end."

Brielle scanned the room around her. "Lay down your weapons. We are not enemies. Not anymore."

And many of the trolls did. Nakia released her nets. A few resisted, but the guards loyal to Brielle moved swiftly, detaining anyone who looked willing to continue the fighting.

I checked that my brothers and Nakia were okay with a glance. And then I looked at Kiran.

But his eyes were on Bleiz, who had shifted back to fae form and sat staring up at the prince, just as aggressively as Kiran studied him.

"I'm sorry." Kiran said softly.

Bleiz stared at him. Tears tracked his cheeks, smearing the blood from their fighting. He didn't say a word. Simply sat and cried. Damara stepped up beside Kiran.

"Fiore would never have wanted this," she said softly, and I moved to her side, gripping her hand. "Fiore forgave Kiran. I know she did."

Bleiz didn't respond. His chin fell to his chest, and he sobbed. Maybe for the first time since Fiore's death.

"Should I have him locked up?" Brielle asked.

Kiran shook his head. "We'll take him back to Devayne Estate. I'll deal with him there."

The troll princess nodded. "As you wish."

Then Kiran looked my way and the breath caught in my lungs. The relief, the fear, the stress of the last few days melted away. Before I could move, he was there. Then I was in his arms and tears were flowing down my own cheeks.

"I'm so proud of you," he whispered in my ear. His own cheek was damp against mine. "So, so very proud of you."

I clung to him tighter, threading my fingers into his hair, inhaling the scent of him. Real, alive, safe. He wavered for a moment, still unsteady after days of being drugged, and I tugged him down to the ground. We rested on our knees, and I cupped his face between my hands.

"I love you," I whispered. "I love you so much. I didn't say it before. I should have. I've regretted it ever since."

"I love you too," he murmured back, pressing a soft kiss to my lips. "*Ashyndah Talehn.* Love of my heart."

Epilogue

Two moon cycles had passed since the fall of Amirah and the release of Kiran, my friends, and all Numeryon. Kiran sent regular patrols to check the borders, and to make sure Brielle was upholding her side of the treatise. Nakia had taken on a liaison position, and the more she visited the troll princess the less we saw her. If it meant what I thought it did, I was happy for my best friend.

Trust between all the races would be a long time coming but, for once, it felt achievable. For the first time in so very long, Numeryon might know peace.

My family had survived the assault on Eldoris. Mama and my youngest siblings managed to hide in the cellar, but Papa had been taken as a captive. Thankfully, he wasn't much worse for wear and he was freed with the others in the glass palace. And even though most of our city, including our home, had been destroyed and burnt to the ground, Kiran had sent plenty of funds and as many fae as were willing to help with the restoration.

I never found out if the face I had seen in the water was real, or if he was the father I didn't know. But I did realize that it didn't matter. I could learn about my siren abilities from so many places. The only father I needed was my Papa. And watching him help rebuild Eldoris, to come into his own light aside from being a fisherman? I was proud to call him such.

Bleiz was biding his time in the fae prison in Lytharius. I hadn't heard from him, and Kiran wasn't accepting his correspondences. Damara thought he should give Bleiz a chance, because she knew the pain he felt, but I understood why he didn't. Nothing Kiran ever did was meant to hurt Bleiz or Damara, or her sister. He did what he had to in the line of duty. Kiran could even understand why those actions hurt Bleiz as badly as they did.

But Bleiz betrayed all Numeryon with his actions. That was vastly different from extracting petty revenge. If he was going to earn forgiveness, it was going to take time.

I stared into the mirror in front of me. I didn't fully recognize the woman I saw staring back. Braids lined my hair, but they were studded with small jewels. A circlet sat at my brow, until I would change it for my formal tiara later in the night. There was a relaxed look to my expression that I had never seen, and even though my pale pink gown completely exposed the scars I wore, they didn't really bother me anymore. They were a part of me, as much as my hair or my eyes, or any other piece of the person I had become. Once, I hadn't been able to see my scars like that. They were another broken piece to a wheel that couldn't turn.

Now I realized that it was the little differences we all carry that set us apart.

Scars that mark our survival. A love of water that contrasts our greatest nightmare. Freckles that remind us of a sister lost.

A dragon form that reminds us of the cage we were trapped in.

And all the courage it took to escape.

"You wouldn't be thinking about me, would you?"

Heat rose in my cheeks at the sound of that voice, his voice. Warmth spread through my chest at the aching familiarity, at the safety and security that he brought with him. And the joy he gave me.

"Kiran, you're not supposed to be here," I said quietly.

He crept up behind me, looping his arms around my waist. "Yes, well. I couldn't keep myself away," he murmured against my neck, pressing long, tender kisses all the way down to my shoulder.

"Keep that up and we're going to be late."

"Hmmm," he mumbled, spinning me around. He pressed his lips firmly to mine, running his hands down my arms in ways that sent pleasant shivers along my spine.

I pulled away with a smile, placing a hand on his chest to put space between us. "Kiran."

"Yes, my rose?" His chest pushed against my hand gently, testing my resolve.

"It's our wedding."

"Exactly why we can be late." He smiled then, that devastating smile that I had once worked so hard to earn and that now came as easily as the morning sun. "No one will go on without us."

"You're a terrible influence."

"You like being terribly influenced."

My fingers curled into his shirt. "I suppose I do." I stepped closer, so close our lips were only the barest sliver apart. Then I whispered, "I'll make it up to you later."

And strode for the door.

His fingertips grazed the skirt of my dress.

I knew if I had been a second slower, I wouldn't have made it out that door. I also knew I wouldn't have wanted to if he caught me again.

Nakia and Damara waited for me, bouquets in hand. I had asked them to stand with me, as Kiran had asked my brothers to stand with him. Aleksei and Kirsi had already pranced their way to the front of the ceremony, dropping swirling Eventide petals on the ground behind them.

We had decorated a section of the garden for the ceremony, but we didn't really have to do much. Once the Eventide Roses had begun to bloom again, they had been unstoppable. Their vines covered the walls around us, their petals swirling in the gentle wind. And as Kiran strode toward me with a wide smile on his face, as we were surrounded by family and friends, I appreciated the idea that our wedding was filled with hope.

Because when I looked around me, when I took in everyone that had come, the joy I felt was boundless. But when I looked into Kiran's eyes, it was so much more.

Love. Safety. The beginning of a new life and a new future.

"You ready?" Kiran asked, taking my hands in his.

I grinned, teasingly. "As ready as I can be."

His returned smile was tender. "Ashyndah Talehn. My rose. My heart."

"I love you too," I said.

And together, we stepped forward into our forever.

The End

ALSO BY
TYFFANY HACKETT:

THE THANATOS TRILOGY

THE GENESIS CRYSTAL SAGA

ACKNOWLEDGMENTS

I joke that every book I publish is fueled by copious amounts of Dr Pepper and lack of sleep, but it has never felt more true than with this monstrosity. I had some very genuine fears that I would never finish her, so that I'm here, that she's in your hands, is more emotional than I can express. And I'd be lying if I said I didn't have a world of support that got me here.

To my Ethee Weethee; (who will kill me for immortalizing that nickname when you're a teenager, I'm sure haha) every year you grow older I'm amazed at what an incredible, brilliant human you are. You're my biggest cheerleader, even when you don't entirely understand what I'm doing or why. I love you to the multiverse and back, my beautiful sunshine boy.

To Corey; who, come what may, still validates and supports me on this crazy journey through authordom. I love you.

To Ally and Sebastian; who have made the impossibly challenging last two years of my life so much easier. I don't know how I would have survived them at all without you two, and I'm eternally grateful for that level of friendship. I love you both, and Mikey, and little bean, to the ends of the galaxy.

To Hannah and Chelscey; who kept me sane when I was beating my head off the literal and proverbial wall. You've both supported me tirelessly and I'll never be able to express the gratitude I feel for that. You're amazing friends and critique partners and I love you.

To Jesikah; DC would not have been done on time without your tireless efforts, your incredible skillsets, and some wonderfull catbutts ;) Your friendship means everything to me. Love you!

To the betas I haven't yet mentioned, AJ and Bri; thank you for sticking with DC even though my beta schedule was truly hellacious. I appreciate every inkling of help you gave me getting her polished.

To Matt, Wayne, and Chris; for existing <3

Special thanks to my girl Karley for naming Rhett! He took on a life of his own and I really hope you love him. :3

And to my readers; for whom these stories take on their own lives. I couldn't do this without you. Thank you. <3

ABOUT THE AUTHOR

Tyffany Hackett is an award-winning author of Young Adult and New Adult Fantasy. Her stories are filled with strong women, found family, powerful friendships, and lots of loveable cinnamon rolls.

Residing in Upstate New York, Tyffany spends her days corralling her little minecraft addict and her nights trying to make the words go. In her down time you can find her killing reapers, darkspawn, or battling for the horde.

Daylight's Curse Playlist

TOP TEN SONGS

Full Playlist on Spotify:

https://spoti.fi/3sVpdQP

• Graveyard - *Halsey*

• Turning Page - *Sleeping at Last*

• Could you Be Mine - *Billy Raffoul*

• Lost it All - *Black Veil Brides*

• Dark Paradise - *Lana Del Ray*

• Cosmic Love - *Florence + The Machine*

• The Edge of Dawn - *AmaLee*

• Between Twilight - *Lindsey Stirling*

• Strong - *Amaranthe*

• All is Found - *Evan Rachel Wood*

Bonus:
• Without You - *Ursine Vulpine & Annaca*

Made in the USA
Middletown, DE
23 August 2024

59097801R00236